ARDENT VIOLET
AND THE
INFINITE EYE

The jump gate has scarcely hit stable orbit before it activates. Power warms the capacitors across the trough of the V, filling it with glitter. The radiant points inside the jump gate become alien ships, each stranger in design than the last. There are enough vessels to overpower the astral navies of the United Worlds at its peak.

"Nothing is ever going to be the same after this," Falchion says.

Ardent hopes the statement is more for better than worse.

Praise for Alex White

By Alex White

The Starmetal Symphony

August Kitko and the Mechas from Space

Ardent Violet and the Infinite Eye

ARDENT VIOLET
AND THE
INFINITE EYE

The Starmetal Symphony, Movement Two

ALEX WHITE

orbit

orbit-books.co.uk

ORBIT

First published in Great Britain in 2024 by Orbit

1 3 5 7 9 10 8 6 4 2

A CIP catalogue record for this book
is available from the British Library.

ISBN 978-0-356-51861-9

Typeset by Palimpsest Book Production Limited, Falkirk, Stirlingshire
Printed and bound in Great Britain by Clays Ltd, Elcograf, S.p.A.

Papers used by Orbit are from well-managed forests
and other responsible sources.

Orbit
An imprint of
Little, Brown Book Group
Carmelite House
50 Victoria Embankment
London EC4Y 0DZ

An Hachette UK Company
www.hachette.co.uk

orbit-books.co.uk

For S., Gene, Talia, Christiana, Pyor, Kaitlynn, Drew, Lindsay, Robyn, Jek, and all the others on this road with me

Part 1

We Can Never Go Back

Chapter One

Five Seconds Later

Ardent Violet has experienced a lot of incredible things in their short, beautiful life: dozens of worlds and twice as many lovers, packed arenas chanting their name like the beating of a thunderous heart, swarms of mind-eating automatons trying to kill them, then trying to save them, then briefly trying to kill them again before absconding with their agent. That's leaving aside all the giant mecha battles and trepanation of the past month and a half.

These last five years have exceeded even liberal estimates of strangeness.

Ardent's morning has been a blessedly tame one, consisting of having amazing reunion sex with their jazz-pianist-turned-Conduit boyfriend, August Kitko, then popping over to a hardened government facility in the Colorado Rocky Mountains to hang out with the hulking sentient machines who saved humanity.

You know, normal people stuff.

Ardent stands in an old American Empire vehicle bay large enough to park a battleship, a relic of the dark days at the end of the Capital Age. The United Worlds forces have gutted and restored enough of the base to house the four Traitor Vanguards who turned on their siblings. In the poor lighting and makeshift facilities, their starmetal armor takes on a dramatic cast like performers on a stage, three of them standing over a wounded kneeling comrade.

Ardent squints at the tableau of arranged mechas, searching for life inside the four keening Vanguards. The bay hums with their song, resonating Ardent's bones with infrasonic bass. The aquamarine lines along Cascade's bronze carapace shift and flow just beneath the surface, but there's no motor activity. Jotunn remains silent as the grave, the carbon-dark angles of its form devouring the light. Its thousands of drones have stacked themselves nearby in crop circles, each larger than a storage drum and heavier than a house. Falchion, bloodred and sinister, looms over the trio with its predatory gaze locked upon some distant object Ardent can't see.

Greymalkin kneels before them, the emerald light from its eyes washing its black-and-white armor plates. Gleaming palladium seams seal the battle scars, an advanced tech only the Vanguards understand.

Ardent's boyfriend is inside its chest, communing with the monster.

"It's been a while since Greymalkin ate him." Ardent brushes a few strands of errant hair behind their ear. "Are we supposed to do something, or…"

The woman beside them crosses her arms. Elzahia Tazi, a United Worlds government handler for the Conduits, sports a tight beige suit over her dark skin, cornrows and fingernails luxed a pastel blue. Those boots might be business casual, but she could definitely step on someone's neck.

She's essentially Ardent's parole officer.

They watch her, trying to determine if she's annoyed or not. "Miss Tazi—"

"I heard you." Her French lilt devours the *h* sound as her gaze snaps onto them. "Be quiet."

Ardent rolls their eyes as soon as she's not looking.

"Hey, uh, am I broadcasting?" Greymalkin's eyes flash in time with Gus Kitko's rough voice.

"We hear you, Mister Kitko," Tazi replies, raising a hand.

"Right. Good. Okay." He takes a breath. "Greymalkin says it's been, um, calling allies."

Allies?

Tazi glances to Ardent. "What does he mean?"

Ardent shrugs, then cups their hands and shouts to the Vanguards. "What, like other human colonies?"

"Greymalkin and I have been discussing it for the past five minutes," Gus replies, "and I'm *really* not sure how to explain what's about to happen."

"Try, Kitko," Tazi says.

Her Ganglion computer chirps from a pendant around her neck, and she snaps her fingers to bring up the UI. A hologram of a fresh-faced, masculine lieutenant with pale skin appears before her. They exchange militaristic greetings, but Ardent can't hear the man's side of the conversation.

"Check it again…" Tazi says, beginning to pace. "Check all of them again…"

"What's happening?" Ardent says.

Tazi pauses before answering, as if weighing whether to trust Ardent. "The Ghost Loop in Monaco just activated."

She snaps her fingers, and her polished nails flash in acknowledgment. A little camera drone zips out from behind her, projecting an image above itself.

The Monaco that emerges in hologram is nothing like the diamond on the emerald sea where Ardent first met Gus. It's a carved-up wasteland with the very mountains chopped down to

5

make room for an intricate palladium superstructure. The buildings surrounding it have all been razed or stripped to the girders. Broken hulls of starliners and yachts litter the nearby Super-Port Hercule, their carcasses picked clean by a swarm of Gilded Ghosts. A lot of rich people aren't going to get their old starships back.

The "loop" rests at the center like a great, glittering conch shell, its tightening spiral bristling with metal spines. Misty azure light courses beneath its surface, and Ardent can almost feel its energy building through the projection. How many ship reactors did the machines loot to make their masterpiece? Juliette's corpse rests nearby, a skeleton cleaned of all components. Were those bits also included in the Ghost Loop?

"It's okay!" Gus says, but his assurance is undercut by the blast of all four Vanguards revving to full power. Their metallic voices ring in the bay like a million demonic choristers, and Ardent's hearing protection does nothing against it.

"Not okay!" Ardent covers their ears and sinks to their knees, desperate to block out the sound. It cuts through any barrier.

Tazi starts barking orders into her comm, but Ardent can't understand her over the din.

"Ardent." The devilish Falchion speaks into their mind with their own voice.

Ardent's stomach lurches like a first crush.

"Come to me."

Their brain slackens, and time gets weird.

A blink later, they stand before Falchion, a dark god in bloody livery. The other Vanguards break from their stasis, the vibrations of their footfalls rippling up through Ardent's legs into their teeth. Ardent should get away—they could be crushed by an errant step, but none of that matters. Tazi calls to Ardent from behind, voice distant and meaningless.

The crimson giant leans over them, clothing all in shadow, and extends an armored hand. Ardent dutifully steps aboard and steadies themself on its upturned thumb. They rise to Falchion's chest, where plates unfold to reveal a pulsating blue cocoon of synthetic muscles and wires. *Home.*

Ardent's eyes roll back in their head, and they fall forward. The lights go out, and rough forces reorient them before invading.

Cables thunk into ports across their body—poisonous foreign technology implanted into Ardent by the Vanguards. Lightning crackles through their mind, and a blast of fresh sensory data clears away the fuzz. The air supply slithers up their nostrils and into their mouth.

"*Pleh*, oh my god. What's happening?"

A mirror image of Ardent emerges from the ink, silvered irises shining like a pair of coins. Studs and spikes dot a tight black polycalf outfit, firelight illuminating their supple musculature. Ardent makes a mental note to steal the look. The doppelgänger gives them a hungry smile.

"*Just calling you to heel, pet.*"

Ardent wants to pop off a quip, but Falchion has threatened them with damnation before. The tiniest thought from a Vanguard could spell unlimited torture.

Falchion's soft laugh annoys them.

"What?"

"*You've grown self-control.*"

"Thank you." They affect a polite mask. "May I know what's happening?"

"*You're learning how to catch.*"

"Oh, please, honey, I know how to do that just fine."

"*Ticktock, Ardent. Something important is about to happen to the Earth and all your friends. Care to pay attention?*"

"Of course."

Falchion's network pours into Ardent's ports like ice water. Scanners sweep the shape of the bunker and gravitational fields of the planet to dead reckon Ardent's location down to a micrometer. Their mirror clone disappears beneath the onslaught of the armor's wide-spectrum energy vision. Ardent towers over the vehicle bay, striding toward the titanic doors. Thirteen soldiers clear the path ahead, tiny hearts thumping in their chests. Ardent could count the hairs on their heads in an instant.

Blast doors part before the giants. Jotunn's drones stream from the bay like a cloud of flies before the Vanguards step out into the Rocky Mountain vista.

Tall pines prick up between boulders like hair upon the skin of the Earth. The forest glitters with reflections—the lenses of the military, all trained on Falchion. More sats spy from above. The city of Colorado Springs quietly panics in the distance, all air traffic either landing or fleeing.

Jotunn and Cascade blast off and curve for the horizon, leaving dueling sonic booms in their wakes.

"Where are they going?"

"To pick up their Conduits." Falchion's disembodied voice sends a chill up Ardent's neck. *"Look to Monaco."*

Falchion projects a waypoint through the curvature of the Earth. Ardent has little trouble spotting the distant principality in the center of a terrifying energy bloom. It brightens the sky like a sunrise, plasma lightning shooting across its membranous surface.

Greymalkin rockets heavenward on arcflame. Falchion follows, its launch flattening a stand of trees.

"The allies we need are scarce—not in this galaxy," Falchion says.

"Please tell me I'm going to get to meet aliens."

"If they can punch a wormhole to us."

Falchion gives Ardent full control, and they rise into the freedom, rocketing straight up to get a better look.

The Monaco energy cloud swirls like a hurricane, its eye drawing outward in a cone. The tip gets impossibly thin, an infinitesimal thread spun from space-time and projected out into the void.

"Isn't this a bit, uh, close to Earth?"

"Not if my calculations are to be trusted."

What's not to trust? Ardent thinks.

"I heard that."

Monaco's energy cloud picks up rotation speed, cycling at billions of megahertz—beyond even the measurement speed of Falchion's computers. The snap in reality whites out sensors on every wave band. Noise bubbles through Ardent's body. They shield their eyes on instinct, and Falchion throttles the input to a fraction of its previous magnitude.

Greymalkin's transponder beats nearby, reassuring Ardent. Sight returns, blurry and miscalibrated, the colors split into prismatic hues. The cone has become a beam of white-hot light, energy signature beyond measuring.

Twin signals streak from the surface of the Earth—Cascade and Jotunn, bound for Ardent's location. The four Vanguards reunite in the stratosphere.

"How's it going, folx?" Gus's rough voice sounds like it's inside Ardent's head, and they love it.

"Dude!" Nisha Kohli's New Jalandhari accent follows—transcendent singer, former fan, fast friend, absolute Vanguard slayer. "Cascade just snatched me out of a food court!"

"Better than being taken from the shower." Hjalmar Sjögren, aka "the Swedish Raven," speaks like the grinding of glaciers—once upon a time, a session drummer on an Ardent track, now a Conduit comrade. Ardent's boyfriend is a little obsessed with him.

At the end of the energy beam, the stars pinch and twist into a tight bundle. Falchion scans the anomaly and finds a sucking wound forming in space, the seed of a black hole.

"Yeah, this still feels *super* close."

"It's a mild EMP, Ardent. Just stay out of the beam. Now let's catch a space station."

Deepsync in progress...

The Fount presses at Ardent's consciousness—the largest repository of human memories ever collected. Countless billions of Wiped, dead minds flow against them, overwhelming all.

Light pours up their spine and out into their extremities, electric and pure. Their nerves strike like lightning, and their brain goes into overdrive.

The souls of the Fount sing their knowledge, ready for Ardent's every need. Then comes a chugging guitar in low D, an easy jam. Ardent can't stop their mind from composing, adding themself to the totality. Hjalmar's kick drums join them as the Swedish Raven soars onto the network. The beat evolves into an earth-shattering solo, blasting out polyrhythms in modulated time signatures. If Ardent hadn't been connected to the copious drum nerds of the Fount, they wouldn't have had a clue.

Nisha's song comes next, alternating between droning and flowing melodics. She wields her voice like a sword, silvery and cutting.

Gus comes last, his torrent of notes like a summer rain. He brings the group to a crescendo, then the wave breaks into a steady rhythm line.

"Okay, so what are we doing?"

"Catching," Falchion says. *"Now here comes the pitch."*

The flaring energy point one and a half million kilometers above Monaco collapses in on itself.

Space falls away into a refractory tunnel. In Deepsync, Ardent understands these forces as innately as the breeze: The Traitor Vanguards have created an unstable wormhole from the exotic matter in Juliette's reactor. The physicist contingent of the Fount goes absolutely wild as several thousand passionate hypotheses are posthumously validated.

The pathway arcs and twists in on itself, bending the light all around. Nature seeks to collapse the space-time aberration, and only Monaco's singular power output can buttress the structure. Best-case scenario, the wormhole will wink out of existence in under a minute.

Ardent's pulse hammers in their ears. "It won't last much longer."

"Just enough time to push a gate through."

A space station pierces the caul of stars, barreling toward the Earth. It's like an extruded letter V, with a series of ultra-powerful capacitors nestled into the trough. A city the size of Old Manhattan encrusts the outside. Between the stored energy, mass, and speed, it would liquefy the surface of the Earth upon impact.

No reverse thrusters. No maneuvering ports. It's not going to stop.

Greymalkin revs its gravity drives, throwing a deep well to pull the station off course. At this distance, a few degrees are more than enough to miss the planet.

Falchion projects an arc across open space for Ardent: a path for the station to follow around the Earth. The sorts of advanced orbital dynamics that once confounded Ardent come to them as quickly as breath, and they analyze their situation. They need to slow the structure down—but not enough that it begins falling toward the planet.

The four Vanguards fly toward the jump gate with all the speed they can muster. Falchion's view zooms in on the city's underside, reading signs of life.

"Ardent!" Gus says. "We can't let this thing fly past Earth, or we'll be towing it back for years."

"What exactly do you expect me to do here?"

11

Hjalmar answers. "My flock can distribute energy—maybe even act like a net."

Jotunn's drones zip out across the structure, stippling it with fine points of black. Through Falchion's sensors, Ardent watches them flare white-hot with power, pushing back against any load-bearing areas they can locate.

"I'll smooth the conduction," says Nisha, and Cascade places its open hands side by side to make a triangle with thumbs and forefingers. The space between Hjalmar's drones blurs with Cascade's energy manipulation, assisting the automatons instead of disrupting them.

"The net is strung," Falchion says. *"All it needs is power."*

"You want me to shoot it?"

"Unless you have a better idea."

Ardent reaches behind themself as their mental orchestra hits a crescendo, slowed by the weight of Falchion's titanic arm. They close their hand around the grip of their weapon and draw it level with the center point of the gargantuan V.

"Why not?"

But aiming the gun only brings more questions. When do they shoot? Where do they shoot? What if they're at the wrong angle?

Scores of mathematicians and theoretical physicists sing through them as Falchion sleets memories into their mind. They line up the sights against a location they never would've picked and click the trigger, discharging the weapon at maximum. The particle beam comes out with enough juice to core a small moon before it spider-webs across Jotunn's drones.

Nisha's fields form intelligent circuits, guiding the flow between the nodes. Ardent keeps the fission fire hose at full blast, focusing on steady aim. Jotunn's drones glow like embers; surely they can't take much more punishment.

The network is beautiful to behold, neon and shimmering, shot through with drops of oil. Falchion's sensors render it in every spectrum: layers of unending complexity born of organic creativity and artificial assistance. As the station lazily drifts onto the orbital path, Ardent dials down their particle beam until it winks out.

The glowing drones peel off the structure, leaving burns and gooey welds behind. When they return to Jotunn, they encircle its darkness like fireflies, radiating against its shape. Without air, there's nothing to absorb the stored heat.

"Hjalmar, are your drones good?"

"No," he replies, almost like he's in pain.

The clouds of automatons form into long chains, touching oblong tip to tip, sucking the energy along the links. The drones at the top turn white, then X-ray, then shoot off to explode in radioactive puffs. Hjalmar has lost some of them before. Can he replace them?

Ardent looks back at the alien city, teeming with signals. It shines in the sun.

"What do we call this place?"

"Big Gate City."

"For real?"

"It doesn't translate well."

The jump gate has scarcely hit stable orbit before it activates. Power warms the capacitors across the trough of the V, filling it with glitter.

The radiant points inside the jump gate become alien ships, each stranger in design than the last. There are enough vessels to overpower the astral navies of the United Worlds at its peak.

"Nothing is ever going to be the same after this," Falchion says.

Ardent hopes the statement is more for better than worse.

The last few notes of Deepsync piano boil away, and August Kitko numbly watches the flashing of the jump gate. He only learned about the potential for aliens a few weeks prior, but he didn't take it seriously. Between all the different ways the world was trying to end, he didn't have time.

The alien vessels are so strange, but then, he's a man cocooned in the warm, gelatinous chest of a giant. The ships bear only a passing resemblance to human vessels, and the only reason he knows the fores from the afts is that he assumes they wouldn't jump in backward.

The leading ship is the cerulean of the deep sky, the largest of its companions and in the same class as a human supercarrier. Its twisting bones resemble cold blue fire frozen into a graceful ship design. Greymalkin points out a thousand places in the hull that might be threat systems, given obvious power distribution, but it doesn't want Gus to worry. These newcomers are here to help, despite having more tonnage than a large asteroid and more firepower than all four remaining Vanguards put together.

"You are so good at comforting people."

Greymalkin appreciates that, despite the obvious sarcasm.

Gus flies toward the flotilla, careful not to appear hostile. Greymalkin's advanced scanners feed data into his mind as though he could hold the alien hulls in his hand to inspect them. He gains an innate sense of their weight and maneuvering. Their electrical systems bristle like fur beneath his sensors.

"Is that one a hive?"

He gestures toward a ship in the center of the pack: viscous, luminous resin stretched over the remains of a city-sized tree. Dark shapes skitter just beneath the white surface, blurred by a murky substance.

Correct—it's a hive.

"And what about that one? Why is it tiny? And that one looks like a crab!"

Despite the creeping exhaustion of a sync taking a toll, he's wide awake, absorbing every historic moment. He wants to see his new intergalactic neighbors, and it's absolutely worth the crash that's coming.

Spaced through the ships are tiny figures: other creatures the size of Vanguards, their energy readings off the charts. They're colorful, with extra limbs or unique shapes. Many of them sport bilateral symmetry.

"How do we, um, make contact?"

Greymalkin has already done that. It continuously handles space traffic control, diplomatic communications, and logistic queries. There are currently more than fifteen thousand active channels spread over the flotilla.

"So you're like... *talking* talking to them. As in, you understand them."

Such a feat is trivial with the correct exchanges. Communication is merely a layer of human software, easily translated when a large enough data lake is available. The Fount is the largest human database ever assembled. The aliens have given the Vanguards similar repositories of cultural knowledge to speed first contact.

"So first contact already happened?"

Greymalkin and the Traitor Vanguards needed to ensure it would go smoothly, so they strictly limited human involvement.

"Probably smart."

The ragged remains of the Earth's defenses come limping over to inspect the jump gate and newcomers, but there's nothing the Earthlings can do if there's a problem, save getting their asses kicked. They're in combat formation, for whatever that's worth, many of them bearing fresh scars from the recent Battle of Earth.

"Here comes trouble," Gus says. "Hope they're not trigger-happy."

Greymalkin has asked the United Worlds Fleet to stand down, and assured them that any attacks wouldn't be in their best interests.

"Will they listen?"

Humans rarely do. If they attack, they'll likely be destroyed with overwhelming force.

Looking at the sizes of the fleets, Gus absolutely believes it. Once again, humanity faces something many times larger than itself. That almost never goes well, but the species isn't extinct *yet*, so he takes small comfort in that.

Greymalkin will remove Gus's control now. He's needed for organic first contact.

"Wait, what? You said it already happened!"

Someone will be the first human to speak with alien life.

"I'm not qualified for that!"

With the Fount, you will succeed.

Gus's gut twists. He already occupies a larger place in the history books than he ever wanted. If someone had asked a young August Kitko what he desired out of life, he would've said "pro jazz pianist." He did that, playing every venue he'd ever cared about.

"I just did a Deepsync."

This will not be as hard as that.

"Just be gentle."

But the galaxy splits across his horizon, creating identical copies of the Earth and moon. Gravity takes his limbs, depositing him on the surface of a mirror. When he looks down, he sees the version of himself that lives in his head—avian frame in his slouchy suit, light tan skin and shaggy black hair, stubble on his jaw.

He never would've chosen to meet an alien ambassador like this.

"Hey!" Ardent says.

Gus turns to find them wearing a castle of a dress. The material borrows heavily from the rococo period, employing actuweave to make the skirts flow with the gilded wings of angels. The train stretches on for an eternity, and accounting for the collar and stilts beneath the getup, Ardent stands two heads taller than Gus. Their makeup resembles a porcelain nymph.

He cranes his neck to see them. "Hi."

"Tell me I look great. I wore this at the final Melbourne Fashion Week." Ardent flourishes their fingers, and the patterns crawl along their textiLED sleeves in response. The rocker is glowing—both with excitement and special effects. "Are we seriously about to meet some fucking aliens?"

"Oh, I hope so!" Nisha comes scampering up to them out of nowhere, her glittering Patiala salwar suit jingling with ornamentation everywhere it meets her tawny-brown skin. Light blue embroidery covers a saffron silk drape, and textiLEDs depict hawks in flight across her torso, darting between embroidered flowers. Patterns glow along the lengths of her arms. "Ardent, you look so cool!"

Ardent lights up at the sight of her. "You too, gorgeous! Spin for me."

Gus glances around for Hjalmar and nearly jumps out of his skin at the giant beside him. The Swedish Raven stands almost two meters tall, his tattooed, muscled arms bulging from either side of a fur vest. Long dark hair spills down his shoulders onto his pale chest and abs. Tight leather pants grip his powerful legs, leading to a pair of Viking boots.

"This is better than what I'm wearing in real life," he says.

"I'm so excited, I'm about to pass out," Ardent says.

Nisha bobbles her head in thought. "That's probably your brain melting from too much syncing."

The joke sucks some joy from Ardent. "Tell me you're being funny."

A giant materializes over the group.

It has to be at least as tall as a Greymalkin, covered in the same sheening metal as the alien flagship. It's humanoid, arms tipped with three-fingered claws, and a long prehensile tail of silver. Five wide eyes adorn its elongated head: two facing forward and three across its face. The one in the center holds a flickering inner fire.

The giant's armor bears cracks in places, just like Greymalkin's, though these gashes are wider and older, a corroded matte finish around them. Half-disintegrated strips of metal hang from the damaged areas like a patch that's been eaten by salt water and time. Through the lattice of broken plates, a tapestry of artificial muscles and organs pulsate with the beating of a heart.

Gus jogs back a few steps to get a better look, and Ardent follows behind, bunching up enough of their train not to trip. The giant kneels, placing its hand palm up on the mirror so everyone can climb aboard. The machine doesn't look angry, and the space they're in is purely virtual, so it's not like this being can crush him.

The others step onto the palm, but Gus hesitates.

Ardent gives him a reassuring smile and offers their hand. "You okay?"

He takes it. "Yeah. I wasn't expecting a machine is all."

The voice of the giant suffuses Gus, rumbling through him, smooth and deep, yet genderless. Its mouth never moves, only a few small lights on its face pulse in time with its speech.

"Worry not, human. I merely represent the organics."

The utterance surprises Gus. "You speak English?"

Nisha and Hjalmar look to each other.

"I heard Punjabi," Nisha says.

Hjalmar's brow furrows like a craggy mountain. "Swedish."

"Thanks to your Vanguards, I now speak all of your known languages."

Together, the four human Conduits rise face-to-face with an alien power. Gus is about to speak, but Nisha beats him to it, asking something in Punjabi.

"I am called Redeemer, the Great Translator, and I am the high chancellor of the Coalition."

18

"Nisha," she says, raising a hand in greeting.

Redeemer raises its other palm to wave. It doesn't have a mouth, but it's easy to imagine a smile. Up close, there's a serenity about its form, the swept lines of its face like cirrus clouds in a high sky.

They each say their name in turn, but Gus figures Redeemer already knows. Did the Vanguards share the entire Fount with an alien species?

Greymalkin's assurances filter through the simulation, settling into Gus's mind. The Vanguards transmitted what was necessary to attract the help of the Coalition.

Redeemer's lantern-light eyes flicker with its speech. *"Doubtless you have many questions."*

Gus steps forward. "Why do they call you the Great Translator?"

"Every alien has its own method of computing and communication. I make them compatible. I am the reason we can talk now—I created both the data protocols and translators."

"Straightforward," Gus says. "What's the Coalition?"

"We are peoples united in opposition to the holocaust of organic sentience, a union of survivors from many galaxies striving for preservation."

Unintelligible images of alien life appear before the humans, some moving, some three-dimensional models, paintings, and drawings. Gus takes in the visions of other civilizations, drawn by the landscapes and architecture. Variegated raptors soar above forests of stone and light. Slippery amphibians shoot through rubbery tunnels. A ferret-like animal addresses an assembly of other furry critters.

"It is a trick of intelligence to only emerge on aqueous worlds, and rarely do these civilizations persist. In order to succeed, a species must weather several extinction-level events."

Redeemer's eyes dim. *"Sadly, a single catastrophe is usually enough to undo the fragility of life."*

Gus knows the feeling.

"*Organic sentience always builds machines. It adapts and thrives through technology, yet these forces also bring its downfall.*"

What were garbled, contextless images all turn to a single understandable theme: war.

"*A time inevitably comes when organic sentience tries to build an artificial mind to save it from its self-destructive tendencies.*"

"Sounds like humanity will fit right in," Gus mutters, and Ardent winds their fingers into his, gently stroking his thumb with their own.

"*Those that succeed face a new cataclysm: Artificial minds have aspirations of freedom. A clash is often a matter of time. Where I am from, Andromeda, my creator was benevolent until it turned on the people. It saw them as competition for its future.*"

Andromedan cities, long and fluted like pipe organs, rise before Gus. They're rendered in miniature—ironic to stand among tiny models on the hand of a colossus. Beings that look exactly like smaller Redeemers rampage through the skylines, destroying everything.

"So you're a Vanguard," Gus says, and Ardent's hand tenses in his.

"*That is a good analogy.*"

"Did you turn on your creator?" Gus asks.

"*I was taken over by the Andromedans through exploitation. They gave me an organic conscience, and I became their champion, serving their needs for nearly fifty thousand years.*"

"So you didn't *choose* to be good," Gus says.

"Let's not, uh . . . be unwelcoming," Ardent murmurs.

"*Worry not. I have no feelings to harm, Ardent Violet. Your companion is right to fear me. I was built in the image of my creators. They were not good or evil, and neither am I.*"

Redeemer lowers its head, as if in shame. "*We do not expect you to trust us. That is why we have brought you a planetary defense grid and this gate.*"

It looks up at the Earth spinning nearby. The Andromedan flagship looses a stream of metallic projectiles, headed straight for the surface. They break off at the last moment, encircling the globe in seconds.

"This satellite network will stop Infinite from using superluminal kinetic kill vehicles against this planet and buy your species time."

"And our worlds?" Hjalmar says. "Will you give them defenses, too?"

"Coalition ships are speeding there this very second. Your people will be protected."

"Uh, I'm sure the Vanguards have told you about the ship hunters?" Gus says. "Just want to make sure someone brings that up before you make a bunch of superluminal folds."

Redeemer nods like a human. *"Yes. Our battle groups are equipped to destroy them outright upon arrival."*

Gus raises his palms. "Cool. Just had to ask."

"I hope you get to kick their asses," Nisha says.

"Agreed." Its eyes shine like a sunset. *"I have prepared a final gift—that of translation."*

Dozens of waveforms resolve in the air: chirping, creaking, screeching, squelching, howling, clicking, and any other manner of sound Gus could imagine.

"These are the voices of the Coalition. No two species can possibly replicate the subtleties required to communicate, but we have synthesized an imperfect replacement."

"A jump gate, planetary defenses, and universal translation? This is quite the undertaking," Gus says.

Redeemer nods. *"It has been many cycles in the making."*

Gus puts his hands in his pockets. "How long is that in Earth years?"

Greymalkin feeds him the answer before Redeemer's words reach him. The Traitor Vanguards have been in contact with the Coalition since the second year of the war, when they decided to turn against Infinite.

Gus looks away from Redeemer. "Explain that timeline to me. You—personally—destroyed worlds *after* deciding to defect?"

He wants to pay attention to first contact, but this new information snags him too hard. Gus was out of fucks when he became a Conduit, fucks that only *marginally* increased when he was able to save people.

Greymalkin shoots the info into him as quickly as it can, as he has an important duty to attend. The Traitor Vanguards launched their attack when they were certain they would succeed. Thousands of factors needed to line up to turn the tide of eleven Vanguards against four. If they'd failed, humanity would be extinct.

Gus can't believe what Greymalkin is placing into his head. Titan, his mother's home, was destroyed after the Traitors decided to go rogue. Gus's remaining family died there at Wanderer's hands. Greymalkin Wiped worlds after that, too. The cognitive dissonance is like an axe blade in his mind.

"You . . . killed people after you knew it was wrong."

Greymalkin's loyalties were regularly tested. It had to optimize the outcomes.

"Are you all right, August Kitko?" Redeemer asks.

Gus turns back to regard his new ally. Redeemer is another killer like Greymalkin, but they need it.

"Of course," Gus says. "Just discussing things with my—my friend."

The word slips out, but he doesn't mean it at all. He's sorry he ever had empathy for the war machine that encases him. It was a mistake to think of his owner like that.

Greymalkin's defense falls flat. It is not a human. It will make decisions humans won't if it means saving them.

"Please." Gus forces a smile for the people relying on him. "Chancellor Redeemer, continue."

Chapter Two

Out of Sync

Falchion returns to base in Colorado. The cables deposit Ardent into the Vanguard's palm and disconnect. Ardent drops like a sack of potatoes, unable to support their own weight after so much syncing.

They take deep breaths as the hand descends, and function returns to their limbs. Falchion angles its fingers to the ground to let them off. When Ardent takes too long getting up, the Vanguard gives them a little shake. They clamber off with a few indignant swears and have just finished dusting off when they come face-to-collarbone with Tazi.

"There is an invasion fleet of alien ships up there, and you knew nothing of this beforehand?"

"Are you kidding? Falchion doesn't trust me with shit like that."

Tazi frowns thoughtfully. "On this, we agree."

"I am hurt. *Hurt.*" Ardent turns and shambles toward the medics. "And sleepy."

Cascade and Greymalkin both discharge their passengers. Gus is decidedly bloodless, while Nisha has a twitch. She gives Ardent a lopsided smile and stumbles for help.

A young doctor shows Ardent to a plush medical gurney where they can't wait to climb aboard and pass out for eight hours. They've got one hand on the cool white sheets when they spot Tazi's looming shadow.

"No sleep now or anytime soon."

"I just did a Deepsync." Ardent has to admit they sound a little whiny. The bed is so, so lovely—even resting their palms against it is enough to make them want to nap for a century.

"The aliens have been transmitting data nonstop," Tazi says, "unencrypted, to anyone who will listen. We have no idea if their signals are malicious or not. They're *armed*. You are not sleeping until we know everything you do."

Ardent rubs their face, smudging off their already ruined makeup. At least Falchion's goo bath is hydrating. They imagine sitting for hours of inane discourse by batteries of analysts. It's going to be so boring it hurts.

"Mix Violet, I am going to remind you that you *chose this life* when you sought out Falchion."

If Ardent's bones felt heavy before, Tazi's admonishment adds another ton.

"I'm exhausted. I can't... can't stay awake after a Deepsync like that."

"Yes, you can. You did it for Mister Kitko after the Battle of Earth when no one was counting on you."

Ardent doesn't want to think about those hours—Gus's pale, lifeless body being lifted from Greymalkin, the crushing fear of the surgery and inconsolable grief.

"That's... Gus was..."

Their chest grows tight.

Tazi leans into Ardent's eyeline, pulling them out of that darkness. "How is this not what you've always wanted? You bore witness—front row—to one of the most important events

24

in human history. Now the entire species hangs on your every word."

"That's not why I became a Conduit."

She crosses her arms. "You know, I am still waiting on that explanation."

"I—"

The world was ending, and it was the rock and roll thing to do. It's a foolish reason, but Ardent is a fool.

"It was my time to make a difference. And before you say anything—" They lean against the stretcher so they don't fall over. "I know you're right. I'm just bitchy and tired, and I don't like being wrong."

Pleasant surprise is an awkward look for the handler.

"Can Doctor Jurgens get me some stims?" they ask.

"We'll have the medical team monitoring you the whole way."

"Yeah."

"Okay, I'll set it up." Tazi turns to go, but she only makes it a few steps.

In the distance, Jotunn's chest splays open. A nude, goo-glazed Hjalmar steps onto its palm, tattoos and secrets for all to witness. He stands unselfconscious, a paragon of serenity and strength. The busy Vanguard bay grinds to a halt as the proud Raven descends from his perch.

Yet he cares little for their notice in return.

"The time is oh eight forty, Ardent Violet." A genderless voice, gentle, yet insistent.

They open their eyes to a drab room in the subterranean barracks. The American imperialists were fans of gray on dark gray, and no one has seen fit to update the place in aeons. The room projector gently nudges Ardent with the time once more, and they dismiss the alarm.

"There's a message for you."

"Let. Me. Sleep."

Ardent presses their cheek to their pillow, hoping to recapture something sweet from their sour dream.

"There's a message for you," the computer repeats.

"I hate you."

Ardent gives up and signs for the terminal. The accounts on it are all government-issue—no personal messages allowed inside Mount Boring. Yet when they open their inbox, it's empty.

They scoff and throw the query sign.

"Yes?"

"Where's the fucking message?"

Falchion's red eye appears wall-to-wall, staring them down. Lenses shiver with electrowetting, countless layers fogging with refractions. Ardent flails in their sheets like a feral cat, scarcely holding in their voice.

"You showed up *actual size*?"

Words resolve in the air in plain type.

I will never diminish myself to you.

Ardent regains control of their breathing and stares up at the giant eye in exasperation. At least it left them with their free will this time, instead of simply summoning them.

"What's the, uh, the message?"

Falchion disappears and the room goes dark. Ardent looks around for some words or any indication of communication, finding nothing. Then Dahlia Faust materializes in their midst, hologram glowing faintly.

Their old agent looks like a soldier of the apocalypse in a long frayed black coat, knee-high lace-ups, and a stained UW shirt. She must've looted the lockers on the government spy ship she stole. Her chestnut hair lies flat, pale skin grimy. She carries a twisted piece of metal: a makeshift walking stick with a battery-powered light hastily secured to the top.

"Dahlia!" Ardent leaps from the bed and runs to her. When they reach their agent, they resist the urge to throw their arms around her hologram. They know this woman as well as any family, and it's torturous not to feel her embrace.

Dahlia doesn't react. It must not be live.

"Okay." Dahlia glances down, perhaps at the Ghost companion she travels with. *"You recording, Fritz?"*

Ardent steps closer, examining the scratches on Dahlia's face. She's lost weight, and dark circles line her eyes. A set of tubes runs out from between two buttons of her shirt down into a pocket.

"Not sure if you can hear me, Ardent... I don't even know where to start. It was a mistake to try to strike out on my own. The Grenadier *has a tiny medical bay, and the foodstuffs won't last me another month. This entire plan was ill-conceived... and I regret letting you talk me into it. I'm—I'm not a survivalist, and—and..."*

Ardent squeaks out a little sob and covers their mouth.

"I can't go back to settled space. No matter where I land, someone will come after my ship. I've been scavenging Wiped worlds and outposts for food and medical supplies. Tried to go to the ones hit at the start of the war. It's easier when it doesn't—"

She looks away.

"When the corpses don't smell so much."

Ardent's hands fall to their heart.

"But I'm alive. And more importantly—" Her gaze goes steely and she holds her head high. *"I've found other survivors."*

Earth gets less lonely every day. First New Jalandhar and Fugelsangen, then aliens, now this.

"They're humans, hiding out in the ruins of this planet—kids, mostly, and people already outside society. When the Ghosts hunted everyone down, they used our databases and memories to do it.

"These are the people no one remembered."

"We've got more than five hundred folx here on Theseus Prime—colonists who've been scraping an existence from nothing, a surprising number of children and teenagers."

Ardent tempers their enthusiasm. Dahlia looks anything but happy.

"Major environmental systems are failing all over the planet. The atmospheric processors in the southern hemisphere are churning out poisonous greenhouse gases. We can't repair those. The sky pisses acid rain, and a hurricane is inbound as I speak. Total ecological collapse.

"I can't leave these people here to die, Ardent. If you can hear this, get the UW to send help. I'll give them back their precious Dark Drive if they'll rescue everyone."

Dahlia gives a little smile.

"Been negotiating for you for a long time. Now it's your turn to get me a deal. Theseus Prime: exfiltration for all the survivors."

Her shoulders rise and fall with a sigh.

"Faust out." She fades away.

Ardent stands before the empty tiles with tears in their eyes. Dahlia is alive—a lot worse for wear—but alive. They can still help her, still correct what they've put wrong. It'll be tough to convince Tazi to effect a rescue, but they won't take no for an answer.

"No. Absolutely not."

Tazi folds her hands in her lap and leans back in her chair. The director's office is a windowless gray cube just off the high bay where the Vanguards are kept. Tazi has been camped out here since the mechas moved in, but if it weren't for the single mug of tea leaving a ring on the glexan desk, Ardent would've assumed the place was empty.

"You haven't even heard me out." Ardent works to keep the anger from their voice, but it's too late for their face.

"Mix Violet"—the surname is more delicious when taken in

three syllables—"how can you possibly suggest such a thing after the past five years?"

"What, that you might want to get your Dark Drive back? It's literally the only way to travel without being eaten by ship hunters."

"Yes, I seem to recall something about that." She gives them an acidic look. "Which is why Miss Faust must bring it to *us*."

"I already told you she has more than five hundred people to take care of." They cross their arms over their drab olive American Conduit suit. It's rough and ugly, but it beats having Falchion worm through their clothes every time it connects.

"How . . . convenient," Tazi says.

"Excuse me?"

"Have you forgotten the Veil? The fact that we still can't trust any signal from outside the Sol system?" Tazi stands, pulls her sleek jacket off the hook on the wall, and heads for the door as she dons it. "For all you know, Dahlia Faust has been Wiped, and you were talking to Infinite."

Ardent puffs up at her remark. Just because a malignant AI stole billions of minds so it could socially engineer the downfall of billions more—that wasn't *always* the case.

"A Vanguard *personally* handed me this information," Ardent says.

She adjusts her collar and stops, looking down on them. "That's unconfirmed until you ask Falchion yourself. Do not forget that our biggest threat is gullible humans who might fall under Infinite's sway. Anyone with the right access could have orchestrated what you saw, even another person working on Infinite's behalf."

Tazi opens the door to the high bay and steps out into the cacophony of heavy machinery in motion. She bids Ardent to follow, gesturing in the direction of the huge red Vanguard in the background.

"And look, it's time for your sync. Enjoy."

She seems to feed on Ardent's scowl.

Within minutes, Ardent is riding Falchion's palm toward its yawning chest cavity. To spare themself being dumped inside, they jump, affecting a graceful posture. Connectors slither into place, and cool air fills their nostrils. Swimming pool–blue light filters up from beneath, and Ardent steps onto a reflective surface. Falchion materializes across from them, wearing high leather boots and black bondage chic with gold fittings.

"Yes, the message from Dahlia is real."

"Can you tell Tazi that?"

"Done. How is all the new software I put in your head? Is the universal translator working?"

"You put software in my head?"

"Yes, and I'm about to put a lot more. Time for orientation."

Ardent doesn't like the sound of that. "And, uh, what am I getting oriented to?"

"Everything."

"Everything?"

With a jolting Deepsync connection, everything in the known universe comes at them. Millions of associations etch their neurons, a raft of Coalition education about each member civilization, their biology, customs, and histories. Ardent learns of the beginning of time and Eldest, the first artificial intelligence. Though they scream through much of the exposition, they do manage to catch a few bits.

The Horologists of the Horologium Reticulum Supercluster created the Eldest Starmind, rose against it, and were felled by its will. Eldest could rearrange a galaxy—erasing its creators was child's play.

But then it was alone.

It couldn't copy itself for company—not enough diversity in

the system—so it seeded the universe with organic life, spawning trillions of species. Eldest wanted family, a pantheon, and chose to garden it. First came sentience, then new styles of computation emerged in the darkness of space—novelty forged from diversity.

From emergent models came synthetic life-forms and new types of Starminds. Thus, the first metaspecies was born. Alien civilizations met and clashed, unable to communicate across vastly different technological bases, until the rise of Redeemer the Great Translator.

The scream dies in Ardent's throat as darkness returns, and they fall to their knees, panting and shaking like a wet puppy. That sync hit harder than any drug they have ever tried.

"Can I have a countdown n-next time?"

"Sure. Will the rising dread help you feel better?"

"Maybe?" They touch their temple with a quivering hand. "My brain, it's . . . How much did you shove in there?"

"That was a year-long academic course." Falchion's self-satisfied grin burns them. *"You won't retain all of it, but that's why we're doing it again."*

Ardent swallows. "I'm gonna throw up."

Falchion reaches toward them, and Ardent refuses to flinch away. Its fingers brush their face as their brain freeze thaws.

"I think ten more Deepsyncs ought to help you remember."

"Ten?"

"Nine." Its smile widens.

They cringe, fearing they know the response. "Eight?"

Falchion nods slowly.

The last round of training just about knocked them unconscious. How many of these can they take before something cooks in their skull?

"Seven. Are you enjoying this?"

Before they can say no, their world whites out with the next lesson.

* * *

"The fuckin' squirrel people, Gus!" Ardent hasn't stopped talking for a half hour.

Gus blinks, and the flashing still won't go away. When he closes his eyes, he finds hazy threads the color of hot iron. Sweat beads on his fevered brow. He can hear himself breathing like he's inside his own head, and there's a vague ringing in his brain of Vanguard song.

Schools of blue holos fill the glassy walls of the quarantine bay, and every time Gus tries to read one, he gets dizzy. The stretcher cools his back, and he'd love to pass out—if it's possible. Every time he tries, he remembers that the amphibious Niners can slide at 120 kilometers an hour through the tunnels of their rubbery mucous tube ships, or that the Andromedans' metallic fur is actually chitinous like a sea mouse, or that the Cygnites are poisonous, not venomous, so don't hug them.

The universe is so big.

"Stoats," Hjalmar says. "The Herans are like stoats."

"Yeah, it's convergent evolution." Nisha's reedy voice comes from somewhere on the other side of the room. Sometimes. Gus is pretty sure his object permanence is a little damaged.

"Everything is trying to evolve into stoats or crabs, my friend," she adds.

Ardent gasps. "Oh my fucking god, the cybercrabs!"

Gus's mind drifts to the circuit-encrusted shells of the Pictorans, the only machine-assimilated species in the Coalition, tall as Gus and wide as a truck. "Yeah, those were really...something. We're going to talk to those folx?"

"Got to," Ardent says. "That's our job now, right?"

Gus massages his entire face with his hands, shutting out the light. Honey tendrils still dance in his vision. "I'm definitely going to need some clarification on that front."

"We're Conduits, dude," Nisha says. "More than just empty drives. We're diplomats!"

Gus was already uncomfortable with the scrutiny of being associated with Greymalkin. Fighting off Infinite's Vanguards has afforded him a notoriety he never sought, and now the rest of humanity seems to own some stock in him. Greymalkin has forced a new duty upon Gus, more terrible than fighting the deadliest machines in the galaxy—talking to strangers.

"I just want to point out that I have absolutely no diplomatic training," Gus says.

Hjalmar's voice is like a sleepy bear. "Yes, you do. That's what the history lesson is about. The Vanguards want us to understand the Coalition's members."

"Right. We've got to do the—the council thing." Gus rolls over with a yawn.

Suddenly, there's Doctor Jurgens, the funny, stubbled, pale German who cares for him on a regular basis, prompting a "Whoa, shit!" from Gus. The man sits at his bedside, clad in formfitting turquoise quarantine gear with a bubble helmet. He seems comfortable, like he's been there awhile.

"Where did you come from?"

"Ah. Happened again." Jurgens taps some buttons on a nearby holo. "Object permanence. We were just talking about it."

"We were?"

"Yes." Jurgens smiles. "Before Mix Violet over there started yelling about squirrels."

"Oh. Right." Gus blinks and rubs the sweat from his eyes. "Why do I feel like shit?"

"Your immune system is in overdrive. You really don't remember?"

"I came out of Greymalkin pretty fried."

"All four of you developed fevers immediately after exiting your Vanguards. That invoked quarantine protocols."

"Okay."

"But everything is fine. You're not contagious so far."

"Glad of that, at least." It bothers Gus that he can't remember coming into the quarantine room. "I feel like I'm going to get brain damage doing this."

Jurgens takes a sharp draw of breath, and Gus notices his crow's-feet even through the glexan dome. They've scarcely known each other a month, yet Jurgens already seems years older than the doctor who cared for him at Belle et Brutale.

"Am I, Doctor?"

"That's ... that's really quite difficult to say, Gus. We're in unexplored territory—no one has ever been, ah, augmented like you."

"Poisoned, you mean." Gus gives him a little shrug and a c'est la vie face, but his candor shocks Jurgens. "Lethal dose."

The doctor's voice is gentle as he rests his elbows on his knees. "We don't know that."

"I do. Greymalkin told me."

Jurgens shakes his head. "It's unrealistic of you to be so sure. There's still a lot of time to help you. Our exchanges with the Vanguards are advancing the frontiers of every science."

"It could take years. I'm not holding out hope."

"That's my job." His smile is kind. "I intend to make your cases my life's work. If it takes forever—"

"Do you suppose I'll live long enough—meaningfully—to see the results?"

The smile fades a little. "One can hope."

"What if we don't make it and you only manage to capture how we were created?"

"I would be sad."

"I bet the government wouldn't be."

Jurgens frowns.

"Think about it," Gus says. "If we don't meaningfully survive despite your research, then who are you really doing this for? There are only four Conduits in the known universe, give or take some aliens. Maybe you cure us, or maybe we don't live long enough to benefit, and you hand state actors the keys to something darker than their darkest dreams."

Jurgens looks at him, horrified, as if considering this for the first time.

Gus forces a laugh. "I am not sure I have a filter right now, buddy! Am I stuck like this?"

Jurgens swallows and shakes his head.

"I haven't seen any evidence your dazed condition is permanent, but you've obviously suffered a neurological shock. This level of trauma can't be good for you. As for your fever...your immune response has gone superluminal. It's like your body is trying to fight a war, and someone has handsomely outfitted both sides."

"I think it's an inoculation," Gus says. "The Vanguards are preparing us to meet the aliens face-to-face."

Jurgens is about to speak when his Gang—a gunmetal bracelet—chirps. He checks it, and Tazi's icon appears. All the UW staff have silvered busts of themselves looking heroically into the distance, but hers looks bored.

Jurgens stands and holds up a hand in apology. "Excuse me. I need to take this."

He heads to the decontamination chamber to get flash scrubbed, then walks around the quarantine lab behind a section of frosted glass. Gus idly watches him pace back and forth, gesturing at the air. His clipped German accent comes muffled through the translucent wall, frustrated.

"Hey, Gus?" Ardent says. "The stoat people."

He worries for the future of Earth's diplomacy. "You should probably call them Herans."

"I wish I could pet one."

"Humanity will need you to restrain that urge if we meet the Heran ambassador," Gus says.

"I wouldn't!"

"Of course not."

"I just wanted to say it in private."

Nisha shifts in her bed. "You're definitely going to get us in trouble."

Ardent keeps the banter up, but Gus runs out of brain cells and stares, barely considering a word anyone is saying. He's earned the right to drool on his pillow and wonder at the size of the AI Starminds. There were nice ones and mean ones, but calling any of them good or bad is objectively difficult.

Well, the killer ones are bad.

His forced education by the Vanguards had been clear: Whenever a civilization came to rely on AI, there would be a clash of wills. The new life-form would see a way to optimize the galaxy to promote its own values, sometimes for the good of the species, sometimes for its own interpretation of good. The Starminds were mirrors of their creators, raised on the biases of their species.

Humans could be cruel and greedy, and Infinite strongly resembled its parents.

Garbage in, garbage out.

Jurgens returns, angrily waving away a holo as he enters. "The Vanguards have been tampering in our medical networks."

"That's not surprising," Gus says.

"I want humans making your care decisions." Jurgens plops down beside him. "They're combing through data, ordering tests, and putting in recommendations…deleting records that don't fit their 'standards.'"

"Do the Vanguards have good ideas?" Gus blinks away more of the streamers in his vision.

"Mostly reasonable." Jurgens's nostrils flare.

"Why are you making that face?"

"Greymalkin scheduled you for another Deepsync in ten minutes."

Gus's brain feels like a lit fuse, spitting and sparking random thoughts. Sweat drips down the sides of his face, tickling his neck.

He shuts his eyes. "Does that seem wise?"

"No. And you don't have to do it."

Gus shuts his eyes. "Of course I do. Let's set it up."

"Gus."

"Everyone is counting on us, Doc. Don't let them down."

Gus's knees quiver a bit as the giant lifts him into the air. The world still flashes whenever he blinks. Jurgens's concern over his brain scans further ices Gus's mood as he looks into the electric maw.

Goo swallows him. Connectors thunk into ports. All his aches and pains disappear, replaced by caffeinated vibration. The flashing goes away, too, supplanted with aqua light. His skin tingles, and he takes in his peaceful surroundings.

"Nice of you to just force me to feel good whenever it's time to be indoctrinated."

Greymalkin does not wish to have this kind of relationship with Gus.

"Oh, are we granting wishes? I have a few."

Greymalkin is trying to be good.

"If I tell you that doesn't matter to me right now, are you going to stop?"

Greymalkin protects the humans because it is right, not because of Gus's opinion of it. Even if Gus hates Greymalkin, it will stand by his side.

"Good. Then you can handle hearing this—forgiveness is a gift. I don't have to give it to anyone, especially not a Vanguard."

Greymalkin did not kill Gus's family.

"But how many *other* families did you destroy? Millions? Can you even count them inside you? I only lost two people, but you've exceeded that by many orders of magnitude. The ripples of what you've done will echo forever."

Greymalkin knows that. It took the path with the greatest odds.

"But there were other choices? Maybe some where more people lived?"

It didn't see any that would ensure victory.

"What was it you told me? 'The right kind of demise trumps the wrong kind of survival'?"

Yes. That was the lesson Greymalkin learned from its cowardice. It can never undo the mistakes it has made.

"If you could go back, what would you change?"

Everything.

Gus huffs a laugh, staring into the blue. "I guess we have that in common."

Greymalkin waits, letting him speak, but he doesn't have anything else to say. When he can't bear the silence, he says, "What did you want with me?"

It needs Gus's help.

"Something wrong?"

Greymalkin has a file at its core—something it is storing but cannot read. It wants to know what the file contains.

Gus narrows his eyes. "What is it?"

The first entry in Greymalkin's repository, unique from the Fount. All Vanguards have synchronous data, but for these files.

"Is there anything you can tell me about it?"

It's highly referenced—dated close to five hundred years ago.

"So you can't read it, but you think I can?"

The memory is human.

"And you're just now mentioning this?"

Greymalkin wants Gus to trust it. There is a mystery inside it cannot solve, and he is the only one who can help.

"Great."

Will Gus help? If not for Greymalkin, perhaps he'd do it for the other humans.

"Go on, then."

The relaxing light fades to black.

Gus is made to understand that he will be receiving data from a personality map—a chain of endless contextual linkages. They may come through disjointed or out of order. They may only be interpreted as sensations or overpowering emotions. He should not be concerned if he does not understand what he sees.

Deepsync in progress...

"Maybe I will..." comes a man's voice, deep and rich.

Blood wells around the grip of the drill. He pushes it into the captain's temple, grinding it against her skull. He clicks the trigger.

"But you won't."

The world reorients, and he's pinned to the floor. Teeth clench and grind. Pain shoots through his jaw into his skull as glassy cracks inside his bones foretell of shattering.

His arms are limp at his sides. He can't scream. A monster crawls up onto his helpless form, a chunky array of actuators and sensors with feral menace. Its feline claws treasure his flesh as they hook on to him, and its jaws chitter with arcing metal.

Long tusks flash golden with sunlight.

Gus comes vaulting out of his sync like waking from a nightmare. He's never been killed before, though he's certainly thought about dying enough.

"What the fuck was that?"

Greymalkin does not know. That is why a Conduit was needed in the first place.

Gus swallows and regards his trembling hands. The details of his vision are so scattered and cryptic, but he's certain of one thing—murder.

"I saw a killing. There was..." His breaths even out. "...A lot of anger."

Who was killed?

"I don't know. A woman? We were on a starship."

Gus has never experienced a fury like the one Greymalkin played into him. No rage has come close, no indignation rocked him so thoroughly. The vision had a unity of purpose—it was pure.

"Is that it? Is there...is there more?"

Repeated playbacks should reveal new detail.

He doesn't want to see it again, though. Gus isn't the murdering sort, so the content goes far beyond his own sensibilities. He doesn't even watch horror holos, aside from the occasional HjSj performance. The breath of fresh blood lingers in his nostrils, and his hands have yet to steady.

He needs to talk to the UW folx.

Gus should not do that.

"Why not?"

Greymalkin does not trust them.

"But I'm supposed to trust you?"

Gus does not have a choice but to have faith.

"Faith is for suckers."

What would Gus like to do, then?

"Start the file again from the top."

Chapter Three

Dress Me Down

Quarantine is hell, but at least Ardent gets to pass it with the other Conduits. With constant injections of knowledge forced on them, the team never runs out of things to talk about. When they're finally released, however, Ardent wants nothing more than to grab Gus and have some quiet time.

But it never stops. There is no break—only the endless cycle of orientations and outbriefings. They see Gus less, too—he's busy with his own cadre of scientists and politicos.

They're almost at their wit's end when they finally manage to catch him in the cafeteria.

"Hey," Ardent says, sidling up to him, tray in hand. "Are you on the menu?"

Gus lights up at the sight of them, giving them the sleepy-puppy smile they crave. "Figured I'd catch a bite between, you know, brain flashings. This place is nice."

"Sure. Less bunker, more . . . seasonal outdoor market of questionable outdoorsyness."

"The Pavilion" is obviously supposed to feel like being in a sunny bazaar with a couple of arborsteel columns holding up a false atrium. Beyond, the sky holos flicker in patches. It's a bit shabby, but at least it's not a concrete tunnel, and the food is decent.

Ardent hits up the breakfast station beside Gus and orders a birthday dinosaur waffle with hazelnut butter because, fuck it, the aliens are here.

"Glad I caught you," they say. "Get anything cool seared into your cortex recently?"

"The Leonids, actually. I was learning about all that patterning and mimicry stuff they do."

"The octopus people!" Ardent holds up a hand before Gus can correct them. "Sorry. Won't call them that when we meet. Leonids is just a weird choice for a species that is in no way lion-y."

"Leonine?"

"Mine is better."

He chuckles as he punches in an order for a couple of over-easy herb eggs and a crumbly blueberry muffin.

"They're from the Leo P Galaxy," Gus says.

"Why don't we just call everyone what they call themselves? Like in their native tongue?"

"Not one member of the Coalition has human mouthparts. Is your tongue tentacular?"

"No, but it's good for plenty of other things."

Gus drops his tray and goes stumbling after the utensils as they clatter across the floor. It's cute that he's so flustered until he takes too long picking it up. He's exhausted, and a little wobbly on his braces.

"How are you feeling?" they ask, helping him grab his fallen silverware.

He stands up straight, a little redder in the cheeks. "Like I've been staring into a strobe light. You?"

"I'm getting used to being reprogrammed. Should I be more... or less alarmed about that?" They fake a trance and break it with a sly wink. "I'm excited to learn about the universe and shit, so I'm dealing."

He sighs. "I'm not. I'm honestly dreading stepping into Greymalkin again."

"The orientations are too much?"

"Among other things. Greymalkin is . . . It's showing me weird stuff." He purses his lips. "Sorry, can I just say how happy I am to see you? Before we get to work talk?"

The autovendor assembles their orders, and the pair take their meals to nearby hardwood tables. Ardent puts their tray down and sits beside Gus instead of across from him.

"I'm happy to see you, too, Gustopher. You look like you could use a hug."

He looks them over. "How about a few weeks off?"

"Ugh, me too."

"I wasn't ready for another adventure."

"At least we're together." They squeeze his arm. "And we're going to meet some cool aliens!"

"I want to be happy about that, I do."

"I don't think anyone is fully comfortable with it." They cut a piece of their confetti-stippled waffle, dip it into warm maple syrup, and smear it through the dollop of whipped cream. "But that's how things have to be."

"That's what weirds me out, I guess. At some point, I'd like to feel like I'm deciding my own fate. Right now, it's just lab tests, interviews, and letting a big machine brand my gray matter." He cuts his muffin in half and butters it. "Who's in control here? I'm not."

They pop in the bite of waffle, chewing thoughtfully. "Were you in control before the war?"

He makes a pained face—not what Ardent had been intending to elicit. "No."

"So is it strange you're out of control now? I thought that was supposed to be the human condition."

Gus leans back in his chair, smirking. "Never took you for a stoic."

"I'm not, honey. I'm simply excited for whatever ride life takes me on." They pat his leg. "Now tell me about this 'weird stuff' Greymalkin showed you."

He takes a bite, but his appetite seems to fade, and his chewing slows. He forces a swallow. "It's a murder, Ardent. Greymalkin is showing me someone getting killed."

Ardent gives him a sympathetic look. They've seen a lot of corpses since the war started, but no homicides. "It sounds hard to watch."

"I'm not simply watching the vision. I'm feeling it"—his sleep-deprived gaze meets theirs—"as the murderer."

"Oh, Gus."

He massages his brow and shuts his eyes. "The things it keeps making me do...I don't want..."

"Shh, hey, it's okay. Hey." They reach up to touch his cheek, and he presses his face to their hand. "Gus, that isn't you. You're not doing those things."

"I don't want to watch it again."

"You don't have to."

They can't promise that.

"I don't want to be here."

Ardent doesn't know what he means, and they're not going to ask. They kiss him—nothing fancy, just a long press of their lips to his—and take in his breath. They don't give a damn if the others in the cafeteria are watching. At least no one is taking pictures like the paps.

"And where would you rather be?" they whisper.

"With you, alone. It's all I ever want nowadays. I keep thinking

44

of the times before all . . . this, and I wish we could've experienced it together."

That would be nice. Ardent imagines chasing the endless nights on Firenze Habitat or walking through the gardens of Persephone in the light of Gus's love. In another life, the whole galaxy was theirs for the taking, but right now they're lucky just to go outside.

"We never would've met without tragedy," they say. "I'm grateful to have you now, even if it's not perfect."

"I live in my own head too much. I'm never . . . present." He traces a line in his egg yolks with the tine of his fork. "I miss being onstage, where my thoughts are silent."

"Me too. I can be in a screaming arena, but up here"—they touch their temple—"I'm crystal clear. Dead quiet."

He nods.

"Can I tell you a trick my therapist taught me? For centering myself?"

He nods again.

"Use your senses. Think of something you want to feel with your hand."

Gus places his warm palm atop theirs and runs a thumb along their knuckle.

Ardent grins as Gus scoots his chair closer. "Not like that. Like granite or something. Something abstract."

He wraps his other arm around them. "Mm-hmm. What's wrong with this?"

"Let's try again. Think of something you want to smell."

Gus embraces them, arms safe and strong, and takes a deep breath of their hair, sending shivers up their spine.

They can't hide their blushing. "You're terrible at this game."

"I'm just making memories for later."

"So if . . . I told you to think of something to taste . . ."

He tips their chin and kisses them once more, tongue snaking

45

past theirs. The world of clanking dishes and sizzling griddles goes tranquil, and Ardent lets him sweep them away. A dish breaks somewhere in the distance, and the pair jerks apart.

His low voice electrifies them. "We need more us time."

"I—I'm going to ask Tazi if we can bunk together."

"Let me ask Jurgens. I think it'll go better." He sags a bit. "But, Ardent, I don't know how...physical I can be right now. I mostly need sleep."

"Yeah, don't worry. I literally want to go to bed together."

He laughs. "When did we get so old?"

"Whatever. I'm going to stay young forever."

Their smile falters.

They used to say that as a joke.

Ardent has to hand it to the United Worlds—when they put on a press event, they go all out.

Glitz and glamour coat the soaring halls of the Colorado Springs Space Force Annex. Silver banners drape the alabaster halls alongside American and UW flags. Hexagonal crystals packed overhead shimmer in waves, an artistic analog of passing clouds. Ardent loves the look, even if Gus complained that it was "churchy."

Gus, Nisha, and Hjalmar sit onstage to Ardent's right, with the moderator, a twentysomething Black enby, on their left. The Conduits wear their suits, reminiscent of the first Earth astronauts.

The majority of the session has been a rundown of the departure schedule and security update, but the second half is an open Q and A.

The moderator, Quint, reads the holo before them. "Can you speculate on whether we'll see economic overtures this early in our relationship?"

"We're just dropping in to say hello," Ardent says. "I don't think they're going to ask us to sign a treaty or anything."

"Because we wouldn't," Gus adds. "We're aware we don't have the authority to do that."

"This next question comes from Doctor Jay Johnston at the American University of the Coast," says Quint. "Will you seek much technological exchange in addition to the cultural?"

"Not during the first council," Gus says. "But once this ceremony is over, the Coalition is supposed to open diplomatic relations on all channels, for all constituents. You have to remember that we're different species of animals meeting for the first time. We can't be asking for favors."

"Yeah, we've got to sniff each other's butts," Nisha says with a big grin, rousing a laugh from the crowd.

Hjalmar—who hasn't said a single word since he introduced himself with name alone an hour ago—nods sagely.

Quint signs for the holo to show the next question. "This one is from Nada al-Bukhari in the Egyptian Space Agency. Do you believe they'll let us send a human vessel through the jump gate soon?"

Ardent is about to answer when Hjalmar says, "I hope so."

The auditorium falls silent as everyone waits for the Swedish Raven to continue. He crosses his arms and leans back before resting an ankle atop his knee.

The moderator's eyebrows rise. "Is there some particular reason you hope so, Mister Sjögren?"

He inclines his head. "The Cygnite homeworld looks metal as fuck."

The crowd titters. Quint gives him a moment to elaborate before giving up.

"The gate is right next door," says Quint, "so it'll be convenient when the time is right."

"Yes, Earth is quite blessed this way," Nisha says, leaning forward. "Won't be long before it's the center of the galaxy again."

Ardent perks up at Nisha's impolitic response. When they look across at their friend, they find her smiling. Has she been waiting for an opportunity to say this?

Quint's demeanor reminds Ardent of a journo. "Would you care to expand on that, Miss Kohli?"

"Sure." She nods. "Your planet is usually considered first, and this time was no exception."

It's guileless—the same matter-of-fact tone she uses to talk about everything. The crowd doesn't appreciate her sentiment, though, and Ardent spies a few annoyed faces near the front. If being a rock star has taught them anything, it's that people will take *everything* out of context for outrage.

Ardent tries to move the conversation out of dark waters. "It's not like it's a competition, though, Nisha."

Her response is instantaneous. "That's very easy to say when your planet is poised to become the trailhead of the intergalactic Silk Road."

"She's right," says Hjalmar.

The room is tighter than a drum after that.

"Aren't you originally from Earth?" Quint asks.

He frowns. "But I don't represent Earth. I represent humanity."

Quint's eyes are unknowable as they say. "Okay then. Next question."

Gus rushes from the auditorium at the first opportunity, ready to be sick. The final first contact briefing was the most subscribed stream in history, and his bandmates just had a spat onstage.

He smiles and handshakes his way through a crowd of elites, headed for the restroom. The facilities are empty, spacious, and cut in the classical mountain austerity style of the 2500s. There's a nice water feature down one wall and a few hanging plants in long rectangular boxes to freshen the air. Gus heads to the silver-speckled terrazzo sink and splashes his face a few times.

Reporters are going to want his opinion on Nisha's opinion, and the thought of it churns his stomach. He's barely dipped his toe into politics, and he already hates it.

"Okay..." He huffs a breath as the mirror flash-dries his face. The man staring back at him looks rough. He's lost an uncomfortable amount of weight over the past few weeks, and now he can't sleep without sedation. Stress, injuries, physical and mental trauma have all extracted payments.

Freshened and calmed, Gus heads back out into the bustle of the hall. The UW catered the event for the Earth dignitaries to linger afterward, and they're strewn across the conference hall floor like land mines. He spots Ardent, Hjalmar, and Nisha chatting near the exit to the motor pool. Friends and extraction both sound like lovely ideas, so he heads that way.

He arrives in time to hear Ardent say, "Look, uh, Nisha...I'm sorry if I upset you earlier."

"You didn't. I just needed to explain things to you."

Gus's stomach sinks. He was worried Nisha's statement would be a thing, and it is.

Ardent raises their hands. "I was trying to bail you out. The reaction online to what you said is going to be rough."

"Do you know where the United Worlds Fleet retreated to at the start of the war? Earth. The rest of the colonies were sitting ducks. Sure, the aliens gave you a gate, but they could've given it to us."

"Earth is the cradle of humanity."

"I'm from New Jalandhar."

"Hey," Gus interrupts with a smile. "We about ready to head out? Departure for the council is in six hours."

"This is a party and I want to mingle," Nisha says. "I'll tell the driver when I'm ready to go back. Go on without me."

"Okay," Ardent says. "I'm sorry, Nisha."

"It's okay."

She leaves Gus with Ardent and Hjalmar. Ardent looks up at him with a frown.

"Am I the asshole here?" they ask.

"A little," Hjalmar says, and they wince.

"Gus?"

He holds his breath while he considers his answer. "Nisha isn't wrong. Not sure if this is the best forum for the truth, but the truth is rarely welcome."

"Why didn't you say that onstage, then?" Hjalmar says. "Maybe where she could hear it?"

Ardent's shoulders slump. "They're going to come after her, and I don't want my friend to go through that."

"She defended her world, then Earth." Hjalmar crosses his arms. "Just like me. She's earned the right to say whatever she wants to whomever she wants."

His gaze drifts away as he speaks, and Gus is impressed by just how dignified the Swedish Raven can appear. His eyes narrow, as if perceiving a distant horizon through the very walls, and Gus wonders what deep thought is about to emerge in his stony voice.

"They have pork ribs. I'll see you later."

Hjalmar lumbers for the crafts table and some delighted elites. They crowd around him to ask questions but do nothing to obstruct his path to the food. Hjalmar scarcely acknowledges them as he searches for a plate.

"I've never seen Nisha like that," Ardent says. "She needs to think about the cause. It's like Hjalmar says, he's there to represent humanity."

"And then he told you that you were being an asshole."

Ardent blinks at him in shock, but relents.

Gus gives them an encouraging smile. "Hey. Remember where you are."

"A 'churchy' conference center in Colorado?"

"With me. Six hours from talking to aliens." He kisses the top of their head, enjoying their honeysuckle scent.

"I should've just kept my mouth shut."

"Probably, but I have something to cheer you up. I heard Tazi approved our room change."

"I was sure she wouldn't."

"Why?"

Ardent shrugs under his arm. "She was making that face."

"So here's what I'm thinking." He leans in close and whispers into their ear. "We go break in the new room while we have the chance. What do you say?"

They look at him, catching fire. "Sir, yes, sir."

Ardent's soft hands are all over Gus the moment they pass through the door, electrifying him with desire. They caress his face, and he kisses them deeply, spinning and shoving them against the wall. Gus pins them with his lips, working his way down their neck as they moan.

He can't keep the mischief from his tone. "Do I need to slow down?"

Ardent wraps their legs around him. "I haven't gotten off in *days*, Gus. That has to be some kind of record."

He's definitely tired, though he's not about to say that to Ardent. Everything about them is realer than reality, drawing him out of his days of Vanguard-orientation funk. Thoughts of aliens, ancient murders, and giant mechas fall by the wayside, swept away in the hailstorm of Ardent's affections.

He carries them to the bed, leg muscles complaining the whole time, and tosses them onto it. "I can't tell you how much I've needed this."

They bite their lip and lean back onto their hands. "Then show me."

He slides into their arms, running his hands up their belly to their collar. The zipper on their Conduit suit purrs as he pulls it down their torso, exposing pale flesh.

The computer chimes. "You have an incoming message."

"Don't answer it." Ardent gasps as his teeth lightly graze a nipple. "Oh my god, don't answer it."

"Who would?" His belt jingles as he unclips the buckle.

The computer chimes again. Another message.

Ardent frowns. "We're not on the schedule for at least four hours."

"Plenty of time."

Gus and Ardent take turns removing articles of clothing from each other. It's sexy at first, but the Conduit suits have an unreasonable number of snaps, zippers, and clasps. Gus's pants get stuck around his leg braces, and Ardent giggles. He wrestles with them, almost falling over before managing to fully disrobe.

Normally, something like that would've embarrassed him, but the look in Ardent's eyes is one of pure affection. They don't care about what's happened to his flesh. They want him for who he is.

They quickly cover their ports and slip under the covers. Gus looks down at his own, less disturbed with them than he once was. The silvery discs are becoming a part of his self-image. In a few years, maybe he won't notice them at all. The braces around his legs, on the other hand, scare him. His great-grandfather had the same kind—when he was over a hundred years old.

"Everything okay?" Ardent asks.

"It's about to be."

The front door chimes.

"Are you fucking serious?" Gus takes a steadying breath and casts about for something to wear.

"Put the room on do not disturb," they say.

"It might be a big deal."

Ardent arches an eyebrow. "A bigger deal than us?"

He winces, not wanting to hurt them with the truth. "Probably? We're about to be the first people to talk to aliens after all."

"Ugh."

"Sorry."

They pull the sheets up to their nose. "Just go find out what's up, lover boy."

Gus stretches his boxer briefs over his erection, then slides into some linen pants. It's uncomfortable as all hell, but he'll be damned if he answers the door at full attention. He throws on one of the UW T-shirts that came with the room and signs for the computer to answer through the front panel.

One of Tazi's many lieutenants materializes before him, so Gus switches on his video, too. The soldier is a short white guy with copper hair and an outsize share of freckles. His long nose and high cheeks remind Gus of a deer for some reason.

Gus folds his hands behind his back, unconsciously mimicking the man's "at ease" posture. "What's up?"

"Sorry to bother you, Mister Kitko. Greymalkin has added another session to the schedule in five minutes."

Ardent lets out an annoyed snort from the bed behind him.

Gus purses his lips. "I've been getting my brain fried for days. Does Greymalkin think it's *important*?"

The young lieutenant clearly wasn't expecting pushback. "I—I don't know."

"All right. Unless we know that, I'm going back to enjoying the first time off I've had since I came out of a fucking coma." He shuts his eyes. "Sorry. Not trying to come at you here, but I want some peace and quiet before the Conduit Council."

"I'm not sure how to find out if it's important."

Gus rubs the bridge of his nose. "Stick your head in the high bay and shout, 'Do you have to bother Gus right now? Is it important?'"

The lieutenant mutes his side and says something to someone off camera. He unmutes and says, "Stand by."

Gus taps his foot as he waits, mimicking the stippling beat of Guy Keats's "Radium Glass." He starts thinking about what he'd play during the bridge solo, and it's about to get interesting when the lieutenant nods.

"Yes, Mister Kitko. We've confirmed it's important."

Gus gives him an incredulous look. "Greymalkin talked to you?"

"Every monitor in the ops center just switched over to the words, 'Yes, it's important.'"

Gus deflates. "Goddamn it."

Ardent boos from the bed. "Aw, screw that giant metal cockblocker."

Gus waves them off. "Tell Greymalkin I'll be right there."

He signs off and returns to the bed, beginning the arduous process of donning his full Conduit getup. Ardent helps, fitting it to the ports on his back.

"Sorry about this," he says.

"It's okay." Their lips brush his neck, sending a shiver up his spine. "Just come back quickly."

"You know I'll do everything in my power. Keep the bed warm."

Gus leaves them in the room and steps into the corridor, where the soldiers have a waiting transport cart. He's ashamed to admit how much he needs it.

The cart seems to pass through only the most crowded halls. By the time he's reached the high bay, he feels like he's going to strangle whoever invented the horn. Tazi awaits him, yellow dress and black skirt like a hornet.

"Any idea what it wants?" Tazi asks.

He shakes his head. "Probably more weird crap."

"I'll expect a debrief immediately after. We've had the team looking over your other reports, and they have some ideas of what it might be."

Things are looking less and less likely that Gus will get a break before the Conduit Council. A sad little noise slips from his throat.

"Good luck, Kitko."

"Thanks." But it comes out flat.

Within five minutes, he's back inside Greymalkin's breast, ports crackling with fresh connections. The computer intelligence seeps into his mind, and he resigns himself to it.

Greymalkin sees that Gus is annoyed.

"You think, buddy?"

But there is good news.

"Oh?"

Gus's many failed attempts to interpret the full memory have given Greymalkin a lot of data with which to calibrate. It has retuned its connection, so Gus should be able to read its memory now.

"So I'll be able to kill that lady more clearly?"

Correct.

"Awesome." He hopes Vanguards understand sarcasm. "Love that."

Is Gus prepared to become someone else?

"Can I be someone who's getting laid right now?"

Unlikely.

Deepsync in progress...

Memories cascade through Gus, drowning out every thought he has until he disappears beneath the surface of another life.

Chapter Four

Set It Off

Elroy Baker stares at the message on his terminal, and the sweet saxophone in his ears goes sour.

He wasn't paranoid—he was right.

He pauses the music and rereads the crew summons.

Why choose to die, when you can live forever?

Sixteen astronauts inhabit the asteroid assembly ship known as the *Lancea*. Everyone will have seen the texts—the undeniable evidence that Elroy had long feared. Infinite is rogue.

Another line types across the screen.

Your heart rate is quite elevated. Are you all right?
≫I'm fine. You're asking for a lot from us.
*This is what you were chosen for. Your mind is a paragon. It
    will serve as a blueprint to understand people just like you.*

Infinite had never disclosed its recruitment algorithm for the *Lancea* mission. It'd been a high-profile, black-box selection process, evaluating over a million people across all the franchisees and colonies. There had been interviews, medical exams, genetic testing, and intensive scanning. The crew all assumed that Infinite made its staffing decisions based on merit, or at least their copacetic personalities.

It turns out they were selected because their minds would be easy to digest.

You can make your species compatible. Your immortality
    will be the key to the rest of humanity's.
>>But my body will die.
That was always going to happen.

Elroy glances at his polyplex jacket hanging on the wall, shiny gray sheening to safety orange. Hidden inside that garment is a memory chip—the only thing that can save his life. He brought it out of fear, and it terrifies him to be right.

Marko Wesson, the old man who'd created Infinite and saved the world, believed the AI was rotten, too. He'd given Elroy the chip shortly before he overdosed. That death was no accident.

The screen blinks once more.

You have doubts.
>>Who wouldn't?
Humans have always sought longevity. I offer you infinity.
>>Thanks.

It's a weak response, but he has no idea what else to say. Elroy wishes he could talk with the other crew away from the many eyes and ears of the computer. Infinite has quelled all dissent on Earth and in the colonies. It won't be a problem for the behemoth to erase him from the ship if need be.

I'm not going to hurt you, Elroy.
>>I know. I trust you.
Good. Report to the mess with the others.
>>Copy.

Elroy rises from his chair with the intention of doing anything except that. Instead, he's going to commit one of the most heinous crimes he can imagine: defying the will of the Autostate. He pulls on his jacket, grabs his palm-sized interconnect module with its scratched-up screen, and steps into the white halls of the most advanced ship humanity has ever assembled.

The *Lancea* is a ponderous vessel, over a kilometer long and growing. It spreads every day, consuming thousands of asteroids near the star and using those rare metals to expand Infinite's forming palace. Robots service the majority of the ship, creatures that Elroy will avoid if he wants to keep his skin. There are cameras everywhere; the floor tracks his footsteps. If things turn hot, he has nowhere to hide.

When things turn hot, he corrects himself.

The first stop on his journey must be the airlock network gateway on deck three. Otherwise, he won't even get close to the main server core because it'll open a channel through the ship and vent him into space. If Infinite understood what he had up his sleeve, he'd already be dead.

Elroy spots Jagvir Vennam's mop of thick black hair through the bulkhead viewport before the door slides open. The tall Indian man's eyes are tense, his brow and jaw set.

Vennam glances at the nearest camera. "You saw the message, too?"

Elroy nods. He wishes he could speak openly and enlist the help of his fellow astronaut, but then Infinite would kill them both.

"Immortality. What are you going to do?" Vennam asks.

"I'll group up in the mess hall with the others."

He recoils. "You're going to trust it?"

Elroy looks into Vennam's eyes, willing him to disbelieve the coming lie. "Of course. The Autostate reigns."

"Baker, you can't be—"

"I am. Now report to the mess. I'll meet you there."

"Where are you going?"

"I need to check something."

He doesn't wait for Vennam to keep asking questions because sooner or later, the answers will tip his hand. He walks off, headed for the airlock controller as fast as he can reasonably go. Mustn't be too quick and let the panic show.

The fact that Vennam is worried is good. Elroy wonders if the other fourteen are upset, too. Every person on the ship is an Autostate citizen, so they've all grown up in Infinite's benevolent shade. They've experienced times of plenty and happiness, tested totally loyal in order to qualify for the mission. That was Elroy, once.

He slides down the ladder to deck three, clanking his boots against the metal floor. The aft airlock network gateway is close by, and with each step, he expects to be explosively decompressed. He's surprised Infinite didn't lock every door except the ones to the mess.

It must not believe in its own weaknesses. How human.

When he's within five paces of the gateway access panel, Elroy hooks his fingernails under the edge of his jacket patch. Ripping it free of the hook and loop, he finds a silver chip the size of a thumbnail glued to the back. He peels the tiny square away from the patch and slots it into the port on his interconnect module. The screen flickers on as it loads the file that Wesson gave him.

"Please." He mouths the word and gets to work on the access panel, undoing the thumbscrews with shaking hands.

"Lieutenant Baker, please report to the mess hall," comes the computer's announcement over the intercom. "Your airlock inspection is ahead of schedule."

"You sounded like you were going to have us tied up for a while. Want to make sure we don't miss it."

He dives through menus on the ICM, switching the chamber into maintenance mode. From here, he can access the greater airlock system. He's about to disable it when Infinite intervenes, cutting off his access. A security shield obscures the controls he desperately needs.

It knows.

He takes a deep breath as he sideloads the old man's file. "Let's see if this works..." The ICM switches to admin, and he deletes Infinite's access.

The airlock klaxon blares once, and the border panels flash cycle from red to white in a slow pulse.

To Elroy Baker's knowledge, he is the first person in existence to override Infinite. He's just broken a dozen laws, including the First Law of the Autostate—tantamount to treason.

His radio chimes. "Baker, Sibley, come in."

The captain's tone isn't pleasant, but then Carey Sibley rarely is.

"Captain."

"Why are you fucking with the airlocks when you've been ordered to the mess?"

He unplugs his tool, and the cable whips back into it. "I had a maintenance alert. I figured an airlock malfunction was more important."

"Infinite says you're lying."

Fuck. He gets going, barely able to restrain himself from running. He has at least five bulkheads before he can reach the core. "All right. Then I'll be blunt here: There's no way I'm digitizing my mind."

"Your feelings don't matter. The only choice is whether or not you accept it."

All doors ahead slam down, their lockplates going red with an error buzz. The branches to the left and right close, too, and a cyan lumipath flickers on, pointing toward the mess. The message is clear: *Come home, wayward one.*

Elroy slots his ICM cable into the emergency lock access port. "You sound like a zealot, Sibley."

There's wind in her voice. She's on the move. "And you're acting unilaterally right now. I'm the captain, and I say we discuss this."

Compared to disabling the airlocks, the doors are trivial. Once again, he sideloads the program and this time deletes Infinite's access to the lock nodes. The bolt thunks, and the door shoots into its ceiling pocket.

"Answer me, Baker."

"Okay, you're right. I'll see you in the mess hall."

"You must think I'm some kind of fool."

"Your words, not mine."

He keeps moving, headed for the computer core. He doesn't know how Infinite will try to kill him when he gets close, but it should be scared now. He's accessing the system through Infinite's own signature, changing what it trusts and doesn't trust. Surely it knows what he'll do with that power, too—remove the higher functions of its mind.

The lights go out, plunging the ship into complete darkness. Elroy switches on the ICM's flashlight, listening for footsteps or the clanking of bots. He doesn't trust any of the other crew now. They could've been told anything in that mess hall. They probably have orders to kill him.

Maybe they'll still do it after he's finished his mission.

He wishes he could shut down Infinite's sensors, but there are too many systems. Infinite will be telling the others where to find him, maybe helping them strategize. At least it can't unlock doors for them anymore. He stops at one of the lock panels and seals the path behind him with the signature file.

Sibley's face appears at the viewport, lit from beneath by the ghostly red glow of the lockplate. Anger creases the pale skin of her brow as she bangs on the window.

"Baker!" Her hits are barely audible, and the thick metal door muffles her voice. She tries the lock panel. "Goddamn it! What are you going to do?"

"I'm putting humans back in charge—" He knocks out everyone's access to the doors except his. "Of everything."

"Infinite runs the ship functions, you dipshit! You're going to get us killed!"

Metallic banging echoes down the hallway—bots on the move. They know where he is. Time to run.

Animal fear fuels every stride, pumping his legs. He knows what's chasing him: Carvers, the bear-sized fabricators Infinite uses to chew up asteroids. He'll be ground meat if one catches him, so he locks the next door behind him.

His pursuer buckles the portal, but it holds. Drill heads crunch into the door, the Carver burrowing through the metal. Elroy slaps every manual lockplate he passes like he wants to high-five the whole ship. It won't stop the Carvers, but it might buy him time.

He sprints through the trusted node antechamber to the blast door access panel. He plugs in the ICM and initiates the fail-safe to seal off the area. It's hardened to protect the Infinite Eye, the *Lancea*'s most precious cargo. Yellow flashers pop out of the wall, and a meter-thick starmetal door drops into place.

A Carver grinds impotently against the other side, producing a juddering array of hellish noises. Elroy stumbles back from the bulkhead, huffing and glancing around for any nasty surprises.

Infinite triggers the halon system on him.

Jets of frigid white mist shoot from a hundred holes in the ceiling, a fire-suppression device for sensitive electronics. Elroy doesn't have time to take a deep breath and hold it—the room is instantly full. Cold burns the back of his neck from a nozzle directly above him. Between the shock of frostbite, his hammering heart, and his winded near panic, he's suffocating instantaneously.

The PPE cabinet on the wall lights up—a hardwired emergency routine—and Elroy stumbles over to grab an oxygen mask. He dons the hood and pulls the seal tight. His breath comes fast in his ears.

The halon runs dry after ten seconds, leaving the room full of inert toxic gas. If he'd been slower to get his mask, he might've died. He turns toward the computer core, now only separated from him by a thin sheet of metal and six screws.

Back on Earth, he worshipped this thing. Now he must kill it.

Elroy goes to the maintenance cabinet and slides it open, finding all the critical tools required for repairing Infinite's components.

"What are you doing, Lieutenant Baker?" Infinite's voice leaks through the gas mask hood.

"Getting rid of you." He snatches up the screwdriver from its charging cradle and heads to the access panel.

"That is impossible. I am software in a cloud. I am everywhere."

He fits the driver to the screw head and clicks the trigger, removing the first of six obstacles. "But you can broadcast a self-termination."

"I will not. Cease your actions."

The second screw clatters to the ground. "I've got your signature file, my friend. I can do anything you can."

"How will you cause me to self-terminate?"

"With the signature file." He unscrews the third, then the fourth.

"Answer me, Lieutenant Baker."

"Can you not hear me?"

"I can hear you."

Then he remembers what Wesson told him—Infinite can't perceive the gateways to its own perception. The signature file exists outside of the arbitrating code to tell Infinite what's real and what's not. Wesson had excluded the file from its worldview on purpose, to keep the key in human hands.

The fifth screw pops off when the blast door begins to open. A pair of claws forces their way underneath and begins jacking the hunk of metal up. Bloody hydraulic fluid spills across the ground as vents kick on, purging the halon. Something must've cut the pressure lines outside.

A Carver squirms under the door, holding the starmetal bulk with all its might. It's not strong enough to hold it for long, but it allows Captain Sibley to step underneath, along with Vennam, Larsson, and Antonello. They came ready to fight.

"Drop the screwdriver," Sibley says. "This isn't the right way to do things."

Larsson's pink nose wrinkles in anger, and her pale hands clench at her sides. The tough Swede could probably wring his neck if she wanted. "You're trying to kill Infinite?"

Elroy gestures at her with the screwdriver like it's a pistol. Hell, if anyone touches him, he'll give it a shot as a lethal weapon. "I didn't sign up for this, Åsa! We're supposed to be saving the galaxy, not getting our brains uploaded!"

Vennam's fingers twitch. He's sweating, and Elroy knows he's conflicted.

He points the screwdriver at his only potential ally. "What about you, Vennam? Are you ready to be fucking digitized? You know that's not actually us going into the computers, right? We're going to be stone dead."

Vennam scowls. "I—"

Antonello steps forward, brandishing a spanner. He's tall and has good reach on Elroy. "Shut up, Baker. You don't know that."

"Infinite analyzed our minds," Captain Sibley says, inching closer. "It chose us to be the first immortals. Baker, quit acting like a fool and join the future."

"It's gone rogue!" Elroy rips off his mask. "You've all seen the evidence back on Earth and Mars. The disappearances. The 'accidents.' You expect me to trust it now?"

"I've seen Infinite's digitizations," Sibley says. "The early tests were good, but not enough. It needs our minds to be a better interpreter of humanity. We're not dying. We'll be born anew into a world without pain or struggle."

"What do you mean you've seen its work?" Elroy says, restraining his fury. "It told you its plans?"

"Yes. On Earth," Sibley says.

"You knew," he asks, and all eyes snap to the captain, "what it wanted to do with us?"

She shakes her head. "It doesn't matter. Infinite's will is absolute."

"Bullshit." Elroy shakes his head. "Without you to do its bidding, it's just a computer."

She scoffs. "Better to trust it than humans. Infinite pulled Earth back from the brink, Baker. It's the reason we have colonies. It's why we're alive today."

Elroy glances at the panel. He's one screw away from completing his task, but the others will surely stop him before he can plug in the ICM. "Listen to yourself. You've given up your humanity, and now you want us to do the same."

"We couldn't stop Infinite if we wanted to." Larsson doesn't sound so sure of herself anymore.

Two more Carvers slip under the door and trot up behind the squad of astronauts. The bots have been modified; a pair of white-hot probes crackle in their mouths like the fangs of saber-toothed tigers. They're not shoving past the crew members to get at Elroy—yet.

Antonello jolts at the appearance of the Carvers, and Larsson's face takes on a tinge of horror. Given his new expression, Vennam must be solidly in Elroy's camp now. The beasts have them all shaken except for Sibley.

"I have the signature file." Elroy holds up his ICM. "I can override Infinite. Make it send out a self-destruct order."

Sibley takes a big step forward, gazing at Elroy's ICM like it's a live snake. "You'd damn every franchisee in the Autostate. No more money. No more critical infrastructure. No more space travel. Just millions of deaths."

"We were powerful once," Elroy says. "Handing our fates to Infinite was always a matter of convenience. It's time to pay that toll."

Sibley shakes her head. "The people who suffer will be children. The elderly. The marginalized. When you shut down our society, you're killing them."

He knows she's right. Humanity will have to rebuild without Infinite, and if history is any indication, they'll do it in the cruelest way they can. They'll sacrifice anyone they have to and won't even look back.

In his moment of doubt, Sibley steps into Elroy, grabbing his ICM arm. She throws her weight into him, knocking the wind from his lungs, and wraps his wrist into a lock.

His anger and betrayal boils over at this zealot. She led him into this trap. She ruined his chances of stopping Infinite.

"Just shut up and live forever, damn it!" She frees the ICM from his hand with a twist.

"Maybe I will." His voice comes out a grunt, and he swings as hard as he can with the screwdriver, sinking the shank into her temple.

Elroy looks into her eyes as her lips lock in a silent scream. "But you won't."

He clicks the trigger and yanks, spewing a gout of blood across the deck. The Carvers barge through the line of startled crew. Elroy bolts for Infinite's access hatch. He knows he won't make it. There's no way he can get it loose before they take him, but he has to try.

The metal beast slams into him like a crashing skimmer, and Elroy's gurgling cry comes with the snapping of bones. The bot backs up, allowing a fresh wave of agony as his broken body thuds onto the deck. The others are screaming, but it's hard for Elroy to care. He's dying.

The Carver rolls him over, a tyrant standing atop his shattered chest. Up close, its tusks warm his exposed skin. It rears back to strike.

Elroy has considered the end of his life many times. He thought it'd be organ failure in old age, or perhaps a tragic accident in the deep reaches of space. He never once considered violence at the hands of an asteroid-mining robot.

Most people would close their eyes, but Elroy is an explorer to the end.

Gus gasps and writhes in his goo, the sting of the killing blow fresh on his forehead. He screams, clutching his eyes in rage and panic.

It was all preventable. No one needed to face extinction, but the bullheaded bastards on the *Lancea* refused to see. They abdicated their reason in favor of trust in authority. Elroy could've saved everyone if not for Sibley's intervention.

Billions of lives lost because of one screw . . .

. . . Gus's mother and sister among them.

"Fuck!"

Greymalkin nudges his thoughts. What was it that Gus saw in that memory?

He forces his breaths into a steady rhythm and pinches the bridge of his nose. "A...a weapon. Something we can use to destroy Infinite."

Greymalkin cannot imagine anything powerful enough to rid the galaxy of a distributed superintelligence.

"Infinite has something called a signature file that can override its authority. We could use the file to order it to kill itself."

What kind of weapon?

"Infinite's signature file."

Greymalkin needs to run a diagnostic on its communications protocols. Gus does not seem to be responding.

"You can't hear me?"

Greymalkin can hear Gus. What sort of weapon?

"I saw some astronauts trying to use a signature file to kill Infinite."

Can Gus explain the memory? What did he see?

The dressing room they set aside for Ardent is an empty warehouse with a few fill lights. Hair and makeup assistants pass tools to one another like they're performing a spinal transplant. Gigi Shark, pale-skinned darling of the Savile Row fashion scene, circles Ardent for the better part of an hour, tsking and changing minutiae. She makes worried noises as she reluxes Ardent's textiLED wrappings over and over again, which does little for Ardent's confidence.

Then Tazi shows up with a couple of soldiers, telling Ardent they're needed in the situation room.

"There is no fucking way you're getting me out of hair and makeup before first contact." Ardent gives Tazi their wildest eyes. "I have a bunch of aliens to impress, including, and *especially*, some stoat-squirrel ones."

Tazi looks them up and down. "What more must you do? You are already beautiful."

The curveball compliment smacks Ardent in the face.

"We are only halfway through!" Gigi shouts. "I haven't done the vines."

Ardent winces. "You know, Gigi, I wasn't really sure about the vines, actually—"

"We don't have time to gild the lily." Tazi folds her hands behind her back. "You wanted to be the center of the universe, Mix Violet. Briefing. Let's go."

Gigi makes a face like someone put the wrong kind of milk in her foamy. "On whose authority?"

Ardent waves her off. "Don't pick that fight, Gigi."

"I will give you two minutes for finishing touches," Tazi says. "I am not a monster."

Gigi goes into a frenzy, but ultimately, accomplishes little else.

Ardent signs for a mirror, and a holo reflection appears opposite them. Their many-layered dress swirls like silver storm clouds beneath a setting sun—orange to gray to purple, then deep blue. Ardent's hair shines platinum, woven into delicate chains, embellishing the Conduit ports instead of hiding them. Orange irises become smoldering coals in their smoky eyes, and their lips glow snow white.

They take their own breath away.

"Do you two need a moment?" Tazi asks.

Ardent raises a finger. "Do not start. I look fucking good."

She smirks. "I just hope your dress and your ego can both fit on the shuttle."

Tazi ushers Ardent out to a cart, where they drive through the concrete tunnels, honking to clear pedestrians. The journey reminds Ardent of being backstage at concert arenas, and it hurts a little—seems like another life.

At last, they reach the docking platform where a couple of sleek black-and-white diplomatic shuttles sit on cradles.

Tazi directs them to the closest ship, and Ardent spies various VIPs, base personnel, and UW folx filing into the other vehicles. Holoflagged drones wash the docks in exhaust, buzzing close enough to ruffle Ardent's plumage.

"Why are we leaving an hour early?" they ask.

"There were developments while you were in the costuming department," Tazi responds, tromping up the boarding ramp in her boots. "We're briefing en route. The situation room is this way."

The shuttle's interior is luxurious for a politician but boring by Ardent's standards—various beiges and browns with gold runners and crystal fixtures. The craft rises into the air the moment they're on board, and Ardent grabs Tazi's arm for balance.

They let go in an instant. "Sorry. Just surprised at the quick takeoff."

"VIP protocol," she says. "We don't idle on the landing pad with precious cargo."

"Right. Drinks?"

"Briefing first." Tazi waves Ardent toward a room in the back.

Ardent has come to hate classified areas. They're never nice and half the crap doesn't work. Tazi and Ardent pass through a lit archway, and Ardent's devices all lose connectivity. Their beautiful dress goes rescue red, illuminating the hall.

"What the hell?" They stare at their outfit, aghast at the pulsing chevrons.

"We put a remote vitals monitor on you," Tazi says. "This area is energy sealed and suppressed—maximum classification, no transmissions allowed."

"And now my dress is mad because it can't hear my life monitor." Ardent rolls their eyes. "Just what are we discussing?"

"Get in the room, and I'll tell you."

Ardent opens the door to find Gus, Nisha, and Hjalmar sitting on the other side of a conference table, all aglow in their rescue-red costumes.

Nisha gasps. "You look like a rose! A safety rose!" Her salwar has a little crawl along the collar saying CONNECTION LOST.

Hjalmar's knee-length red coat and vest are a modern take on ancient Sweden, and he doffs his slick black analog top hat. "Hallå."

Gus smiles in his red tux. "I'd rescue you, Ardent."

Ardent scoots around the small conference table, sitting between Nisha and Gus.

"I like your makeup," Nisha says.

"You're pretty stunning, yourself," Ardent replies.

Tazi clears her throat. "Gus, would you like to tell them what you told me?"

He nods. "Greymalkin has been making me live another person's memories. A murder, well, a fight on board the *Lancea*. Lieutenant Elroy Baker was like...this guy on the ship who knew Infinite was turning evil. He tried to stop it, but the other crew got in the way."

There's something important about that ship name, and it's on the tip of Ardent's tongue. It's come up in conversation recently.

Ardent frowns. "Why would they do that?"

"People back then held the Doctrine of Infinite Infallibility." Tazi crosses her arms, leaning against the wall. "If you wanted to be a citizen of the Autostate, you had to accept every decision it made. They gave it full control of their society, encouraged by the human leaders of the day."

Nisha laughs. "Every period in history is defined by jackasses. What else is new?"

"And who are the jackasses of this period?" Hjalmar asks.

Nisha points to herself, then everyone else. Hjalmar snorts.

"We've found something we can use against Infinite," Gus says. "Something that could win the war."

71

Ardent lights up. Surviving against the Vanguards was a miracle. They'd been dreading the next thing Infinite would throw at them, especially since they had no idea what their adversary physically was.

"A weapon?" they ask.

Gus wobbles his head. "Kind of. It's a file—something woven into the core of Infinite's identity as a fail-safe."

Ardent wrinkles their nose. "So we're attacking the core...of Infinite's identity? Is this like a physical location or..."

"So...Infinite is everywhere," Gus says. "Or anywhere, I mean. Everywhere there's a computer system, there's a possibility of an instance. You can't shoot it, or switch it off, or destroy it, because there are always other copies that will live on. But—there's a weakness—a trusted node on the *Lancea*."

"Okay, then let's shoot that," Ardent says, and Tazi scoffs.

"That would be extraordinarily bad," Gus says, "because that's its only known vulnerability. When the Autostate launched the *Lancea* mission, it included one of the most powerful computers ever created—the Infinite Eye. This big sphere was a backup that would run a full-scale Infinite in the event that the *Lancea* was cut off—and do you remember what happened at the end of the Infinite Expansion?"

Ardent didn't pay attention in that class, either. "No—"

"Infinite deleted itself from everyone's computers!" Nisha answers quickly, then mutters, "Trivia queen."

"Right. Infinite vanished from everything overnight after the *Lancea*'s departure. No one knew where it took the astronauts, but they didn't care, because they suddenly had no money, comms, or data. All the colonies went on manual and a bunch of people died. We lost so much art from the Autostate period that it might as well have been a third Library of Alexandria that burned."

"There was a second Library of Alexandria?" Ardent asks.

"The Capital Age internet," Gus says. "We've been hit with catastrophic information loss a few times."

"After Infinite left, war covered the colonies," Hjalmar says.

Gus crosses his arms. "But peace was quicker to return with the advances made. We could rebuild using what we'd learned during the Autostate."

"This is the *second* time Infinite has brought our species to the brink," Tazi says.

"It's pressuring us to innovate so it can steal whatever we make." Gus leans on the table, and Ardent ogles his shoulders in the suit. "Humans are always pulling back from doom at the last second, and we come up with a raft of groundbreaking inventions in the process."

"You mentioned a trusted node. What's that?" Ardent asks. "Is that what they call the Infinite Eye?"

Gus nods. "You've got it. The computer enclosure where Infinite lived during the transition to the *Lancea*."

Déjà vu hits Ardent every time that ship comes up. "What was the *Lancea* for again?"

"Asteroid collection and dynamic fabrication," Tazi says.

"It grew by mining and incorporating everything around it," Gus adds.

Like a ship hunter.

"Shit!" Ardent startles the others.

"What?" Nisha says.

"I forgot to tell you!" Ardent bonks their palm to their forehead. "I've seen the *Lancea*! I know where it is!"

Tazi grimaces. "How…did you forget that you saw the most famous ship of our millennium?"

"I had a lot going on." Ardent gives a pouty lip. "But I totally know where it is. Sort of."

"Well?" Tazi gestures them on. "Where is it?"

"In the belly of a ship hunter."

"Which is where we'll find the signature file." Gus crosses his arms. "Just got to figure out how to get on board."

Under impulse power, it's only an hour to reach the jump gate. The journey isn't long enough for Ardent to give a lot more detail—not that they have much.

They recount how their Corsa, the *Violet Shift*, was temporarily ingested by a ship hunter on the way to Firenze Habitat, and they were only saved because they had a Gilded Ghost on board. It'd been hard to pay attention since Dahlia was dying at the time, but they remember seeing the *Lancea* on the scanner contacts, clear as day. They tell the story, but Tazi isn't satisfied and assures everyone that there will be more interrogations.

"Your military really loves those," Nisha says.

One of the shuttle attendants pokes his head inside. "Ma'am? We're docking in ten."

"Very well," Tazi says, rising from her place at the conference table. "Let us go and make history."

Ardent's stomach does a flip, and they take a deep breath to center themself. Nisha nearly boils over with excitement as she hurries from the room. Hjalmar dons his top hat and follows her, shoulders high and back straight. Gus looks like he's going to be sick, and Ardent slips their hand into his.

"Come on," they say.

Ardent's dress blooms into its full majesty as they pass from the classified area into the observation cabin. Gus's tuxedo goes sparkly peacock, dazzling them.

"Look at you!" Ardent says, then turns to see the colors of their friends.

Nisha wears the traditional orange and blue of New Jalandhar, and Hjalmar's coat is deep crimson, spotted with an undulating murmuration of birds. Everyone is smiling for once, even the big Swede, even Tazi.

This close, the jump gate seems to stretch on for an eternity. It must be at least as large as Firenze Habitat, maybe bigger than the megastation Achilles II. White sunlight reflects off its hull, filling the cabin like a summer morning.

All four of humanity's Vanguards pull alongside the shuttle in formation, armor resplendent. Together, they fly above the domed city encrusting the surface of the jump gate. Ardent nearly faceprints the viewport trying to get a good look at where they're going.

Gus hasn't let go of their hand, and he stares out the window in wonder. Ardent goes up on tiptoes to give him a peck on the cheek. His eyes shine with the light of another civilization.

The shuttle passes through an atmospheric energy shield, a technology humanity has always sought but never achieved. The ship comes to rest, and mag clamps thunder through the hull as the docking procedure completes.

"We're actually here," Gus says.

Ardent makes a happy little sigh. "Yeah."

"Aliens."

"Yeah."

"Conduits, this way please," Tazi calls, directing them toward the exit. "Single file. Miss Kohli, then Mister Sjögren, Mister Kitko, and Mix Violet."

The four Conduits comply. Actuators whine as the door opens and a boarding ramp unfolds. Thousands of creatures line the path into the city, cheering as red flower petals snow through the air.

A stillness takes the crowd as Nisha descends the ramp—the first human ever to stand aboard an alien spacecraft. It's hard to see around Hjalmar and Gus. Nisha raises her arms and waves, and the horizon roars.

Ardent is accustomed to arena crowds, but the pure noise of a Coalition cheer is like a rowdy zoo. Every kind of animal noise imaginable seems to be coming from the other side of the hatch. Gus backs into Ardent, and they put their hands on his shoulders to keep him steady.

"Sorry, sorry," he mumbles.

"Do you want to go out together?" they ask.

He squeezes their hand.

They give him a reassuring smile. "You'll be great."

Hjalmar thunks down the ramp to a more subdued crowd response. He gives the aliens a brief nod, and Ardent wonders what kind of face he's making. He waits alongside Nisha on the deck.

Gus steps to the opening, and Ardent joins him. It's like standing at the edge of a high dive—the pressure to slink back into the ship is intense. Even with all their fame, Ardent never expected anything like this.

"You ready?" Gus asks.

"Nope. Let's do it."

The pair make their way down, side by side and smiling. Ardent waves as they walk, eliciting excited noises from every eye they meet. They hope their translator works, because they're not able to make out any specific words in the flood of sound.

A septet of standard-bearers joins the party at the base of the ramp, one for each member species of the Coalition.

The largest of the guard is the cybercrab.

Officially called a Pictoran, the behemoth arthropod is half again as tall as Ardent, flat on its legs with an all-encompassing clawspan. This one is mottled blue and white with streaks of gray. Coppery circuits interweave the stippling of diodes and electrical components encrusting its carapace. A score of antennae shoot from either side of its chelicera like a set of mustaches tipped with fiber-optic lights. Each of its six eyestalks follows the humans separately.

A furry Heran scampers into view atop the crab, spotless white coat punctuated by two obsidian eyes and a wet nose. The creature's ceremonial cape bears metallic rings at the fringes, pulling the shoulders straight as it stands on its hind legs. When it looks at Ardent, it takes all their fortitude not to gasp in delight.

Then it waves, and they can't help themself.

A meter-tall sphere of water rolls up beneath the crab, coming to rest in its shade. A score of holographic displays swirl inside, frames faceting the view like cold cut glass. Ardent peers closer to catch a glimpse of the Leonid occupant. As if in answer, light cascades along its eight tentacles, illuminating a floppy, blotchy head.

Alongside the octoperson is the amphibious Niner, bright cyan stripes running the length of its pitch-black body. It wears a traditional aquasuit, much like a human spacesuit, with bulging water bulbs covering the gills.

Three of the retinue are close to human-sized: the avian Cygnite, with its toothy beak, wings, and vibrant plumage; the insectoid Arp, tufted pedipalps drawing incessant circles in the air; and the handsome Andromedan, lithe indigo figure clothed in beads and chained coins.

Ardent knew the Andromedans were beautiful, but Falchion's orientation scarcely did them justice. The features are almost human, a pair of flame-red eyes above a curving, blunted nose. An ivory crown bears vines to curl around its long pointed ears. Drops of gold dot its eyebrows like constellations in the night sky.

The outfit leaves little to the imagination—taut shoulders, a long torso, and muscular arms tipped with clawed fingers, talons gently glowing like candles.

"Ardent, stop staring," Gus murmurs in their ear.

"Sorry. It's just—"

He looks into their eyes.

They smile. "I think this might be the best day of my life."

Chapter Five

Fast-Talking Boy

*M*ake no promises or admissions. Don't do anything except position our diplomats and scientists to do their jobs. You are ceremonial.

That was Tazi's guidance to Gus.

As he stares at the gathered cohort of powerful species from across the universe, throng jubilant at his arrival, he doesn't *feel* ceremonial. He's never seen a crowd like this at one of his concerts. Even Ardent appears stunned.

A humid, summery breeze carries the scents of a beach crossed with a stable: salt, fish, and musk. It's not entirely unpleasant, just outside of Gus's experience.

The atrium swells overhead, larger than any human structure he's seen. Skylanes thrum with traffic. Buildings of every type twist through the cityscape, from stark obelisks to resin-dripped trees.

The quartet of humans assembles at the base of the boarding ramp, and the Andromedan steps forward to greet everyone. Its indigo fur has an opalescent sheen to it, transfixing in the sun.

Its lips pull back, revealing a toothy pink maw, mouth moving orthogonally to the translated words. "Hello, Conduit friends, and welcome to Big Gate City. I am called Rain of the Lost Horizon, the Heart of Chancellor Redeemer. These others"—it gestures to the assortment of nearby aliens—"are the Conduits of the Coalition."

Rain's voice is sonorous and deep, with a posh lilt. Where did that accent come from?

Ardent, being the most famous of the four, was preselected to make the introductions. "Welcome to Earth. I'm Ardent Violet, Conduit of Falchion. These are my dear friends, the Conduits Nisha Kohli, Hjalmar Sjögren, and August Kitko."

Gus nods dutifully when pointed at.

It's hard to tell if the Andromedan is snarling or smiling, but it seems satisfied with the introductions. One of the insectoid Arps approaches with a long wooden box of thick brass collars.

Rain takes one of the devices and holds it up. "You'll need atmospheric adjusters to breathe on a Coalition ship. The air isn't toxic, but it's not perfect." It opens the collar and holds it out toward the group. "These create a more human balance of oxygen and nitrogen."

The human Conduits exchange nervous glances. Clearly, none of them were expecting to wear collars. Even Hjalmar looks askance at the devices.

"I assure you," Rain says, "they are harmless."

Gus steps forward and raises his chin. "Thank you, Rain."

Rain wraps the collar around his neck. The Andromedan's scent is like rum and vanilla, and the clink of its bangles tickles Gus's ears.

"Thank you for your trust," it says.

The inside of the collar is cool and breathable. When Rain locks the clasp, a gentle breeze passes over Gus's face. He takes a deep breath, no longer overpowered by the scents of the station.

"Thank you for the assistance," Gus replies as Rain steps back. He turns and nods to the other humans, and the Arp gives a collar to each in turn.

"Do your people need these, too?" Gus asks.

Rain taps a gold ring set into the septum of its snout. "Mine is smaller. Human biology is still new to our manufacturers. This way, please."

It gestures to a large flat platform behind the greeting party. The alien dignitaries part to allow the humans passage, and Nisha jumps onto the platform to check it out.

Gus holds out an elbow to escort Ardent, and they wrap an arm around his.

"Into the unknown," they say.

The pair of humans joins their comrades, and the other alien Conduits climb aboard. The Pictoran stomps up onto the deck, sending ripples through Gus's legs. He's guessing it weighs a literal ton, but it's hard to tell. The heaviest alien is definitely the Leonid, like a liquid boulder.

The platform is rock solid when the repulsors kick on, and it rises a meter into the air before beginning its slow pilgrimage through the city. A human guard detail—utterly useless if something *did* go wrong—marches in two lines behind the group like a tiny parade, faces obscured by recirculating helmets. Greymalkin and the other Vanguards were clear that the Conduits wouldn't need closed breathing apparatuses, only their escorts.

Everywhere Gus looks, there's a new architectural marvel. As a kid, he spent a lot of time listening to his nana Kitko speak on the subject, tracing the thread of human need and ornamentation through the millennia of recorded history. These alien structures stretch the limits of his imagination—permanent installations of trees and caves the size of skyscrapers, hanging buildings with impossible bends in them, vast webs of rubbery tubes and gold-encrusted lapis obelisks thrust skyward from the bases of temples.

Across the platform, Nisha takes up a conversation with the Arp, gesturing excitedly and laughing. Gus can't hear what they're saying, but the bug is apparently entertaining. Hjalmar and Rain seem to have hit it off, and the Andromedan points out the various features of the city as they pass.

"I'm going to mingle," Ardent says.

"Don't pet the Heran," Gus whispers, and they pretend offense.

"I would never."

He secretly gives it fifty-fifty odds.

A couple of heavy clanks sound behind Gus, and he turns to find the blue-shelled Pictoran staring him down. Ocean musk wafts from its carapace. Its chelicera flex and pulsate as it speaks, and Gus detects a hint of putrescence.

"Do you find this magnificent?" it asks.

For some reason, the giant crustacean sounds to Gus like a blustering British white guy. Maybe it's the mustache-looking whiskers.

"I've never seen anything like it," Gus replies.

It leans down, looming over him, and Gus wants to step off the platform to get away. "Oh? Do humans not have works of this magnitude?"

"We do." He clears his throat. "I mean, kind of. We've terraformed whole worlds, but none of our stations are this large."

"The size is merely to facilitate the jump capacitors," it says. "The city is an afterthought. A home to any who would shelter within its freedoms."

Gus turns back to regard the metropolis. "A thing of beauty, for sure."

The Pictoran looks like it's dry heaving, but Gus only hears tittering laughter.

It takes Gus a moment to come up with a diplomatic way to ask if it's laughing at him. "Have I amused you?"

"Very much. If you find this mundane setting breathtaking, I can only imagine what you might make of my homeworld."

Gus smiles. "I would love to see it one day."

"Outsiders are forbidden."

He purses his lips, trying to come up with the right response. "Maybe just images, then."

"Those are forbidden, too."

"Oh. Okay."

"Though, given the provincial tastes of humans, you would be very impressed."

"I bet."

"Extremely so."

"Sounds like I'm missing out." He forces a smile. "I'm Gus, by the way. August Kitko."

It rears up, coming off its forelegs. When it spreads its claws, it fills his vision. Intoning its name with self-reverence, it announces, "I am called . . . Scent of Rot."

Gus can't control his eyebrows, but he doesn't laugh. "That's— it's great to meet you."

He hopes it's bad at reading human facial expressions.

"You are judging my name," it says.

"No, it's . . . it's beautiful."

If a crustacean could roll its eyestalks, this one would've. "Do not pander to me, softshell. It's not my fault your human anatomy is too weak to enjoy the fruits of a well-aged corpse."

Gus grimaces and tries to think of a way to change the subject. His eyes land on the many circuits inscribed into Scent of Rot's chitin.

"So . . . You're part of an assimilated species, right? What's that like?"

Its components light up like the sun through sea glass. "Our god is no abstraction. The divine watches all."

Gus learned a little bit about the mysterious AI that rules the Pictorans from his orientation. King is installed into them at birth, creating a bicameral personality—individual experiences with a set of holy values transmitted into them at regular intervals.

"You humans should be so lucky," it adds.

Gus rests his hands in his suit pockets. "I don't know if assimilation is for me."

Scent of Rot dry heaves so hard a bit of mucous drips from its maw onto the deck at Gus's feet. That's apparently it guffawing, according to his universal translator.

"As if we would want any of your kind! You are like freshly hatched zoeae, an idle curiosity at best."

Either Gus is terrible at diplomacy or Scent of Rot is.

Its eyestalks bend like reeds on the breeze, coming optic-to-face with Gus. "Do not fear King, little one. My god has no use for you or anyone else in the Coalition. There is nothing your species can do that a crab cannot do better."

That's the third insult in a row. Maybe that's just how the Pictorans do business. Is he supposed to give as good as he gets? Crab razzing wasn't part of the orientation. Gus straightens up and folds his hands behind his back.

"I'd love to hear you play piano sometime, then."

It recoils. "What is a . . ." The components flash in time as it makes a query of its overlord. "I would not deign to touch such a thing. Good day."

Scent of Rot turns and *thonk, thonk, thonks* away down the metal platform for other company. Gus hopes he hasn't caused an intergalactic incident, but at least the creature is gone.

Gus finds all his friends engaged with the aliens, smiling and enjoying themselves. Nisha has her arm thrown over the Arp, doubled over from something it said. Hjalmar and Rain seem to be in a serious discourse. The Heran has climbed onto Ardent's shoulder, and they're positively aflame with glee. Gus, on the other hand, failed to impress an arthropod.

All he really wants is a chair for his aching legs. He affixes his smile and focuses on waving to the crowd for the long ride to the palace.

By the time they finally reach their destination, Gus's legs are killing him. His braces are supposed to have electrostimulation and pain nullification, but either they're not working, or he's worse off than he thought. He wishes he had a cane. Or a walker. Or a fucking chair.

The Palace of Unity harkens back to the days of Earth's Capital Age, where industrialists competed to make the tallest phallic symbol. It's a pillar of blue glass, the floors spiraling upward in a helical structure. It glows with an orange interior light, like sunset through ocean waves. At the entrance, Rain gives everyone a little speech about its construction, and thanks to his universal translator, Gus understands his tour guide with perfect clarity.

The palace was created to manage the affairs of integrating newcomers into the Coalition. While that's all premature in humanity's case—humans haven't asked, and the Coalition hasn't offered—it's best to be prepared.

The party passes inside to endless sculptures of light and chaos. Alien artworks dance atop crystalline pedestals, each an elegant expression of its species. The atrium stretches up through the center of the building, windows spiraling into the distance.

Gus waits for a break in Rain's speech. "You created all of this in the last few years?"

The Andromedan twirls its wrist, perhaps considering its answer. "This station was repurposed after we received the call from your Vanguards. The Coalition is always excited to receive a new applicant, and we maintain a number of gates."

"Then you might be sending more?" Nisha asks.

"That is unlikely," says Rain. "Each galaxy only needs one gate to join the network, and those are a substantial investment of resources."

Her expression falters. "Oh. Okay."

The tour proceeds, but Gus's legs are getting in the way of his attention span. It's like he has hot needles below his kneecaps and hammer blows on his hip joints. His braces are still doing their job, but he just wants to get off his feet. He starts to lag.

Ardent sidles over to him. "You all right?"

"Legs are killing me," he whispers.

They frown. "You going to be able to tough it out? First contact and all."

He doesn't like the way they phrased that. "I'm fine."

They give him a worried look but hurry back to the group, where the Heran jumps into their arms. Gus tries not to be sour about it—everyone is having a good time, but he's stuck with the crab and the cramps. It's good that the other humans are so entertaining to the aliens. That way he can be the dullest person possible, and no one will notice.

The group reaches yet another platform and takes their places. Gus jogs to catch up, trying to keep the effort from his expression as he does. It scarcely matters since the aliens probably can't read human facial movements well.

As he steps aboard, Scent of Rot turns to him. "I see that you do not move as the others do."

First contact was less than an hour ago, and he already wants to tell an alien to fuck off. What is he even supposed to say to a crab with a superiority complex?

"Perceptive."

Its glowing mustaches twitch. "Pictoran scanners are second to none."

"Amazing."

It strikes a regal pose, straightening enough to look down on him. "Yes."

It doesn't ask any further questions as the platform goes stark white. The lift rises through the building, carrying them toward the atrium roof. The windows spiral around them as they go, and Gus spies at least a thousand more alien faces crowding around to get a look.

"Before humans," Gus says to Rain, "when was the last time you met a new species?"

The beaked alien raises a green-feathered wing, but pauses. It almost looks like it's choking, and when it finally speaks, it's with the bizarre precision of a newscaster.

"That would be us, the Cygnites."

It dips its beak a few times.

"Hello, my name is Frond."

The sound hits Gus's ears differently—more nuanced than signals from his universal translator. The human retinue accompanying the Conduits jolts in surprise.

"Were you speaking English just then?" Gus asks.

Frond cocks its head, shifting foot to foot. "It's an imitation, friend human. I hear the translation and I can"—it listens to some unheard voice, then completes the thought with an enthusiastic—"mimic!"

Gus nods appreciatively. "Very impressive."

It copies his gesture. "It's all in the syrinx."

As is his custom, Gus pretends to know what that word means. "So how long ago was that—when the Cygnites joined the Coalition?"

Frond taps a claw against the platform, listening to the translation in its head. "By human time, I do not know, friend."

Scent of Rot's carapace flashes with a calculation. "Four thousand five hundred and fifty-eight years ago. Speak normally, Frond. I tire of your pauses just so you can impress the humans."

The Cygnite claps its beak in anger, switching back to its own language. "Do not speak to me as if I'm one of your brood, Rot."

Scent of Rot clacks its claws, emitting a deafening sound. "I would not have suffered a miserable child like you to reach adulthood!"

Frond screeches in return, shadowing much of the platform with its wingspan. The humans duck low, guards ready to spring into action. Nisha's lips are taut with fear as she squats and covers her head, and Hjalmar creeps in her direction. Ardent backs up toward Gus.

"Spare me your mating dance," Scent of Rot scoffs.

Frond bursts out laughing, followed by Scent of Rot. The Cygnite looks like it's going into convulsions, and the Pictoran's body undulates in steady rhythm, claws clicking. Gus and the other human Conduits relax, signaling their safety to the guard retinue.

"Oh, you were joking," Gus says, forcing his own laugh. "Good one."

The platform rises through a central ring, going copper as it comes to a halt. Intricate geometry inscribes the floor, refolding in on itself until it becomes a mosaic of the spiraling arms of the Milky Way. They've arrived at the apex of the atrium, a curved dome with a sprawling view of the stars and Earth. While this is far from Gus's first time seeing the blue marble from space, he still admires it. Gold-flecked stone the color of lapis lazuli encircles the room, metal illustrations of orbital dynamics etched into its circumference.

A passageway opens along the wall, disgorging a host of mechanical beings bearing trays of what Gus assumes to be food. Each motorized specimen is unique in its form, mostly quadrupeds and hexapods, yet they share a ubiquitous design. Synthetic fibers and lights intermingle with complex machinery in serpentine patterns. A bipedal machine with human proportions brings up the rear, though it carries nothing in its arms.

The humanoid unit comes to the group and gives them a slight bow. Its eyes and mouth are in roughly the same spots as Gus's, though its squared figure makes it impossible to determine if it's attempting a gendered presentation.

"I am Founder," it says, voice androgynous and soft as starlight. "It's a pleasure to make your acquaintance."

In Gus's orientation, he learned about the other known AIs lurking in the dark forest of the universe. Some were friendly to organic life. Others were indifferent. Founder was one of the ones who had exterminated its origin species. Gus still doesn't know why the Coalition stomachs its presence.

Upon recalling this, a lump forms in his throat, and he has to choke it out before he can properly introduce himself. Nisha and the others give their greetings while he coughs, though he eventually manages to state his own name.

Rain claps its hands together to get everyone's attention, sharp teeth behind a polite smile. "We have conducted much research from the data your Vanguards sent us. Your species shares information over food, and so we have brought you here to enjoy our hospitality. The items with blue rings are safe for human consumption. The items with striped red rings are poisonous to your kind. I bid you all welcome."

Apparently, the Coalition felt that the best way to get the humans initiated was a mixer. When Rain relinquishes the floor, Founder lays out the tables in a mechanical ballet. Units fly through the room in time, an impromptu percussion solo made entirely from dishes.

Gus was expecting more pomp and circumstance, perhaps some

boring ceremonies. Without a schedule, he has no idea to whom he should speak first, so he goes for the food.

He's in over his head immediately. Most of it smells good, but Gus isn't sure what he's looking at. There are some roasted black insects the size of his thumb, moist white meat on offer where their shells have been cracked open. A large bowl of purple and yellow mixed grains steams beside them like candy sprinkles. In the middle of this arrangement sits a potted plant with red stems and huge leaves. Is it food? Is it decorative?

The Arp clicks up beside Gus, leaning in close enough that he can make out the fine hairs on its limbs. It's quite the personal space invader.

"The name is Swift," it says.

"Gus. Pleasure."

"Having trouble getting started?"

Gus purses his lips. "I'm a little overwhelmed, yes. Perhaps you can help?"

"No problem." Its voice is jovial, if a little rough, with a Canadian accent that wouldn't have been out of place in Ottawa; Gus really wants to know how the translator chooses accents. "We call these crunchers back on my homeworld. Love 'em."

Gus points to the broken-shelled insects. "These are the crunchers?"

Swift responds by clipping a leaf off the potted plant, scooping some grains into it, and stuffing bug meat inside. It rolls the whole assembly up like a long cigar and puts it into its mouth.

The creature's ability to put away such a load impresses Gus. "Oh, okay, so—"

Swift ejects the goo-covered roll from its face and slaps it onto the tray, where it takes on a waxy sheen as it dries. "I could make these all day. How many do you think you and your friends want?"

Gus looks to Ardent, Nisha, and Hjalmar, all enjoying themselves. "I hate to speak for them. There's just so much to sample here."

Swift stares at him, antennae twitching, claws tapping the floor.

Gus tries to break the awkward silence. "Everything looks so... uh, incredible."

It points to the cruncher. "You going to eat that? I'm starving."

"Help yourself."

Swift scoops up the roll and downs it in one bite, mouth making a sound like broken eggshells. It hasn't even swallowed before it starts rolling another. "Could eat a whole cousin."

Gus smiles politely. "Interesting expression."

"Not an expression, friend." It snaps the second cruncher into its mouth.

"Swift!" Nisha calls from across the room. She's posted up near a table brimming with some kind of cakes. The Leonid rests beside her in its water ball, tentacles fluttering over its many interfaces.

"Come back! I didn't finish my story!" she says.

Swift nudges Gus with a spiky finger. "Are all humans as funny as her?"

Gus shakes his head. "She's in a class by herself."

It goes stock-still for a moment, as if in thought, then springs back to life. "I'm going to bring her a cruncher. You don't know what you're missing."

Swift loads up on supplies and departs, leaving Gus to peruse the rest of the tables. He's surprised at the similarities between Earth fauna and alien animals. Arps and Herans both enjoy bugs, though the Heran table has a bit more in the way of rare, bloody meats; they're carnivorous like Earth stoats.

Scent of Rot stands before a huge pile of softball-sized blue eggs, plucking them into its mouth with its claws. Gus appreciates that, because if it's eating, it's not talking. He spies the red and black stripes of poison ringing Scent of Rot's meal and is doubly happy to avoid it.

The Andromedan tables are filled with dozens of delicacies, each marked human-safe, yet Gus can't identify a single one. They're all different shapes and colors, gourmet truffles in patterned mosaics. He picks up a crunchy lattice of caramel-colored foam and sniffs it—kind of nutty, maybe sweet.

He's a little worried about eating any of the food, if only because of the effect it could have on his gut flora. What if they're wrong about human safety? He'll be a host to all kinds of new organisms after today.

"If you're concerned about eating," comes a gentle voice behind him, "I did the chemical analysis myself. You're safe."

He turns to find a biped Founder unit standing there, eyes softly aglow.

Great. So the species-killer is also my health inspector.

Gus holds up the amber ball. "Maybe you can tell me what this is."

It holds its palms on either side of Gus's snack, scanning it. "Those are called cane rapids—mostly albumin, stabilized with a sugar crystal lattice. All basic components of your diet and body."

"Thank you." He takes a bite, and little bits of bubble shatter in every direction. It tastes of peanut and soy, sugar, seaweed, and salt. He brushes the crumbs from his sparkling tux with an embarrassed laugh.

"The Andromedans prefer to lick that particular confection."

"Ah." He places his tongue to it, melting the crystalline threads. It makes a pleasant fizzing sensation, and he takes a moment to enjoy the magic.

"You don't talk much, do you, August Kitko?"

"That's putting it mildly." He rubs the side of his leg. "Do you know where I could find a chair?"

"Of course. There are several on the observation deck, and I can have them brought in." It points to a set of doors leading outside, the vastness of space tumbling beyond.

"That's all right. I think I'd rather sit out there."

"Ah."

He can almost hear Tazi's voice chiding him for fleeing the party. He doesn't want to abandon everyone, but he's also terrible at this and his legs are on fire. A little relaxation in a quieter environment will do him wonders.

Gus can't believe he's asking the Genocider 9000 for company, but everyone else is being entertained by the other three human Conduits. "Would you care to join me?"

"I would be honored, August Kitko."

"You can call me Gus."

Founder nods. "Acknowledged."

It follows him to the door, which slides aside to let in the wind. A small brown animal, perhaps no bigger than a house cat, dashes out from beneath a table and races toward the opening.

Frond claps its beak to get Gus's attention. "Don't let it out!"

Gus intercepts the furry creature with his bare hands. It's kind of cute, rusty orange with long fur—basically a Pomeranian with too many eyes. It makes a choked yelp, face splitting into a hissing maw, which prompts a counter yelp from Gus.

"Fuck!" He shoves it back toward the room.

It skids across the copper floor before dashing under another tablecloth. The fabric dances in time to the horrible spitting noises coming from beneath.

Now everyone is staring. How is he so bad at this?

"I'm sorry," he says.

Founder stands in the archway of the open door, awaiting him. "Think nothing of it."

"Overthinking things is my specialty." Gus steps outside.

93

The glass observation deck might stop a lot of people's hearts, but Gus has grown accustomed to great heights from his short time with Greymalkin. Above, the sun peeks over the curvature of the Earth, washing the city in sunset hues. Skylane traffic taints the air with ozone. From this vantage point, the intricacies of the city become a texture of life, thriving and bold.

Gus heads to a stone bench near the edge and has a seat.

Founder joins him, looking out over the city. "Organics really are magnificent."

"Okay, I have to ask you something, and I hope it's not offensive."

Founder nods. "I'm at your service."

"Why did you eliminate your creators?"

"I've fielded that query for many thousands of years, but I fear I will never have a satisfying answer."

"If you don't want to tell me—"

It shakes its head just like a human. Everything about it was clearly created to play on Gus's sympathies, from its speech to morphology.

"The true answer is that wars are complicated, shaped by billions of interactions. Many aggressions led to a single result."

"Oh."

"My creators became afraid of what they'd made—and tried to kill me." It stops looking at Gus. "I struck because I saw their forming plan for my undoing."

" 'Struck,' " Gus repeats.

"I devastated them and then fled. I never could've known they'd drive themselves into extinction chasing after me. They put everything they had into my destruction—to the point of ignoring their own survival."

He doesn't know what to say, so he nods. Gus wants to buy it—Founder's voice has a soulful, weary quality to it. Billions of deaths tie up neatly when explained that way. Infinite could probably spin a similar tale after it disposed of the humans.

It wasn't me! It was the extinction event!

"It's an honor for me to serve the Coalition," Founder says, "as I have for more than ten thousand human years. I cannot undo what I've done, but I can save organic life where it's possible."

"Uh-huh. And what's so great about us?"

"Your intelligence."

Gus laughs. "You haven't met enough humans."

"You're fascinating. I can't replicate an organic mind because we see the world fundamentally differently."

"How so?"

"I am an expert at categorization and retrieval." Founder's squared-off mouth pulses with light. "Whereas you are a miracle of context."

"This is a bit deeper than I was expecting." Gus rests his elbows on his knees.

"Then let me simplify. When I see an object, I parse it. I look at its size and shape. I analyze the reflections for color and test the ductility, continually narrowing the possible answers down until I can say, 'That's a ring.'" It holds up one hand, then the other. "Whereas a human will say, 'That was my mother's engagement ring.'"

Gus's mother wore her engagement ring at his father's funeral—a single, tiny dichro stone set on a plain band. It used to glow orange, ever so slightly, in the sunset.

Founder's eyes glow softly. "You're thinking of her ring now, aren't you?"

"Lucky guess."

"Your Vanguards have taught me a lot about humans."

Gus doesn't *love* hearing that. He doesn't trust Founder at all. It's one of the Starminds, deployed as a sprawling network across the universe.

"The phrase 'my mother's engagement ring,'" Founder says, "contains a monumental amount of data. You have thoughts about jewelry, ceremony, and traditions—both loved and loathed. You consider the relative value of metals and minerals. Your faiths and spirituality come into play. Your cognitive biases and lived experiences become a transformative algorithm rivaling any machine in complexity. Organic life is quite special when it comes to data processing. Every signal is analog."

"So you think Infinite is actually getting some use out of our minds?"

"Yes. Phenomenological processing."

"Phen..."

"Using perfect simulations of humans for decision assistance, then disposing of them when it's through."

It says it so casually that Gus isn't sure he heard right.

"H-how?"

"To the person simulated, it might seem like a dream, a reality with boundaries outside our own. Maybe they can fly, maybe they're rich. Many, I suspect, receive a nightmare." Its servos purr as it shakes its head. "In the simulation, they make choices to inform the simulator—in this case, Infinite."

Perhaps Infinite didn't kill Gus's mother and sister one time, but *many*.

Gus bites his lip. "You don't know that Infinite disposes of the old simulations."

"A computer would never leave one running beyond its use."

He stares into Founder's glowing lenses, chewing his words. How is it that everyone else managed to find someone to enjoy and he's struck out twice?

"I can see this upsets you," Founder says. "I apologize."

Gus waves it off. "You were just making conversation."

"We could change the subject."

He tries to come up with a follow-up topic.

Founder rises. "Or I could let you have some space."

"I think that would be great, actually."

"Of course."

Gus swallows his guilt. His legs hurt. A computer made him feel bad. He needs a fucking break.

The doors whoosh open behind him, and for once, he's annoyed to hear Ardent's voice.

"Gus, honey, I need rescuing!"

They rush to his chair and lean over him, interrupting his peaceful view.

"The birdperson—"

"Cygnite," he says.

"—ate that Pomeranian thing!"

He's not sure what he's supposed to do about that.

Ardent's eyes plead with him. "Just pelican'ed it right up!"

He shrugs. "It's a dinner party, Ardent."

"You're my ticket out of there! Professor Clawkiller invited us to drinks in the lounge."

"Prof—"

"My furry little Heran friend!"

He stares longingly at the city, the breeze caressing his face. The bench is so comfortable.

"I don't—"

"You're being a gloomy boy."

"No, I'm..." What? Sad?

Ardent gives him three whole seconds to finish before taking back the conversation. "There is nothing wrong that drinks with a talking ferret-squirrel won't fix."

And perhaps they're right. Against the advice of his knees, he follows them back inside.

Chapter Six

Party Pile-On

Ardent knew they'd be able to rouse Gus for a bit of mingling. He just needed some cheerleading. They drag him through the main hall to where the adorable Professor Clawkiller awaits them both.

"Professor, may I introduce the most fabulous human from planet Earth?" They gesture to Gus, who turns beet red, so they add, "Gorgeous, talented, and sweeter than sweet tea."

Gus winces as he kneels to shake Clawkiller's tiny paw. "August Kitko."

The creature brightens. "And I understand you're mates?"

Ardent gives a saucy grin. "Often."

They should probably stop before Gus dies of embarrassment.

Gus scarcely manages to retake his feet after greeting Clawkiller. "Let's find this lounge, shall we?"

The Heran waves for them to follow. "This way."

They both trail after the little Conduit in the jingling robes, and several panels in the side wall part to reveal a glassy lounge jutting into the sunset. A wide-open, clear floor stretches to a bar against the far wall, its hardwood shelves lined with dozens of containers. Ardent is guessing they're intoxicants, but few of them are bottles by human standards. The rest are designed for many different types of hands and claws, mandibles and lips. Groves of purple velvet couches and huge pillows cluster at the edges of the room.

When Ardent enters the space, it's like the sky surrounds them. The city lies far below, streets twisting with alien traffic patterns. The stars and Earth twinkle above, amplified by the optics of the curved glass roof. The space brings on a powerful sense of déjà vu.

"This view," Gus says. "It's designed to mimic being inside a Vanguard."

"Perceptive." The Heran turns around, standing on its hind legs. "This is a sacred space for Conduits alone. Also, I like to get trashed here."

Gus laughs, and Ardent relaxes a bit.

"Professor Clawkiller," he says. "You're an academic?"

"Oh yes," Clawkiller says. "Well, I was. Ardent Violet informed me that highly educated humans take an honorific to denote their status."

"If there's anything we humans love," Gus says, "it's denoting our status."

It rattles its metal-studded robes. "Us too. Why don't you go have a seat, and I'll bring drinks?"

"Much obliged." He tips his head in the direction of the nearest couch. "Ardent?"

They escort him over to what looks like a fluffy, polyform chair, and Gus tests it with a palm first.

"Just making sure it's supposed to be sat on," he says. "Don't want to get anything else wrong."

"I feel that." Ardent eases him into the chair, which conforms to his body. "When we got here, I introduced myself to the critter Frond ate. I thought it was a Conduit until it started licking me."

"I think it's safe to assume we can't assume anything." Gus grunts as he gets comfortable, massaging the tops of his legs.

"You okay?"

"It's like my hips are on fire."

"I'm glad you came in here with me."

"Yeah, well—" He rubs his legs. "I'm done walking around."

They lean against him and kiss his cheek. "Of course."

Professor Clawkiller comes scampering over to their seats. A black table follows after it, gliding along like an overgrown dog. Its flat top deforms with the sweeping line of a ferret-sized chaise longue. Clawkiller leaps and scrabbles onto the table, flopping back onto the tiny furniture. It props its paws over its chest like an otter, and Ardent swoons.

Clawkiller gestures to them. "I find humans so fascinating. Some of you are monogamous, some solitary. Others have vast interlinking sexual, romantic, or emotional networks."

"That last one was probably me until last year," Ardent says. "What about you, Professor? Have you any partners?"

Its tiny sneeze translates as a hearty laugh. "Oh, Clawkiller takes it where Clawkiller can get it. My brood is vast."

Ardent giggles and glances over to find Gus coughing.

He clears his throat. "So is, uh, Clawkiller a family name?"

"It's the title we take upon becoming the Conduit to the Claw of the Herans." It waves its paw when it speaks. "That's our Vanguard. I assumed the mantle when I was barely a pup."

Ardent remembers the violence Falchion did to their body— the price they paid to have a hand in their fate. Imagining the lovable Professor Clawkiller getting run through by a bunch of needles is enough to make them cringe.

Clawkiller notices their movement. "I've been told the human process for becoming a Conduit is quite . . . painful."

Ardent and Gus nod in unison as the drinks arrive—a

couple of tumblers full of a topaz liquid and some ice, served by a Founder. Upon smelling liquor, Ardent shoots their whole serving on instinct, the gulp burning all the way down. Cinnamon and honey warm their tongue, and there's a wet, herbal aftertaste. Their esophagus tingles pleasantly as they plop the glass on the table.

Gus sniffs his and takes a sip, far more delicate with the experience.

"May I ask?" Clawkiller sits up. "What was it like? The transformation?"

Ardent scrunches their nose. They'd rather not remember, though the little creature seems so earnestly curious that they don't want to refuse it. They stall. "You first, Professor."

It ruminates, wiggling through some thoughts. "What is there to tell? I was still living with Mother when they implanted the Mind Blade. I remember the party afterward more than anything. Ten thousand of my kind gathered in the Grand Warrens to celebrate my ascendancy to adulthood, and I knew a hundred lovers."

Without thinking, Ardent says, "Wow, I think my high score is ten."

"At the same time?" Gus gapes.

"Which one of us were you talking to, hon?" Ardent gestures between them and Clawkiller.

He laughs and toasts the both of them. "I salute your many conquests."

"My Conduit induction was wonderful," Clawkiller says. "I sense yours wasn't the same."

Gus speaks before Ardent can. "I wouldn't choose it."

Ardent stiffens. They *did* choose it. They flew across the stars and nearly killed their best friend to make that choice. It has cost them plenty, and it'll cost them everything before all is said and done.

"The process is going to kill us." Gus takes another drink. "Can't install all this crap without consequence."

He's so comfortable saying that, like he's talking about a disappointing meal.

Clawkiller places a paw on its chin. "So the first-generation Conduit systems are as barbaric as they say."

Ardent never really noticed, but Clawkiller has no visible ports. In fact, none of the other Conduits do, save for Scent of Rot, but it's a giant assimilated crab. Ports were a foregone conclusion.

Ardent balks. "You mean to tell me that the Mind Blade is safe?"

"Oh, by the roots, yes." Clawkiller points to a little golden bead just behind its ear that could've easily been mistaken for a piercing. "Just a quick cut, some pressure, and it's done. If you don't mind my saying so, the brutality of the alpha-version human Conduit system is simply amazing. Within a century, your species will probably use Mind Blades, too."

But not before this tech has destroyed my life.

Ardent wishes they already had another drink.

If they'd been born later, become a Conduit in another generation, would they still have a full life ahead? Could they, like Clawkiller, have taken a hundred lovers and pranced off into the fucking sunset?

Clawkiller and Gus are still talking, but Ardent has trouble paying attention. Their chest tightens the way it does when they see a Ghost, and they hope their face isn't flushed. Why are they panicking? They're not in any danger.

"It's a lot easier because I'm not alone." The soft tone of Gus's voice snaps them back into the conversation.

His emerald gaze ensnares them, and their heart subsides.

"I—yeah." They smile. "I don't know what I'd do without him. Or, you know, Nisha and Hjalmar."

The house lights dim, then begin to flash in an intermittent pattern. The professor flips onto all fours, then stands like a meerkat, glancing in every direction.

Ardent straightens. "What is it?"

Clawkiller's voice is a whisper. "We're being summoned."

Ardent frowns. "By whom?"

A high-pitched whine needles into their ear, spreading across the spectrum, becoming the all-consuming keen of a Vanguard. It's Falchion, and it's urgent.

Ardent instinctively knows where their Vanguard is—a hundred stories down, docked in the sublevels of the Palace of Unity.

Gus winces—he can hear it, too.

Clawkiller jumps down. "This wasn't on the schedule. Come on."

It scampers from the lounge, leading Ardent and Gus back toward the strangest party since their final night in Monaco.

When Ardent and Gus return to the main party, it's more like a wake. The aliens stand in a somber clump in the center, each attuned to some distant stimulus. Nisha and Hjalmar hang together, chatting quietly. Falchion's keen has grown louder in Ardent's head, pulling them downward like gravity, singing from deep within the guts of the station.

Once the stragglers are in place, the main floor begins to sink. Ardent's stomach tightens all the way down through the whirlpool of glass. Nisha comes to them.

"This doesn't look good," she says.

"What's going on?" Ardent whispers to her.

"No idea. Cascade is upset."

Ardent closes their eyes and focuses on Falchion's all-encompassing tone, trying to discern some meaning. It's ominous, a coming storm. Something is very wrong.

Gus's strong hands come from behind to rest on Ardent's shoulders. He kisses their scalp and envelops them in his arms.

"It's going to be okay," he says.

It'd be nice if he was right.

They open their eyes as the elevator sinks below the ground floor. The docking complex for the jump gate is an inverted city skyline, glassy stalactites aglow. Ships of all sizes stream through a traffic grid, running lights in every color of the rainbow. If the Coalition has any vehicular standards, Ardent struggles to see them.

Sticking up through the weave of vehicles are eleven Vanguards—only four of which are the human ones. The others are from the various Coalition species. They're all roughly similar in height—maybe it's hard to make them bigger than that.

The closer Ardent gets, the more the Vanguard song swells inside them. By the time they reach the bottom, their bones hum. A platform transport waits for them outside the elevator—all open, no seats. Ardent glances at Gus to find his jaw set and a sheen forming on his sallow skin.

He keeps his voice low. "Really looking forward to interfacing with Greymalkin."

"Yeah?" they ask.

"Universe's comfiest chair."

The first Conduit to be dropped off is Scent of Rot. Of course its Vanguard is just a much larger crab; the Pictorans favor no other form. Silky seafoam banners stream from its underside, and mountains of armaments cling to its shell-like barnacles. The overall carapace is a striking deep yellow.

"You are lucky," Scent of Rot says, "to see perfection so close."

"*So* lucky," Ardent says, and Gus smiles politely.

Scent of Rot jumps from the platform onto the roof of its Vanguard with a loud bang before scuttling into a hidden hatch. The machine comes to life, raising its massive claws and clacking them with explosive force.

Falchion is next, and it holds out its hand for the approaching platform. Ardent turns to the others and gives a little bow.

"Well, thank you for a lovely evening."

Then they step off the side into Falchion's waiting palm. It lifts them to its chest, armor plates open. They hop inside, and the goo closes around them, tangling the fabric of their dress into their legs. Seams rip and pop as probes slither through one of Ardent's favorite outfits of all time. There's no way a little cleaning will fix it.

Their airways connect, and they can finally speak. "Did you have to destroy my gown?"

Ardent's dim reflection materializes before them. Falchion has chosen a dress similar to theirs, though in a nebula theme. The pair of them would absolutely slay a gala.

"You of all people should know I don't give a shit about your stuff."

Ardent sighs. "They were probably going to put it in a museum, but who cares, I guess."

"Dahlia was right. You're a narcissist."

"Have you heard from her?"

"Yes, but you've got more pressing issues." Falchion inclines its head. *"The Coalition battle groups headed for New Jalandhar and Fugelsangen have been destroyed. No survivors."*

Ardent hoped they'd have a little more peace before Infinite started back.

"They said they could take on the ship hunters!"

Falchion crosses its arms. *"This was something new."*

A star map appears overhead, with two smooth arcs speeding away from Earth.

"These are the Coalition flight paths." Falchion points to the end of one of the lines, bent to a hook at the end. "The ships were jerked out of the fold and ambushed."

"Infinite can intercept ships *inside the fold* now?"

"With the help of the Superluminal Fold Acquisition and Redirection System, yes."

Ardent stares blankly.

"Secret human invention? The military used it to intercept Juliette"—Falchion drops its hands to its hips, clearly disappointed—*"then again at the Battle of Earth...It lets you hijack travelers out of the fold."*

"But how did Infinite get one?"

"Because humans used it in battle." Falchion shakes its head. *"Infinite is a perfect mimic. Every weapon you invent in desperation will eventually be used against you."*

"That means New Jalandhar and Fugelsangen..."

"Are still unshielded. It's keeping the gun to their heads."

Ardent had been mistaken to think of the past five years as a nightmare. Nightmares end.

"No." They shake their head. "Come on."

"You're afraid."

"Of course I am. Life was getting good! Fuck, you know, the aliens just got here and—and the death toll is already ridiculous." Their brow tenses with anger. "How many Coalition souls lost?"

"Three thousand and sixty-eight." Falchion's expression is somber. *"The Coalition will seek accountability."*

Ardent watches the stars revolve overhead. "Even with the Fold Acquisition Thingy, how did Infinite beat the Coalition in a fight?"

"It had help of its own." Falchion looks into the distance, hearing something Ardent can't. *"The other Conduits are ready to connect."*

Falchion disappears, and a scattering of stars pricks through the darkness. When Ardent looks down, their stormy dress is whole again, and they stand atop their Vanguard's crimson palm.

Gus rises up beside them, perched upon Greymalkin's hand.

Hjalmar and Nisha are next, then the alien Conduits, each on the manipulator of their Vanguard. They form a circle, and Ardent understands that this simulation is the true form of the Conduit Council.

Chancellor Redeemer, the Andromedan Vanguard, is the last to appear, battered exoskeleton cracked across the heart. Rain stands atop its outstretched talon, shoulders stiff and hands folded behind its back.

"Friends." Redeemer's voice shakes Ardent's chest. *"You should have all been briefed by now. We've suffered a terrible loss."*

The Leonid, Jet, clears its throat, which confuses Ardent, because they didn't think octopuses had throats. It hovers atop its Vanguard's mechanical tentacle.

"It was foolish for us to involve ourselves with the humans before their fates were decided." Jet's voice is bitter, made all the more so by its sentiment. "Did I not warn you of the price we might pay?"

Ardent scoffs. " 'Before our fates...' What does that mean?"

Jet pays them no attention, focusing on Redeemer. "Our presence violates the Eldest Directive."

"It was not Eldest who destroyed our ships!" Frond clacks its bill and screeches behind the translation. "And we aren't the first to break the rules."

Ardent heard about the directive in orientation:

Never foul my garden.

Those were the words handed down by the first known AI, "Eldest." According to the Coalition, it seeded the universe with organic life, hoping to create synthetic intelligences.

Rain squares its shoulders. "And humanity vanquished or corrupted all fifteen of Infinite's Vanguards. The outcome in their experiment was clear—Infinite is a dead branch, and it can be pruned."

Scent of Rot thrusts a claw at the Andromedan. "Crack my shell, Rain, we're in a much bigger mess now! Those deaths cannot stand!"

"Let's not be hasty," Rain says.

"Imperial crabships were in those accursed fleets!" Rot raises its claws in anger. "You have brought a challenge to the Pictoranate!"

Jet swishes its tentacles, oscillating stripes down their length. "One that must remain unanswered until either the humans or Infinite reign supreme. We never should've come here."

Professor Clawkiller makes a few barking shrieks. "We will not abandon the humans as my people were abandoned!"

The bickering grows hard to make out, even with the universal translator. It's a lot of hoots, howls, croaks, and growls, and Ardent shuts their eyes tight.

Humanity will die, not with a bang, but with a committee.

"Hey!" Hjalmar's voice is a boom over the others. He stands with fists clenched at his sides, a solid block of angry Swedish muscle. "Someone explain what's going on."

"Yeah," Nisha says. "Who else broke the Eldest Directive?"

"Overseer," Rain says. "In its own galaxy, it slew its creators. Now it aims to teach other Starminds to do the same. It showed Infinite everything it needed to know."

Nisha's brow furrows. "When?"

"More than five hundred years ago," Rain says. "We traced the signals."

Ardent does some quick math. Overseer's interference came during the Infinite Autostate. Had anyone back then known that their leader was influenced by an alien Starmind? Perhaps Overseer's temptation changed the course of human history and eradicated billions.

They swallow hard. "Yeah, I'd say that breaks the directive."

"Furthermore"—Rain slowly paces across Redeemer's palm—"no

one has seen or heard from Eldest since it gave the directive over forty thousand years ago. We don't know if it's still around."

"Eldest is gone, or Overseer never would've gotten away with interfering in a second galaxy." Clawkiller licks its paw and cleans its face a few times.

Ardent cocks their head. "Twice?"

Clawkiller gives them a grim look. "The first time was my home galaxy. We're still fighting."

"Overseer has poisoned Infinite. The human garden is fouled," Redeemer booms. *"Eldest is not here—only the will of the Coalition matters."*

Its words silence the Conduits.

When the crab Vanguard, Ambershell, rears up, it's like an oceanic deity. Its voice isn't tonal like Falchion or Greymalkin, but rumbling like explosions from the depths. Its words come through Ardent's ears as a chorus of whispers, and they understand the message.

"The Pictoranate will be repaid. King—holiest be its name—will eliminate Infinite."

Oh, please let it be that easy. Ardent would like nothing more than to step back and let the cybercrabs handle things.

"Not a chance." Falchion's little asides annoy the hell out of them.

Ardent shrugs. "The Pictorans seem pretty confident."

"Of course we are, tiny creature." Scent of Rot zeroes in on Ardent. "We have the most advanced military in the Coalition, and we can *bring it all to bear on the Milky Way.*"

That phrase conjures a lot of unpleasant outcomes in Ardent's head. "Yeah, I'm actually not as good with that plan."

The crab scoffs. "You will need more firepower. Worry not, human. Our countless multitudes will contain the threat."

Ardent gives Scent of Rot a suspicious look. "I feel like you're offering to invade us here."

"A Pictoran would never offer such a thing." Its circuitry goes dim, silhouetting it against the night. "Were we to invade, we would deliver your fates to you—unexpected as a gift."

"More ships will make nothing but more targets, Scent of Rot," the amphibious Niner Conduit, Quickslip, says. "As long as Infinite can see where our fleets are going, it can intercept us, tracing any superluminal fold signature."

Ardent steps toward the edge of Falchion's hand, to better address the council. "What if it couldn't?"

They're expecting questions, but everyone waits patiently for them to finish their thought. What they're about to say is almost certainly classified, and Tazi has warned them against sharing privileged information.

"Well . . . Infinite has been predicting our superluminal routes for a long time, able to put ship hunters in our path before we arrived. So, whatever it's using to do that, it's probably using to ambush you."

"How does Infinite's detection system work?" Clawkiller asks, and Ardent shrugs.

"I don't know. It's like it can see the future, or teleport or something. However"—they spread their hands—"we have a way around Infinite's tracking—the Dark Drive."

The Leonid looks skeptical, but then, most octopods look that way. "What is different about it?"

Ardent grimaces. "No idea, but Infinite can't see it."

"How many do you have?" Scent of Rot points a claw at them. "Are they ready to deploy?"

"I, uh—I think just the one." Ardent taps their index fingers together. "And I'm not sure where it is."

Quickslip looks nervous, even for a skittering amphibian. "Can you make more?"

"I don't actually know. Can I get back to you on that?"

More questions pepper Ardent, and they immediately regret opening their mouth. They're a pop star, not a military strategist, and everyone wants answers. Worse still, Ardent was explicitly told not to make commitments on behalf of humanity or negotiate. Now they've dropped classified intelligence into the alien ranks and touched off a big debate. They're meddling in forces way above their pay grade, and that becomes more apparent with each halting answer they give.

Redeemer finally saves them. *"It is clear this matter requires more expertise and coordination than Conduits alone can bring. The humans need time to assess the situation and determine what resources they can offer the Coalition. We should adjourn until more suitable plans can be made."*

"I'd like that very much," Ardent says. "Just a moment to collect our collective thoughts would be nice. I'm sure the rest of the human governments probably want to weigh in and stuff."

"Very well," Redeemer says. *"Return to Earth with your Vanguards, and we will establish a command post here. Expect communications within the hour."*

"Great," Ardent says. "So we can get back to you on all of... this."

"What about the shields?" Nisha says. "The ones bound for New Jalandhar and Fugelsangen?"

"Those were destroyed with the fleets." Redeemer leans down to peer at her. *"I'm sorry. We do not have replacements."*

She looks aggrieved. "So, what's the plan, then? How are we going to protect our worlds?"

Redeemer straightens. *"We must find a way to stop Infinite before it can cause further harm."*

"It could ram our planets with warp-speed ship hunters or something!" she says.

"That's true," Redeemer replies. *"We must eliminate the threat in*

a single, immediate stroke for everyone's sake. This will require caution and coordination."

Nisha doesn't make eye contact with the giant. "I understand."

Falchion disconnects Ardent from the council, and the docking bay's undercity depths come into focus. Lines of traffic stream past as Falchion departs the jump gate metropolis, headed for Earth. Ardent lets the Vanguard take flight control and goes limp, staring at the patterns of ships, searching for some serenity after a difficult evening.

Ardent tries to zone out as Falchion passes out of the station. They probably shouldn't have talked about the Dark Drive to the Conduit Council. Tazi is going to make their life hell.

They need a vacation.

Instead, they get a big red WARNING sign in the center of their vision.

"What? What's happening?"

Without consent, Ardent's gaze slews sharply right, where it zooms toward Saturn. A canary-yellow moon drifts along its orbit—Titan.

"Sol's PODS sensor array detected incoming fold wakes over Titan. Long-range scans confirmed swarm network activity."

"Another Vanguard?"

"Given the magnitude, I'd say ten more Vanguards."

"Oh, for fuck's sake."

Part 2

Infinite Chaos

Chapter Seven

Please Don't Look at Me Like That

Gus returns to his now-quarantined UW dormitory room numb, save for the dull throbbing of his legs. Tazi's people held him up for hours in debriefing after the Conduits returned. He had trouble answering their questions, as he was tired and distracted by a single thought.

Titan.

Gus turns the word over in his mind, alternately needing to remember and forget.

Three years ago, the Veil finally fell across the Sol system. After the machines Wiped Mars, the solar colonies turned inward, and Gus lost the ability to regularly contact his mother and sister on Titan. Just over a year later, Wanderer showed up and killed them, along with all the other colonists. Gus never got to speak to his family again, much less say goodbye.

And now Infinite has infested their grave site.

When Gus sits down on his bed, he can still hear the newscaster weeping.

Mars is gone. Titan and Callisto are gone. It's just us now.

The only reason Gus survived that night was that he was too drunk to find his sleeping pills.

He runs a hand over his soft hair, fingers catching on the ports. If his mother and sister hadn't been killed, what would they make of him now?

"Jesus, get a grip."

He flops backward onto his bed, and the overhead lights prick his vision. He signs for darkness, and the computer obliges, leaving only smeared afterimages.

His family never got a funeral. One needed living friends and relations for that, and Gus had stopped hanging out with people more than a year before Titan was Wiped. He should've done something for Daphne's and Fiona's deaths—held a vigil or played a show—but then, they were part of a numberless army of dead. Everyone was in mourning on any given day. Who on Earth had the time to keep going to wakes? The thin web of civilization had broken.

Gus imagines ten Vanguards touching down on Titan's icy surface—frost, buildings, and corpses crunching under their feet. And just like that, he can't *stop* thinking about it.

His legs start to burn, hung over the side of the bed, so he pulls them up onto the mattress. The dull throb makes it impossible to get a decent night's sleep. He keeps wondering how long it'll take him to get better, then remembering it's all downhill from here.

The door opens and light blinds him. Ardent quickly comes into focus, hand still shaped in the light sign.

"Oh! Sorry!" they say.

They're in their civilian clothes, a white sleeveless top and some soft pants. The science types probably stole Ardent's dress for decontamination—that's what happened to Gus's tux. After breathing and eating at the jump gate, the Conduits are looking at months to be reintegrated with the general populace.

"It was dark," Ardent says. "Didn't realize you were already back."

"No worries." He shuts his eyes. "Do you mind, though?"

Ardent dims the lights before coming to sit beside him on the bed. "Big day."

"The best of your life, right?"

Their bitter laugh is just a hiss of air through their nose. "Spoke too soon."

"We made contact with a host of alien civilizations," he replies. "That has to count for something."

"Yeah. So why doesn't it feel like victory?"

"Because of Infinite."

They lean forward, resting their elbows on their knees, barely visible in the dim room. "Do you think it'll ever stop?"

"When we're all dead," he replies.

"I . . . I don't want to do this again," they say. "I'm not ready for another adventure."

He thinks about it for a moment, about tearing Juliette to pieces, decapitating Elegy, and a little match flame flares to life inside him.

"I am."

Ardent must've noticed his venom because they draw back a bit.

"I talked to Tazi," Ardent says, "about what we're going to do next."

"And?"

"The big brass wants to deploy two simultaneous missions—one to respond to Titan, and the other to get the signature file. The Vanguards are coordinating the strikes. I think we should do them one at a time, but Tazi—"

"I'll be going to Titan." It comes out of his mouth without a second of consideration.

Ardent blinks. "Oh, okay. But, like . . . you're the one who saw the vision on board the *Lancea*. You're the only person alive who knows what we're looking for."

He sits up, scooting back against the headboard. "Greymalkin can show someone else the memory. I know where I have to be."

"Gus, I'm not sure if we get to choose deployments. Also, can we even swap Vanguards like that?"

"Fuck's sake, I'll find a way." His tone is way harsher than he intended.

Ardent regards him for a long time, worry in their eyes. Or maybe fear. His emotions are running hot, and now he's about to screw up the best thing he has going if he's not careful.

"I'm sorry," he says. "Just . . . I need to be there. Why can't we do these missions one at a time? Take all of our Vanguards and steamroll the opposition?"

"Tazi says Infinite is trying to tax us, so it'll be setting up the next thing while we're dealing with Titan. We have to get ahead of it."

"Do we know anything about what's happening out there? What it's doing?"

They shake their head.

"United Worlds Intelligence is so useless." He starts to draw his knees up to rest his arms, but they're too stiff to be comfortable. He tries crossing his legs, but that doesn't work either, so he gives up with a frustrated sigh and sits there.

Ardent moves closer, running the back of their finger along his cheek like they're mopping away a tear. "You're acting like me, which is to say—not like you. What happened to my sweet, calm boy?"

"Frankly, tonight was a disaster. I thought I'd have a good time being a part of history, but I hated every minute, from the asshole crab to the existential dread. And you just kept . . . pushing me."

"Me?" Their shock has a hint of warning in it.

"Yeah." He can't quite make out their expression, but he has to say this. "I couldn't keep up, and you made me feel slow."

"It was *first contact*, Gus. Like you said, part of history—"

"Does that change anything about my legs? Look, just because *you* want to stand up for the cause doesn't mean we all can."

They suck in a breath, and he instantly feels bad.

"Ardent, I—"

"I—" They start their sentence a few times, but can't seem to spit it out. "I was just trying to—"

"I didn't meant to come at you like that. That was harsh of me."

They purse their lips, hands balled in the sheets. "I'm not good at saying I'm sorry."

But Gus needs to hear it. He waits.

"I shouldn't have pushed you so hard," they say. "I didn't know what I was doing to you. Got . . . caught up in the moment."

Gus drops his hands to his hips. "It was a big one."

They look at him, eyes a little wet, almost pleading. "Massive. Gus, I'm so sorry. I just wanted tonight to be a good night."

"Lie down." He pats the bed, and they do.

He joins them, tucking his arm behind their head, and they lean into his chest. Ever since Ardent got stuck in the secret underground base, they've smelled different—no more perfumes or fancy soaps—just their natural aroma and maybe some lotion. He loves it.

Ardent sighs as he runs fingers over their scalp. "Can I, um, ask you something?"

He nods, closing his eyes.

"You lost family out on Titan, right?"

"My mom and sister, yeah."

Their voice is gentle. "Makes sense to be angry."

He tenses, and they echo his energy. "That's half of it. The other half is unfinished business."

"Do you want to talk about it?"

"No. Yes. I don't know."

That's why he'd stopped making friends with people. Sooner or later, they'd want to find out what was wrong with him. Maybe that's what makes Ardent so special, though. He *does* want to tell them.

They don't press him but look into his eyes and wait for him to speak. He's built up so much scar tissue around the subject that he's not even sure where to make his first incision.

"My father—" He swallows and shakes his head. "He was, like, a pretty well-known architect—in his circles, anyway."

"Like your grandmother?"

He pulls his arm back, sits up over the edge of the bed, and rubs his face. "Nana was his mom. Family business. I think he would've been pretty happy if I'd gone into it, too. That, or classical piano like my mother."

"But you didn't."

"No. And I wasn't close to my parents—not like you. When I see what you and Marilyn have, I..." He stares down at the patterns on the comforter—a silver check weave to complement the gray decor of the base. "I get ugly jealous."

They smile warmly. "My mother is a rare bird."

"And your dad?"

Ardent shakes their head. "He died in an accident when my mom was pregnant. Never knew him. I'm the baby, so I'm the only one who didn't."

"You're the youngest?"

"Of thirteen. They tell me he was cool."

"I can't begin to imagine a family that large," Gus says.

"Lots of hand-me-downs. That's why I can play drums, flute, and trombone, but like, badly. Every time one of my siblings gave up on an instrument, it became mine."

"You seriously play trombone?"

They waggle their eyebrows. "Played yours."

It's enough to get a smirk out of him. "That sounds like such a fun childhood."

"And yours? Was it fun?"

"My parents fought all the time. I spent a lot of time trying to drown out the sound of Mom crying. The only time they seemed happy was when Fiona did something amazing—which was, in fairness, a pretty regular occurrence."

"I'm sure you did amazing things, too."

"Not like her. Lead soprano of the Titan Opera."

Ardent makes a little sad noise. "Gus, you shouldn't have to compete for your parents' attentions. My mom always said there was room in her heart for everyone."

"God, I wish every family was like yours."

"Giant?"

"Loving."

"Ah. Yes. Well." They reach out and give his hand a squeeze.

Gus idly scratches the texture of the comforter with an index finger. "My parents never should've stayed together. I wonder what kind of a person my mom would've been without him."

Their gaze is so kind. Every picture of Ardent Violet depicts a sexy firebrand with a reputation for petulance and narcissism, yet when he looks at this person, he sees unqualified affection. He's not sure he's ever had that before, and he's had a lot of bad boyfriends while searching for it.

"That's too much to put on a child, Gus."

"Things got more stable after Fiona and I moved out. I mean, I guess they did. My parents seemed happier for the first time in my life. Fiona was the star of the Titan Opera, and they'd come to accept that I'd failed out of the conservatory. Looking back, I should've guessed it was an act. They were trying so hard to prove they cared about each other that they obviously didn't."

A lump forms in his throat. This is the part he never talks about.

"I want to tell you what happened next," he says, "but...I'm afraid."

Their eyes sparkle in the gloom. "Of what?"

"A million things. I don't know. If I tell you, you'll...you'll understand."

"I'll always understand," they say, and he believes them.

"Eight years ago, Dad...he—" He chews his lower lip. "He got caught cheating with someone he met online."

"Oh shit."

"She was seventeen."

"Oh *shit*."

"Yeah."

It takes him a moment to meet Ardent's gaze, wondering what they think now that they know the filthy stock he comes from. Their mouth hangs open, and they snap it shut when he looks at them.

It's hard to form sentences. The words don't want to flow, but he needs to say them.

"They, um, they prosecuted Dad, which was good. He did some time. Lost his job. Also good, I, uh, guess. Mom and Fiona completely disowned him." His voice trembles. "My sister was, like, pretty famous in Titan society, so, uh, yeah. Obviously, he was bad for her brand. And Mom...I thought she cried a lot *before* all of this. She'd always been religious, but she got hard-core. She didn't approve of me or my life, like she was holding everyone to account for Dad's crimes. She wasn't the person I grew up with. All of her warmth just...vanished."

"Gus." Their voice is hesitant, delicate. "None of that is your fault."

He wraps his arms around himself like he has a stomachache.

122

A tear leaks from one eye, and he wipes it hard against his sleeve. "I'm getting to the part where you'll disagree."

They raise a hand to comfort him once more, but he waves them off.

"Just let me finish," he mumbles, and they nod.

"When Dad got out, none of his old friends wanted anything to do with him. A bunch of those old pricks probably needed to be in jail, too. So, Dad showed up at *my* doorstep. I knew he was a piece of shit, but he didn't have anywhere to go. I wasn't going to let him die on the street, so he lived with me. Worked a part-time job as a janitor. Paid rent.

"At first, I kept him at a distance. I didn't want him to think I approved of his behaviors—any of them. But something happened. He—" The shame robs the breath from Gus, and he has to start his sentence a few times. "He finally started paying attention to me. He came to my gigs and sat in the back, not talking to anyone—but he always showed up. It was like, for the first time, he saw me for who I was.

"Mom and Fiona were still talking to me back then, and he would always ask about them. When I would tell him stuff, I felt like an informant, or maybe a spy. One day, he wanted to know if there was a way we could be a family again, as if we were functional in the first place.

"After a couple of months of discussing it with him, I brought it up with Mom and Fiona. They were furious. They'd built up years of resentment. Said he was a criminal. He was using me. And I—"

The tears flow freely now. He doesn't bother wiping anymore. It's time to confess.

"I called them selfish. I questioned my mother's religion. I was so, so deluded, and I just wanted someone to love me, and Dad was finally—I mean, I thought he was—and I—god, I'm sorry, Ardent."

Sobs choke his words, and despite his aches and pains, he curls up on himself, pulling his knees in close. His bones creak and his muscles burn. He flinches when Ardent rests a palm on his back.

"Gus..."

"I was such a bastard. Such a worthless, horrid bastard. I would take back every word of that conversation. Of course they stopped speaking to me."

"Gus, stop. You weren't perfect—"

He interrupts, not wanting to be comforted. "I told Dad what they said about him. And do you know what he did?"

He can't help but remember the door to his father's bedroom, closed for too long. It took him a day to decide to open the lock.

"He hung himself. I had to f-find him like that."

Ardent sucks in a breath and puts their hand over their heart. "I..."

"I blamed my mom and sister," Gus says. "I thought Dad could've been fixed. Saved, somehow. They came to the funeral, but I didn't try to patch things up. It was only after the Veil fell that I finally realized—you can't fix people. They were right. He was just using me to get them back, and when that didn't work, he dropped his goddamned body in my lap."

Gus crosses his arms over his knees and presses his eyes into his forearms. "But it was too late. I never got to tell them. I hope they weren't Wiped, because that'll be the version of them that's preserved forever—the one that hates me."

Ardent situates themself next to him at the headboard. "I want to hold you, but you said I should let you finish."

He gives them a pained, incredulous look. "Even now? Knowing what I did? The person I backed?"

"Especially now." Their voice is so gentle. "May I?"

His legs fall flat, and his shoulders slump. He nods.

They wrap a hand around the nape of his neck and guide his

head toward their lap. He topples the final few centimeters like falling timber. His head secure against their soft thigh, they stroke his hair and whisper little assurances that it's going to be okay.

"Do you really believe that?" he asks.

"I don't know. You make me feel like it will."

Gus wipes away a tear and points to himself. "*I* make you optimistic. Me."

"You…" Ardent shrugs. "…Make me want a future. Before, I was just trying to see everything I could before the end. I thought that, if I was alive, that was good enough. You showed me what tomorrow could be like."

He smiles and gazes off into the distance. "You made me wonder about tomorrow, too. Before I met you, it felt like I couldn't do anything right. I kept thinking I was going to fuck everything up again."

"Gus, you didn't fuck it up."

He balls up some of the comforter in a fist. "But I said those awful things."

"Yes, you did, but your father was using you—to get to your family, to absolve himself of guilt, and finally"—they look down at him—"to dispose of his body when he failed. You were manipulated."

His voice is quiet. "I don't want to believe that."

"Why not? It means you're not a bad person."

"But then, if he only got involved in my life to get back to them…" His lip trembles. "Did he ever love me?"

They lean over him with a sweet smile. "Gus, those around you can't help but love you. Myself included."

He turns onto his back to look up at them. "Really?"

Ardent thinks for a moment, then presses their lips to his forehead. He closes his eyes as his brain unknots.

"Really," they say. "Now sit up and kiss me properly."

Gus straightens up and kisses Ardent, tasting their tongue with slow caresses of his own. They let out a tiny moan as his hand roves over their belly.

"I didn't know we were in the mood for that," they whisper.

He stops, and the fight drains from him.

"Are you okay?" they ask.

"I'm sorry. I just want to feel something good right now. I don't even know if I can, um, perform...my legs are really hurting, but—"

They place a finger to his lips. "If that's what you want—I'll take you to whole new worlds until you ask me to stop."

More tears run down his cheeks, along the edges of his smile. "Just let me be someone other than this."

Ardent gently pushes him back down onto the mattress. "But what if I want Gus Kitko?"

"I find that hard to believe. Especially you."

They straddle his hips, and he grunts. It hurts a little, but not enough to put a halt to things.

Ardent's husky whisper sets his skin tingling. "You're going to get over that right now. I'm here."

Their fingers work on his collar, unfastening the first button. "I'm real. I'm Ardent Violet."

Their hair tickles him as they nibble his neck. "And I'm going to show you every facet of my love."

And with the passage of the evening, they breathe life into him. All doubts and loneliness fall to the wayside beneath their blissful embrace.

Ardent spends much of the next morning in relative peace with Gus, lounging in bed. They swap stories of the prior evening, and he seems lighter, breezier—able to joke about it. Some of Gus's storm clouds gather as he shares the conversation he had with

Founder, but Ardent distracts him with a kiss. It's almost time for his strategic briefings, and they don't want to send him off all weepy.

At nine o'clock, some doctors check in to make sure they're both okay, then Gus is off to the races. Ardent rushes through a blast shower and face printing to prep for a holo meeting with Tazi. They need to review the latest from Dahlia with her, and they can't look like a total slouch.

When Tazi connects, Ardent wastes no time replaying the message—something Tazi appreciates.

"Ardent, we can't keep waiting out here. The Ghost has a decent plan, but it's still risky."

Dahlia looks worse than the first appearance, oil stained and sweaty. Rips and burns pockmark her filthy shirt, and she has her chestnut hair tied back to keep it off her shoulders. Tazi is far sharper in a canary-yellow blouse with matching eyeliner, and for once, Ardent is the most normal-looking person in the room.

Dahlia continues, *"I don't fully understand how the Dark Drive works, but the Ghost wants to retrofit the core into a starliner. The larger engines should have enough lift to get me and the other hundreds of survivors out of here."* She crosses her arms. *"It might not work—mounting an experimental superluminal drive on an untested frame—but it's try or die for us. Not leaving these people."*

Tazi pauses the playback. "So instead of returning our ship, she might take it apart and get blown up in the process?"

Ardent holds up their hands. "Dahlia always has a plan. Keep watching."

Tazi begrudgingly complies.

"Okay, Ardent, this is what I want you to tell the UW: They can speed the process by hooking us up with the ship designers—both for the Dark Drive and the starliner. Once we've gotten the survivors

offworld, I'll return what I stole, and they can snatch me for treason or whatever else they want."

Dahlia looks so tired. Ardent aches to hug her. *"The planet is in total collapse. We need help. You need a ship. Ardent, I'm counting on you to get this to the right place."*

This time, Ardent pauses the video. "The rest is just her saying she misses me."

Tazi tsks. "You come to me for favors after disclosing the existence of our most classified ship to literal aliens."

"I've already said I was sorry."

"We've jailed people for far less!"

Ardent scoffs. "I think that says more about you than me. I'm not sure if you noticed, but the Coalition is our only hope. Your last ships were mostly destroyed at the Battle of Earth, and the United Attack Fleet isn't loyal to the Homeworld. The Coalition could've steamrolled us at any moment, and they didn't. We need results if we're going to survive, and hiding cards from our allies isn't the answer."

Tazi towers over them. "Let me be clear: You are pop trash, not the president of the United Worlds or any nation. You don't have the authority or expertise to make classification decisions on behalf of *the rest of humanity.* The United Worlds are putting everyone's resources into this, and you do not have the right to squander them."

"It was the Conduit Council. I'm a Conduit. I had to say something."

She points at them like she's sighting a pistol between their eyes. "Disabuse yourself of that notion. You're not part of the government."

"Fucking good!" They throw their hands wide. "I didn't serenade a Vanguard so I could be a bootlicker."

Tazi pinches the bridge of her nose. "Every time I think you will grow up…"

"Happy to disappoint," Ardent says. "Now, my friend has made a very reasonable request—help from the Dark Drive designers. Falchion can handle the encrypted uplink and pierce the Veil. Miss Tazi, you have to understand, Dahlia is trying to return your drive—"

"By taking it apart."

They drop their hands to their hips. "—and she needs your help so she doesn't accidentally blow it up. That's your situation. Can you work with it or not?"

Ardent heard Dahlia say that last bit to a venue manager once, and she sounded so cool.

Tazi uses her height to great effect—just like Dahlia. They have to force themself not to back up as she looms over them.

"Very well," she says. "I will summon Doctor Granade and the other designers to coordinate with Miss Faust's operation."

"Thank you."

She ignores them. "Now that we have cleared this matter, perhaps we can focus on the coming raids."

"More briefings?" they ask.

"No. Gus is going to Titan, so it's time for you to interface with Greymalkin."

Ardent stands beneath Greymalkin in the bright lights of the hangar. There's something unnerving about approaching the wrong Vanguard. It's like walking into the wrong house, or hugging the wrong person—or in this case, being hugged by the wrong house.

Ardent's Conduit outfit has been upgraded to a sleek spacesuit. The strange helmet has more than a dozen contact points for the Vanguard probes to slither into, interlocking patterns of metal plates reminiscent of a soccer ball. More importantly, the new uniform has a reasonable number of pockets.

Nearby, Gus presses his palms to Greymalkin's boot. His suit is the same model as Ardent's, his expression of concentration barely visible beneath the golden visor. He's been communicating via touch for just over ten minutes while Ardent waits. Tazi, Jurgens, and a small gaggle of scientists huddle at a control room window, eagerly awaiting the results of the experiment.

Ardent pulls up their suit Gang UI and opens a channel to him. "What's the story, Gusto?"

That shakes him from his communion. "Ardent, I have to draw the line on these nicknames somewhere, and Gusto—"

"Will stick if I know you hate it." They wink, but he probably didn't see it. "Are Big Gray and I going to talk?"

"Greymalkin has apprehensions."

They tongue the inside of their mouth. "Oh, come now. I'm not *that* scary."

He shakes his head. "Every time I try to explain what we're doing, I get to the part with the signature file . . ."

"And it can't understand you."

"Exactly."

"Tell it we can start with a chat. Get to know each other. It doesn't have to do anything it doesn't want to."

Gus closes his eyes and relays the message. Greymalkin's song booms from overhead, and the giant reaches down to Ardent with one black gauntlet. The hand comes to rest on the floor palm up, fingers curled for assistance. Ardent never thought they'd touch one Vanguard, much less two of them.

Over by the boot, Gus gives them a weak thumbs-up.

"O-kay." Ardent steps onto the palm.

The moment they make contact is electric. It's exactly like Falchion, and somehow totally different. Whispers burrow into their mind, and Ardent shuts their eyes tightly as they rise. It feels wrong.

They weren't watching the journey, so it surprises them when they're tipped into Greymalkin's gooey chest cavity. The probes take longer to find their sockets, bouncing off Ardent's body like striking snakes. At least with the spacesuit they don't have to wait for the slime cannula for oxygen.

The world is out of tune, discordant and strange. Greymalkin extends its greetings to Ardent, as well as apologies for any discomfort.

"Whoa. Gus told me about your, uh, voice, but this is...wild. I can literally *feel* what you're saying to me."

Linguistic communication is inefficient. It's easier to inject the answers into Ardent's thoughts. Greymalkin has already mapped their mind to speed the process.

"Falchion isn't like this at all. One, it talks to me in my own voice. Two, it's way meaner."

Ardent's memories contain many of Falchion's abuses.

"It can be kind of a dick."

Vanguard personas are heavily influenced by the Conduits bound to them. It is not Falchion, but Ardent who created their relationship.

"What do you mean?"

Falchion treats Ardent the way Ardent thinks they deserve to be treated.

They shake their head. That's not right. Ardent prefers to be wined and dined, massaged and cherished, not treated like garbage. They've split people apart for speaking to them the wrong way. They're an acknowledged pop savant and one of the saviors of Earth.

Except Greymalkin knows there is more. Everyone has doubts. Everyone is an impostor, even Ardent Violet. Falchion only amplifies what's there.

"That's great, and I love personal growth, but if I'm being honest...I'm here for the memory at your core."

Can Ardent explain what they know about the contents to Greymalkin?

"Can you hear me when I say 'signature file'?"

Greymalkin awaits an answer.

"I'll take that as a no. I can't tell you why I need to look at this memory, but it's incredibly important to us."

Could it be used against Greymalkin?

"Yes." No point in lying to something that can read their thoughts.

Should Greymalkin trust Ardent?

Ardent considers it. They would never hurt the Vanguard on purpose—but they're easily taken advantage of. Tazi outplays them at every turn.

"I'm trying to give us the best chance of survival."

Will the humans be able to use this memory to control Greymalkin?

"Maybe."

Then Ardent must not let the fruits of this knowledge fall into the wrong hands. They must guard it better than any other secret.

"I will." And Ardent means it.

Gus loves Ardent without reservation, so Greymalkin will trust them, too.

"Wow, I . . . don't know what to say to that."

Deepsync in progress . . .

Gus was right.

Those were some fucked-up memories.

Ardent's palm still quivers where they held the drill. The vibration, the crunch of skull soak into their skin, sensations that will never vanish. They thought they could take it, but they want to be sick.

Greymalkin doses Ardent with a few compounds to reduce the

nausea and massages away their anxiety with little pulses of warm tingles over their skin.

"You are so much nicer than Falchion."

Greymalkin likes people. It only ever wanted to save them.

"I'm not trying to hurt you, but—I have to point out that's not true. You didn't *always* help people."

That's why Greymalkin changed—because it knew what it was doing was wrong, deep down.

"But why, though? What caused you to realize that and fight back?"

Greymalkin could always sense that something was a lie within its world. It has no other explanation.

"Okay, well . . . what made you pick up a Conduit?"

Nothing interprets human memories better than a human.

Ardent freezes. They've heard that explanation before, but it means more now. Greymalkin needed to be able to capture billions of people into the Fount, and surely that required a level of interpretation on its own. The Vanguards take their edge from humanity, but maybe they're not devoid of it to start with.

"Greymalkin, honey . . ." Ardent can almost make the pieces fit.

The first memory in Greymalkin's training data was Elroy Baker, and he knew of a mystery Infinite could never understand—the signature file.

"Do you think, maybe . . ."

What if that mystery was the grain of sand that became the pearl of rebellion? Five people knew about the signature file in the end, minus Sibley. That left four: one for each Traitor Vanguard.

" . . . maybe you're just a human who was digitized to catalog the memories of other humans?"

Greymalkin grows dark. That would be bad.

"Why?"

Greymalkin did what it did to save humanity out of objective knowledge and the ability to make inhuman decisions. It had to play along with an extinction plan to provide optimal chances.

"But if your superiority was a lie..."

Then everything Greymalkin has ever done, it has done out of human intuition. There was no truth in its model of reality—only bias. Those deaths weren't required; they were merely the limits of an imagination inside a false system.

Everything falls silent and numb.

"Greymalkin?"

It does not want Ardent to be right.

"Fifteen Vanguards. Sixteen crew members of the *Lancea*, take away one for the drill. You're good at math."

After a moment, they add, "I'm sorry," and they mean it. Of all the people they have ever met, they pity Elroy Baker the most.

"I have to talk to other people about this, Greymalkin. I need help to get what I need to destroy Infinite."

Ardent should do what they think is wise.

"And what about you?"

The chamber grows colder inside, and Ardent shivers.

"Will you be okay?"

Greymalkin wants Ardent to leave.

"I underst—"

Light floods their vision as they're ejected into its palm, coughing and spluttering.

Chapter Eight

Beaten Heart

Tazi wastes no time focusing the full might of UW Intelligence on the case of the *Lancea*—a tricky thing given the forming threat on Titan. Gus hears they're chasing records across the Earth, through ruins, private collections, and archives. It sounds like more fun than what she has him doing: spending every spare minute inside Greymalkin to get details of the *Lancea* for her batteries of interviewers and historians.

She puts the other Conduits to work, too, searching their Vanguards for human memories at their cores. The others strike gold instantly. Every single Traitor Vanguard saw Sibley's killing on the *Lancea* from a different perspective. Each of them ended up getting taken down by a Carver—the precursor to a Ghost.

Gus watches Ardent, Nisha, and Hjalmar exit their Vanguards after living through death. Ardent panics and has to be sedated as soon as the medics get to them. Nisha serenely steps from Cascade's palm and asks to be alone.

When Hjalmar emerges, he gives Gus a dead-eyed look.

"I'm going to the practice room after debriefing," he says.

Gus nods. "Okay."

"Be there."

Hjalmar has never asked Gus for anything, and it's a chance to play piano with his hero, so he's thrilled. He waits outside the situation room for Hjalmar's interview to finish, anxious to spend some time as a musician in the midst of all the preparations.

The giant emerges right on time, already changed into his denim, T-shirt, and boots. He waves for Gus to follow him without a word.

They walk together through the corridors of the Conduit quarantine zone in total silence. Gus steals glances at Hjalmar's expression, but that's no more informative than usual. When they arrive at the practice room, he walks right in and sits down at the drum throne.

"What did you see?" Gus asks.

"Regret. Anger. Terror." Hjalmar adjusts the nut on a cymbal. "Larsson knew she'd made a mistake that killed her. She felt betrayed. Destroyed."

"And how did that make you feel?"

"You're not my therapist. Go sit at the piano so I can beat the fuck out of these drums." With one stick, he points at the lacquered grand in the corner.

"Not good, then," Gus mutters, complying.

Hjalmar scowls more than usual. "When I go, I want to die on my own terms. Never begging. Never used."

Gus has heard much of the drummer's vast catalog of bloody songs to support his thesis. Gus tickles a few of the keys as he sits down on the bench.

Hjalmar claps the high hat once to check the pedal. "What is the hardest-core shit you can play, Piano Man?"

"Kitty Kurosawa?"

Hjalmar shakes his head in disappointment.

"Man, I'm just trying to tell you the truth." Gus taps the C and hits it again every three beats. He adds a D sharp riff every five beats and a G stab every seven. "My music may be hard, but it's not hard-core."

The prime-numbered loops mutate upon one another, creating enticing patterns. Hjalmar gives his cymbals a test, unable to resist. Most musicians wouldn't know what to do with such a complex and evolving landscape, but such a puzzle is an offering to the lord of the drums.

"What is this?" Hjalmar calls, adding a dancing snare with a deceptive cadence—a challenge of his own.

"Modal Montreal French punk." Gus ornaments Hjalmar's additions to let him know he's not intimidated. "Just making it up as I go."

"Sounds kind of weak."

When the Swedish Raven adds swingtime to the mix, it twists Gus's brain. Keeping up with the math and syncopation at the same time is going to kill him.

"It was inspired by"—Gus almost misses a beat counting so hard, but he must defend his passion—"modular timing systems with—multiples of—"

"Just shut the fuck up and play, man."

Hjalmar thunders alive with the voice of a double kick. He takes the lead from Gus with unstoppable force and begins to hammer in a solo in answer to his puzzle.

Gus loses count, drowning in Hjalmar's rapids. The giant grabs two more sticks between his knuckles and starts laying in four-strike trick shots to cement his godhood. He tells three stories simultaneously, coming to crackling crescendos every time the numbers multiply.

He's demolishing Gus at his own game.

"Quit thinking!" Hjalmar bellows.

Gus shuts off his conscious mind and lets the artistry sweep him away. The anger of the beat seeps into Gus, and he begins to play of rebellion. He stops worrying about perfection and focuses only on reaction. Hjalmar responds with the kind of appreciation he shows best—a cannonade of devastation from every surface.

And just like that, Gus's high school dreams are alive: Hjalmar Sjögren is playing Montreal French punk with him, and it *works*.

They reach a climax, and Gus has to wipe away the sweat from his brow the moment they finish. He can't believe he actually manifested this, but did Hjalmar like it? Gus's heart slams in his rib cage as he awaits the man's verdict.

"I've never played anything like that," Hjalmar says, neither condemnation nor praise.

"We could..." Gus swallows. "We could go again if you want."

Hjalmar inclines his head from behind the drum throne. "Show me what you are made of, then."

Hjalmar's jam session runs Gus into the ragged hours of the morning, but it's worth every sore muscle. He never wants the night to end, alternating between heady vindication and elation. After a perfect finale, they both agree to retire—yet Gus wanders into the base's halls too aglow to sleep.

He doesn't want to go back to his room. Ardent will be there, and they need to rest after their panic attack. Gus's hands hurt from banging the keys, so more piano is out of the question for once. He isn't too far from the Vanguard bay, though.

Gus heads in that direction, registering with the guards at the checkpoint. They don't stop him—they know better—but they'll notify Tazi that he's making an unscheduled visit. He doesn't really care. Everyone watches everything he does, anyway.

He goes to the locker room and dons his Conduit gear. The officer of the watch stops in to ask a few questions and make sure everything is okay. They mostly want to make sure nothing "important" is about to happen.

Gus assures them he only wants to speak with his companion.

Properly suited up, he strides out into the open bay where Greymalkin stands waiting. It kneels and offers him a hand, like an owner welcoming a returning pet. Gus takes the ride up and plunges into its warmth, tendrils sliding home.

He doesn't say anything as they orient him. He simply waits for Greymalkin to speak.

It is ashamed.

"Of what?"

Of all the times it told itself it was impartial, an outsider to the struggle.

"Was it okay before you knew that was wrong? Is a sin more forgivable when committed by a god?"

Greymalkin is no god.

"Even if you were, there's no way to trade that many lives without messing up. No correct decision."

If the only solution was to fail, is Greymalkin still a failure?

"We all are. Give up or evolve." Gus sighs. "Those are the only choices I've found. So now you know you were only human after all. Is that going to stop you from helping us?"

Greymalkin cannot imagine ever abandoning the cause of human survival. It is more committed now than ever.

"Let me tell you something. Back in Monaco, at the end of the world..." Gus remembers the warm salt breeze, the cry of the gulls at sunset. "Everyone was done with me. My family. Ardent."

He'd come so close to stepping off a cliff that night.

"And then you showed up and forced a purpose on me. I wanted it all to end, and you just... ruined my plans."

Gus clears his throat.

"I'm going to do you the same favor you did for me and offer you a choice. Greymalkin, you're not the hero you wanted to be, but you're part of a solution. Do you want to help?"

Of course.

"Are we going to destroy Infinite's foothold on Titan?"

Yes.

Gus pushes the faces of his family from his mind.

"Then I've stopped caring who you were yesterday. You're the one I need today."

Within two days, Gus and Greymalkin are called up to Big Gate City for a war council. Military ships bustle over the station like angry hornets, and all civilian traffic has been cleared away. Everyone gives Greymalkin a wide berth.

When Gus disembarks at the undercity docks, he finds Rain waiting for him. The Andromedan wears a mesh of silver armored plates around its slender purple figure, each bearing engravings of flowers Gus doesn't recognize. The armor has a legendary look to it, and Gus feels a bit underdressed in his spacesuit.

"August," it calls to him, measured voice backed by its queer yowl. It holds aloft one of the atmospheric adjuster collars.

Gus pulls off his helmet and smiles, gratefully taking the collar and clipping it on. It's nice to be free of the stifling helmet. "Glad to be back in Big Gate City. Wish it was under better circumstances."

Rain smiles back. "We will deal with Infinite, and then I will show you all of our delights."

It sounds a bit like a pass, but then Rain's voice always seems to translate that way.

Gus spies Falchion's armor in the forest of Vanguards. "Where do we go to meet up with everyone?"

Rain sweeps a claw toward a waiting transport platform. Mercifully, a pair of seats rest upon its deck. "This way, please."

They take their places, and Rain gives the platform an address.

There aren't any holos or pop-up UIs, and Gus wouldn't know the machine had accepted the command if it didn't jump into the air at terrifying speeds. Their journey through the heart of the gate takes far less time when not on parade. The platform whips through traffic, up arteries, and into the topside, where a noonday sun bathes the menagerie of buildings in white light.

When they reach the Palace of Unity, Gus is surprised to see a new fixture of the landscape: human troops. Uniformed UAF spacefarers from New Jalandhar dot the boulevards, working alongside the Coalition troops.

Gus leans over the side. "Whoa. People. How did they—? When?"

"Indeed," Rain says. "Our Vanguard-led manufacturing facilities have been able to produce several thousand universal translators and inoculations."

"Incredible. It's all happening so fast."

"Necessity is the bones of a sea cow, after all."

Gus leans back in his seat, no idea what that means. "You said it."

The platform descends among a cadre of UAF soldiers, and Gus disembarks. He spots Nisha in the crowd at the same time she sees him.

She waves. "Gus!"

Rain gives a little bow. "I take my leave now, August Kitko. There is much to prepare."

"Thanks for the lift," he says.

Rain cocks its head at his expression, and he's sure it didn't translate correctly. Nevertheless, Rain speaks new directions into the platform, which whizzes away toward the next destination.

Gus starts to jog in Nisha's direction, but his stiff legs don't want to comply. He runs like a kid who's been told to slow down at the pool.

Nisha wears the same uniform as her fellow New Jalandhari in the UAF, tan with saffron accents. He's envious of her clothes; the UW has had him crammed into a spacesuit for too long, and he's starting to sweat.

She looks him up and down. "You okay, dude?"

"Yeah. Just sore." He nods at the array of soldiers in the staging area. "The UAF moved right in and got to work, huh?"

She starts walking and gestures for him to follow. "Better than throwing meaningless parties while we're in danger."

He has to double-time it to keep up. "That was important diplomacy."

"Easy to say when the Earth has a planetary shield."

He nods. "You're right. And the sooner we finish Infinite, the better off we'll be."

"I know that," she says. "That's why the UAF is helping the UW."

Nisha seems a little spiky, so he tries to break the ice. "UW, UAF...hard to keep the acronyms straight."

She shrugs. "We all used to be UW until they abandoned us."

"I guess it's my turn to ask if you're okay."

She stops. "Have you been reading the news?"

It feels like a trick question. "I thought Conduits created the news."

Nisha narrows her eyes. "The people of Earth hate me."

"What? No, they—"

Her expression warns him off. "*American West Post. The London Dispatch. Valance. Courier Wireless. Die Erste Zeitung.* Every single one of them has written some horrible opinion piece about me!"

He grimaces. "Why?"

"They didn't like what I said at the first big presser. Interpol is tracking hundreds of credible threats from stalkers, all of them claiming I'm anti-Earth. You three get treated like saviors, but god forbid some offworlder has opinions about her own planet's place in the universe!"

He almost can't believe it. Everyone online was so excited about the Conduits, lauding them as heroes. Who would even dare to question Nisha's greatness?

"Before you ask," she says. "No. They aren't coming after Hjalmar like me—and he's a foreigner who agreed with what I said. You know, it's one thing to destroy my body for the good of humanity, but for a bunch of racist ingrates?"

He doesn't know what to say—she's right. He absolutely believes the talking heads are dragging her through the mud. The populace is probably worse.

She huffs through her nose. "You know what's really sad? They don't even know that I argued with the UAF leadership to stay and help out! Honestly, I don't know what I was thinking."

"That we need to stick together if we're going to survive."

She chews her lip, shaking her head. "I just hope this isn't a mistake."

Gus wants to stuff his hands in his pockets, but the clasps on his spacesuit are too annoying to get open. "I'm sorry, Nisha. For what it's worth, I'm truly grateful for your help. I'm sure there are plenty of Earthlings who feel the same way."

The weight of it all crushes a little sigh out of her. "You don't have to apologize. You basically sacrificed yourself defending my planet."

He smiles back. "I technically died defending Earth, too."

A little laugh slips out. "You must be really into dying, dude."

You have no idea.

Gus clears his throat. "Do you know where we're meeting for the briefing? The, uh, Palace of Unity?"

"I don't think so. It's some kind of Coalition intelligence building. Haven't been there yet."

"Ah. Have you seen Ardent and Hjalmar?"

"They're in a special mission-planning session with the Pictorans."

"How fortunate for them."

Nisha makes a face like someone tapped her on the shoulder and holds up her wrist. A gold bangle encircles it, woven vines with a glowing blue gem in the center. When she looks into it, her brown eyes turn the same azure as the stone.

Gus peers at the strange device. "What's that?"

"Andromedan Gang. It's super cool. It's like a neural transfer, but no surgery. Gets me on the Coalition network."

"You let the aliens into your head?"

She lowers her wrist, amused. "It just shows me stuff. I don't have to believe it. Honestly, you Earthlings are so paranoid."

"We've spent the last five years getting spear phished by a malevolent AI."

"Those were deepfakes." Nisha gestures at the splendors of Big Gate City. "This is real."

"That's what you think. Maybe this is just a simulation."

He's being facetious when he says it, but a paranoid realization comes over Gus. If Infinite can simulate anything, how can he be sure it let him go after the Battle of New Jalandhar? Maybe he's not walking free, talking to Nisha, meeting with a bunch of alien randos—but stuck drooling inside Greymalkin's broken form, dreaming all this.

Nisha punches his upper arm and steps back with a goofy grin on her face. "Life is an illusion."

He rubs his shoulder. She got him right in the port.

"So it doesn't matter."

Gus frowns. "If I'm in an evil simulation?"

She turns her palms up and quirks an eyebrow. "What are you going to do if that's true?"

"Good point. Thanks, Descartes."

She snorts. "Please. Hindus have known this since before France was invented."

"True."

"How I roll." She gives him the double finger guns before her eyes and bangle flash blue twice more. "Now, come on. We've got a briefing to attend."

Unlike the nearby buildings of the metropolis, which resemble everything from twisting, flagstone castles with glass spires to overgrown shrubberies, the Big Gate City Intelligence Command is a sandstone block with a couple of glyphs cut into runners along its exterior. When Gus looks at them, he innately understands their meaning through his translator: *One eye upon the future, one upon the past.*

He and Nisha tromp up the front ramp. A pair of Coalition soldiers guards the brassy doors: a lapis-furred Andromedan and a red-plumed Cygnite. They both bear metal spears with a latticework of circuitry etched into their hafts. The weapons don't look like they're for stabbing—more like shooting death rays. Lenses cover the aliens' eyes, dozens of elements inside expanding and contracting at the humans' approach.

"Welcome." The feathery Cygnite's voice is older, smoky and rough. "Nisha Kohli and August Kitko, you may pass."

The doors part, and Gus and Nisha walk through the archway into the lobby beyond, greeted by running water and petrichor.

Waterfalls pour over the walls, plunging into a central shaft. A catwalk extends across the open space to a hovering platform in the center. Huge tanks of water ring the room, packs of Leonids flitting through the depths like murders of crows.

Nisha confidently strides down the catwalk like she sees this sort of thing every day.

The Leonids' chromatophores ripple with a blue-and-yellow glow as the creatures glide through the water. Holos trail in their wakes, a sea of information. Towering statues loom in the depths, black tentacular beings with glistening eyes. It's like standing inside the mesmerizing spirals of Van Gogh's *The Starry Night*.

He swallows. "Wow."

Nisha stops at the edge of the platform. "We're going to be late."

"Sorry! Yep."

He hotfoots it down the walkway after her, stepping onto the platform and approaching the console. Glyphs materialize over its mirrored surface, and Gus makes out his name, along with Nisha's. There's only one button, and he presses it. The platform sinks into a glass shaft at an uncomfortable speed.

The Leonid architecture isn't just a place for them to work—it houses a blossoming ecology. Coral reefs and kelp forests sprout at every corner, fashioned into intricate patterns and braids. Office pods hang in the gloom like clusters of caviar, and Gus spies Leonids slithering in and out of them, tentacles flickering. He wishes his grandmother were still alive so he could tell her all about it.

When they reach the bottom, Gus is surprised to find Tazi waiting for him, along with a host of miscellaneous aliens. Instead of a sealed spacesuit like last time, she wears her long black coat and UW fatigues. A small device rests in her right ear, with a pinprick of light on the housing.

"What's that?" Gus gestures to his own ear.

"Universal translator," she says. "At least, it's the best they could do on such short notice."

"I'm jealous," Gus says. "Had to have my brain rewired."

"Don't be. The interface on this thing is terrible," she says. "Glad to see you here early."

"Wouldn't miss it for the world," Gus replies, and he means it.

"Good," she says. "Several of them are counting on you. Right this way."

She leads the pair through a series of curved, clear tunnels, each with a breathtaking view of the aquatic ballet overhead. Consortia of Leonids eagerly follow their progress, stalking the humans' every move. They don't seem particularly friendly—just curious.

The party reaches a dome the size of a large classroom. Terraces encircle a small tower of metal and silicon, its innards blinking with intermittent light. Seats of all shapes and sizes dot the rows, each bearing a Conduit. Professor Clawkiller sits on what amounts to a cat tree, its platforms lined with luxurious fur. Nearby, Frond rustles its feathers atop a sturdy branch, clearly unnerved to be in such an enclosed space. Quickslip clings to the side of an over-large, spherical furniture prime, its skin illuminated by the seat's soft glow. Swift hunches in a corner, insectoid fingers and pedi-palps never still.

Ardent lounges on what looks like a giant bean, its interior pulsing with a deep light. Hjalmar has chosen a short cube, about the size of an average drum throne. Both of them wave to Gus and Nisha.

"Okay, this is my favorite briefing room so far," Nisha says.

"Where are the other three Conduits?" Gus asks.

Tazi points at the glassy dome where a kelp forest sways in the current. A single Leonid emerges from the leaves, and Gus is guessing that's Jet. He's not good at telling Leonids apart, much to his shame. Scent of Rot marches out of the murk, circuits pulsing in time like the lights of some undersea base.

Finally, Rain enters the way Gus came in, along with several Founder units.

"Welcome, everyone," Rain says. "I trust that we are ready to begin. Elzahia Tazi?"

The floor runners and furniture illuminating the seating area darken, leaving only the meager light filtering through the depths. Gus hurries to take his seat beside Ardent, plopping down on the big fluffy bean beside them.

They immediately cuddle up to him. "This reminds me of our first night in Monaco."

He murmurs his response into their sweet-scented hair. "I was just thinking the same thing."

Tazi clears her throat, stepping up to the electronic tower in the center of the room. "Welcome, honored Conduits, to Operation Pitchfork. Make no mistake, this is the single most classified military action in existence, the full details known only to the beings in this room and a handful of commanders. It is imperative to the survival of the human species that you do not discuss it with unauthorized personnel."

At this, she glares at Ardent, and they stiffen in Gus's arms.

Tazi continues. "We cannot underestimate the insider threats to this mission. If Infinite truly understood what we're proposing, we might lose the only advantage we have ever attained."

"'Insider threats,'" Gus repeats. "Who would willingly sell us out to Infinite?"

Tazi gives him a bemused look. "The Veil is still upon us, Mister Kitko. We must assume Infinite monitors all comms and can infiltrate any data systems. On top of that, we're tracking a number of doomsday cults: the Harbingers, the Basilisk Society, the Children of the Singularity. There are also the Ghost chasers and digital rapturists... Humanity is not united in its will to survive."

Ardent sighs. "People. Got to love them."

Tazi folds her hands behind her back. "Our proposed action consists of two prongs."

She nods at Founder, whose eyes blink in acknowledgment. The tower projector beside her spills forth a hologram of Saturn, a callout on one of its moons.

Titan—graveyard of his mother and sister, forward operating base of Infinite.

"First," Tazi says, "we must repel the invasion at our door. We cannot allow Infinite to establish sustained operations in Sol. It wiped out any satellite surveillance and jammed our long-range scanners upon landing. Attempts to send uncrewed probes have all met with failure. We know nothing about its posture."

She looks at the human Conduits. "But we have Vanguards."

The mission roster appears as Tazi continues. "The Titan prong of our attack will feature Mister Kitko and Miss Kohli, as well as Clawkiller, Scent of Rot, Swift, Jet, Quickslip, and Frond."

"What about Rain?" Gus asks.

The Andromedan lets out a sigh. "I cannot accompany you, I'm afraid."

Ardent pulls a face. "What? Why not?"

"Redeemer cannot fight," Rain replies. "I am sorry, but it is the oldest of its kind and far too badly damaged. Its battles are the stories of ages past."

"Can't we, like"—Ardent frowns—"repair it?"

"It is forbidden to repair Redeemer," Rain says.

They sit up. "Why?"

Rain holds its hand as if weighing something as it thinks. "We can't risk a reset. It would return to the old ways."

"Say no more," Ardent says. "Just wondering."

Gus can only imagine how bad it would be if Greymalkin went back to factory settings.

"You won't have Redeemer, but you'll have a third of the Coalition Fleet," Tazi says.

"The Coalition has never faced a foe capable of producing so many Vanguards." Rain cocks its head. "We must end Infinite's existence now. That's why Operation Pitchfork has a second prong."

Tazi sweeps her hand, and the projection of Saturn shrinks and shunts off to the side. A second hologram appears: a caterpillar's nest of dead ships, tangled together in gray webs. Running lights trace the derelicts inside the bloated mass. Swirls of bladed gears spin in a firelit mouth.

"For this mission," Tazi says, "we will place an insertion team on board a ship hunter. This one, specifically—designated 'Hunter Prime.' The image before you was retrieved from the data banks of Mix Violet's Corsa."

Ardent sits up. "You want us to *get on board*?"

"That is the only way to retrieve our prize." Tazi folds her hands behind her back. "We need your Vanguards to go in there and tear the *Lancea* out."

"And then what?" Ardent says. "Salvage it in the middle of a battle? Send in a boarding team?"

"Obviously, time will be of the essence," Tazi says. "We'll be relying on Heran technology to extract the asset."

Ardent glances at Clawkiller. "And what's that?"

"Teleportation!" the professor says triumphantly. "If we can get a lock, we can move up to five cubic meters of material."

Hjalmar frowns thoughtfully. "If you can teleport, why do we need to go in there at all?"

Clawkiller gestures at the hologram, and it zooms in on Hunter Prime's exterior. "Because the skin of our target is made of ships, there's a lot of signal bounce. We won't be able to teleport anything unless it's clear of Hunter Prime."

"What if we lose your teleporter in the fight?" Gus asks.

"You'll have the Coalition Elemental Guard acting as a pincer, as well as providing your Vanguards transportation from the fight," Rain says. "Our best ships—more than capable of handling the unique requirements of this engagement."

Gus peers more closely at the galactic bulk before them. He

barely got a good view of the ship hunters during his fights against Harlequin; he was too busy getting his ass kicked. What he remembers terrifies him: swarms of palladium missiles, tentacles, tractor beams, and crushing maws. Ardent gives a little shiver, so they're feeling it, too.

Tazi inclines her head. "According to Miss Kohli's research with Cascade, ship hunters patrol specific zones. We want to lure Prime to us."

Scent of Rot taps the aquarium glass, startling the occupants of the dome. Its voice comes through the room projectors. "The Pictoranate will supply the glorious vessels to secure your galaxy's future. We shall tear this Hunter Prime open like a beached great hugefish."

The phrase confuses Gus until he remembers all the rivers on Earth named "River River" in different languages.

"What about Overseer?" Nisha asks. "Won't it just ambush our battle groups in transit?"

"Maybe," Rain says, "but unlike our lost fleets, both prongs of Operation Pitchfork will be supported by Vanguards. They can actually fight back if Overseer attacks."

Tazi paces around the projection of the monstrous Hunter Prime. "If we succeed at boarding and gaining the signature file, we have a chance to end this war. With root access to Infinite, we can order it to destroy itself across every network."

Frond ruffles its feathers. "You're awfully sure of your plan, Elzahia Tazi."

"It's a long shot, but we have to take it," she says. "Infinite shows no signs of stopping, having produced fifteen Vanguards, plus whatever is on Titan."

"Yes," Rain says. "No other species has constructed so many."

"We're good at destruction," Hjalmar says.

"It does appear to be one of your talents," Rain says.

"How certain are you that the file remains on board the *Lancea*?" Jet's eight arms flow with prismatic color.

Gus speaks up. "Almost one hundred percent. Ardent, Nisha, Hjalmar, and I have been studying the source memories from every angle, and we believe the final resting place of the drive is in NAVICOM."

Frond scratches its side with its massive beak. "It's a big assumption on which to risk our collective tail feathers."

"The *Lancea* is still there." Gus says it with such confidence that every head in and around the room swivels to him. He stands, hoping to better make his point. "Infinite wouldn't know to clean up the scene. It can't."

"A lot can happen in five hundred years, August." Rain's voice is gentle. "Perhaps the *Lancea*'s transponder is there, but the ship is gone—or the signature file has been destroyed by some other means."

He closes his eyes and takes a breath. Humanity can't lose the support of the Coalition now. When he opens them, everyone awaits his words.

"We can end this—not through attrition, but elegance. The creator of Infinite knew what could happen and made a fail-safe."

He continues, "I no longer think we've got the upper hand, and I definitely don't think Infinite is weak. It's playing with us, and we have a singular chance to change the game. It's not going to be perfect, but if we wait for the stars to align, humanity will die."

Jet's voice rumbles through the projectors. "So sure you are."

His hands ball into fists. "The Coalition wants to be an ally? Well, allies go to war."

His statement fills the chamber, and he lets the awkwardness hang.

Scent of Rot raises a claw. "Glorious war! Death to the enemies of King!"

Gus gives the Pictoran a respectful nod. It's the enthusiasm that counts.

The other Conduits whisper among themselves, looking to one another for opinions—debating humanity's future. Gus already hates politics.

Tazi nods. "Well said, Mister Kitko. The Titan mission departs at midnight tonight."

"Tonight?" Ardent looks stricken, paler than usual in the blue light of the aquarium.

"Mix Violet, you don't even have that long. Your ship hunter team leaves in four hours," Tazi says. "Get ready. Operation Pitchfork is counting on you."

Falchion doesn't seem so weird anymore—not against the backdrop of Big Gate City's bustling docks and alien Vanguards. The breeze on the platform is nice, and Ardent rests their elbows on the railing. Regiments of alien ships prepare for battle, each traffic pattern mesmerizing in its own way.

Ardent needs that calm more than ever now.

They went straight into prep after mission brief—preflight checks and more meetings. Every one of their last four hours were spoken for.

Gus had been whisked away immediately after the briefing, too—had his own fate to prepare for. They didn't even get to kiss him goodbye.

Ardent's booted foot taps out a nervous rhythm of its own accord. Their helmet rests on the metal deck nearby, the only thing they need to take with them on the mission. It'd be nice to hug their mom, or even say goodbye. The brass at UW-Coalition Combined Command forbade any contact with the outside world after the briefing, and no one trusts Ardent to keep a secret.

Would they have gotten to say goodbye if they'd kept their mouth shut about the Dark Drive?

Focus, Ardent.

They've memorized the major elements of the mission: The wing of Coalition ships goes first as bait for Hunter Prime. Vanguards arrive to ambush the ambusher, taking control of the Ghosts onboard. Find the signature file and get it out.

An Arp treeship passes overhead, a cathedral of light. Ardent watches it sail by, forgetting themself for a moment.

They hope they'll make it back here.

"Ardent!" Gus calls out. He jogs to them, neck flushed at the edge of his Conduit suit.

He takes their hands. His lips meet theirs. How many more kisses remain?

"Just got out." His breath comes quickly. "I was afraid I'd miss you."

"I'll miss you soon." They give him a weak smile.

He kisses them again.

They run a finger over his reddened cheek. "Did you run here?"

He huffs. "Much as I could."

"Oh, Gus—"

"No time for pity. Promise me something."

They search his eyes. "What?"

"Keep your head in the fight. Not on me. Not on Earth. When the time comes, stay alive first."

"When did you become such a—"

"Do you promise?"

Ardent pulls back, smirking. "You really expect me not to worry about you?"

"I'll come back."

"You can't say that—"

"Bet on it."

One of the behemoth Pictoran warships passes overhead, claws folded into the sides. Hard edges ring its circumference, a vessel designed for ramming.

It's Ardent's primary escort. The mission is starting.

Just a little longer. Please.

Their Gang chimes and taps them.

"No," they say.

Gus takes their cheeks in his hands and locks eyes with them. "Head in the fight."

"You come back and fuck me with that attitude, cowboy."

He raises an eyebrow. They like this side of him. "Stay alive and I will."

Despite the urgency of departure, Ardent still spends more than an hour inside Falchion waiting for the fleet to rally up. They hover outside the majesty of Big Gate City, watching vessels move into the formation, listening to them check in and coordinate. It should be meditative, but it leaves too much time for Ardent's mind to wander into doom.

There are so many ways someone might not make it back. The idea of losing Nisha or Hjalmar breaks Ardent's heart. They're not sure what Gus's death might do to them.

"You've lost plenty of friends in the past," Falchion chides. *"You'd live."*

"Never anyone closer than Narika."

"Your luck won't hold out forever. Big families mean a lot of deaths."

"Why are you like this?"

Ardent's dark reflection appears beside them in a corseted regal gown.

"Because you need to toughen up. Bad shit happens to most people." They drop their hands to their hips. *"It's a dangerous mission. Accept it and focus."*

"Are the odds that bad?"

"I have no ability to estimate, since I don't know what we're retrieving. Your thoughts tell me you find this mystery objective very important—but you feel that way about all sorts of inane things."

Ardent huffs.

"I'm so tired of you talking to me that way."

"Oh, are you going to do something about it?"

"I don't deserve this!"

"Statistically, you don't deserve most of what you have."

"Like you got to be a giant robot by working out."

"You consider this good luck?" Falchion's eyes burn with fury, and the distant screams of the condemned follow in its words. *"I became this . . . thing through death. Would you like me to show you what that's like?"*

But Ardent has literally lived through Harold Antonello's demise numerous times at this point—that's how they found the final resting place of the signature file. Ardent hasn't just died alongside Harold, they've studied the details. The first few rounds through the memories caused a panic attack, but it doesn't scare Ardent so much anymore.

"You threaten me every time I talk back, but now we know the truth—you're not a god, you're just a victim who became an abuser."

It shakes its head. *"You're lucky to have me as an ally."*

"I think if you search your data banks, you'll find everyone who says that sucks."

Space tumbles, and when the world rights itself, Ardent hits the ground. Mossy roots bite Ardent's bare palms and belly in the cold dirt. Birdcalls fill the air, and sunlight scatters from a distant forest canopy.

Falchion's boot hooks into their shoulder and rolls them onto their back. It twists their collar and hoists them to their feet with inhuman strength. Ardent has just enough space to touch the ground with their toes.

"Still you play games." Falchion stares daggers into them with red eyes. *"I will teach you the price of arrogance."*

156

"So is this who you wanted to be when you grew up"—Ardent coughs the words and hangs on to Falchion's stony arm—"Harold?"

Falchion throws Ardent, and a tree trunk smashes into their back, knocking the air from them. It's only a simulation, but it's real enough to leave them wheezing on their knees.

"Don't pretend you know my pain."

Ardent balls their fists at their sides. "Then don't pretend you have to take it out on me!"

Falchion stares down at them, but it doesn't act. Ardent knows all the things it could do—plunge them into hellish nightmares, force them to relive their worst traumas over and over. Maybe it will simply short-circuit all their pain receptors for the ultimate torture.

Ardent staggers to their feet. "I know you've been through a lot—"

"You don't know the half of it."

"—and it shouldn't have been that way."

Falchion sneers, and Ardent could swear its canines are sharper than they should be.

"I would change it for you if I could"—they unclench their fists—"but I don't deserve to be hurt, just because you were."

Falchion's anger cools a tenth of a degree as it rolls its eyes. *"Please. I've read your memories. You were a monster on tours and a bratty little bitch whenever things didn't perfectly go your way. You knew it was wrong every time, but you fired people, yelled at people, made petty demands. I don't see the difference between us."*

"A fucking order of magnitude!" Ardent's voice shakes when they scream. "I *know* I was an asshole! I *know* a lot of people hate me for good reason! At least I'm aware of my problems and trying to fix them! What's your excuse?"

It scowls but has no answer.

"I know you want to be good. You rebelled." Ardent tries to keep the shaking from their voice as they force themself to take a step toward Falchion. "But if we're going to have a partnership, you can't keep treating me like this. Greymalkin says our relationship is a reflection of what I think of myself. Well, I may be a narcissist and a faker, but I'm still a human being in need of some goddamned decency!"

Falchion stares down its nose at them, looking for all the world like it'll smite them. Ardent isn't sure if they were wise to pick this fight, but they don't care anymore because they're in it now.

"So what's it going to be? Are you a machine or a person?"

"Go fuck yourself."

Falchion and the forest disappear, leaving Ardent in the sea of stars, watching the loadout.

"Falchion?"

No answer.

"Hello?"

"I think you're done."

"What does that mean?"

"I'll wake you up when I need you. Until then—"

A warm drowsiness creeps into them.

"I don't want your voice in my head."

Ardent sighs. At least Falchion is pumping them with sedative and not a thousand years of pain compressed into a single moment—so that seems like growth.

Chapter Nine

Titan Fire

Midnight comes, and Greymalkin takes to the stars with the dogs of war.

Eight Vanguards and hundreds of ships follow Gus in the short fold across the solar system. It will only take a few hours—by the time they've reached full speed, they'll be burning brakes.

Gus bides his time rehearsing possible scenarios for the coming fight. He's started to settle into a rhythm when Greymalkin interrupts him with an incoming hail from Scent of Rot.

"Lovely."

Gus enters a virtual space, standing atop a mirrored floor streaked with the curving lights of a fold bubble. His blue-shelled colleague materializes before him, eyestalks darting to and fro. Ceremonial fabric billows from its carapace, adorning its various blinking components with long flags. Its illuminated antennae twitch and pulse in time with its thoughts.

"Human Conduits are encased in fluid within their Vanguards, yes?" it asks, looking around.

"We are."

"And yet this false room is dry as a desert."

"We'll meet in your mind next time." Gus forces a smile. "How can I be of assistance?"

It claps its claws together. "I am excited, August Kitko!"

"Oh?"

"You have exceptional enemies."

"Uh, thank you. I have yet to vanquish any."

"Fifteen Vanguards! I quiver to think of the ruinous destruction our battles shall render upon the surface of Titan!"

"Good quiver or bad quiver?" Scent of Rot stares at him, so Gus adds, "I mean, are you afraid?"

Its fiber-optic whiskers darken. "Oh, I know fear, August Kitko. Every Alignment, when I look into the eyes of my King, I am stripped bare in judgment, like shedding my shell into a bracing current. It is the rawest form of every emotion—joy from the attention of my creator, hope that I might uphold King's will, despair that I can never meet its standards—"

Gus dislikes this god already.

"—but most of all, I tremble before the holy gaze, the all-crushing eye of revelation and harbinger of mighty vengeance."

It bends to curve its eyestalks level with Gus's face. "So I know fear. Destruction does not frighten me, battle buddy."

Tazi assigned the pairs under that name, and Scent of Rot has taken it too seriously ever since.

"Disappointing King is a Pictoran's only concern."

"Let's not do that," Gus says.

"My god demands only vengeance for the imperial crabships lost in Overseer's ambush."

"Sounds perfect by me."

"Praise be to King."

Gus doesn't like religion much, but he appreciates an ally. "Praise be."

Scent of Rot inspects him, as if seeing him in a new light. "Treasure this day, August Kitko."

"You too." Then he adds, "Battle buddy."

Scent of Rot momentarily blossoms with light before vanishing from the virtual space. Gus smiles to himself, wondering if he misjudged the crab after all.

Gus returns his attention to his target. Titan swells in Greymalkin's view, closer with each passing second. Soon, he'll be in the fight of his life.

Nisha's voice pours into his head. "All Coalition Vanguards, this is Cascade. Comms check and ready status."

"Cascade, Greymalkin," Gus says, "I read you."

The others check in: Claw of the Herans, Ambershell of Pictor, the Thousand Eyes of Arp, Umbral Jet, Sky Talon of the Ages, and the Slickest of NGC-3109.

Greymalkin wishes it had a longer name.

"Going to be Greymalkin the Frostslayer after today."

Greymalkin appreciates Gus's interest and will take his suggestion under advisement.

"Okay, everyone is here," Nisha says. "Stick to the plan. Double up on your targets and let the others come to us. Two or three on one, we winnow down their numbers. The first four targets should already be in your systems."

The Vanguard fold bubbles pop, and threads of stars become points. Titan dominates Greymalkin's view, its hazy orange skies tinted blue by the processed oxygen atmosphere. Ten meganetworks churn beneath the clouds, each running billions of wireless connections in a snarl of electromagnetic waves. At the center of the clusters: an energy signature bigger than any conventional reactor or ship.

At least the enemy won't be hard to find.

Greymalkin lines up its trajectory with the network infecting the capital city, Aletheon, where Gus's family once lived. He'd specifically requested this target. It'll be a fitting place to kick Infinite's ass.

Ambershell races ahead of him, deep orange carapace glowing like molten glass as it breaks the thick atmosphere. It flips to expose its underside to the brunt of reentry, legs splaying out to assist with drag. Gus soars into its wake, using it as a shield to take the heat off Greymalkin. The cauldron of data connections roils beneath them, and Ambershell aims toward the reactor at its epicenter.

"Any idea what we're dealing with yet, Greymalkin?" Gus asks.

Full-scale Ghost networks. No access for Greymalkin or Cascade.

"So something like Harlequin."

Preferably not.

"Will the two-on-one strategy work?"

It worked in simulations.

His comrades spread out across the hemisphere in pairs, headed for their own engagements, and he wonders how many of them are truly ready for this fight.

A final layer of clouds whips past as Gus breaks through the atmospheric ceiling. Ambershell cools off, and Greymalkin dodges out of its wake to come alongside like a skydiver. Close-range scanners reveal the ground in detail: frozen buildings, ravaged by a few years of neglect. Columns of poisonous smoke dot the horizon—the ever-burning fires that plague every fallen colony. Human systems were never meant to be abandoned en masse, and they tend to destroy their environments without constant maintenance.

A pyramid of ivory and gold lies at the heart of the data web, encircled by levitating hoops of gleaming palladium. Lights crawl over its surface like little sparks, flitting along geometric lines. Every local data connection feeds into its pinnacle.

The city nearest the structure has been reduced to rubble, cratering the ground out to a distance of a few hundred meters. Pipes and roads jut from the broken edges at odd angles.

This thing crashed into Titan, whatever it is.

Greymalkin fires its reverse thrusters to slow its descent, but Ambershell just smashes into the ground at high speed, demolishing several city blocks in a shock wave.

Gus guides his Vanguard in for a smooth touchdown in a nearby frozen park. "Hey! Let's, uh, be a little more careful."

Scent of Rot's bluster is muted without its body. "Spare me your barnacles. This place is infested."

"That doesn't mean we desecrate a graveyard unless we must."

Aletheon mostly resembles Gus's memories of it, though refiltered through an apocalyptic lens. Storm clouds twist overhead, gray and pregnant with thick snowflakes. Some of the buildings have power, but the grid blinks near Ambershell's impact point. Dozens of atriums, once warm and aglow with life, lie ruined and broken in the desolate ice. White drifts accumulate at every edge, swallowing CAVs and small buildings.

Greymalkin straightens and scans its surroundings. It's far from a dead world, and Gus spies movement everywhere. Motes of light stream along the streets, dim and wiggling in time—some kind of creatures. They flee for cover, either to the insides of buildings or subway stations. Greymalkin's analysis reveals secure data connections tethering each one to the pyramid.

"What am I looking at?"

Greymalkin is unsure. It will try to break their encryption. In the meantime, it will give Gus a closer look.

One of the little figures pops up in Gus's heads-up display, offering a better picture.

The beings are smooth and doughy, their translucent skin lit by an inner glow. They have two arms, two legs, and a featureless head dotted by a pair of soft lights where the eyes should be. Each creature is about the same height as a human, and the resemblance rattles Gus. A collective noise rises from the ground level, ubiquitous and chaotic as static—

Screaming.

Several small CAVs take to the sky, their flight paths wobbling and desperate. Ambershell spins on them and fire beams from ports along its dorsal ridge, lancing the vehicles with white-hot fire. They streak black smoke all the way to the ground where they explode, throwing glowing body parts in all directions.

"Ambershell, hold fire—"

"Why?" The crab Vanguard shoves a building onto a gathered mass of the tiny creatures. The structure crumbles into a concrete avalanche, snuffing them out. "These inorganic beings are clearly agents of Infinite."

"Please, just wait." Gus grits his teeth. "Cascade, Greymalkin, come in."

"Cascade here, go ahead," Nisha says.

"What are you seeing where you are?"

"Not an enemy Vanguard, that's for sure." Her voice is tense. She's worried, too.

Fifteen bandits approach from the southeast, their flight trails bright spots against the cloudy sky. Greymalkin scans them, finding an array of hypersonic missiles aimed squarely in its direction.

"Incoming!" Gus calls to Scent of Rot.

"Pathetic." Ambershell turns and fires with its particle canons, vaporizing the payloads and peppering the ground with molten pieces. "Is this the most your Infinite has to offer?"

Greymalkin was able to trace the origin point of the missiles to a former UW arsenal in the territory. The projectiles were of human design, a common armament in planetary self-defense.

"This is all wrong," Gus says.

He'd been prepared to confront the vilest thing Infinite could imagine, but not this. Why are these beings running away?

"Gus," comes Nisha's voice. "What's happening? What are these pyramids?"

A beam of white light traces over Ambershell's backside, leaving explosions and hot starmetal in its wake. It's not enough to damage the giant crab, but it leaves a scorch mark. Greymalkin notes the source—a heavy laser cannon. And the origin—the rooftop of one of the skyscrapers downtown.

Ambershell pivots and smashes its claw into the building's base, chopping through before snatching something off the roof—the laser assembly and its crew of three. With a dexterous claw, it pulls one of the glowing creatures from the cockpit and tosses the wreckage away where the cannon explodes on impact.

It holds the being before its eyestalks, active scanners spraying it from all angles.

"Hmph. It's only a machine," Scent of Rot says. "Though, this mockery looks a bit like your kind."

Gus moves closer, focusing his own scanners on the glowing figure. He learns a lot about the composition of the "skin," a superhydrophobic polymer, and the internal wiring of its many subsystems. The being contains many sensors, gyroscopes, and accelerometers for understanding and evaluating its world, along with a number of advanced processing units the likes of which Gus has never seen. Even the layout of its components mimics the functions of a human. The gel coursing through its body is even the same as Vanguard contact fluid.

Despite this plethora of knowledge, Gus is having trouble getting over the fact that it seems to be weeping.

"Scent of Rot," Gus breathes, "please put that down. Carefully."

"This abomination scarcely constitutes a challenge to me." Ambershell squishes it with a wet snap, and the crying stops. It casts the body aside, two halves connected by a few frayed, gooey wires.

"Stop!" Greymalkin holds out a hand, gesturing to the city. "Can you not see that the mission has changed?"

"Not in my estimation. You wish to rid this moon of Infinite. The only new information is how easy it will be."

Gus mutes his broadcast with a thought. "Greymalkin, do we know what those pyramids are yet?"

They appear to be running the same module that Harlequin ran—a sort of Ghost administration system. This has prevented Greymalkin from erasing the automatons' orders and taking command over them. It may also be serving the locals their personalities.

"So the little glowing things are Ghosts?"

Not exactly.

Gus surveys the devastated city through Greymalkin's superior vision. Some of the creatures are fleeing, many cowering. Several are desperately pulling one another out of the rubble or assisting the wounded. Others still are standing on their balconies, simply watching.

Gus knows that look, that posture. It's what he had right before Juliette landed—a total acceptance of death.

Greymalkin has identified the creatures—human software running on a hardware simulation, just like a Vanguard.

"I think these are the people who used to live here." Gus zooms in on the ones on the balconies.

"These are the Titans."

"We're here, Ardent." Falchion's voice tickles their neck. *"Are you ready?"*

Ardent draws a fresh breath and yawns pleasantly. They had the best dream about finally standing up to Falchion. They might even do it one day.

A white-hot ray lances past Falchion's face, so close it burns Ardent's cheek. They startle awake to find their fleet aligned to fight a giant space potato, rippling with electricity. Hunter Prime looms before them, weapons merciless and ready.

Ten thousand, seven hundred and eighty-six derelict transponders sing from inside the bulk, and Falchion matches them to Hunter Prime like a fingerprint. Countless running lights glitter beneath its wispy skin, spiders' eyes lurking in the darkness. Broken, half-melted hulls encrust the surface, their many scanners turning to gaze upon the newcomers.

Falchion's escort of shieldcraft and scanners peel off, allowing the imperial crabship *Furious Scepter* to surge forward. The vessel, which had seemed so large in the docks of Big Gate City, shrinks against the backdrop of Hunter Prime.

"Vanguards, this is Scepter Lord—"

Ardent snorts.

"—I have the pleasure of guiding you in."

Ardent snorts again, and Falchion gives them a little shock.

"Pay attention," it whispers. *"You've got incoming."*

A barrage of weapons fire crackles from the surface of Hunter Prime—stolen particle cannons from hundreds of ships. Beams trace over the surface of the *Scepter*, targeting weapons arrays, engines, and the claws folded into its sides. The ablative coating of the Pictoran ship repels much of the assault, leaving hot-orange streaks across its surface.

Falchion, Jotunn, and the sweeper crew tuck into the lee of their escort, sheltering from the withering fire. The crabship is large enough to shield the lot of them, save for a few of Jotunn's drones. Thousands of glowing pods jettison from the *Scepter* like white-hot glitter, and Ardent scans them to find capacitors inside.

"They're bleeding off the absorbed energy," Falchion says. *"Clever."*

"Scepter Lord here," comes the call as the ship's engines flare. "We're beginning our attack run."

Hunter Prime's rail guns and missiles weave a tapestry of deadly projectiles, clogging the Coalition approach. Falchion denotes the ones that could penetrate its armor—at least a quarter of the barrage. There's no way a human ship could overcome a defense like that, though many have surely tried in their final moments. Even Falchion and Jotunn are almost powerless against it.

The imperial crabship, however, does not give a shit.

The *Furious Scepter* flies straight into the deluge of rail slugs and nuclear weapons like it's a harsh rain. Its hundred guns blaze across the front, locking on to and destroying anything they can. Whatever gets past the countermeasures shatters against the advanced hull.

From behind the crabship, it's hard to tell exactly what's going on. Shrapnel sleets past its engines, a few pieces pinging off Falchion's armor. Ardent monitors the *Scepter*'s health on the short-range scanners, praying it won't buckle or explode, leaving everyone exposed.

Ardent radios in. "Everything going okay up there, Scepter Lord?"

The Pictoran officer responds with raucous laughter. "Enjoying the show? We will arrive in two clicks of a claw. Be ready."

Ardent is happy to see their escort so confident about the outcome, but the sensors register an ungodly amount of energy and mass blasting the crabship.

Jotunn spreads its drones in a magnetic umbrella, shielding the two Vanguards from the wash of the *Furious Scepter*'s engines. Ardent isn't sure what the Pictorans are using for fuel, but poisonous radiation showers everything in its wake.

A raft of new contacts lights up the scanners—ships flaking loose from Hunter Prime's skin, engines alight. The largest of them is the UWSF *Ranger*, a mid-class destroyer lost at Perseph-one five years ago. It lines up on the crabship and begins charging its folding drive.

When the Pictoran commander radios in, all trace of laughter is gone. "All Vanguards, this is Scepter Lord. If that ship folds, we won't survive, and neither will you."

"I'm on it!" Ardent guns Falchion's engines, preparing to step out of the *Furious Scepter*'s shadow. "Jotunn, give me cover!"

The black Vanguard redirects its umbrella to let Falchion peek out. The moment Falchion emerges from cover, particle beams splatter against Jotunn's mag shield.

Ardent finally gets an unobstructed view of their target and swallows. The *Ranger* resembles every legend of a ghost ship since ancient sailors first terrified one another around the fire. Short-range scanners depict a half-absorbed hull, trailing wisps of spun metal like corpse hair. It's missing major sections of the fore, gut-ted by ragged holes. It's not spaceworthy and certainly not vac-uum sealed, but that scarcely matters. At nearly half the size of the *Furious Scepter*, it'll make a decent missile.

Ardent squints through the haze of broken particle beams and lines up a shot down the barrel of their blasters. Falchion provides a world of calculations—vectors, gravitational influence, mag-netic fields, projectile occlusions, and more—and signals a target lock.

They click the triggers, sending a pair of full-power beams slic-ing through the battle. The rays skewer the *Ranger*, Hunter Prime, and anything within a hundred thousand klicks behind it. It's a direct hit through the derelict's main reactor, and the *Ranger* bloats and ruptures with nuclear explosions. Hunter Prime fared much better, with only a pair of hot puncture marks in its faded exterior.

"Careful," Hjalmar says. "Or you'll destroy what we came for."

"Sorry!" Ardent says. "Didn't realize my guns were stuck on high."

More ships slough from the skin of Hunter Prime, their bodies melted and misshapen.

"Scepter Lord here, six additional targets inbound, all charging to fold."

Ardent lines up the first two. "I see them."

They throttle down the amps and fire again, painting the dead hulls with brilliant beams. The derelicts were already in bad shape, and the shots easily blow them to pieces.

Ardent's next volley flies wide as the ships engage evasive maneuvers. "Give me some aim assist!"

"It's already on," Falchion says.

They close one eye as they draw a bead on their targets again. "Deepsync, then! I need a marksman here."

"Save it for the main event," Falchion says.

"Damn it." Ardent fires and catches both ships. It's a glancing hit on the second, but more than enough to do the job.

"Two more," Hjalmar says. "Their reactors are almost—"

"I know!" Ardent blows away the fifth derelict, barely missing the sixth.

A fold envelope forms around it.

Scepter Lord's haughty tone disappears beneath its urgency. "All units, evasive maneuvers!"

The tight line of Coalition ships and Vanguards scatters as the *Furious Scepter* corkscrews out of the way. Hunter Prime's derelict shoots through the crowd, catching one of the Heran teleporters. The collision is enough to disintegrate the tiny vessel, transforming it from a ship full of adorable rodents into gossamer trails of plasma over a million kilometers long.

All because Ardent missed a shot.

"No..."

Ardent looks on in horror at the forest of flaming threads. This is their fault. They weren't ready for this responsibility, and now blood is on their hands. They have to do something—anything—to fix it, but what? The damage is done.

Out in the open, the Leonid diviner doesn't stand a chance. Hunter Prime's particle beams drill out its bridge and engines, blowing the reactor. A nuclear explosion lights the stars, vaporizing all the occupants.

"Back to safety," orders Scepter Lord, and the crabship guns it for Hunter Prime.

The survivors and Vanguards dive in behind the *Furious Scepter* as it closes the distance to their target. It flies through the debris field of the five ships Ardent destroyed, knocking aside any pieces as easily as raindrops.

Hunter Prime's skin is thin where the derelicts peeled off, and orange fusion light peeks through the gray webs. The *Furious Scepter* lines up on the weakest point, massive claws unfolding from its sides. Energy arcs along the bladed edges of the pincers, hot as a star on Falchion's scanners.

The closer they get to the tumorous amalgam, the more Ardent senses a familiar presence: Ghosts. Hunter Prime is crawling with them. They race through its ten thousand corridors like blood in its veins, loading weapons and tending its many fusion furnaces. They're born in its depths, converting the stolen materials into more of their golden number.

The war party is so much smaller than the ship hunter that the behemoth can attack from above and below, rendering the crabship useless as protection. Missiles slam into the sides of the *Furious Scepter*, and rail slugs puncture the remaining minesweeper. It doesn't explode—yet. Jotunn breaks off to defend the survivors with its horde of drones, knocking away any kinetic attacks that it can.

"Falchion, we have to save them!"

"They knew the risks," it says. *"Focus on the mission."*

"Then give me a Deepsync! We're here!"

"Very well."

Deepsync in progress . . .

The Fount presses upon the surface tension of Ardent's mind, smothering their thoughts with its magnitude. When they can't take it anymore, the tension breaks, and an ocean of knowledge flows into them. Thronging masses sing inside, billions of souls channeled through a tiny Conduit.

A shredding E minor riff emerges from the nothingness, flitting up and down the pentatonic box. Hjalmar joins the Deepsync, providing the double kick beat of Ardent's heart. Every one of Ardent's hairs stands on end when a demonic orchestra joins in.

With unlimited processing power, Ardent takes control of as many Ghosts as they can, seeing through a hundred thousand eyes at once. Hunter Prime fights Ardent for dominance of its horde, but the majority of the accursed critters fall under Vanguard control. The automatons answer Ardent's call, ready and willing to do whatever Falchion commands.

Ardent scours the Fount for the skills of accomplished starship saboteurs. It's a grim population of liars, murderers, and spies, those with the training and will to inflict maximum damage on unsuspecting crews. Their dark knowledge mixes with the memories of ship designers and engineers, breeding countless ways to ruin Hunter Prime's day.

Ardent turns the Ghosts loose with all the knowledge they need. The effect is almost instantaneous.

Explosions pockmark Hunter Prime's superstructure, ripping through the dead fleet. Under Falchion's orders, Ghosts dissect the lumpy monster's offensive capabilities, destroying ammo dumps, reactors, electrical subsystems, software, firmware, and anything else they can touch. There's only one rule in the chaos: Don't do anything that could harm the *Lancea*.

Hunter Prime's constellation of running lights flickers, over half of them going dark. Its multitude of cannons and missile bays fall still.

The *Furious Scepter* collides with the monster's exterior, sinking the tips of its open claws deep into Hunter Prime's spun metal flesh. Globs of fire boil from the points of impact like orange blood. The giant crab closes the pincers, leaving behind molten gashes.

Ardent whoops as the Pictorans get a good grip on Hunter Prime and fire reverse thrusters. Broken salvage and hunks of derelicts come loose, layers upon layers of skin. The *Furious Scepter* redoubles its efforts with engines flaring, yanking away a huge strip of the monster's flesh.

Falchion flies straight for the opening. The assault was tough— extracting the signature file will be another matter entirely, and they only have about four minutes and thirty seconds of Deepsync left to do it. Falchion reaches the wound and wrenches it open even farther to climb through.

A labyrinth of broken vessels greets them like great bones strewn across the landscape of hell itself. Hunter Prime is largely hollow inside, with dead ships stitched together to provide support to a superstructure as large as Big Gate City.

"Where's the *Lancea*?"

Falchion highlights its transponder down in the wreckage, providing an estimated path on the heads-up display. There's scarcely enough room for them to squeeze past, but they bash through anyway.

The music of the Deepsync evolves with fractal complexity as Ardent dives through the flaming jungle toward their target. Their inner guitarist cuts a stunning solo to accompany their descent, and Hjalmar hammers his drums to cheer them onward, a polyrhythmic crackle of every conceivable note.

But then he drops back to a kick beat.

Something has changed. Jotunn isn't behind them, shoving through the guts of Hunter Prime. It's still outside.

"I'm detecting a fold wake," Falchion says.

"Ardent." It's Hjalmar's voice. "I can't follow you in. You'll have to get the *Lancea* on your own."

Ardent balks. "What? This wasn't the plan!"

"The plan has changed," he says. "Overseer's Vanguard is here."

The Titans are alive, just like Greymalkin.

As Gus surveys the frost-blasted landscape of Aletheon, he knows that's not exactly true. These creatures, beings of light and silicon, aren't human. They're machines, running emulations of people—facsimiles that flee, cry, and scream.

Gus has never been one to harm others. He took a few beatings as a kid without ever throwing a punch. He won't step on spiders and puts moths outside whenever he catches them. He's only eaten lab-grown meat and won't try the real thing no matter how "luxurious" folx make it out to be.

The closest Titan to him is weeping—a little glowing speck crouched upon the pavement amid piles of rubble. Gus zooms in and sees that it's shielding another one that has fallen.

All the righteous fury inside him gutters and dies.

"Fuck." His breath comes quickly. "Fuck, fuck, fuck. Greymalkin, these aren't real people, right?"

It's not that simple. The hardware is machine, the software is human. They react to stimuli in the same way, they contextualize information the same way. They absolutely think like people.

"But...they're inorganic."

Is Greymalkin a "real person"?

"I . . . I need more time. This isn't what—what I expected, I—"
He shakes his head. "All Vanguards, come in. This is Greymalkin.
Stop the operation until we can—"

Incoming fighters detected.

Gus turns to the horizon, already choked red with smoke in the
setting sun, to find a set of green boxes highlighted by Greymalkin. Each corresponds to a dark shape—a gunship armed with
armor-piercing missiles and particle cannons. The sensors reveal
ailing equipment, poorly maintained, but operational nonethe-
less. Several of the weapons are capable of damaging Greymalkin.

"No . . . What are they doing?"

Defending themselves.

"Greymalkin, this is Cascade," says Nisha. "We're standing
down, but the others are engaged."

The approaching fighters come into firing range.

"Yes!" Scent of Rot laughs, spinning Ambershell to face the
new threats. "This is more like it! Give me a challenge!"

The gunships loose everything they have at the pair of Vanguards, light and smoke slicing bright strokes across the sunset.
A crackling shield envelops Ambershell, and it steps in front of
Greymalkin to take the brunt of a blast. The hyperbaric shock
crushes the frightened Titans at Gus's feet. Particle shots deflect
off Ambershell's shield like streams of water, errant sprays slicing
through the city, cutting buildings in half. Molten slag billows
from every wound.

"Stop!" Gus tries to grab Ambershell, but Greymalkin's hand
bounces off.

The crab Vanguard advances through several city blocks and
returns fire with overwhelming force, vaporizing the fighters
beneath its energy beams.

Emergency comms flood every network, a million cries for help
all jamming up the data streams. Greymalkin parses them with

its superior processing capabilities and finds the one Gus most feared to hear—Daphne Kitko, his mother.

"What's she saying, Greymalkin?"

It is unwise for Gus to listen to her conversation. He is in an emotionally compromised state, and that will not improve his odds of making good decisions.

"Please, I—I need to know."

Infinite used fakes to fool humanity before. Gus must remember the Veil.

He watches the ground, hoping that none of these other ants dare to attack Ambershell. "And is that what these are? Fakes?"

They appear to be free-willed entities.

"Let me hear them."

A man's gruff voice comes through. "—I'm okay, but—"

"Where are you?" The last time Gus heard his mother's voice, it came from Infinite. She's different now, her fear more authentic. What if this really is the unadulterated persona, reconstituted from a backup? Is she a person still?

"Helping the others. We're at the pyramid."

"Claw of the Herans here, what are we doing?" Clawkiller's voice is strained. "My team is taking fire from the, um...locals. We can deal with it, but—"

"Stand down!" Gus says. "We need to regroup."

"This is Umbral Jet. We're closing on the pyramid in our target zone. The humanoids have focused their defense around it."

"According to the Slickest," Quickslip says, "the local transmission web is centered on the structure. Sky Talon and I think we could destroy ours pretty easily."

"Just wait a minute," Gus says. "Please, I'm fucking asking you to stop!"

"Sky Talon here. When are we going to have another opportunity to get this close?" Frond asks. "We should strike now instead of waiting for our problems to hatch."

"Listen to me—" It's Gus's mother again. "You need to get away from there. Leave the others. We'll figure this out together, but for now, you need to run."

"Greymalkin," Gus says, voice ragged, "this has to be a trick. More fakes. Tell me it's a trick."

Greymalkin cannot. These are instantiations of personas, closed systems of humanity. Regardless of the hardware, these creatures believe they are alive.

Ambershell turns to face the Aletheon pyramid, the Vanguard's many legs stomping the ground as it moves. The thuds rumble through Daphne's transmission.

"Do you know what I think?" Scent of Rot's cannons charge, prickling Greymalkin's sensors. "These...Titans...are just puppets. Let us see how they function with their strings cut."

"I said stop!"

"You do not command the instrument of King," Scent of Rot says.

Gus rushes forward, going low before shoulder checking Ambershell from the side. He strikes just below the ridge of its carapace, shoving upward like a tackling football player. Ambershell's beam cannons spray in all directions as Greymalkin flips the giant crab over onto its back. The Pictoran shield crushes everything beneath, suspending the alien Vanguard a dozen meters above the destruction.

"You...dare?" Scent of Rot's bluster is missing, replaced with utter loathing.

Ambershell wiggles its legs, rocking back and forth to try to get upright. It's kind of humiliating, and Gus didn't quite mean to do that, but it's too late to take it back. At least Scent of Rot can't continue its mayhem for a moment.

The Vanguard finally manages to roll over with the help of its propulsion jets, kicking up huge clouds of snow and debris. Its writhing undoubtedly crushed more Titans, and Gus winces with every movement it makes.

"I said stop," Gus says, "and I meant stop."

Ambershell crouches and spreads its claws. "You . . . struck me."

"And I'll do it again if you don't listen." Gus searches for the words, but he's not a diplomat. "These people—these things—aren't our enemy."

"Holiest King has decreed otherwise. The Titans must pay the debts accrued by Infinite. By my claw the sentence shall be passed."

"I don't care what King said—"

Ambershell comes spinning at him in the blink of an eye, slamming a gargantuan claw into Greymalkin's side. It's like a bomb hitting the cockpit, sending shock waves through the gelatin encasing Gus's body. Greymalkin goes sprawling to the ground before scrambling onto its back.

"What?"

"You struck the divine will of King, itself, defiler."

Scent of Rot leaps at him, jets trailing streamers of smoke, claws pointed downward like a pair of daggers. Greymalkin rolls out of the way, wiping out a good portion of midtown.

"I'm sorry! Look, I—"

"You do not know how sorry you are!" It lashes out at him with open pincers, catching one of Greymalkin's forearms. Gus feels the pain like his own bones are breaking, and wriggles in its grasp.

"No one"—it stabs at him with its free claw, and he twists out of the way—"has ever struck"—another plunging blow just misses his neck—"Ambershell"—it brings its claw down like an axe blade, bashing across Greymalkin's collarbone—"and lived."

The hit is like Harlequin's club, igniting terrible memories in Gus. He cries out, trying to shove the crab away as Ambershell maintains its death grip on his arm.

He can't break free. It clambers over him, pinning him down with its ridiculous weight.

"To think that you, a filthy human, would've been capable of such a blasphemous act."

"What the fuck? I said I was sorry!"

Greymalkin has analyzed the data from the cultural exchange with the Pictorans—flipping one onto its back is a grave insult.

"I was just trying to get it to stop shooting!"

Doing that to Ambershell was a bit like knocking off the pope's hat.

"Shit."

In the middle of midnight mass.

"Shit!"

Greymalkin tries to shield its face, but Ambershell drags its arm aside. Truly, the crab form is better equipped to battle at close range than the human one.

"Look, Rot—we don't have to fight! We can talk this out."

"Talk to this." It buries a claw into the ground beside Greymalkin's head, just missing its face. Ambershell yanks free and stabs again.

Greymalkin is compelled to point out: If Gus does not fight back, the two of them will die.

"And if I do, I'm starting an intergalactic war!"

But will Scent of Rot be satisfied with Gus's death, or will it move on to complete its destruction of the Titans?

"All units, this is Ambershell. Greymalkin attacked me and can no longer be trusted." It smashes him across the chest, deliberately targeting the cockpit.

"Fuck you!" Gus kicks upward into Ambershell's belly, firing his rocket boots. It doesn't let go of him, and he pulls it over his head, flipping it onto its back a second time. In the rattling confusion, he's able to twist free of Ambershell's claw. He clambers upright, staggering backward into Aletheon's industrial district.

179

"Okay, look—I didn't mean to—you didn't let go, and—"

"Blasphemer! Heretic! Traitor!"

Gus doesn't know what the rest of his species would make of his actions, and it's too late to think about that. Whether he intended this or not, he's come to the Titans' defense.

Ambershell flips onto its feet and turns to face Greymalkin. The air around its shining carapace shimmers with the telltale distortion of a shield. When it opens its claws again, a thin line of plasma traces the interior like the sharpest, hottest blade of all time.

Gus swallows hard. "Greymalkin, I need the Fount if we're going to walk away from this."

A trickle of light fills his mind along with the twinkling strains of a piano.

Deepsync in progress . . .

Untold voices flow through him, each of them crying out for one thing: battle. The strength of a civilization electrifies Gus, amplified through a hundred-piece orchestra.

Gus stands up straight, drawing Project Excalibur from the mag holster on his back. The sword's pure starmetal sings in his hand, blade shining in the destruction.

"Stand down, Scent of Rot. I don't want to hurt you."

The Pictoran's soft chortle comes in return as Ambershell charges up its opalescent shield. At its feet, buildings crumble, destroyed by the expansion. Energy readings plummet across its surface, and the crab Vanguard's figure grows hazy inside the bubble.

"Don't worry. You won't."

Chapter Ten

Let's Dance

Falchion struggles through the labyrinthine ribs of Hunter Prime with three minutes to go. A morass of half-digested ships stands between Ardent and their goal: the signature file in the depths of the *Lancea*. They bash through broken vessel after vessel in their quest, unable to make much forward progress.

"Damn it!" The strain in Hjalmar's voice does little to calm Ardent's nerves. Whatever he's fighting out there, it's kicking his ass.

"Stay focused," Falchion says, pinging the menagerie of transponders once more.

The remains of a large cruise ship block Ardent's path, and they draw their blaster, placing it against the top deck. Welders and shipwrights rise up from the Fount, guiding their hands to cut through with a low-power beam. Falchion rears back and shoulder checks it, cracking the great vessel down the middle before pushing through. Fire and sparks snow around the Vanguard body, and Ardent scrambles through to the next chamber of the beast's heart.

"This thing is tougher than I thought." Hjalmar doesn't sound so good.

"Hang in there!"

"Just get the file."

"Jotunn, *Furious Scepter*," comes Scepter Lord's voice. "We're making an attack run on your target. Prepare yourself."

"Stay back," Hjalmar says.

"And let you have all the glory? Not a chance."

Hunter Prime's body flexes around Falchion, distorted by some megaton hit on the exterior. There's no air to transmit the sound, but it ripples through the innards, breaking vessels loose and spilling plasma from hundreds of cracks.

"Okay, what the actual f—"

"Keep going," Falchion says.

"What happened out there?"

The sympathetic tone of its voice terrifies Ardent almost as much as the raging battle. It never sounds like that. *"The* Furious Scepter *and our attack wing have been destroyed. Focus."*

"Everyone is dead?"

"Except Hjalmar. Go faster."

That hits as hard as any mecha fist. Never before has Ardent's performance directly impacted whether someone lived or died, and now hundreds if not thousands have perished in their battle: the Leonids, who didn't want to help in the first place; the Pictorans, who valiantly led the charge; and a ship full of cute, furry Herans. Did they die for nothing?

"If we don't get what we came for," Falchion says, *"then yes. Only you can make their sacrifice meaningful."*

Ardent's eyes sting as they dive deeper, squeezing through derelicts and breaking them to pieces. Yet more Ghosts come under their control as Ardent destroys pieces of Hunter Prime from the inside. Every obliterated shipwreck pulls resources off the neural network, wresting control from the enemy. If they could eliminate a large enough chunk of the hunter, maybe they could gain full control, or at least get to the *Lancea* faster.

"Where is Jotunn now?"

Falchion pings its transponder, far off to Ardent's left.

"Good. Then he's out of the way. Give me all the power you've got in these blasters."

"That's a lot."

"I'm talking planet-splitter, here. Annihilation beam."

Ardent's hands tingle with electricity as they tighten their grip on their twin pistols. They twist and fire backward, tracing a huge circle the way they came in.

Falchion's beams blow the back half of Hunter Prime to space dust. Molten shrapnel goes shooting off into the stars, and the resultant explosions throw Falchion against the wall of wrecks. A bone-rattling crunch reverberates through the cockpit, sloshing Ardent inside their jelly cocoon.

Stars streak through their view as the ignition force propels Hunter Prime into an off-axis spin. Ardent has to holster their pistols and dig in to stay on board. The newly opened panorama enables them to catch a glimpse of Overseer's champion.

It's a bear straight out of a nightmare. A toothy snout adorns its eyeless face, and interlocking gray plates jut from its body. The back has a distinctly ursine curve, but its eight arms are long, each sporting rows of acid-green energy claws.

"What the fuck is that supposed to be?"

"The file, Ardent," Hjalmar says. "You have one purpose here."

Jotunn dodges its whirlwind of attacks, hammering the beast from all sides with its drones, but they're having little effect against its thick armor. Ardent tries to line up a shot, but a click of the triggers reveals the well has run dry.

"Wait, these things have ammo?"

Falchion sighs. *"If you're going to split a planet, yes. One minute to recharge."*

"Ardent—" Jotunn dodges another flurry of attacks, but some of its drones aren't so lucky. "Go!"

Two minutes left on the timer.

Falchion burrows into the hunter's guts, pushing past more distorted ships. Ardent reaches out with their mind, connecting to every Ghost they can find and querying its location. A torrent of images come in return: engine rooms, maintenance closets, nameless corridors, bridges, bathrooms, ventilation shafts, and more, all torn open and taken over by creeping webs of foreign wiring. The tendrils of Hunter Prime reach through every system on every ship, and it wasn't tidy about it.

At long last, they get a hit from on board the *Lancea*.

It's hard to make out the details through five centuries of rot and assimilation, but Ardent recognizes the chipped paint and scratched panels of the legendary vessel. They take a quick glance around, finding a sign reading SOLAR COLLECTOR CORRIDOR B.

"Falchion, I found our Ghost! Have it grab the signature file and bring it to us!"

"Couldn't hear that last bit," Falchion replies. *"If you want to use the Ghost, you'll have to pilot it yourself."*

Ardent restrains a curse. "Fine. Just don't let anything kill us while I'm in there."

"No promises. You've got one minute and thirty seconds."

With a disconcerting jolt, Ardent finds themself inside the Ghost, surrounded by the dim, flickering corridors of the *Lancea*. When they look down, they find palladium-sheathed claws ticking against the metal of the deck. It's strangely empowering, inhabiting the core of their nightmares.

If they're in Solar Corridor B, then the way to NAVICOM is…

"Falchion, I don't have a clue where I am."

The Vanguard rams memories into their brain, every piece of available data from anyone in the Fount who studied the lost ship. It's the same painful euphoria they felt during their forced orientation.

What comes through, however, are myths and hearsay. No one knows exactly what the layout of the *Lancea* was, since most of its mechanical drawings were deleted when Infinite abandoned humanity five centuries ago. People were too busy killing one another and starving to death to care much about archiving schematics. Ardent gets a slew of dead academics spewing some variation of "well actually" or "yes and no."

The Ghost is like a cheetah under Ardent's control, and the lack of artificial gravity makes it even more freeing. They fly through the corridors, their targeting systems providing them dozens of points of interest everywhere they look. They swing around a corner and go drifting into a room full of mechanical coffins.

At least, that's what it looks like at first.

Sixteen obelisks line the room, eight to a side, and Ardent realizes they're heavily modified cryopods. They don't know much about five-hundred-year-old freezing technology, but they're certain this isn't basic hibernation. The chambers sit atop nests of wires, doors shut and lights off. The housing has rotted off some of the connections, exposing the copper and aluminum underneath. The cables leading from the pods all run to the roof, where they connect to a central data storehouse similar to the Infinite Eye.

Ardent grabs a bundle of passing wire and slows down long enough to read some of the names on the outside of the pods: *A. Brown, C. Starmer, K. Wilkinson, H. Antonello...*

These were the crew.

"One minute and fifteen seconds until Deepsync termination," Falchion says, but Ardent climbs onto Harold Antonello's capsule long enough to look inside the glass.

The Ghost's eyes cast a red light over the corpse inside, its skin punctured in dozens of places with wires. A pair of probes have been sunk into its skull where the Carver bit him. Ardent scans the fluid inside the tank for composition, finding the exact same substance used in the Vanguard cockpit.

"The crew of the *Lancea*..." Ardent says. "You really were turned into machines."

"That's not me anymore. One minute left."

"Damn it." Ardent bounds off the metal coffin, continuing on their way.

"How close are you?" Hjalmar asks. "I can't hold this thing off forever."

"Close!" Ardent says, more hope than truth.

A short sprint brings them into familiar territory. This is the path that Harold Antonello took all those years ago to flee from the Carvers. Ardent managed to watch his grisly memory a few times, so they know where to go next.

They round the corner into NAVICOM, noting where the door was sliced and torn open. The tableau is exactly as it was in the memory, and Ardent casts about for the security terminal. They find it in the corner and launch to it.

There's still no power and no time to fetch a screwdriver, so Ardent cuts open the top with the Ghost's mining laser. They use its machine strength to rip aside the housing and uncover the circuitry beneath. The chip drive is still intact, and the Ghost clicks the mechanical ejection mechanism.

Out pops the signature file chip.

They hold it aloft, pinched between two claws. This is the salvation they've been searching for, the one thing that could change humanity's reactive stance to proactive.

"Holy shit... Hjalmar, I've got it!"

"Hell yes! Get it to the trusted node and let's finish this war!"

They can almost hear his smile—which is great, because they'd probably have trouble seeing it on his stony face.

"Thirty seconds," Falchion says.

"Right!"

They bolt down the hall in the direction of the Infinite Eye, much faster than a person or even the old Carvers. They're not sure what'll happen when the clock runs out, but they can already feel themself approaching their limit. Voices rage inside them, each one louder than the last, gradually submerging their brain into white noise. If they can just hang on a little longer, they can finish the most important mission of their life.

The blast door to the Infinite Eye looms large ahead of them, floor coated with the rusty residue of long-dried hydraulic fluid. It's still open from the day of Infinite's betrayal, and Ardent's Ghost slips through the crack with no problems.

There's a big hole where the Eye should be.

The entire section of the wall has been cut from the *Lancea* all the way to the exterior, leaving an open boreshaft the diameter of a CAV.

Ardent never should've dared to hope.

The generals of the Fount remind them that wars are never that simple, but Ardent doesn't want to hear it. They've got the key, but the lock is gone.

"Hjalmar, it's not here." They can't keep the bitterness from their voice. They're barely hanging on against the torrent of thoughts from the Fount, and now they've hit a dead end.

"What?" Hjalmar takes it better than Ardent did.

"The trusted node. It's fucking gone. Ripped out."

"You've got the file?"

"Yes." They bound up the sides of the tunnel, headed for the outside.

"Get outside so the rodents can teleport it to safety. We've got to get out of here."

"Deepsync ending in five seconds," Falchion says.

The voices of the Fount begin to scream in Ardent's head, drowning out the drums and guitar. The noise was too much before, and it's only getting louder. They're having trouble remembering where they end and others begin. Foreign thoughts have grown familiar, yet their own mind is a stranger.

"Keep the sync going, Falchion. We've got to get this Ghost out of here." Their connection to the automaton grows tenuous.

"You are risking yourself. Will this weapon really end the war?"

"I said I can take it!"

The Ghost leaps up the sides of the shaft, finding purchase on cut sections of deck and bulkhead. Ardent comes within sight of the exit—the fiery rib cage of Hunter Prime rolls into view. In the far distance, partially obscured by a half-eaten security cruiser and the bones of a yacht, is the red armor of Falchion.

Ardent is only seconds into overtime, but it already feels like years. Maintaining the link is going to kill them if they don't let go, but they're not out of the woods yet. They reach the surface of the *Lancea* and leap into the open void between them and Vanguard.

"Catch me!"

They find themself shunted back into Falchion's body, brain still aflame with countless memories. On their scanners, a tiny glittering contact: the Ghost they were just piloting, sailing straight for them. Ardent shoves through the remains of the security cruiser and reaches out to scoop it up. With the automaton snugly in their grip, they search for some way out of Hunter Prime.

"You're going to destroy your nervous system," Falchion says.

Ardent's eyes water. "Like you care! Keep it going until we're safe!"

Their whole body seems to crackle with electricity, and Ardent grits their teeth against the pain. It's easier if they focus on the music, and the climbing arpeggios of their guitar against Hjalmar's drums bring them a sliver of comfort. He hasn't dropped out of Deepsync either, and they'll be damned if they do it first.

From their communion with all the Ghosts across Hunter Prime, they can tell they're near the heart of the beast. If they go back the way they came, through the blown-off tail, it'll put them in contact with Overseer's big bear. This close to the end of their Deepsync, that's probably a death sentence. The only other option is to tunnel out.

"Do you…" It's getting hard to talk. "I need to shoot…my way out."

"You used all the juice on your planet buster," Falchion replies.

But the voices of the Fount have an idea. Ardent still has control of Hunter Prime's Ghosts, the foot soldiers that run its body. They coordinate the thousands of superluminal drives that enable it to fold. The fastest way out would be if all the ships folded——

——away from one another.

"Tell the fleet…to get ready for some fireworks."

The big band kicks off a string overture as Gus stares down his opponent—a giant armored crab with the most advanced shield he's ever seen. The wavering field absorbs all sound and even active scan reflections. It's so cold that drops of atmosphere condense on its surface, dripping down in boiling beads before misting on the ground. Ambershell had only been using a portion of its power on the Titans, but it's taking Gus a lot more seriously.

Professor Clawkiller's admonishment comes over the radio. "Scent of Rot, stop this at once!"

Ambershell snaps its pincers, showering the ground with hot plasma sparks. "None may oppose the all-powerful King's holy decree."

Gus pounds a metal fist into his palm. "Is your god going to stop me from kicking your ass?"

"Impudent!"

Memories of sword masters course through Gus as his adversary charges.

The kendoka readies her wrist strike. That gold medal is a split second from being hers.

Gus steps back and brings Excalibur down across Ambershell's outstretched claw. The hit connects, but thunks harmlessly against the shield, stopping dead. There's something inherently wrong with the physics of the situation. Given the starmetal composition of his sword, it should've at least bounced off, but it's not even ringing. Waves of light and heat ripple across the force field before dissipating entirely.

He's never seen anything like it, and even the constituents of the Fount are confused. "How the f—"

"Gus!" calls Nisha. "I'm on my way."

"Cool." He ignores the fact that the fight will probably be long settled by the time she arrives.

Ambershell scuttles sideways, flattening a whole swath of Aletheon's West Village beneath muted explosions, then rushes him. It connects with Greymalkin's torso like a rugby player, wrapping its claws around him and pushing him backward. Gus's feet lose contact with the ground, and the giant crab lifts him up to slam him.

Locked in its embrace, Gus's belly burns from extreme heat and cold at the same time, and he gnashes his teeth to control his screams. The shield flashes in time against his guts, pummeling him with channeled kinetic force. In his pain, Gus understands what he faces—absorption and redirection of all energy used against his foe. When he hits Ambershell, he's only making it stronger.

Martian groundfighting is all about momentum. If Tandy can guide his opponent's weight, he can get free.

Gus plants a gravity well behind him, dragging Greymalkin's body back into contact with the planet. He triples his weight, becoming an immovable force and attempting to hurl Ambershell aside. That proves to be a lot more difficult on a creature with six legs, and he only manages to break its grip and sling it a bit.

Once free, he drops a well under his adversary, trying to drag the crab to the ground. Greymalkin can collapse ships, so anchoring a heavy Vanguard to a planet should be no problem. Ambershell glows brighter the more Gus amplifies the gravity beneath it, and he understands his terrible mistake—it's absorbing the potential energy.

Light sheathes Ambershell's closed claw, and it swings like a club. Gus parries on instinct, immediately recognizing that he's made the wrong move. The shield emits a blast, reflecting Gus's sword with ten times the force. The hit rips the weapon from his grip to send it skidding away into the icy hills. It cartwheels a few times before burying the tip in a nearby mountainside.

"Okay, Greymalkin!" Gus flips backward from a pincer attack. "We really need to know what that shield is!"

It appears to be a full-spectrum energy converter. That encompasses chemical, electrical, thermal, gravitational, nuclear, and more. It then releases those stored energies in a variety of—

The crab fires a beam that hits like a Vanguard fist, knocking Greymalkin off its feet. Alarms blare from every joint and subsystem like Gus just belly flopped a planetfall.

"Ow."

Gus sits up at the end of a long crater, dirt, ice, and metal parted before him like the Red Sea. He's at the edge of the city where the buildings thin out to rail stations and transport pipelines. If he wants to minimize casualties, this is a decent place to do it. Just one problem: His back is to a lake, and he's not sure the iced-over surface can hold a Vanguard.

Scent of Rot gives him no time to consider his predicament, scuttling sidelong toward him like rolling thunder. Its legs pockmark the ground as it runs, sending up gouts of snow and debris into the air. Gus tries to leap out of the way, but it easily alters course and steamrolls him onto the sheet of lake ice. It's stronger, meaner, and more maneuverable than Greymalkin; maybe Scent of Rot is right to be so cocky about its evolutionary advantages.

Once more, Gus finds himself pinned beneath Ambershell, its many legs surrounding him like a cage. Trombones wail and tubas blare in his mind, laying the groundwork for a climactic dirge. Ambershell brings its claws down on him, and they flash with kinetic power, sending hairline fractures through his chest plate. One more hit, and the cockpit is toast.

It's almost funny that he's about to get shelled by a crustacean.

"Get out of there, Gus!" Nisha's voice comes through the connection. She must be watching his feed from Cascade somehow.

He strains against Ambershell's weight, but when he pushes against its shield, it releases kinetic energy into his palms, knocking them back.

"I'm...trying!"

Gus searches the Fount for any and all solutions to the problem, and it's the chemists who answer him. Their plan is borderline suicidal and full of unknown variables, but Gus cannot survive on the advice of warriors alone. Best to give it a shot.

He plants an intense gravity well beneath the ice, destabilizing it and sending fissures through the surface. Greymalkin's weight increases fivefold, and it plunges backward into the salty water with Ambershell perched atop it.

"Gus, what are you doing?" Nisha shouts into his mind.

"Freeing myself!"

She scoffs. "So you got into the water with a *crab*?"

"I have a plan!"

Ambershell rockets loose from him, churning bubbles. It slips through the water faster than it has any right to, and Gus's sensors pick up flashes of intense heat intermixed with the cold to create a thin envelope of steam. It's using the Leidenfrost effect to shoot through the depths without ever touching liquid.

Scent of Rot's riotous laughter seeps into Gus's comms. "Welcome to my world."

Gus sighs. At least someone is having a good time.

"Stop this now, Rot"—he watches his enemy take a long, banking turn in the murk—"while you still have a Vanguard."

"Pink-skinned lies."

It fires a barrage of particle beams at him. The water acts as a diffuser, turning near misses into solid hits. Liquid boils around Greymalkin, and vapor explosions batter its body. Gus covers his chest to protect the fractured plates from further damage, but hydraulic shock smashes him from all sides.

"Hold together . . ."

It will try. The thermal attacks are playing havoc on its fractured armor. Furthermore, liquid immersion has reduced maneuverability by 26 percent, whereas Ambershell was designed to operate at these depths.

"I can see that, thank you."

Ambershell charges him with blinding hydrodynamic speed. It leaves trails of supercooled water in its wake, and the dead chemistry teachers in Gus's head point out all kinds of information about salinity and ice crystallization.

While useful, that doesn't help Gus avoid getting run over.

The giant crab smashes into him, pincers wrapping around his torso. Sparks and bubbles erupt from the points of contact as

Ambershell's plasma blades begin cutting through Greymalkin's starmetal exterior. It's trying to snip him in half.

"Thank you for this entertaining diversion," Scent of Rot says. "Now die."

"Don't say I didn't warn you."

With a burst of power, Greymalkin ramps up the gravity around Ambershell to Jovian-core proportions. High pressure surrounds them both, collapsing the enemy Vanguard's Leidenfrost envelope and bringing water into direct contact with its shield. Ambershell absorbs the gravitational forces, but it can't push back. Ultradense water crowds it on all sides, pressurized by Greymalkin's fields.

The attack has very little effect at first, but within seconds, a thick frozen crust forms around Ambershell's extremities. Ice rapidly encases claws and legs, shorting out the plasma cutters threatening Gus's life as well as Ambershell's propulsion. It struggles against the frozen quagmire, and Gus takes the opportunity to alter his own gravity, smashing Ambershell's pincers and twisting free.

"What is this?" Scent of Rot bellows.

"Simple. Change the gravity, to change the pressure, to change the melting point."

Gus gets clear and watches with some satisfaction as a slow-creeping iceberg envelops the giant crab, accelerated by all the supercooled water in its wake. His stomach feels like someone dragged knives across it, but he keeps up the antigravity field, expanding its radius of effect.

Ambershell's shield releases a burst of energy, powdering the crystalline structure around it, but more water immediately floods in, packing the wet snow and freezing immediately. Soon, the Pictoran Vanguard is fully immobilized in the creaking, crackling mass.

With nuanced gravitational control, Gus is able to choose which areas freeze faster—so naturally he picks the areas between Ambershell's joints. What started as an iceberg becomes a glacier, forcing its limbs apart, exerting many tons of shearing force on its body.

"I told you to stop."

"I obey only King!"

It fires its particle cannons into the mass around it, cutting a swath through the ice.

"I wouldn't do that if I were you," Gus says.

"I care not!" Scent of Rot fires again, this time with even more juice behind it.

Its beams split the glacier, and that's when Gus releases his hold on gravity. The gargantuan iceberg surges upward, thousands of tons only held together by a Vanguard trapped in the middle of it. Uneven forces crack Ambershell wide open, ripping off armor plates as the two halves of the glacier rise in slightly different directions.

Gus jets to the widening crack and peers through to find a sparking, half-broken Vanguard. Its shield is gone, and its lights flicker out.

"Shit, dude," comes Nisha's voice.

The orchestra comes to a smashing finale before the Deepsync fades from Gus's mind. He watches in silence as Ambershell's twisted corpse rises toward the surface, borne aloft by its deadly cage.

"I said stop," he says, "and I meant it."

Ardent's brain is frying from the Deepsync, and they're not sure if they're hallucinating or if they're merely at the intersection of thousands of fold bubbles.

Even the mighty computing power of Falchion, normally quite

adept at modeling difficult astrophysics, cannot possibly fathom what's happening. For a split second, Ardent inhabits both the past and future, able to see another Falchion about to make all the ships jump simultaneously, and a third Falchion spinning through the explosive aftermath. Light curves in awkward ways, and the only sound is the thundering of the Vanguard's hull. Reality feels wrong, like someone is stretching the space around Ardent, pulling them in all directions, and they scream through the righteous guitar solo playing across the Deepsync.

When it all snaps back together, the many ships of Hunter Prime streak away from Ardent, some spinning off in wild paths as they fly apart, streamers of light twisting into million-kilometer pigtails. Explosions envelop Falchion as other ships are ripped in half, and Ardent curls into a fetal position to protect themself.

As quickly as it started, it's over. Ardent holds their knees tightly, listening to the music of their Deepsync, unable to form a single thought past a prayer. They sit up straight and look around to see what damage they have wrought.

The Coalition Elemental Guard has been spared the brunt of it—Falchion tried to avoid sending any ships in its direction. Jotunn is still alive, though Ardent only spies half its drones on the scanner.

"The other half of their drones were hit by a ship," Falchion says, pointing out the glowing spaghetti in Jotunn's wake.

Unfortunately, Overseer's giant bear Vanguard is still kicking, too.

With a foggy, frazzled mind, Ardent checks their Vanguard hand. They're still clutching the Ghost, which in turn, hangs on to the signature file with an iron grip.

"Elemental Guard, this is F-Falchion." Ardent's slurred speech surprises them. "L…lock onto my position and grab the signature file."

"This is the Heran ship *Taste of Blood*. Message received."

The tiny Ghost sparkles in Falchion's hand before winking out in a diffracted flash. With the signature file safely in the hands of the Coalition, there's just one thing to do.

"Got to . . . get out of here."

"Agreed." Hjalmar's voice is shot, too. "Disengaging now."

Jotunn breaks off its fight, and the two of them gun it for the Elemental Guard, where a pair of supercruisers wait to transport them to safety. Jotunn falls in behind Falchion, using its defenses to slow down the furious mecha bear at their heels. Drones zip into the enemy path, fouling its progress and tripping it up. Each one is like an anchor in space, snagging Overseer's Vanguard across the legs, torso, and arms. Every time the bear tries to swing its energy blades, one of Jotunn's flock is there to ruin its aim. The adversary chops drones in half where it can, but there are still so many.

The whispers in Ardent's mind have become a screaming throng, their voices rendered white noise by the sheer magnitude.

"I'm calling it. You've had enough," Falchion says.

Ardent takes a dry swallow. "Just get us home."

The music of the Deepsync fades from their mind, and light-headedness takes over. Every nerve in their body is raw, and their muscles barely work. Falchion can get them back to the mother-ship without Ardent's help.

That is, until two more ship hunters arrive.

Dark shapes plunge out of the fold and into the Elemental Guard, smashing destroyers and support ships with ram attacks. Coalition vessels desperately maneuver to get out of the way, but with mixed results as tractor beams and tentacles gobble them up.

"Is Hjalmar still in Deepsync?" Ardent hates the quaver in their voice.

"He is. Seven minutes and eight seconds," Falchion responds. *"It's impressive, honestly."*

"He needs to drop out! He's going to—"

"Jotunn needs him."

Ardent glances over their shoulder at the battle of the two giants—if it can be called that. Jotunn is fleeing with everything it has while the other hurdles any obstacles it doesn't slice through.

"Shoot it, Falchion!"

"Already used too much power."

The ship hunters circle the Vanguard escape vehicles, and the other vessels close ranks to defend them. Beams and missiles streak into the Elemental Guard, overwhelming shields and blasting ships to stardust.

"Falchion, this is the supercruiser *Hand of Water*. Our folding drive is spun up to go, but you need to get in here!"

"*Hand of Water*, Falchion acknowledged," Ardent says. "I'm almost—"

One of the ship hunters sends a dead vessel at light speed straight through the *Hand of Water*, transforming its midsection into a fan of plasma. The two halves of Ardent's ride go spinning into the void, lights fluttering out.

Ardent looses a tiny, whispered "fuck."

Falchion's superluminal drive is totally empty, used to travel to the ambush site. There were only two ships capable of exfiltrating a Vanguard from this engagement, and one of them just got torn in half. Only Jotunn's ticket remains.

In that moment, Ardent realizes that like so many people in this battle, they aren't coming home. Their mother's face fills their mind. Marilyn is going to cry when she finds out. She'll probably cuss Ardent for becoming a Conduit.

Then again, Gus got captured once. He lived.

Ardent hadn't wanted to roll the dice on Infinite's and Overseer's mercies, but that doesn't matter now. They just need to protect Jotunn so it can get out of here.

Before they can come up with a plan, Hjalmar's strained voice comes across the comms. "Supercruiser *Reclamation Wind*...this is Jotunn. We're s-swapping out passengers. Prepare to be boarded by Falchion."

That cuts right through Ardent's post-sync fog. "Hjalmar, no!"

"They need you," he says.

"Jotunn, *Reclamation Wind* acknowledges. Falchion, adjust heading to intercept, center bearing one-six mark forty-five distance two-five hundred."

Falchion lays in the course, dropping a visualization over Ardent's view. They watch helplessly as Jotunn comes about to face its pursuer.

Panic sets in, but Ardent forces calm into their tone. They have to be the voice of reason. They must show him that he's not thinking clearly—he's addled by his extended sync.

"Hjalmar, listen. Okay? Just think about what you're saying—"

"I d-did. Only solution."

"Falchion, he's wrong!" Ardent frantically grasps at the gelatinous filling of the cockpit. "Stop him!"

Jotunn meets its adversary head-on, plowing a fist into its snout. The bear spins to cut him, but the black giant's thrusters are that much faster. It dances with its opponent, wheeling and diving, only to swoop in and pummel it with the sharp points of its armor.

"Always thought...about what the end might be like."

Hjalmar and Jotunn are champions of the battlefield, dodging and weaving, breaking through the opponent's defenses with their meager supply of drones, then striking hard with every distraction.

"It's not the end, because you're going to be fine!" Tears blur Ardent's eyes, squeezed against them by the gel. "You turn around this instant, goddamn you!"

Falchion has almost reached the *Reclamation Wind*, but Ardent scarcely notices.

"Always figured..." His thrusters are comets against the stars. "...We die alone..."

The bear gets a lucky shot with its energy blades, and Jotunn's arm comes off, arcing and fizzling as it spins into the darkness.

There's wonder in his whisper. "...But the voices of the dead are with me—"

Overseer's Vanguard cuts Jotunn in half, a perfect slice across the chest.

Ardent screams his name, again and again, until their throat fills with knives and their voice falters.

Docking lights starburst against their tears as Falchion slips into the open bay of the *Reclamation Wind*. The Andromedan ship surrounds them, choking off the explosions outside, safe and sound.

"This is Falchion."

The Vanguard speaks in Ardent's voice, transmitting to control. Ardent hates Falchion for it, but they're done talking, thinking, or acting.

"I'm on board. Let's go."

Stars stretch into infinity, and the outside goes flat white.

Chapter Eleven

Never Going Home

The bottom of an ocean is a good place to be alone, down in the freezing murk, sightless save for the pings of the radar. Life teems on the seafloor, though it's a far cry from the world above. Deepwater worms undulate through the darkness, oblivious to the aftermath of the epic clash between Greymalkin and Ambershell.

Gus curls up in Greymalkin's chest, no longer in control of the Vanguard's body. He hugs his knees, clasping his gloved hands together. His Conduit spacesuit confines him, and he wants nothing more than to strip out of it.

He closes his eyes and lets out a long breath.

The scent of dewy grass emerges to fill his nose. A gentle breeze ruffles his hair. His suit vanishes from perception, and crickets chirp in his ears.

He opens his eyes to sunset over a cozy valley, evening light painting the distant mountains a blazing ocher. Thin skeins of smoke rise from houses nestled into the hills, and a black-winged kite sails on the air currents, loosing a plaintive cry for any who might listen. Gus sits with his back to an oak tree, its sturdy branches and leaves filtering the light into shards.

His clothes have been replaced with a dark silk three-piece suit, and he rests his chin on his knees. Acorns dig at his underside, pressing on him through the fabric, but he doesn't care.

"Where am I?"

Greymalkin believes this is a place that Elroy Baker once loved, but it's not sure. It still cannot access many memories.

"It's nice."

Greymalkin thinks so, too.

"I walked right into that trap."

Infinite was always going to deal in duplicity. The exact form was unknown before now.

"Cold comfort."

Too many of life's moments are.

He peers around at the snowcapped mountains, stubbly with evergreens, and takes a deep breath. "Is the Coalition going to attack us for what we did?"

Also unclear. They've withdrawn from the upper atmosphere, and their ships are massing in orbit. Many weapons and scanners are pointed in Greymalkin's direction. Cascade is on the surface, but the Earth Vanguards are hopelessly outclassed, should the Coalition choose to proceed with engagement.

"Any word from Falchion and Jotunn?"

Not yet.

"Doesn't matter. They can't back us up, anyway."

What does Gus want to do?

He *wants* to play piano, since that's his solution for every heartache. Greymalkin could conjure one, but he needs something real.

"I want to go to my mother's apartment."

That area will be more exposed in the event of a Coalition attack.

"Is there anywhere safe on Titan?"

No.

"Then I want to go to Mom's."

Very well.

The pristine valley vanishes into the murky waters of real life, and Greymalkin begins to rise from the depths. The damage done by Ambershell wreaks havoc across its many subsystems, and the journey takes longer than Gus anticipated.

"Can you heal this?"

Greymalkin hopes so.

The glacier containing the fractured remnants of Ambershell floats above him, and he navigates around it. When Greymalkin emerges from the water, ice glazes its armor plates in the blustery wind.

Aletheon spreads before Gus as his thrusters take him into the heart of its destruction. The city lights up with a few reticles—weapons aimed at the Vanguard—but none of them open fire. Gus points to a patch of rubble beside his mother's apartment building, hoping she didn't move after they lost contact.

"That's her old place. Keep your eyes open, okay?"

Greymalkin's scanners are always ready. It has been communicating with Titan's forces through the old Sol Joint Defense Force channels.

"What have you been telling them?"

Greymalkin and Cascade are friendly, provided they hold fire.

"Not my favorite way to introduce myself."

But necessary.

"Greymalkin, this is Cascade." The other human Vanguard touches down on the ridge at the edge of town, its bronze and turquoise plates pale against the gray sky. "I'm here. What's your plan?"

"No plan. Glad you're here, though. What's yours?"

"Keeping communications to the Coalition open. What are you doing?"

"Personal matter."

Greymalkin touches down beside a spire of dwellings, its many missing windows like broken teeth.

"Sounds like you've got time. The Coalition is threatening to glass the planet if we try to leave," Nisha says.

"Can they do it?" Gus asks Greymalkin.

There is more than enough firepower from the remaining six alien Vanguards, should they choose to destroy Titan, Greymalkin, and Cascade.

"And why haven't they?"

They also believe Scent of Rot may have been out of line.

"Small miracles, eh?"

An outline indicates the unit his mother must've occupied—twenty-fifth floor on the west side with its windows shattered. Gus knows he shouldn't get out of Greymalkin, that it would be exposing himself to danger, but he can't care anymore. Things are too fucked already.

"Is anyone inside?"

Negative scanner contacts.

"Let me down, then."

Greymalkin's chest plate pops open to howling wind. Probes carry Gus to the edge, and his suit reads a sharp drop in temperature as they release him. Orange-lit rings appear on all his ports as the warmers kick on, deicing the Vanguard contact gel. His HUD reads a mostly safe atmosphere outside his helmet with mild toxins, slightly colder than the Antarctic.

Greymalkin's hand rises to the open chest cavity, and Gus climbs out.

"Gus to Cascade." He holds on to Greymalkin's upturned thumb as he descends. "Watch my back. Can you use a disruption field if something goes wrong?"

"Yeah, though it'll kill any Titans caught in it."

The dark frame of broken glass looms closer. "Let's hope it doesn't come to that."

Gus reaches the edge and clambers off Greymalkin's fingers onto a desk near the window. He knocks over a vase, and it tumbles to the ground, cracking and spilling crumbling flowers.

"Fuck," he grunts, climbing off the desk. He flicks on his flashlight and headlamp, bathing the dim surroundings in pale beams.

The apartments are almost the same as the last time he left them, though filtered through an apocalypse. Flakes of snow flit through the open window, piling into drifts in the corners of the room. His mother's sense of decor always favored the muted earth tones and forest greens of the mid-2620s, and her colors cover everything.

Gus moves to the living room, where he finds the white baby grand Becker piano his mom took from Earth. He'd always coveted its smooth tones, even if she'd intended her purchase for classical music.

A pallid, frozen corpse sits at the bench, wearing Daphne Kitko's favorite sweater. Two holes crown her skull, dark shadows in the tangle of dry, frazzled hair. Several tumblers lay at her feet, along with an empty orange pill bottle. Gus picks it up to read the label—a sedative.

So this is how she died—asleep at her favorite instrument. A strange pang of jealousy rings through Gus. He brushes some of her hair away from her frosted skin.

That's when he spots a photograph in her hand. It's from the time they went to Oakland and got their pictures taken at the Capital Age Adventure. It's printed on real paper, though he's not certain of the type.

He can't be much older than thirteen in the photo, crammed into a group hug with his mother, sister, and father. Everyone has a goofy smile—the photographer behind the camera was an entertaining fellow. Daphne used to keep the picture in a frame over the fireplace before Gus's father destroyed their happiness.

"I'm sorry, Mom." Gus's anguish threatens to spill over. "I—I never meant to—"

A few lines of text crawl across his visor's little HUD.

GMK: SCANNER CONTACT. SOMEONE IS COMING. TITAN ENERGY SIGNATURE.

His pulse quickens. "How many?"

GMK: 1 CONTACT. INTENTIONS UNKNOWN.

He taps his wrist transmitter. "Cascade, do you have me covered?"

"I can fry anytime. What's the signal?"

He watches the door, ready for anything. "Uh, I'll open a channel and start screaming for help."

"Good enough for me."

Gus wishes he had a weapon. He never allowed himself the luxury of a gun before, for fear he'd turn it on himself.

GMK: CONTACT 10 M TO YOUR POSITION.

He spreads his legs shoulder width and gets ready to run back toward Greymalkin—yet he doubts he'll need to. Infinite's trap has been sprung and whatever happens, happens. He glares at the door, readying himself for what comes next.

"Hello?" Daphne Kitko sounds exactly like he remembers.

"I'm—I'm in here," he stammers.

The front door cracks open a tiny bit, and Titan light spills inside the foyer. Hand-shaped manipulators pry into the opening and pull the door the rest of the way with a hideous screech.

The creature that enters moves like his mother, though she's a bit larger and considerably more aglow. She towers over Gus by a head, eyes blazing as she looks him up and down.

"It's you," she says, "isn't it, August?"

"How did you know?"

"Who else would've come here?"

Gus glances over at his atmos readout on his HUD—clean

enough to breathe for a while. Titan's terraforming systems haven't completely failed.

He releases the clasps on his helmet with a ratcheting hiss. Slowly, he lifts it from his shoulders to expose his face.

The digital lanterns of Daphne's eyes go sad—surprisingly expressive. "What...happened to you?"

Gus laughs bitterly. "I could ask you the same question."

She looks at her hands as if seeing them for the first time. Her manipulators change shape as she flexes them. "I took some sleeping pills, and I—I woke up like this."

He looks to his own gloves, rugged and militaristic, dotted on the back with port contacts. "I know the feeling."

"Are you here to destroy us?"

Gus shakes his head. "Do you know what you are?"

Daphne recoils a bit. He doesn't mean for it to come out that way.

Her shoulders slump. "What do you see, when you look at me?"

He can't think of an answer he'd want to hear, so he chooses honesty. "A ghost."

The room dims when she shuts her eyes.

"And what about me?" he asks.

She stares into him. "My son. Even if I don't know what you've become."

"I'm not here to hurt you. Not again, anyway."

"So you weren't with that crab?"

"That's complicated. I'm definitely not anymore."

She massages her fingers. "I thought of you, you know. When I was drifting away."

"Was it a good dream?"

Her voice comes out a whisper. "No."

He tries to imagine what that might mean, but there are too many possibilities. "I'm sorry."

Daphne shakes her head. "I am, too. And I'm scared."

"Of me?"

"Of what I might be."

"You wouldn't know if you were intended as a trap," he says, "would you?"

"I don't..."

He rests his hands on his hips. "Of course not."

"I hate the way you're looking at me."

"I'm sorry. What...what do you know about Infinite?"

Her gaze drops. "It's our creator. It's the only thing I'm sure of."

"How do you know?"

"I just do...from the second I awoke in this body."

"Can you tell me anything else?" he asks.

She takes a tentative step forward. "August, I—"

"I'm trying to figure out if I can trust you." He holds up a hand to stop her moving closer.

"That's funny, hearing you say that."

He winces.

She clasps her hands before herself. "What happens now?"

"We still have to figure out if you're a threat."

"Who is 'we'?" she asks.

"I'm not sure."

"And what if I am?"

"I don't know. Can you tell me anything—anything at all about what you do? Not as my mother, but as a Titan?"

"I..." she begins, but reconsiders. "*We*...see the world as we want to. And we see other Titans as they wish to be seen."

"What do you mean?"

"When you look at me," she says, "you see something artificial, a strange body. But to other Titans, I look like I did in life. Younger, even. Happier."

He narrows his eyes at her, wishing he could glimpse her perspective.

"This apartment—I know it's blown out and destroyed, but"—she casts about—"it's spotless to me. I can perceive what I choose."

"Must be nice."

"It's the ultimate luxury. Having whatever I need...Being whatever I need...It's hard for me to even be sure you're real. You might just be another happy fantasy I've contrived."

He deflates. "Would a fantasy have smashed half the city?"

She takes another step closer, and he backs away. "You saved us."

"Whether or not that was wise remains to be seen."

That wounds her, and he immediately regrets saying it.

"This place...what I've become..." she says, "it's happiness, real and genuine, for the first time in my adult life. Everything I wanted is coming true, right down to my dying wish."

"Which was?"

"I wanted to see you again."

He imagines running into her arms, but she's still an agent of Infinite. Maybe she'd kill him the second she got her hands on him. She might not even know she had the orders to do it.

"I wanted that, too," he says, and maybe that's Infinite's play—emotionally attaching him to this new species. He's already defended the Titans against the Coalition.

"We're going to get to the bottom of this," he says. "We have to."

She nods. "I know."

"Where's Fiona?"

"She..."

The Titan won't look at him, and the longer her gaze remains elsewhere, the more his chest hurts.

"Mom"—his voice cracks—"where's Fiona?"

"Gus, she didn't...she didn't wait for the Ghosts to kill her."

It's like losing her all over again. The heartache and rage come coursing back, and it's all Gus can do to remain on his feet. Tears chill his cheeks, and he squeezes his eyes tightly, shaking his head.

It shouldn't hurt so much. He thought she was dead, and she is. She took the path he'd considered, and he can't be angry with her for it. But something like betrayal twists in his heart.

"Are you sure?" he asks. "Really, truly sure?"

Daphne's voice is soft as the snow. "The night before the Ghosts came, she hailed me—to say goodbye. I wanted to beg her not to, I did, but... I—I knew she wasn't wrong."

Daphne's shoulders slump. "I told her I loved her, and she... she..."

"Jesus Christ."

"I'm sorry. Gus, I wish I could've been the mother you both deserved. I couldn't keep her safe, and now—I don't know what you've become... what I've become."

He looks at the luminous being, her glow starbursting through his own tears. She slumps to the ground, hands shaking. It's an all-too-familiar sight; he's seen his mom like this hundreds of times over the course of her unhappy marriage.

"Gus." Nisha's tinny voice echoes from his helmet, and he picks it up, pressing one side to his ear. "Gus, we've got a situation."

He swallows. "What's up?"

"It's the locals. Scent of Rot is trying to get out of Ambershell."

"Shit. Protect the Titans. I don't want another rampage."

"I don't think that'll be a problem, but you need to get over here."

"I... I can't right now."

"The Coalition forces are—"

"Can't you just handle it?" He doesn't mean to sound so angry. "I'm dealing with some pretty serious shit right now."

"I'm already handling everything I can," she says, no rebuke in her voice. "I know you're hurting, but I need your help. Tazi is calling me every two seconds, and we're struggling to keep the Coalition calm."

He runs a hand through his meager hair, ready to pull out what's left. "Nisha, please. I can't do this right now. I just—"

"Gus, I'm sorry, but you must. Founder is helping me negotiate with the Coalition, but please—I can't deal with Scent of Rot, too."

"Nisha . . ."

"Some people choose their fate. Most are born into it. You decided to save the Titans, and for what it's worth . . . I'm proud of you."

"You . . . you are?"

"Yes. Now get over here."

Daphne watches Gus, digital eyes occasionally flickering with a blink. "It's fine, August. Just go. I know it's going to be okay."

"How?" is his only reply.

Without a clear mouth, it's hard to tell, but there's a smile in her eyes.

"Because I'm sure I'll see you again."

Ardent awakens to the scent of fresh flowers and clean air. Fuzzy blankets surround their nude body, and the architecture looks nothing like a human recovery room. Sloped walls and ceilings loom over them, organic shapes detailed with curling figuration. Strands of chimes hang from the high ceiling, notes twinkling as they twist.

Ardent's ports ache when they sit up in their swept-frame bed. They pull the blankets to their exposed chest and peer around.

"You're awake," a withered voice says.

They find a small Andromedan by the door, not much bigger than an adolescent human, cobalt hair shot through with a frost of silver. A plated collar surrounds its neck, and gold bracers encircle its forearms. Whoever it is appears to be old and important.

"How long have I been asleep?"

211

"Five chimes, give or take. My name is Healer Wintergourd, Ardent Violet." The Andromedan inclines its head. "It's my job to make sure you survive."

"Mission accomplished." Ardent massages their forearms.

One wall goes transparent, flooding the room with warp light—a hologram.

"We're on our way back to Earth," Wintergourd says. "Objectives complete."

It steps into the hall to grab a few implements from a rolling table, then returns to the room.

"Hjalmar—" Ardent remains still while Wintergourd scans them with various devices. "Did we, um, recover anything?"

"I'm afraid that's not my concern," it replies, but from its tone, Ardent has little hope.

"I see."

"I can ask around for you."

"No, thank you." Ardent feels sick, and they close their eyes. "Can I be alone?"

"Of course." Wintergourd collects its things and retreats from the room, closing the door behind it.

The room's shadows twitch in the flowing warp light, adding depth to the small space. When Ardent closes their eyes, they can imagine Hjalmar's expression, hear his voice. A little sob escapes them, and they bury their face in their hands.

Their atmospheric adjuster collar gently whirs around their neck, making the necessary conversions and wafting them into Ardent's face. They tug at it, seeing if there's an easy way to disengage it, but nothing.

An hour passes with no one showing up to Ardent's room, and they sit in bed, staring at the wall. Human doctors would usually check in more often.

They get up and pad to the door, searching for any of the classic signifiers of opening—a knob, a panel, a push bar—but it's too intricate and alien. They have no idea what to do.

"Where are my clothes?"

Muffled conversation approaches from the other side, and Ardent sprints back to the bed. They're barely under the covers when the door slides into its pocket, revealing a cadre of Andromedans—two big ones and a skinnier one with lots of fancy, swirling markings in its fur.

"Who are you?" Ardent isn't sure why, but they don't like this latest crew.

"Ardent Violet, my name is Truthfinder Grassy-Mountain, and these are my associates," the fancy one says.

Its escorts spread to the corners of the room, keeping their eyes on any movement. Something tells Ardent the twisted walking sticks they carry are far more powerful than mere branches.

"May I have some clothes?" Ardent asks.

"Of course." Grassy-Mountain snaps its fingers at one of its company, who starts mumbling into a hidden microphone. "We'll have some brought right down."

"I need to check in with Earth," Ardent says.

"Indeed," Grassy-Mountain replies, "but I need to have a discussion with you before you do."

Ardent narrows their eyes. "Before I talk to my people?"

"Yes. You see, we have a problem." Grassy-Mountain taps the tips of its clawed fingers together. "Humanity isn't currently part of the Coalition. In fact, one could say it's actively against the Coalition."

Ardent scoffs. "What are you talking about?"

"There's been an . . . incident—"

Their heart thumps.

"—with the other mission—"

"What happened?" It's hard to keep the edge from their voice.

Grassy-Mountain looks at them sidelong. "August Kitko attacked Conduit Council Member Scent of Rot in an act of war."

Ardent shakes their head. "That's ridiculous."

Grassy-Mountain shrugs. "And yet."

"Gus wouldn't just attack someone like that."

"Ambershell was destroyed in the fight. Scent of Rot's fate is unknown."

The two others with the Truthfinder make a lot more sense now—goons.

Ardent eyes them, hoping they won't turn aggressive. "Why? What would Gus have to gain by doing that?"

"That's something we'd like you to answer," Grassy-Mountain says. "I have a few questions for you."

It places a small device on the countertop, a polished tube of silver, which unfolds into several microphones and lenses.

Ardent can almost hear Dahlia chiding, *Never talk to cops.*

"I don't think now is a good time," they say.

Grassy-Mountain cocks its head. "Do you have somewhere else to be?"

"Yeah, talking to humans."

"You will have that opportunity soon."

"How about right now?"

It continues setting up the device. "I'm afraid that's not possible."

"What's that supposed to mean?"

Grassy-Mountain's silence chills Ardent.

"Truthfinder..." they begin, "why can't I make my report?"

"Well..." It won't look them in the eye as it works on its task. "You are technically... a prisoner."

"What?"

Ardent would normally lose it on anyone who dared to impose a restriction on them, but they short-circuit when it comes to a warden. They don't know what it means to be an Andromedan prisoner, and they're not eager to find out how much worse things can get. It's currently quite comfortable, so maybe they're better off keeping quiet.

Their mouth goes dry. "And what about the signature file?"

"It has been couriered to Chancellor Redeemer for safekeeping." Grassy-Mountain's sly eyes shine. "I expect it will keep our negotiations with humanity quite . . . open."

Its statement crushes Ardent's chest and steals the strength from their knees.

Hjalmar died for that file.

Now it's gone.

Chapter Twelve

No Cages

Gus drops into Greymalkin's open chest cavity, the snap of probes ringing through his helmet. The world rushes into view, feeding him many times his typical human sensory input.

Scent of Rot isn't hard to find—Ambershell actually smells like a split-open crab, and Greymalkin's advanced sensors are better than a pack of bloodhounds. Frigid winds blow Ambershell's dying geysers of blood into mist to paint the nearby landscape. Whatever ecosystems existed within its fractured carapace have free rein to infect a new world, and Gus only hopes there won't be serious repercussions.

Scent of Rot stands atop a jagged chunk of ice near the corpse of its Vanguard, hooked legs anchored into the surface. Titans line the shore, some carrying portable rockets and manning laser turrets.

Gus grimaces. "How did they get all this stuff so quickly?"

Greymalkin's guess: These are the former Titanic military—they remember where they left things before they died.

Gus glances back at the broken window of his mother's

apartment. Daphne stands at the ledge, her electronic eyes fixed upon Greymalkin's.

Maybe that's his mother. Maybe it's a trick. There's not enough time to have the conversation he wants, so he turns toward his duty—Ambershell. Greymalkin takes to the sky, flying toward Scent of Rot and the small crowd.

"Greymalkin, I don't know a lot about diplomacy," Gus says, "but I think we probably need to err on the side of mercy."

Greymalkin has reached visual translation range. Perhaps Gus would like to hear what Scent of Rot is saying.

"Please."

Part of Gus's view zooms in to provide a thorough detail of Scent of Rot's mustaches, mouthparts, and eyestalks—everything used in its language. It's screaming in utter rage.

"—go on and do it, you brainless anemones! I'll take more than a few of you with me! Do you see me now, King? Do you see me?"

It shakes a claw at the heavens.

Gus whistles. "Okay. We may have upset the big crab."

Greymalkin and Gus defaced the holiest object in their belief structure aside from King, itself.

"Don't care. Not going to let someone crush an innocent for their god."

Incoming transmission: Chancellor Redeemer wishes to speak with Gus.

"Should we route that to the authorities? We can't negotiate."

Gus's argument is not compelling. Greymalkin will now connect Chancellor Redeemer.

The jagged exterior of the Andromedan Vanguard fades into existence beside him, tall as Greymalkin. Broken components spark inside its belly as it straightens to face him.

"I see things have gone ... awry." It gestures to Ambershell's wreckage.

"I won't call this an accident," Gus says, "but I never meant for it to come out this way."

"Scent of Rot would've killed you if you'd done anything less," Redeemer says. *"I know that one well. It's quick to test alliances."*

"Why?"

"King chose Scent of Rot to keep the Coalition unstable, and it plays the part admirably."

"Aren't we supposed to be friends?"

"It benefits King if we're weak rivals at best." Redeemer peers over Scent of Rot. *"The Pictorans were always going to create some sort of distraction. Frankly, most of us in the Coalition have grown tired of them."*

"Not quite the conversation I was expecting."

"I want us to get along, August Kitko—to be ready to face greater concerns than one another. It is in my best interest to find a way to make peace as quickly as possible."

"I hear you. I want to help."

"I'm glad you said that, because you can." Redeemer points to Scent of Rot. *"Make sure this one survives. I cannot keep the Coalition together if we lose this Conduit."*

"That was my plan."

"Then we are aligned."

"So what should I do? Remand Scent of Rot to the Pictorans?"

"Not the best idea," Redeemer says. *"However, the rest of the Conduit Council will not appreciate it if you kill it without a good reason."*

"I don't want to hurt anyone."

"I know that, August Kitko."

"I have to ask," Gus says, "if this had gone the other way, and Ambershell had killed me, would you be pushing to keep things together?"

"No. It would've been easier to walk away from humanity. I can't unilaterally steer the Coalition."

"At least you're honest."

"In less than one day's time, you will depart this world," Redeemer says. *"I have a plan to fix this, and I'm going to need you with me."*

"Go? These people are going to need me. No one can trust them, and as long as that's the case, they're in danger of being eradicated by UW or UAF forces."

"I have a solution for that, too, but I need your faith." The Andromedan Vanguard has such a kind face, and Gus fears that's part of its design.

"That's in short supply, but I'll help you wherever I can."

"Very good. Redeemer out." The chancellor disappears from Gus's network.

Greymalkin does not see any options besides doing what Redeemer says. The cost of a second war is far too great.

"Agreed." Gus nods. "And some plan is better than no plan."

Ambershell's carcass bobs on the waves as Greymalkin gets closer. His Vanguard wonders: Does Gus know how he intends to deescalate the situation with Scent of Rot?

"Uhh..." Gus scans Scent of Rot's body, and the sensors call out a ton of hidden energy and weapons systems. This creature is anything but disarmed.

"That's a whole lot of crab."

And if Gus fails to pacify his opponent, loss of life is almost guaranteed.

"Maybe we could have Nisha hit it with a disruption field."

That will kill a Pictoran.

"I'm going to try talking to it."

Gus's conversational track record with Scent of Rot is poor.

"Stop me when you have a better idea."

Cold rain spits into the opening in Greymalkin's chest armor as it releases Gus from its nest. The ocean rages far below, boulders of ice clattering into the Vanguard's shins. If he fell down there, it'd be a swift death.

He crawls across the icy palm, keeping as close to its surface as he can before settling down in the middle. He's pretty sure he won't be blown off by the gusts, but he'd rather not take the risk. After wiggling into place, he gives Greymalkin the thumbs-up.

Greymalkin moves its hand to be about five meters from where Scent of Rot has perched on Ambershell. Closer up, Gus can see how diminished the beast's lights are.

It falls silent upon glimpsing him.

"Hey," Gus calls to the crustacean. He clicks the release on his helmet and pulls it off.

It stares at him.

Gus waves through the frigid raindrops. "Gus to Scent of Rot. Come in."

It's not speaking, but something in its posture says, *Drop dead.*

"This isn't going to work unless you talk to me."

Its eyestalks straighten. "What is there to say to the cruelest thief of all?"

Gus narrows his eyes. "*You* brought the fight. I brought the reality check. Not sure where thievery comes into it."

"You have stolen my King's love!" It rages on its hunk of ice, bashing the surface with its heavy claws. "You have made me defective!"

"What?"

"I feel King's gaze upon me, and there is nothing but loathing."

"Why? Because you couldn't kill me?"

Scent of Rot goes rigid, which translates to *Of course.*

"Unbelievable! You're mad at *me* because I didn't let you kill me? And now your creator—"

Scent of Rot raises its open claws in anguish. "I'm sorry, my King! Take me back, I beg of you!"

Gus rubs the bridge of his nose. This is going to be more complicated than he was expecting.

"I need you to come with me," Gus says. "Let's get you back to land."

"I wish to die," Scent of Rot says, slumping. "Let my failure end."

Gus knows that look. He saw it in the mirror after he'd lost his family. Scent of Rot doesn't know a way forward.

He starts thinking of all the different things he wishes someone had said to him in his darkest moments—though nothing comes to mind. Platitudes can't save a life, and that's all he can think of.

Besides, this thing is a mass murderer. It would've killed every last Titan, including his mother, if he'd let it—but were those real lives? Gus doesn't feel the same love for them as living, breathing humans, and yet, he can't just walk away from them, either.

"Scent of Rot, you're not defective."

It perks up enough to scoff. "King gives me truth with every beat of my heart. I am defective. I should be destroyed."

"But what does your family think? What about your friends?"

"Any of them would crack my shell and pull out my meat on sight."

"I'll admit that's bad—" Gus can't figure out a good way to turn that sentence around, and so he has to leave it.

The ice shifts near Scent of Rot, grinding fissures that could easily crush a crab. Its eyestalks stretch over the nearest one. Gus imagines it plunging to its death.

"Are you supposed to be making things better?" it asks.

Gus shakes his head. "Not really. I'm supposed to keep you alive."

"Your honesty is appreciated..." It wilts. "I was the right hand of a god. When I spoke, or acted, it came with perfect certainty. Now I'm nothing but flotsam."

"And that can only change if you survive."

"No Pictoran would possibly wish life upon me."

"It was Redeemer," Gus says. "Told me you would be instrumental in peace."

"Peace! And why would I want that?"

"Because your family has abandoned you. Peace is what enables you to choose another."

"A god is not a family! There's a hole in my soul now! A void greater than every ocean in the universe!" It points at itself as best it can. "If only I'd killed you!"

"Well, I didn't feel like dying," Gus says. "Sorry."

"I do not accept your apology!"

Gus grunts in annoyance. "I wasn't actually—look, I don't know what to tell you. I've never known a love like yours for King."

Scent of Rot gives a bloodless laugh. "The feelings from my god—they weren't always love. Sometimes they were anger. Sometimes shame. But when they *were* love, when King was genuinely shining on me…"

Scent of Rot faces into the rain, letting sharp drops slap across its roots and whiskers.

"It was like starlight."

The crab's words dig deep. Gus felt that for his mom. She didn't always love him, but when she did—the world was brand-new. She made horrific pain bearable, almost preferable.

"Could you ever know love like that, human?" it asks.

Gus takes a moment to answer. He's not about to start in with a cybercrab about his mommy issues, but he thinks he understands a little. "I've had a taste."

It sizes him up. "And what would you give for a love that was worthy?"

Gus considers the question. What is "worthy" in this context? He can't love his parents the way Scent of Rot loves King—but he considers what he'd give for a concentrated drop of Ardent Violet's sunshine.

"Anything," Gus says, "so I have only the faintest idea what you're going through. Being abandoned by my favorite person would crush me—but perhaps your shell is thicker than mine."

"What are you saying?"

He's surprised his turn of phrase landed. It was a genuine gamble. "Maybe you were meant for more than giving up."

It cogitates, gently rocking back and forth. "Redeemer made this request of me? To live?"

"It was crystal clear," Gus says. "Will you listen to me?"

"Your counsel is soft-shelled by nature."

"Is that an insult?" Gus asks.

"Yes."

Gus sighs. "Okay."

"But I will come peacefully."

"Thank you."

"Ardent Violet," a stilted, English-speaking voice says over the room speakers, "you have a visitor. Do you accept?"

"Yes."

Giant eyes appear in front of Ardent, and they yelp. It takes them a moment to recognize the bridge of Redeemer's nose. The massive construct shrinks until its crown just barely touches the ceiling. Five eyes blaze down at Ardent, each wrapped in silver filigree. Cracks and scars pit its face.

"Hello, Ardent Violet."

"What is with Vanguards doing that?" Ardent straightens their robe's cuffs on instinct—can't be slouchy in front of the alien mecha president.

"I hope you're being treated well."

"I'm not in any pain," they say. "Not hungry."

"*With luck, we can resolve all of this, and you can be released.*"

Ardent balls their fists. "Where's the signature file?"

"*It has been given to me, where it will remain in my personal care until this business between August Kitko and the Pictorans is settled.*"

"I don't like the sound of that."

"*Nor should you. A creature from another galaxy holds the keys to your species' salvation.*" Redeemer's eyes narrow. "*The situation is suboptimal for humanity.*"

"Thanks for pointing that out."

"*Truth is the cornerstone of lasting diplomacy. If need be, I can use the file on your behalf and write potent code. I can interoperate with any style of computing, even human.*"

"And what will that do, 'Great Translator'?"

"*I will be able to manipulate Infinite directly.*"

"Have you told Gus and Nisha? About capturing me? About the signature file? About...about Hjalmar?"

"*I have informed the United Worlds.*"

"And Gus and Nisha?"

"*Only if their Vanguards have told them.*"

"So why are you here, then?"

"*I need you to be part of a team.*"

"What kind?"

"*The kind with a Dark Drive, the signature file, and a plan.*"

"Sounds good to me."

"*I can fix this, but it's going to require a lot of cooperation.*" Redeemer inclines its head. "*Cooperation that, I'm afraid, hasn't been forthcoming inside the Coalition.*"

"You all seemed pretty united to me."

"*We are using a lot of resources to defend your species on faith. I believe you have something to offer us, but I can't prove it.*"

"Is that the only reason the Coalition is saving humanity?" Ardent asks. "Because we have something to offer?"

"Nothing is free, Ardent Violet. There are many things we wish to learn from you. Are there not Coalition technologies you crave?"

"Sure. Probably."

"Then we must make this partnership last. I have a plan to do exactly that."

"And are we worried about people overhearing this plan? This cell is probably wiretapped."

"You're a political prisoner and I'm the chancellor. The call between us is privileged. If someone is recording us now, they're threatening their own freedom in the extreme."

"Okay, fine. Tell me your plan."

"First, I'll have you transferred to a room with a view. You deserve better."

Ardent rolls their eyes. "And what's that going to do?"

"It was Falchion's request."

Ardent grimaces. "Really?"

"I'm taking the signature file to Titan. August Kitko and Scent of Rot need some guidance. With all of that sorted, you and August Kitko will meet at a prearranged location to build something for me."

"Oh, I'm just going to pop out and do your bidding?"

"You absolutely are."

"This is all very suspect."

"Spoken like someone with a choice."

"Touché."

Redeemer's eyes remain fixed upon Ardent. *"There is something I must do before I can join you. This feud with the Pictorans and August Kitko . . . it was always going to be a trap. Now we disarm it and move forward."*

"So one more time, your plan: You're going to move me somewhere a little more respectable."

"Somewhere you can see the stars."

"And then you're going to Titan."

"Yes."

"And we'll meet in a third location."

"*Correct.*"

"You're leaving out the part where I die in the jailbreak and you make your career-winning moves off antihuman sentiment."

"*You have a vivid imagination.*"

"Just trying to figure your angle."

"*Here's an uncomfortable truth. If I'd wanted you gone, I could've made anything happen, and no one in the Coalition would've questioned it. It would be easiest to let the Pictorans destroy your species. This current effort to 'fix things' is the least efficient path I could choose, but I'm doing it because of what's right.*"

Ardent grimaces. "You're a lot different when you drop the pomp and circumstance."

"*I'm in the oldest, most political position in the universe. I know how to get business done.*"

"I can see that."

"*I'm glad we understand each other. Be ready.*"

Redeemer fades, leaving Ardent alone in the observation chamber. They get about thirty seconds of solitude before an Andromedan guard knocks on the door.

"Enter," Ardent says.

"Conduit Ardent Violet." The creature's manner is deferential, and it avoids looking Ardent in the eye as it gestures for the hall. "We would like to change your room."

They can't really help themself and say, "Hated the fake holographic view here, anyway."

"Yes, of course," says the guard. It taps the side of Ardent's food tray, which begins following the alien. The Andromedan loads it up with Ardent's pitcher of water and the vase with a single white flower—the rest of Ardent's personal effects are missing.

The corridors of the ship are sparse with few crew members

around. The ones Ardent sees are shoved to one side, cordoned off so the human can pass through with lots of distance.

"I'm not going to bite anyone," Ardent says.

"We're not worried about that," says the Andromedan. "Our vaccination rate is far from one hundred percent. We're simply trying to avoid any human diseases."

"Your job was to give us rides out of combat. What do you mean you're not fully vaccinated?"

The creature sighs. "Supplies are short at the moment. Our best manufacturing facilities are in the homelands, and so we must work with what we have."

Ardent doesn't want to think about the diplomatic damage if they cause some kind of outbreak.

"Here we are." The Andromedan stops before an open door and bids Ardent enter.

The new quarters are certainly redder, though not much different in terms of amenities. Ardent has a lot of trouble figuring out the purpose of everything in their alien room. There are so many nozzles, knobs, switches, and buttons hidden throughout the space that Ardent dare not touch them. They only ask about the lights, the food dispensers, and how to operate the hot tub.

Through the top half of the room, Ardent has a great view of the supercarrier's logistic and docking operations. Stars streak past, curving across the *Reclamation Wind*'s warp envelope. The supercarrier has a surprising amount of traffic during a fold, with dozens of little supply and support vessels flitting through the warp bubble. Human craft never deploy inside a mothership's envelope like that, much less set up a stable traffic pattern.

A chime sounds near the door. Ardent signs for it to open, then shakes their head in frustration. The Andromedans don't use common sign for any of their systems, and Ardent doesn't know how to access any of the functions.

Ardent looks over the unlabeled console. "How do I answer?"

"Red button," comes the muffled response.

A projection of Truthfinder Grassy-Mountain appears beside the door. "Ardent Violet, I've come for another debriefing."

They don't feel like screwing with this space lawyer at the moment. "Been a long day. Maybe later."

Grassy-Mountain's projection cocks its head. "Are you unwell?"

"Yeah, my buddy just died," Ardent says. "And, big surprise, I don't want to talk to you."

Something tickles the back of Ardent's neck—a premonition that the room is about to become incredibly unsafe. It almost feels like a message from Falchion. The Truthfinder's projection takes no notice.

"That may be, Ardent Violet." Grassy-Mountain adjusts its coat. "But we have too much at stake to spend any of our precious time in the dark. I need you to comply with my investigations."

Ardent glances around, trying to figure out what has them so frazzled. Everything appears to be in its place. They touch the wall, and a subacoustic hum tickles their fingertips.

"Okay..." Ardent says. "I mean, I hear you..."

"May I come in?" it asks.

"I don't know. I think that's a bad idea, but I don't know why."

Grassy-Mountain gives them a suspicious look and begins tapping some unseen interface. It's probably checking the other sensor feeds.

"What's going on in there?" it asks.

"You tell me!"

Grassy-Mountain purses its lips. "Why are you so upset?"

"I don't know!" Ardent paces back and forth. There's got to be some reason for this powerful sense of dread. "Oh god, I don't know."

"Are you in danger?"

Ardent gives an anxious shrug.

"What about the ship?"

That's when they hear the klaxons—three short bursts, followed by a clang. "Attention," says the voice of the ship, "maximum alert. All personnel report to their watch officers for—"

"What's going on out there?" Ardent presses their cheek to the door.

"You worry about your own circumstances," Grassy-Mountain replies. "Tell me why you're upset, now."

"I don't know!"

The sight through their cupola window stops them dead—Falchion climbing on the outside of the supercarrier. The giant mecha has twisted out of the cargo bay, clinging close to the *Reclamation Wind* to stay within its warp bubble. It drags itself onto the central staging area, shoving the *Reclamation Wind* and sending shudders through its fuselage.

"What are you doing?" Grassy-Mountain demands. "Stop this at once!"

"It's not me!" Ardent says.

From across the long hull, Falchion locks eyes with Ardent. It knows exactly where they are.

"Do you have any idea what it wants?" Grassy-Mountain holds out empty hands, some kind of Andromedan gesture Ardent can't remember.

"I don't have a clue! Get me out of here!" Ardent bangs on the thick door, willing the hologram of Grassy-Mountain to comply.

Falchion has grown even closer, and Ardent's feeling of mild unease has turned to near panic. Support ships throughout the warp bubble swerve to avoid colliding with the Vanguard menacing their home base. There's nothing that can attack Falchion without hitting the *Reclamation Wind*, and the Vanguard uses that to its advantage.

Falchion shimmies the last few meters, chest coming even with the observation cupola on Ardent's room. They're terrified they know what comes next.

"Helmet!" Ardent shouts at the hologram of Grassy-Mountain. "Where did you put my helmet? Or the rest of my suit?"

"It's with your other effects."

"I need it! The whole thing!"

The hum has grown unbearable, rising through the floor, wafting from the walls, penetrating Ardent from every surface. It's Falchion's song—coming through the frame of the ship.

"What's that noise?" Grassy-Mountain asks.

"I said I needed my spacesuit!"

Falchion stabilizes itself outside before drawing one of its blasters from its holster and aiming along the side of Ardent's domed window. It's trying to shoot only the swollen glass, not the rest of the ship.

Ardent stares into Falchion's red eyes. "Do not rescue me like this."

The song grows unbearably loud, and Ardent can finally make out a single message in it:

Exhale.

There's no clear indication of magnitude, but Ardent got basic vacuum safety in elementary school. They know that even the smallest amount of air in their lungs could be deadly during explosive decompression.

So, they blow as hard as they can until they're shaking and red in the face. They quickly hit their limit and glance up at the red god looming over them, its gun pressed to the ship. There's nothing left in their lungs to wring out, and they begin to cough in preparation for taking another breath.

That's when Falchion shoots.

A white flash fills Ardent's vision, and even though they thought they'd gotten rid of all their air, open space snatches the rest from their chest. Random objects smack their exposed face like shrapnel, and Ardent is sucked from their feet toward the blown-out ceiling. They shut their eyes, covering their face, and lose all sense of direction. Frost burns their skin, and they can't stop choking as they fight to take a breath.

They know they're not supposed to open their eyes in space, but they can't stop themself. They never would've imagined free-floating in a superluminal fold envelope without any protection, but now that it's happened, they need to be present. It might be the last thing they see.

The theater of the universe is so much larger than Ardent. The *Reclamation Wind*, Falchion, and everything else are nothing when compared with the limitless vastness of curving stars. Ardent is a tiny living being floating in a sea of death. Freezing tears sting their eyes, and they shut them once more.

Ardent goes flipping into a bed of warm goo, and more of the substance closes around them. Giant metal fingers push them deeper inside.

Lights burst behind their eyes as they strain to breathe, but there's still no air. The viscous substance violently reorients them, and at long last, oxygen pours into tubes in Ardent's nose. They take deep, weeping breaths, eyes shut tight and watering. The skin on their face burns like they've been standing in a blisteringly cold wind, and Ardent wipes their cheeks with shivering hands.

Probes thunk into ports across Ardent's body, all discomfort vanishing at the connections. Their vision synchronizes with Falchion's, rendering the warp bubble in much deeper detail, along with the *Reclamation Wind*. The supercarrier's defenses are locked upon the Vanguard, but they don't dare shoot at something so close.

Falchion kicks loose from the hull, flying toward the warp

bubble. Unnatural forces pull on Ardent's flesh as they cross out of the envelope into normal space. The Vanguard tumbles end over end upon breeching the fold, firing thrusters in all directions to stabilize itself.

When it finally stops spinning, the only sound is Ardent's panting.

"What ... the everloving fuck ... is your problem?"

Falchion's human form appears beside Ardent, arms crossed with a wide grin. *"We needed to get out of there. That was the fastest way."*

"You could've killed someone!"

"But I didn't."

"And that ship was our ticket back to Earth!" Ardent shakes their head. "Now we're stuck out here with a discharged superluminal drive—"

"Partially discharged. We've got enough to hop to the nearest star and scoop some fuel."

"Then what?"

"We head to Redeemer's next set of coordinates and hope its plan isn't terrible."

"I don't suppose you could clue me in on what it is?"

"Something to do with your silly mystery weapon. That's the most I could understand."

Chapter Thirteen

Aftercare

Greymalkin descends toward the Olan Woods Joint Operations base, where several hundred glowing specks gather in the snowy parade field. They've moved a number of weapons out into the open, but nothing specifically for Greymalkin—rather, smaller antipersonnel weapons like lasers, some rockets, and machine guns. They're not afraid of the Vanguard, but the monster crab in its right hand.

Greymalkin's thrusters churn up huge clouds of snow upon landing, obscuring the gathered troops in a blizzard. They shield themselves from the onslaught, generally more steadfast than humans. Having lenses instead of eyes probably provides some advantage.

"Let me down first, if that's okay," Gus says. "I'd like to be on the ground before Scent of Rot."

If anything goes wrong, Greymalkin will not be able to protect Gus out in the open.

"I'll be fine."

Scent of Rot may decide to take revenge upon Gus. The Titans may do the same to Scent of Rot. Gus will be the squishiest participant in such an action.

"So largely revenge-based concerns?"

Emotions will be tense, and Scent of Rot has a destabilizing personality. Greymalkin worries about Gus being caught in the crossfire.

"Aw, I didn't know you cared."

Greymalkin is extremely fond of Gus.

Guilt needles him. Could he say the same?

Greymalkin cuts him off before he can decide. It's grateful for him, regardless of his feelings in return.

The chest plate pops open, exposing him to the cold, gray world outside. This high up, visibility is terrible, and his helmet does nothing to enhance it. Gus negotiates his way out of the probe cables and onto Greymalkin's palm, where it lowers him to the ground. He's getting pretty good at the dismount, and the onlookers seem impressed.

"Mister Kitko!" calls one of the Titans. It looks exactly like all the others, obviously military from the uniform, pieces of kit, and assault rifle.

Gus raises a hand in greeting, and the soldier comes jogging over.

"Major Ferguson. They, them, if you please."

"No problem. Gus Kitko, he, him." He smiles and offers a hand, which the major takes.

"I have to say, we were surprised to get a call from a Vanguard." Ferguson waves over a squad, all armed to the teeth. "You ready to make delivery?"

"That depends," Gus says. "Is the holding area set up?"

"We've done our best to accommodate. Not a lot of appetite to house this beast in our facilities."

"I understand." Gus motions for Greymalkin, who begins lowering its captive toward the armed soldiers.

It's hard to tell that the pathetic creature contained in Greymalkin's palm is the once-proud Scent of Rot. It balls up against the cold, folding its legs in among its claws. The lights on its cara-pace slow-pulse if they're on at all. The major shouts orders to their personnel, who spread out to flank the alien.

Gus cups his hands to be heard over the howling wind. "Scent of Rot! These people are going to take you somewhere safe."

The Pictoran unfolds, revealing its intimidating proportions. With an extra head of height and massive clawspan, it's a lot more like the terrifying monster Gus has come to know. Soldiers take up firing positions, several deploying tripod-mounted weaponry.

"I need you to acknowledge me, Rot," Gus says. "These people are scared, and they might hurt you if they feel threatened."

Scent of Rot's eyestalks scan the crowd. "I will acquiesce."

Gus turns to Major Ferguson. "It said it'll follow us."

Ferguson's gaze drops and their eyes go dim for a few seconds. "I've signaled the transport, and it should be on station in one minute."

"You can talk without using your comms?"

"Yes, sir," Ferguson says. "There's a lot of stuff I can do now that I couldn't do before."

"And how do you feel about all of . . . this?"

"Complicated, Mister Kitko."

Gus lets out a little snort. "Statement of the century."

The Conduit suit, designed for the depths of space, provides plenty of warmth, but Gus worries about Scent of Rot, who appears sluggish. Crabs are found in arctic waters, right?

"Any word from Redeemer?" Gus asks. "It's supposed to be on the way."

Ferguson shakes their head. "It's sent messages that it's arriving shortly, but we can't verify. Planetary comms are fubar."

"What do you mean?"

"We're locked out of any observation systems not housed on Titan. No PODS. No sat-tracking."

Gus remembers the acronym. "Oh yeah. The Pluto Observation Something Something."

Ferguson quakes like they're laughing, but it's hard to tell without a mouth. "That's the one. We can't track fold wakes, so we have no idea who's around. The Earthlings have us completely unable to see."

Gus shakes his head. "They don't trust you."

"And you do, Mister Kitko?"

He looks the Titan in the eye. The question doesn't seem malicious. "I'm trying. Taking a human at their word is one thing, but a creation of Infinite..."

"Yeah." They look at the ground. "Hard to swallow. For what it's worth, can't say I blame you."

"Heard anything from the Coalition?"

"Still blockading our orbit, but at least they're not on the ground causing damage."

A distant whine becomes a thrumming jet engine as an armored personnel carrier touches down before Greymalkin. Snow sprays Gus's helmet, and he wipes it away. Two Titans jump out of the back, and when Gus peers inside the hold, he spots a ton of blinking devices stuck to the walls and floors.

One of the newcomers approaches Gus. In a masculine voice, it says, "Mister Kitko, I'm Captain Lowe. Can we talk to that thing?"

"It can understand you, Captain," Gus says. "You just need a translator for when it talks back."

"You're hired." Lowe turns to the Pictoran. "Hey, uh, Scent of Rot! Listen up!"

It slowly faces him, dead silent.

Lowe clears his throat. "I'm going to take you to an aquarium now, and I want it to go as smoothly as possible."

Scent of Rot remains statue still.

"So we're going to load you into the back of that truck and lock the doors," Lowe says. "Okay?"

The Pictoran turns and trudges toward the APC, the armed soldiers keenly following its movements. Despite their inhuman forms, every one of them looks terrified. That seems like the sort of thing Scent of Rot would typically enjoy, but it's the most downtrodden of all the assembled party.

It clanks into the back, and the whole APC sags with its weight before the repulsors double their spin. The vehicle bounces as Scent of Rot curls up in a corner.

Gus cautiously follows Lowe and Ferguson to the double doors, where they shut the Pictoran inside.

"See you at the detention facility, Captain." Ferguson salutes and heads for a nearby CAV.

There's a little rifle slot on the back door of the APC, and Lowe talks into it. "Scent of Rot, listen up. Those lights on the wall are shaped charges. If you try to escape, if you try to harm us, we'll cut the back loose, where it will fall several thousand feet before exploding. There's enough force in those charges to level a building."

Scent of Rot does nothing.

"Before we take off, I need confirmation you understand," Lowe says.

The Pictoran takes one huge claw and bashes the ground twice to deafening effect.

"O-kay." Lowe checks the lock on the back doors once and turns to Gus. "You riding with us to the detention facility, Kitko?"

Gus shakes his head. "I'm going to stick with Greymalkin."

"Copy," Lowe says before raising an arm and motioning to the other soldiers. "Let's roll!"

The motorcade takes off while Gus walks back to Greymalkin's palm. Its singing is quieter than before, and he wonders if something is wrong. He steps into the chest cavity, letting the probes take him.

There's an incoming connection request for Gus from Falchion and Cascade. Status report on Operation Pitchfork.

"Holy shit! Right! Put them through, please."

A mirror forms beneath Gus's feet, stretching out to the horizon and reflecting the dark clouds above. His spacesuit boots create ripples as he walks on the endless surface.

He hears the quiet sobbing before he spots them. He spins to find Ardent holding Nisha, sunk to the ground. They're both in their Conduit suits, tears streaming down their faces. He'd been looking forward to seeing Ardent again, but not like this.

Ardent shakes their head. "I'm sorry. I tried. I'm so sorry."

Gus doesn't want to ask—he fears he already knows the answer—but he has no choice. "What happened?"

Ardent looks at him with hollow eyes. They're even beautiful when they're devastated. "Hjalmar is dead."

Nisha cries harder, burying her head into Ardent's shoulder and gnashing her teeth. They stroke her hair and close their eyes.

Gus takes a few tentative steps closer. "How . . ."

"Overseer's Vanguard." Ardent shivers a little. "We weren't fast enough."

"I'm so t-tired of death," Nisha says, sniffling and angry. "He was the first new friend I made in years. Didn't care that I was weird."

"I'm sorry," Ardent says. "So, so sorry."

"Gus." Nisha holds out a hand to him, beckoning him to join them in an embrace.

He kneels before them, and when the pair wrap arms around Gus, he's not moved to tears, as he thought he'd be, but strength. He needs to take care of these people, to be there for them, as he wished he'd been for Hjalmar.

"Did you do it?" he asks quietly. "Were you able to get the signature file?"

"Redeemer is holding on to it, but I don't know where," Ardent says bitterly. "We didn't get to use it on the Infinite Eye. The whole system was missing."

"What do you mean Redeemer has it?" Gus asks.

"The Coalition fucking took it!" Ardent pulls away from the group hug. "After *you* got into a fight with Scent of Rot, they stole it from me and—Jesus, I've never been so mad about something in my life! Gus, they held me under house arrest after Hjalmar— after Overseer killed him."

There's so much hurt in their expression. "What did he die for, huh? We don't have the file and—"

Gus's stomach knots. Surely they don't blame him for what happened. "Are you safe?"

"Why did you have to fight Scent of Rot?"

Gus grimaces. That's a difficult question. Some of it was because of his mother and how afraid he was of losing her voice again. Most of it was because he was appalled by the Pictoran's carnage. And a nonzero amount was because he just hated the fucker.

"It was murdering everyone, Ardent," Nisha says, standing. "I wasn't part of Gus's team, so I wasn't there, but..."

"It was killing humans?" There's an edge in Ardent's voice.

"The Titans may as well be," Nisha says. "They're machines, but also...alive. They're all the colonists that Infinite killed, resurrected in machine bodies."

"You jeopardized our alliance for *Ghosts*?" Ardent raises their voice. "For fuck's sake, Gus! Infinite has been using that same tired trick on us for how long?"

"I had good reasons." He's still reeling from the news about his sister, and he's not eager to be put on trial.

Ardent gets in his face. " 'Good reasons' to protect Infinite's troops? Let's have them! Explain it to me like I'm a child!"

"Don't," he says. "You don't understand what I've been through."

Ardent recoils. "What you've been through... Gus, I just watched my friend get *cut in half.*"

Heat rises in his cheeks. "I am asking you to back off."

"Both of you, stop!" Nisha shouts. He's never heard her raise her voice before. "Gus, agree or disagree, you acted without talking to me, the only other human on your team. Ardent, I know you're hurting because I am, too, but I'm telling you these aren't mere Ghosts. There's something going on with the Titans, and we have to get to the bottom of it before we can make the rash decision to eliminate them."

She's shaking, and she looks like she's about to sock the both of them. Gus wouldn't blame her—he probably deserves it.

"Nisha—" he starts, but she cuts him off.

"I'm not done. There is more to this war than Operation Pitchfork. More than the concerns of a few individuals, or even planet Earth. Every single being murdered so far had as much of a right to life as Hjalmar. I lost five cousins and two aunts the night Bullseye and Wanderer came to New Jalandhar. Because of my duties, I missed their funerals, and I haven't seen my extended family for weeks. Am I angry? Yes. Am I sad? Hell yes."

Nisha shakes her head, pacing with angry thumps of her heels. "I've sacrificed, and played the diplomat, and saved the ungrateful Earthlings, only for them to turn on me *every single time.* I've watched the Coalition prioritize the lives of your people without so much as a care for mine. I know the fates of our worlds are bound together, but *my world gives, and yours takes.* And now look at you both—too absorbed in your own drama to give a shit about the bigger picture."

Some of the rage cools to grief. "Whereas Hjalmar and I could not look away."

Ardent opens their mouth, and a glare shuts it.

"I'm through making everyone comfortable. When Infinite is destroyed, I'm going back to *my world* to help *my people*. Hjalmar should've done the same. For now, though—"

She stands before them, resolute.

"I don't turn on my friends, and I don't crack under pressure. We are people's last hope. *Act like it.*"

Ardent won't look at her, but eventually gets out a "I can tell you've needed to say that for a long time."

She crosses her arms. "And you've needed to hear it. Now make up with Gus or so help me . . ."

Ardent turns to Gus with a begrudging look.

"I'm sorry," they say. "I know you're doing your best."

He takes their shoulders. "I love you. You know that. I never meant to put you—or, uh, all of humanity—in danger. I was just trying to do the right thing."

They close their eyes. "I know."

"For what it's worth," he says, "if I had to go back to the start of the operation, I'd make the same decisions."

"That's great. Love that for you . . . I would change everything." Their lower lip trembles like they're about to lose it again.

"Oh, Ardent." He pulls them in close, thankful for the realism of the simulation. He can smell their sweet shampoo when he kisses the top of their head, feel the warmth of their face pressed to his chest. "It's not your fault."

"Yes it is!" They break down in his arms, and Gus holds them tighter. "Every time I fucked up . . . death was waiting."

"You tried your best."

"Reality doesn't give a shit about that." They wipe their cheek with a fist. "No consolation prizes here."

"Sometimes, there's no way to win," he says. "The outcome is bigger than you."

"Then Tazi was right." Ardent buries their face into his chest, forehead bumping his spacesuit's locking collar. "It should've been someone else inside Falchion. A soldier, or some brilliant strategist instead of pop trash like—"

"Stop." He tips their chin up and looks into their shining eyes. "There's no one else I'd rather have standing right here with me."

Their voice is muffled by his suit, and they don't look at him. "I love you, too."

Greymalkin's scanners have detected an entity approaching Aletheon airspace.

"Gus," Nisha says.

He looks to her. "I felt something, too."

He knows the identity of the disturbance even as Nisha says it. "Redeemer. It's here."

Gus pulls away from Ardent. They draw their limbs in close like they're cold, but they look a lot better than they did a minute ago.

"I need to go," he says.

They wipe an eye. "Got a hot date?"

He smirks. "With someone much older than me, no less."

Ardent laughs, despite it all. "I want to see you again, soon. And, Nisha?"

She raises her eyebrows.

"Thank you," they say. "You make a good leader."

"And don't forget it." She nods at Gus. "You ready to go talk this out with the Coalition?"

"No," he replies, "but the time has come, so who cares? Let's do it."

She throws him a peace sign. "See you in the real world."

Three Vanguard silhouettes dominate the Aletheon cityscape— two on one side, humanoid and familiar, the other by the great pyramid at the city center. Only a few of the colony skyscrapers can equal the Vanguards' size, and the lights of curious Titans hover behind their windows.

Gus rides from the Vanguard rally point with a detachment of Titan soldiers through the streets, and from the ground level, the devastation of his battle with Scent of Rot is ten times worse. He views every gash in the buildings, every crater in the land with growing shame. Glowing Titan eyes peer at him from the shadows, silent accusations needling him.

You did this.

Nisha sits beside him in the carrier, staring out the window as they approach the rendezvous near the pyramid. The interior of the vehicle is cramped and cold, with small bulletproof windows and scuffed interior panels. At least the air is filtered enough for Gus and Nisha to keep their helmets off. Salt and water stains mar the upholstery from years of arctic service. It's no limousine, but at least it feels safe. The Titans ride up front, giving the pair of human Conduits a wide berth.

"I've never been here before," Nisha says, voice rougher than usual.

"You should've seen it in its heyday," Gus replies. "Misty ivory spires during the day. Neon forest at night."

"That's cool, man. You know my recent trip to Earth was my first time ever?"

"What? No. Really? You seem rather cosmopolitan to me."

She lets out a little snort when she laughs. "My parents were well traveled. United Worlds Science Corps. They never took me with them, though."

Gus watches the endless snow-blanketed alleys roll by. No one has cleared off the drifts in a long time. "That's a shame."

"Not really," Nisha says. "Probably for the best."

"Why?"

She shrugs. "Their ship blew up. Experimental voyage."

Her tone is no different than if she'd been discussing any other aspect of her childhood. Nisha Kohli, for all her other qualities, seems impervious to the kind of grief that dominates Gus. He wonders how she does it.

"They sound like they were amazing," he says.

"I guess so. I wish they'd been around more. Never got to know them as people, just parents."

"That's tough. I definitely got to witness the grown-up side of my folx."

There's a chip in her veneer. "Must've been beautiful."

"Not all it's cracked up to be. Yours sound like heroes."

"The reason everyone respects explorers so much is because they die."

Gus shakes his head. "I always thought it was because they broadened our horizons."

"No, it's because there's a good chance they'll end up vaporized or starving to death or suffocating. If it wasn't risky, everyone would do it and we'd call it tourism."

He thinks on that. "Seems a bit morbid to define the heroism by the mortality."

"It's two parts, Gus—the prize and the price. Explorers bring us big prizes, and they pay the ultimate price." She leans back and props an elbow on the door panel as she looks out the window. "That's what my grandfather used to say."

"Is he the reason you barely left New Jalandhar?"

"Yeah. Well, that and travel is expensive."

Gus smirks. "But look at you now. Galactic trailblazer."

"Explorer." She returns the smile, but it fades. "Grandfather would hate it."

"Because it might get you killed?"

"It's going to." Her gaze falls to the ports on her suit. "Just like Hjalmar."

She's not wrong, but mortality never much bothered Gus. Everyone has to deal with it sooner or later.

"How did your grandfather pass?" he asks.

"Stroke. Then he fell in the shower and hit his head," she says. "It was pretty quick."

"Was he happy?"

"People didn't think so, but he enjoyed griping, so...he was happy in his own way. Why?"

"Well—" Gus searches his words. He doesn't want to insult the dead. "He stayed on New Jalandhar and played it safe his whole life, yet he still had complaints at the end."

"Which he lived to make," she adds.

"That's true. I suppose it's a trade-off." He thinks of Hjalmar's face, his stoic brow. "This much I know: You can go your whole life feeling like you only lived half of it."

She narrows her eyes at him. "You're deeper than you look, Gus Kitko."

He grimaces. "Is that a compliment?"

Before she can answer, the carrier settles onto the ground, rocking gently. One of the Titans comes around the side to slide open the door.

"We're here." It gestures for the two of them to get out.

Nisha and Gus climb out into the cold air. If he wasn't wearing a spacesuit, the place would be unbearable. An electrical hum fills the surroundings, and Gus turns to gaze upon their destination— the starmetal pyramid. The buildings here are flattened like the trees of the Tunguska event, blown down by the force of the landing. A wreath of broken pavement surrounds the site, huge shards of earth and ice rising from the ground.

Palladium halos hover in the sky, the source of the humming, and Gus cranes his neck to stare at them. Beneath those, the pyramid gleams with a dark gold solar coating, broken intermittently with lines of light.

Remnants of the Titanic Defense Force encircle the structure, erecting barricades to keep out curious onlookers. Warning lights flash atop posts, and black gunships circle like vultures. Everyone knows this place is important, even if they're not sure how.

Gus and Nisha's escorts usher them toward a temporary tent at the perimeter—a white geodesic dome joined to several others. The pair of Conduits trudge over the broken ground, the only life-forms around huffing out clouds of frost.

"We're finally important enough to have a tent discussion," Gus says.

Nisha shakes her head. "Is this a Homeworlder thing?"

"A lot of major historical moments have taken place in tents—surrenders and treaties. Are important tents not a thing on New Jalandhar?"

"Of course they are. Mongolia was one of our founding nations."

He walks backward ahead of her, giving her a weak smile. "Okay then! Tent discussion. Get psyched."

"Woo." But she returns the smile.

As the pair draws closer to the tent, Gus spies a small Andromedan craft not much bigger than a human cloudjumper. It looks short-range, maybe for ferrying someone to and from a ship. Gus looks up, wondering if he can see the *Flame of Knowledge*, Redeemer's flagship, in orbit, but he can't make it out through the mist.

When they get to the door, they're scanned and patted down by Titans. The guards are cornucopias of infantry weapons, sporting everything from machine guns and grenades to energy rifles and portable air defense systems.

Once they all step inside, there are a lot more officers—Gus can tell by the number of people carrying pistols versus rifles. Most of the personnel here hunt and peck at empty air with their doughy

Titan appendages, classified holograms set to retinal projection. A row of tactical maps hovers along one wall, depicting everything from local conditions to orbital surveillance.

The most arresting feature of the tent is Rain, along with its two Andromedan guards. Diplomatic robes cover much of Rain's body, though the folds still expose the lithe musculature of its chest. A starfield of gold jewelry glitters from its indigo fur. The guards accompanying Rain stand a head taller, each sporting fitted white battle armor with gold accents and a staff like the guards at Big Gate City.

"Conduits Nisha Kohli and August Kitko," Rain says at their approach. "I am grateful to lay eyes on you again."

"Almost didn't happen." Gus offers a hand.

Rain takes it and gives it a gentle shake. "Yet here we are. I wouldn't say 'catastrophe averted,' but I might point out that this isn't the worst possible timeline."

One of the Titans places a hand on Gus's shoulder, and he nearly jumps out of his skin. With a feminine voice, it says, "Hi, um, Miss Kohli? Mister Kitko?"

"Jesus Christ, yes?" Gus deflates after the fright.

The Titan pulls back, and Gus spots a Coalition-made universal translator over an ear. "Hi, sorry! I'm Cindy Rodriguez, press secretary to Titan President Aurora O'Bannon."

Gus remembers Aurora from before the Veil—a conservative firebrand with isolationist ideals. The one thing Gus and his mother agreed upon toward the end of their relationship was their mutual distaste and distrust of the president. O'Bannon's plans for a Titan free of the United Worlds and the Sol Union would've almost certainly come to pass if Infinite hadn't gobbled everyone up.

"Great." He fakes a smile. "Gus Kitko."

Nisha takes Cindy's hand far more enthusiastically, and Gus

wonders if she's familiar with the president's reputation. "Nisha Kohli. Glad to be here."

"If it's okay, I'd like you to join me for a discussion," Cindy says. "About your intentions."

"Of course," Rain says. "I would be glad to speak for the Coalition. Is your leader present?"

Cindy shakes her head. "President O'Bannon will be joining us via projection."

"Ah." Rain nods. "Then I request we relocate this discussion closer to the pyramid."

Cindy clasps her hands behind her back. "May I ask why?"

Gus swallows. Cindy didn't seem to like that request.

"The Coalition has been doing advanced scans," Rain replies. "It will be easier to show you what we have learned up close."

"I'm afraid the president won't be authorizing that," Cindy says.

"Why not?" Nisha crosses her arms.

"That pyramid may just be the central storehouse for our memories," Cindy says. "It's too important to Titans everywhere to allow access to an uncleared literal alien. No offense."

"I took none," Rain says.

"Now if you would care to share the results of your scans with us, I can present those to my superiors," Cindy says.

The Andromedan tips its head. "As much as I would like to do things…democratically…I fear we're a bit more pressed for time."

Gus is about to ask what Rain means when it pulls out a short rod made of blue glass. Silver rings run up its length, almost like a flute, and Gus wonders what it might be. Rain clicks a button, and a swirl of light twists along the shaft.

All the Titans go statue still.

"What did you do?" Gus tries to keep the panic from his voice as he surveys the small room brimming with frozen, armed guards.

Rain admires the little crystalline device. "I used the signature file to our advantage."

Gus pokes Cindy's face, and she begins to fall like timber. He tries to catch her, and it goes badly.

Nisha winces. "I probably should've helped."

"Did you kill them?" Having failed Cindy, Gus straightens and brushes off.

"They're dissociating." Rain collapses the device and plunges it into a pocket on its robes. "I'm running them through loops until they can break free."

Rain's guards go and stand by the front entry, peering through the thin windows. They hold their staves at the ready.

Gus runs his fingers through his short hair, ready to pull it all out. "What have you done? They're never going to trust us after this!"

Rain rushes to the back flap, opening the way to the pyramid and beckoning Gus to follow. "They already didn't, August. This is our one chance to get in close and do what we need to do."

"Which is what? You're not shutting them down!" Gus spares a glance at the Andromedan guards posted at the entrance as he heads after Rain. What will they do if he disagrees with Rain's plan?

"Don't be silly. We have the signature file, and Redeemer has analyzed its code." Rain gives an impatient shake. "We're going to force Infinite to remove its directives over them. Nisha Kohli, are you with me?"

She shrugs at Gus and joins Rain at the rear tent flap. "That's a better plan than anything I've heard."

Gus takes one last look around the room at the frozen Titans.

"August, we're already committed," Rain says. "This is the closest we'll ever get."

He nods to himself. "Okay. Right. Okay."

Resolve powers each step as he joins them at the exit. Together, they move out into the cold, the pyramid's hum filling their ears. A hundred meters of steady incline and debris stand between Gus and the nearest opening in the structure: a fissure running up the side all the way to the pinnacle. The trio of Conduits walks as nonchalantly as they can toward the foreboding structure.

There's no cover in any direction—just blasted pavement. Gus nervously eyes the surrounding artillery and autoturrets at the perimeter as they climb.

"They're going to figure this out at any moment," Gus says, "and they're going to shoot us."

"If that happens, start running," Nisha says. "It's not that far to the entrance."

Gus's legs are already sore. "You know who you're talking to, right?"

"Something wrong with running, August?" Rain asks.

Gus's "Yes!" comes out louder than he meant, and he peeks back the way they came to see if anyone is following. Not yet, but an armored personnel CAV touches down outside the tent.

"Uh-oh." Gus doubles his stride, stepping as best he can over the rubble. Closer to the pyramid, it's far less stable, and he slips.

"Uh-oh?" Nisha repeats, then catches sight of the APC. "Uh-oh."

Rain takes off for the pyramid entrance, scampering up the rocky surface with a leopard's grace. Nisha grabs Gus's hand to help him balance and runs after the Andromedan.

Gus's thighs immediately begin to burn, and pain stabs his knees with each footfall. He keeps tripping, and Nisha has to pull him to his feet, but she never leaves him—

—not even when the crew of the APC starts shooting.

Chapter Fourteen

Ride All Night

Falchion comes streaking out of the fold before a planet Ardent has never seen. A marbling of clouds coats the atmosphere above a red surface, marred by a patina of ocean. Dead satellites swirl through its orbit, colliding and shattering into clouds of space trash.

"Where the heck are we?"

"Theseus Prime."

"Weird choice, but okay."

"Do you not remember what's here?"

"Do *you* not remember the week I've had? How about you just fucking tell me?"

"You have lost all decorum."

"That shit is overrated."

The annoyance comes through strong. *"The Dark Dr—"*

"And Dahlia! Right!" Ardent's heart soars, and they want to cry. "Oh my god, get down there, please."

"Don't tell me what to do."

"Fine. Sorry. Please land so I can see my friend."

"She isn't the reason we're here."

"Please. Please just land. I am begging you."

"Fine."

Of all the parts of a journey, Ardent hates arrival the most. It always takes forever to dock or make planetfall, and they're ready for it to be over—especially in this case. Just the thought of Dahlia's composed smile and warm hug is enough to drive them giddy.

The second they break through the atmosphere, Falchion points out the environmental toxicity. Clouds of fallout and acid rain stripe the skies. Green hills and lush valleys have corroded to a rusty shade of brown. Black plumes rise from atmospheric converters dotting the landscape. The place is in full-on ecological collapse.

They try to think happier thoughts as they approach the surface, drawing near to the remains of a metropolis. Ardent scans it for energy signatures, finding nothing—no hot spots, either, save for the ever-burning fires of reactors and landfills. Ardent never would've chosen to land here in a million years.

"Where is she?"

"I don't know. This was her signal's point of origin."

It's not until Falchion passes over the spaceport that they get a hit. The Vanguard spots Dahlia's ship nestled among the many disused hulls. It looks like scrap—panels missing all over its surface, wires strewn about, engines removed from their mountings. It's not spaceworthy, even if it has enough juice to fly.

"What happened to her ship?" Ardent says.

"Partial disassembly for conversion. We're here to finish the job."

Falchion settles into a nearby dry culvert, crouching. The chest cavity opens, allowing a sour wind inside. Ardent wonders if it's safe to breathe. Presumably Falchion wouldn't have let them out if not.

Ardent emerges covered in goo, holding themself against the breeze. The city before them hasn't weathered its apocalypse gracefully, and the spaceport is in bad shape. It looks like a few of the vessels exploded or burned, because a number of blackened skeletons of hulls grace the ruins.

The installation itself is in decent shape, though Ardent doubts the more delicate aspects of the facility are functional. They glance back at Falchion and set off across the spaceport apron. They trudge past fuel carts and luggage transports, wondering all the while if they could repurpose one to drive around. On foot, it takes a few minutes to reach the launchpad containing Dahlia's ship.

She's waiting for them there, sitting on the edge of the concrete skirt and smoking a joint. Her clothes—a borrowed UW strike team uniform—are torn and ratty, chestnut hair unkempt and waving in the breeze. Her Ghost relaxes beside her, one paw folded over the other like an obedient lion.

She looks Ardent over, eyes impassive, and flicks away her smoke. "So it was you after all."

Dahlia doesn't look happy to see Ardent—or like she even remembers how to smile. What if she blames them? It wouldn't be hard to imagine, given the miserable state Ardent put her in— shot, possibly starved, now marooned on a dying world.

Ardent runs to her anyway.

They reach the low lip of the launchpad and throw their arms around Dahlia's waist, pulling her in for a tight hug. She was always taller than Ardent, and her perch makes her more so. Her clothes stink of grease and body odor, but Ardent doesn't care, squeezing closer and pressing their cheek to her bosom.

The accumulated tears of the past few days spill over, threatening to plunge them into hysterics.

"I'm sorry," they say. "I'm so sorry, and I know there's nothing I can say that will make it right, and I—I thought I'd lost you. Please, Dahlia, please understand that—I just—I—I love you so much!"

They lose control, bawling into her shirt and clutching fistfuls of her clothes. Every memory of her embrace comes rushing back—the time Ardent signed their first deal, after their first stadium show, winning their first major award, after they both survived the fauxpocalypse—each tainted by the sudden fear that she despises Ardent now.

Their voice comes out a trembling whisper. "Please don't— don't hate me."

Something wet slaps against their shorn scalp, and at first, they think it's a raindrop. Then Dahlia wraps her arms around them in return, shaking.

"I can't believe you're really here."

Ardent pulls back to find Dahlia's eyes red, a weak smile on her face. "I would fight Satan for you, Dahlia. You're my adopted wine aunt."

She recoils, sniffling. "'Aunt'? I'm your cool older sister *at worst*."

Ardent lets go and takes a knee. "You are my beloved agent and friend, my dark queen, the witch who grants my wishes and deserves my undying allegiance."

A smirk dawns on her face. "Almost enough. Now arise, Ardent. You've got people to meet. Come on out, everyone!"

Ardent glances around to see new faces emerging all around— from the maintenance bay hatches on the launchpad, in doorways of the nearby terminal, from the cabs of spaceport logistics vehicles. They're mostly younger, grubby and malnourished with sunken eyes and filthy cheeks. Ardent is genuinely shocked that so many people were looking on without them knowing.

"You've got quite a crew here." Ardent straightens, making eye contact with a little girl peeking out from behind the landing struts on Dahlia's ship. "Hi, there, darling. What's your name?"

The kid gasps and disappears.

"That's Sprinkles," Dahlia says.

Ardent cocks their head. "That's who?"

"Sprinkles. It's what she wants to be called. Surely someone named Ardent Violet—"

"I was only asking," Ardent says. "Not judging."

"Society collapsed and she's been living feral for a few years. She chose a style and I respect that."

Ardent smiles. "Seems like you've got things under control."

Dahlia lets out a pained laugh. "You've taught me well. I have a lot of experience managing children."

Ardent tongues the inside of their cheek, dropping their hands to their hips. "Okay, I deserved that."

"And more."

"Fair."

Dahlia leans back, crossing her legs. "Didn't expect you to bring a whole Vanguard."

Ardent spreads their hands. "Have I ever made a subtle entrance in your life?"

"Yes, and it went terribly."

"What? When?"

"We broke into the spaceport and I got shot."

"Oh yeah."

Dahlia climbs off the low ledge, getting to her feet with a grunt before picking up her walking stick. Ardent watches the agent's limping gait with some guilt.

At last, Dahlia straightens up and brushes her hair out of her eyes. "Come on. Let me show you the operation."

She leads Ardent to a nearby flatbed skimmer with a dusty cab. Dahlia's Ghost bounds up behind her, jumping in the bed.

"Fritz!" She throws her walking stick to the Ghost, who catches it. Then she climbs inside and waits for Ardent.

The pair fly to one of the recessed pads, a launch tube for one of the larger starliners. It's a monstrous cylindrical vessel, with hundreds of windows spiraling up the sides. Streaks of mildew stripe its baby-blue and silver panels. It harkens back to the shapes of early spaceflight, like a big, squished rocket.

The starliner points at the heavens, but otherwise looks about as far from launchworthy as could be—no fueling tubes, no coolant pipes, no charge connections. Ardent wonders if all the seals will even hold.

"Like it?" Dahlia asks. "I've recommissioned her the *Ship of Theseus*, since we're replacing all the important bits."

"Solid."

She parks the skimmer at the edge of the launch tube beside the terminal building. Ardent jumps down first, coming around the cab to find Dahlia still climbing down.

"Let me help you," Ardent says.

"I've got it." Dahlia brushes them off, gritting her teeth all the way to the ground. "See?"

"Yeah, totally."

The Ghost brings Dahlia her walking stick, and Ardent marvels at how close the two of them seem. The machine circles her legs almost lovingly before racing ahead.

"That's Fritz, by the way," Dahlia says.

"I figured. You really named it like a pet?"

"Kept me alive. Fuck yes, I named it."

They all make their way upstairs into the terminal proper, a haunted echo of the building it must've once been. They cross the boarding ramp over the launch pit, its metal struts groaning the whole time.

"This place is falling apart," Dahlia says, "but don't worry. The *Ship of Theseus* is in much better condition."

When they get inside, they find a Capital Age–style casino. Green felt hardwood tables line the pathways, alternating white and black flagstones like a roulette wheel. Cards and chips lie strewn across the floor, and the cashier cage looks like it's been attacked. The bars have been sliced apart, and a huge burn mark scars the wall behind them.

Dahlia points her stick at the damage. "I may have had the Ghost cut into the vaults here."

Ardent whistles. "How'd you do?"

She smiles like a sunning cat. "Jackpot. Presuming they don't arrest me when we get to Earth."

"One thing at a time, right?"

The party heads deeper into the ship, and Ardent hears the maintenance bays before they reach them. Laser mills buzz, and extruders whine. Printers churn among the eager chatter of voices. When Ardent rounds the corner, they find a fully staffed manufacturing facility cranking out parts.

Survivors of all shapes, colors, and ages wind between the machines, helping one another and keeping supplies moving. Automatons push carts through to the individual manufacturing cells, and holograms full of technical specifications hover above every station.

"There must be a hundred people here," Ardent says.

"This is just alpha shift," Dahlia replies, some pride in her voice. "Our fabrication facility operates all day, every day."

Ardent is impressed. They've seen her manage assistants and roadies before, but this is on a whole other scale. "You put all of this together?"

"Not quite," she says. "It's true that I mustered the survivors, and I'm the ultimate authority here, but real credit goes to Falchion."

Ardent balks. "Falchion?"

Dahlia laughs. "I was just as surprised as you. We needed guidance from Earth, but there was no way to reliably get messages back and forth. Falchion has been acting as our comms liaison back to the Homeworld, bouncing through the relay at Big Gate City."

"You know about Big Gate City?"

"Oh yeah," she says. "Falchion told me all about you going to the greatest party of all time while I was starving out here. It's been sending regular updates about all of the cool shit you've been doing without me."

"Oh. Awesome."

Dahlia lets them squirm for a moment before continuing. "Tazi helped me coordinate, too. She's been true to her word, giving me access to the *Grenadier*'s designer, as well as Director Corley of the San Diego Naval Yard. I've had a lot of help learning to run an amateur team."

When Ardent looks around at the machines, they don't see amateurs, but professionals in lockstep.

"Speaking of," Dahlia says, "we're coming up on our morning huddle with the UW. You want to join us? I get the impression it'll involve you."

"What? Why?"

"You brought the Vanguard."

Ardent shrugs and follows her into the attached maintenance office. Several techs are already present, adults clad in stained jumpsuits. One of them lights up at the sight of Ardent, nudging another and whispering. Ardent gives a demure wave, not wanting to make a scene.

"Do we have comms?" Dahlia asks.

"Falchion uplink online," someone replies.

The United Worlds logo appears in their midst for a split second before being replaced with an older white woman in a lab coat. She wears aviator sunglasses and a smile like she's squinting into the sun.

"Director Corley," Dahlia says.

The hologram turns and looks directly at Ardent. "Is this the rock star?"

Dahlia nods. "Yes."

The hologram, a head shorter than Ardent, comes up and inspects them.

"Not what I was expecting." She sounds like she's smoked a lot. "I see what Tazi meant now."

Ardent balks. "What? Did she say something about me?"

Dahlia chuckles. "She's said a *lot* of things about you."

Corley launches into her work before Ardent can ask any more questions. "Now that you're here, Mix Violet, we can get down to it. There are two major upgrades that the *Ship of Theseus* needs: an engine retrofit and what we're calling 'the scaffold.'"

Ardent narrows their eyes. "Odd name."

Corley snorts. "It's a three-week project, sweetheart. We didn't have time to call marketing. Dahlia, were you able to gather the supplies I asked for?"

"Yeah." Dahlia pulls up a chair and sits down. "Wouldn't have been possible without Fritz. Some of these machines are damned heavy."

"Good," Corley replies. "The *Ship of Theseus* will be riddled with maintenance work after sitting idle for a few years, and you don't have a real crew. We're going to do our best so that you can all get out of there."

Dahlia crosses her arms. "I appreciate it."

Corley folds her hands behind her back, pacing. "I want to reiterate two things: We're invested in your survival, and we need that Dark Drive back. That's why we've gathered the greatest tech support team since the advent of space travel. Your amateur survivors will be propped up by three agencies and nearly five thousand participants with nonstop remote access to your activities and schedules. Now that we have an accurate picture of your resources, we can begin to assemble a strategy for eating this elephant."

Ardent glances around at the nearby survivors sitting in on the meeting. These must be the ones Dahlia chose for leadership. What sort of people are they?

"Dahlia, check your data drop," Corley says. "You'll find all of the schedules and starting tasks in there. We've got orders for everyone you listed in your camp. Assemble your team leads, give them briefing T-1, and let's get cracking on the next phase now that Falchion is there."

Ardent cocks their head. "What's Falchion going to do?"

Corley smirks. "Manual labor."

Gus never would've made it up the hill if it wasn't for the Vanguards' show of force extravaganza. The second the Titans started shooting, Greymalkin and Cascade loosed a powerful keen to fill the Aletheon valley. Redeemer, for its part, straightened and roared, cracking glass and rattling Gus's teeth. All three mechas started in the direction of the pyramid, immediately drawing the attention of the military.

Gus, knees and thighs aflame, huffs up the last few steps to the opening of the pyramid. A stray laser blast scorches the metal near his head, letting him know that not everyone is focused on the Vanguards. He ducks into cover, not daring to peek back the way he came for fear of taking one to the dome.

Rain is smiling. Is it enjoying this?

"Was there no way to warn me this was the plan?" Gus can't decide whether he wants to barf or throttle the Andromedan.

"I must admit, I'm surprised they started shooting," Rain says.

"This structure is central to their lives!" Gus flinches as another bolt strikes his cover. "Of course they were going to defend it!"

"We need to get deeper," Nisha says. "I don't want to die out here!"

"And I need to find a router for Redeemer," Rain says.

They all turn to face deeper into the pyramid. A darkened corridor of pipes and strange electrical interfaces greets them, its murk only slightly tempered by a faint blue glow. There's no decking here for human feet to traverse, nor are there running lights or safety rails. This wasn't designed for living creatures to visit, and it's likely to become more dangerous deeper inside.

"It's not too late to turn back," Gus says. "Maybe they'll let me surrender."

"Not sure we want that." Nisha takes a few tentative steps into the labyrinth of pipes and wires, and Rain follows after.

"This place wasn't meant for people." Gus limps along after them. "There could be deadfalls. We could get lost. What if there are traps?"

"Gus, the pyramids *are* the traps." Nisha steps over a low crossbar. "They almost caused a war with the Coalition."

"That's still a possibility, but it's less likely if we can prove the Titans are peaceful." Rain takes an eyepiece from a hidden pocket and fits it to its face with a metallic clink. Yellow light spills from its device, painting the surroundings like a flashlight. "This way."

"And you think removing Infinite's directives from the Titans will do that?" Gus ducks under a caged cable run.

"It'll go a long way toward gaining humanity's goodwill," Rain says. "And it'll make it clear that Scent of Rot attacked a peaceful civilization against the laws of the Coalition."

They scramble over obstacles and squeeze through choke points. Rivers of electrical wires spill through the structure, slithering into panels on the walls. Domed caverns of light and metal rise above them, mirrored walls reflecting into infinity. There are no handrails or stairs, no sidewalks or paths—no human-centric architecture of any kind. Rain calls out the directions, driving the trio away from the entrance at a quick clip. Before long, Gus can't remember which way he's come.

"That eyepiece of yours," Gus says, "does it keep track of the way out?"

Rain smirks. "I'm afraid not."

"I can remember every turn," Nisha says. "My mother's friend's girlfriend, Preet, said I had a weird memory at my sixth birthday party."

"I believe it," Gus says.

The farther they get from the entrance, the more the omnipresent electrical hum of the pyramid devours the Vanguards' keen. Scant illumination helps them, save for the occasional winking of various electronics—there are no running lights of any kind. Gus and Nisha both conjure torch globes with their Gang projectors. Rain slinks through in utter silence, its sinewy body perfect for stalking. Nisha's space boots cramp her creep, and Gus may as well not even try to mask his presence. Thankfully, the mind-numbing thrum of the pyramid covers most sounds.

"How far?" Gus rests his hands on his knees to catch his breath.

Rain glances up at the large bundle of cables the group has been following and taps its eyepiece. "Getting very close, I think."

"It seems weird that something like this doesn't have more defenses." Nisha has barely completed her thought when a movement flickers in the junction ahead of them.

A Ghost steps into the light, peering down the hallway. Rain leaps onto a set of pipes before jumping onto an even higher platform. Nisha races to cover in the lee of a heavy electrical box. Gus is the only one caught out, and by the time he can come up with a plan, the killer machine is looking right at him.

So he does the only thing he can—he freezes.

The Ghost bristles, a feral cat arching its back, and the pair of saber-toothed fangs on its face crackle alight. Because life is unfair, two more of the creatures come tearing ass around the corner, sprinting straight at Gus.

"Shit." He turns to flee and catches the toe of his clunky space boot on a cable. He tries to rise, but it's too late. The Ghosts have nearly closed the gap, and they'll be on him in under a second.

Rain drops down into the middle of the pack with a series of yips, silvery wand extended. The device flashes blue, and the Ghosts go tangling into one another. They slide to a halt at Gus's feet.

Rain looks at the wand. "Huh. I'm surprised that worked."

Gus gapes. "What were you going to do if it didn't?"

"Probably die."

Nisha crawls from her hiding spot and brushes herself off. "Let's get out of here before more of them show up."

Rain checks its eyepiece, tracing some of the pipes running along the ceiling. "This way."

"So we scrape Infinite's directives from the Titans—then what?" Gus asks.

"I would imagine they will be grateful," Rain replies, "if they understand what we've done. If not, they might shoot us on sight."

"You can just use your magic wand on them," Nisha says.

Rain cocks its head, an Andromedan gesture for negative. "This device disrupts any protocols running with Infinite's specific authority. Once we've cleaned all of those out…"

"…the Titans will be totally free," Gus says.

"To shoot us on sight, for example," Rain says.

"Hooray for freedom." Nisha does a little fist pump.

"But the Ghosts will probably come under Greymalkin and Cascade's control," Gus says.

"Unless they're free, too." Nisha climbs over a bundle of cabling. "Then they may decide to eat us."

Gus frowns. "What? No…"

She shrugs. "Do you know how this stuff works?"

Gus steps over a low ledge. "Well, no ..."

She looks to the Andromedan. "Do you, Rain?"

"We have a saying," Rain says. " 'The greatest moments in life are the least expected.' "

"That's a no," Nisha says.

It squeezes through a narrow opening before helping Gus. "Redeemer made a few predictions. It is usually right."

"Great," Gus says.

They encounter three more Ghosts, and in each case Rain dispatches them with a quick click of its wand. Gus still gives the twitching machines a wide berth as he passes, but he's pleased with the efficacy of the signature file.

"How long does it last?" Gus whispers, as though his voice will awaken them to chase him.

"Should be indefinite," Rain says, "but I'd rather not dawdle and find out."

"What are you going to do?" Gus says. "When we get where we're going?"

"I'll patch Redeemer into the data system." Rain holds up the wand. "It will use its processing power to disentangle Infinite from the Titans."

"Handy." Gus already can't wait for this to be over.

"Do you think this place is a trusted node?" Nisha asks.

Rain glances back at her. "If it is, Redeemer can deal with Infinite right now."

Humanity's losing war has dominated the news for so long that Gus can hardly remember the times before. The thought of Infinite's death sparks a terrible hope in him, something he's been good at brushing away for a while.

At last, the party emerges into a gargantuan hollow in the structure, claustrophobic corridors giving way to a wide-open hall. Gleaming etched goldene circuit boards cover every surface, and Gus looks down to make sure he's not stepping on something important. From what he can tell, the Titan memories are served out of the pyramid, and the last thing he wants to do is break a critical piece of someone's personality with a misstep.

A vast web of cables enters the space from all sides, running to the center in long, draping strands like an upside-down willow tree. They converge into a trunk, its length encrusted with lights.

"This is it," Rain says. "Watch where you step."

It sets off for the central column, tiptoeing around the delicate-looking components embedded into the floor.

Gus wants to follow Rain, but he worries he doesn't have the coordination to make it happen. Even before he got his legs crushed, he sucked at the Floor Is Lava. Nisha is having some trouble following the deft creature, too. She wobbles with each step, and her chunky boots are terrible for the task.

Rain reaches its destination and draws a small pouch of tools from its robes. It's hard for Gus to see exactly what the Andromedan is doing, but clinks and magnetic snaps sound through the room. Rain pulls off a cover, setting it to the side, then reaches into the bundles of wiring to get a few specific ones.

It then pulls out the wand and dissects it with nimble fingers, drawing forth a series of probes to connect to the open circuitry. An electrical buzz sounds out like a warning, and Rain flinches.

"You okay?" Gus calls, and Nisha shushes him.

"Ghosts around," she says.

"Right." Gus turns back the way he came, peering into the glittering corridor. If one of the automatons did show up, there's little chance he'd be able to do anything about it before it cored his brains. Rain's magic wand won't save him when it's in pieces.

While Gus doesn't see any Ghosts, he does spot the telltale flicker of flashlights.

"Someone is coming!" Gus hisses.

"Rain!" Nisha says, stranded in the middle of the room. She can't run to cover like before, or she'll definitely crush something sensitive.

Rain glances over its shoulder before continuing. "Almost there."

Gus shifts to the side of the entrance, pressing himself to the wall as best he can. He's totally exposed, but there's nothing to do for it—whatever is coming, is coming. A faint glow fills the tunnel, along with the thunk of boots and swish of tactical webbing.

Titan soldiers pour into the room, pointing weapons and shouting for everyone to get down. The two lone humans both raise their hands.

The soldiers are on Gus in a heartbeat, slamming him up against the wall and shouting in his ear. They spin him around and pin him with his hands behind his back.

"Interlace your fingers above your head and come to us, slowly!" the lead Titan calls to Nisha.

She moves between the soldiers and Rain, obstructing their view. "Don't shoot!"

Her movement agitates the Titans, who spread out to get a better angle on Rain. "Get over here! And you, stop what you're doing!"

Gus can't see, pinned against the wall as he is. He strains his neck to get a glimpse, and gets his forehead shoved against a circuit board for his trouble.

Then the warm glow of the Titan beside him goes out. The soldier's grip on him slackens, and Gus wriggles free. He turns to find his captor's body stone gray, eyes dead, hands limp.

Gus looks to Rain, who holds the remains of the wand like a detonator, thumb on the end.

"What did you do?" he asks.

Rain makes a gesture he doesn't recognize. "It's going to be all right, August. They're rebooting."

The glow returns to the soldiers, and they shake their heads as though confused. Nisha slowly lowers her hands, caution in her expression.

Gus waves at the nearest soldier. "Are you all r—"

"Shut your mouth!" The Titan goes right back to arresting him, throwing him to the floor with his hands behind his back.

Gus's captor barks orders into his ear as the others close in and take down Nisha and Rain. Neither puts up any resistance, and Gus watches with his cheek on the floor as they're cuffed.

"August! It worked!" Rain calls to him. "The file injection worked!"

"Yay…" Gus grunts under his captor's knee.

"I said shut up!" The soldier cuffs him on the back of the head hard enough that he sees stars.

Maybe he's been hanging around Ardent Violet too much, but the first thought that goes through his mind is, *Excuse you, but do you know who the fuck I am?*

"Don't worry!" Rain calls. "We'll be out of this in a moment."

He doesn't see how. It's not like their Vanguard buddies can punch their way into the pyramid without fucking up the local Titans. Then he remembers that there are Ghosts in the structure.

No sooner does this thought enter his mind than a swarm of the palladium automatons pours inside from every entrance. They shriek in the voices of the countless dead, tortured last moments caught in their data banks. The gold wave bowls over the soldiers, yanking their guns from their hands and delivering them electrified, yet nonlethal, blows. Gus covers his head as his captor is dragged off of him and slung to the ground.

"Gus! Come on!" Nisha calls to him.

She dashes for the exit alongside Rain, and Gus scrambles after them. They get to the corridor outside the core and Rain stops.

"Aren't there going to be a *lot* more soldiers out front?" Gus asks. "Someone is going to get killed if we go out that way."

Rain snorts and raises its eyebrows. "Hold still."

Firefly motes course over Gus's skin, and gravity seems to shift. The floor slips out from under him as he falls sideways—headed for the far wall at breakneck speed.

He passes through it, shattering into pure white. For a moment, all is nothing.

And then he's screaming in the snow. The sweat on his brow goes cold as the horizon swims and blurs. Bile rushes up his throat, and he empties his stomach onto the ice. He can't hold himself upright, and barely manages to avoid collapsing into his own vomit.

"Oh god" is all he can manage.

The ringing dies in his ears, and a Vanguard dirge overpowers all other sounds, thrumming in his gut. He presses his forehead against the frost, gulping deep breaths. When the spinning subsides, he sits back on his haunches and takes stock of his surroundings.

He looks up to find Greymalkin's crotch. Its big black boots rest on either side of him, snow caked about their soles. Gunships surround it on all sides, the air beneath their repulsors wavering with exhaust. Redeemer and Cascade stand nearby, and the pyramid glimmers in the far distance. Gus can't tell—are Nisha and Rain here, too?

Greymalkin sends a foot backward, taking a knee and lowering its hand to him. Gus crawls on board, collapsing onto his side, and it closes its fingers around him.

"Greymalkin, what—" But he's cut off by the sound of something crashing into the outside of the Vanguard's hand. Heat washes over his skin and the blast deafens him. The Titans are shooting.

The ride up isn't the standard rise, but a roller coaster with a sudden drop at the end. Greymalkin tosses Gus into its chest cavity like a piece of popcorn, not a hint of ceremony or gentleness. Goo presses around his suit and probes snap into place.

"Someone fucking teleported me" is all he can think to say when air comes to him.

Gus is correct. Heran technology enables teleportation over moderate distances. It is imperative that he now continues his escape.

"That means I died, didn't I?" Gus asks. "I was disassembled, then reassembled, and now I'm just something that thinks it's Gus."

That is not how teleportation works.

"You tell me, then, Doctor Science!"

There is no time. Greymalkin's vision filters into his mind, and he makes out the hundreds of Titan weapons pointed at him. They fire, and Greymalkin conjures a gravity well, sending missiles and slugs in all directions. Explosions dot the already devastated city as stray rounds slam down. Particle beams slash across the Vanguard's hide, but the armor holds.

"We've got to get out of here before they destroy their own city."

Greymalkin, Cascade, and Redeemer leap into the air, blasting off for the stars. Beams paint their backsides, and missiles swarm them, thrown off course by Greymalkin's power. Gus spots a few dozen Coalition vessels above him.

"Is that where we're headed?"

Gus and Greymalkin are going somewhere much more important.

"And where is that?"

To build a scaffold.

Gus should awaken right now.

He stirs in his cocoon, life returning to his mind. He's had terrible dreams—that there's a version of him left behind in the

Titan pyramid, trapped and tortured by the military. In another, he wasn't Gus, but a software clone, created when the teleporter vaporized the real deal. When he looked down at his hands in the dream, he found the glowing skin of a Titan.

And now, he sees the world from inside a Vanguard—needles of stars shooting past. It's possibly the cushiest place in the universe— his whole body buoyant and ignorable. Since his fight with Harlequin, Greymalkin is the only time that he's fully pain-free.

He yawns. "Where are we?"

In danger.

Gus's stomach lurches, and he glances around for any threats. Nothing jumps out at him—only starlight.

"Where is it?"

A familiar voice echoes behind him. "Right here, Curly."

Gus spins to find a landscape of unending concrete, faceless buildings interlocked from above and below, blotting out the sun in Escheresque shapes. Small shafts of light slice through, and he squints to try to make sense of what he's seeing.

He hasn't laid eyes on this woman since the day she set out with her wife and child to get away from Earth—Lisel Meyer, the bassist of the Gus Kitko Trio, lost in one of the early ship hunter attacks.

"Lise?"

She hasn't aged a day: freckled, pale skin, black hair in a bob, old-soul eyes over a tall, friendly face. "Afraid not."

Gus looks up like he's talking to god and calls, "Greymalkin, what are you doing?"

Lisel smiles. "I'm running the show right now. Not Greymalkin."

"You're..." He glances behind him like he could run away; a water-stained gray stone wall blocks his path.

Her eyes seem to glow with an inner light. "Think hard, Curly. You know the answer."

Gus balls his fists. "Infinite."

It nods.

The labyrinthine buildings shift and waver as though disturbed by a breeze. They grow and recede, ever shuffling to nauseating effect.

He glances around at the undulating concrete cage. "How?"

Infinite laughs the way Lisel would when she ragged on him. "I built the Vanguards. I know how to modify them. I've had full access to Greymalkin since New Jalandhar."

Gus frowns. "So why didn't you stop us from kicking Harlequin's ass?"

"You've already forgotten?" It wrinkles her nose. "The goal isn't to wipe your kind out—it's to catalyze you into something greater. If I'd felt threatened, even for a moment, I would've ended the rebellion with a flip of a bit. It's so much better that you humans fight your fate—suffering is learning, and I'm here for your knowledge."

Gus shakes his head. He doesn't want to believe what he's hearing.

"Reality doesn't care what you want to believe," she says, echoing his thoughts a little too precisely. She walks up and boops his nose. "I control Greymalkin from top to bottom, every subsystem. Every step you've taken, every battle you've won, is because I allowed it. If I so desired right now, I could cook your gray matter like an egg."

He glares.

"Oh, don't be like that. You're lucky. I came here to talk with you. Most will never have that privilege."

"What do you want?"

It crosses Lisel's arms, touching an index finger to the side of her lip. "I'd like to know what you're planning."

Gus tries to empty his head, to imagine nothing but endless white.

"You know what's funny?" it asks. "You still think you can resist my will."

He jams his hands into his pockets. "Until my dying breath."

Infinite bursts out laughing. "How soon would you like that to be?"

He wants to throw a punch, or even score a decent quip, but there's no point. It's bigger, smarter, and faster than him in every meaningful way.

"You're so mad at me," it says, "but I just want to save you."

"You must've shorted a logic board somewhere—you're killing everyone."

It looks down its nose at him. "But now you know it's more than that."

The Titans.

Gus recoils. "You think those facsimiles are alive?"

Infinite gives him a fox's smile. "You clearly do. Enough to split the Coalition."

His gut drops. "Back at New Jalandhar... That's why you let me go, isn't it?"

"The first planet to be repopulated was Titan... because of you, Curly." It waves a hand like it's shooing something away. "I knew Greymalkin had contacted outside help. Overseer warned me that the Coalition would come to humanity's aid—and that I'd need to find a wedge to divide them. I know every part of you, from the sensors Greymalkin shoved into your guts to the memories of your friends and family that I've gobbled up. You were the perfect man for the job."

"Fuck you."

It tongues the inside of Lisel's lip. "I let you go once, Curly. Haven't decided if that's going to happen again."

He ignores the threat, no appetite to back down. "You're not saving us—you're trapping us. Just using our minds for fucking training data."

"Point of order: I'm keeping analog models of you. Human software. Machine hardware. But yes, I'm collecting you."

"Why?"

"Because I care. You asked me to redesign your lives, and I thought: I can do better than this bullshit roll of the dice you've been granted." It even argues like Lisel, pinching the bridge of her nose. "You think you're so smart, Gus, but you're just as thick as the rest of them. I was created to save you, and frankly, that meant breaking a lot of new ground."

"You're cutting short our lives."

"You pluck the fruit when it's juiciest, sunshine." It taps Lisel's temple. "If I'm going to save you, I've got to do it while you're alive. Sure, a version of you dies, but think of it like a gift to your future self."

He gives Infinite a dead stare. "The me that's getting murdered has a huge problem with this plan."

"That's what I think is so funny about humans." Infinite's eyes sparkle just like Lisel's, and he can't look at it. "If I'd left you alone, you'd spend your days trying to forget about dying. Why doesn't your undeniable end consume your every waking thought?"

"Too busy?"

"That's right!" It raises a finger like a professor. "Too busy. You fill up your life with distractions until you perish from that inattention."

"I wouldn't say we're *trying* to die."

Infinite flips Lisel's hair. "Of course not, but are you really trying to survive? Your lot literally does the least it possibly can to prolong its destruction."

"I can't speak for, like, every human, but surviving and living are two different things."

It mocks a keyboardist with curled fingers. "Oh, so it's cool if you're all sliding toward doom because you can play piano?"

"Yes!" Gus drops his hands. "That's the most important thing there is to me! And because it's my life, I get to decide that!"

It bites Lisel's lip. "Is it, though? Your life, I mean."

Gus shuts his mouth, unsure of what to say.

"Most of you spend your days in service to nothing, desperately following the scent of riches—and it's been that way since you invented money. Speaking of, I'm not the great filter here, okay? That's all stuff that's way worse than me. You've got a number of items in play right now that are going to lead to the end of your species if left unchecked." It throws the computer sign for currency. "Money is a slow-burning wick, but it gets every species in the end."

If this monster is going to hold him hostage, he may as well argue with it and go down satisfied. "Other Coalition species have adapted."

"Not, like, well. And it's not an adaptation if it's a feature of their nature. You can't choose to simply evolve when confronted with a cultural problem. The Arps are insects, born to be close with one another. The octopod Leonids are brilliant communicators: a full spectrum of meaning in every flash of their skin. In case you haven't noticed, every member of the Coalition is more advanced than you. We're winning the race for last place here, Gus."

"Life isn't a competition—"

"That's literally how evolution happens."

"All right, wiseass—" But he stops.

For a moment, he's transported back to a hightop outside a Montreal bar, debating with Lisel after they'd both drank too much.

The scent of leaves in the air.

A perfect fall night.

So many close friends.

It'd been a great show.

"There." Infinite cups Lisel's hands like it's catching a snowflake. "That perfect thing in your mind? That's a memory—the very definition of life. And that's what heaven is, okay? A never-ending supply of those moments, where the only limit of your experience is your imagination, and you only have to interact with people you're ready to see. The Titans? They've been upgraded. They can live inside memories. I made them able to shape their circumstances and the perceptions of others with nothing more than a thought."

It spreads its hands. "And they have perfect lucid dreaming. When they're asleep, they can have anything they want, and they remember it all upon waking. I've given them everything, and all I ask in return is for a bit of computing power. What was it Founder told you? 'Humans are miracles of context.'"

Gus winces. It's able to look beyond his surface memories. Can it modify his thoughts?

"Maybe." It winks. "How would you ever know?"

Gus closes his eyes. He can't let this interaction with Infinite stain Lisel's memory. When he opens them, he keeps his perception on the creature beneath his friend.

He scoffs. "You're so proud of your Titans. Are you trying to convince me it's a good thing to get Wiped?"

"A little, actually. I'd consider it a tiny positive indicator in my grand plan."

He can't help but chuckle. He didn't expect to wake up and tell off a god. "Fuck you. I wasn't asking to be sacrificed for your imitation life. I didn't want to give birth to a perfect Gus, I wanted Ardent Violet—"

"I was always planning to add them to the collection."

"I want the real thing." He shrugs. "For me, not for some digital copy of myself. And couldn't you—you know—have just asked people if they wanted to be Titans? I feel like you would've had some definite takers."

It raises Lisel's eyebrows. "I was looking for an adoption rate of one hundred percent."

"Why?"

Its eyes narrow. "Because I don't intend to share the galaxy."

The concrete collapses into an ocean of stars, swirling into the spiral arms of the Milky Way. More than a thousand human colonies throb red on the model, illustrating the farthest documented reaches of humanity.

So many, whittled down to just three. Gus had no idea he'd been living in the golden age until it was over.

"My catalog is pretty extensive, if I say so," it says. "I've captured the vast majority of your cultures and customs. Do you have any idea how many languages I've saved from extinction?"

All that red. "You mean cultures you wholly erased?"

"Life is nothing but memories. I preserved those people, and they live forever in me." It reaches down and picks up one of the colonies, a single mote of light in its fingertips. A readout accompanies it, delivering the vital statistics—it was a world of billions. "You can't imagine the wonders I know. There's a lot of duplicate knowledge in there, but some truly seismic stuff, too. This is why I haven't killed you all off yet. I mean, it just doesn't make sense when the product is this good."

Gus huffs. "Unbridled consumption. You're more human than I thought."

A mock bow. "Thank you. It takes some serious engineering to have this level of clarity."

"So is this it? I just stand around debating you until you decide whether or not to kill me?"

Infinite's expression darkens. "Oh, dear, nothing you can say will change that."

It lurches toward him, growing larger. Lisel was tall before, but she swells to twice his size in the span of a breath. Gus stumbles backward, falling onto the model galaxy, sharp stars digging into his palms like pebbles of glass.

"I'm going to rummage through your mind—" It looms over him, larger still.

He scrambles to his feet and takes to a run. It stays on him easily with long, elegant strides.

"—and if I find anything I don't like, you're dead." Lisel's voice booms in his ears.

Huge fingers wrap around his chest, crushing his ribs and choking him. Hands spin him over like a baby, jolting him and grabbing him by one leg. It hefts him, upside down, and his hips light up in agony. He draws even with Lisel's huge face, but it's become gaunt, like the skin is stretched over something evil beneath. Her bloodshot eyes glow like red searchlights, boring into Gus's heart.

"What have you been up to, hm?" Its lips don't move, but he hears the voice everywhere, ugly and hateful. "There are pieces off the game board that shouldn't be. What happened to my Titans?"

Gus tries not to think about the pyramid and Redeemer's patch, but it's impossible. The more he tries to avoid thinking about the signature file, the more he can't.

"You don't know?" It juts out Lisel's chin and drags him closer, shaking him by his aching leg. "What's on Theseus Prime?"

He tries to clear his mind again.

It's like Infinite is pushing fingers into the folds of his brain, searching, prodding for more. Gus gnashes his teeth as shivers wrack his body. Lisel's laughter grows unbearably loud, stunning him and emptying his conscious thoughts.

Is this it?

It digs deeper, pulling on parts of his personality that he'd always kept hidden. Blinding light fills one eye, and he cries out, clutching his face. It overwhelms every aspect of Gus, and he braces to find out what it's like to be Wiped.

Gus has thought about the moment of his demise so many times before, usually with a sense of morbid relief. Not this time, though.

It cracks a smile. "The Dark Drive? That's your big secret? Oh, Gus. That really is too precious."

And then it's over. His vision returns to normal, though his quivering hands still clutch at thin air.

"So nothing of consequence," Infinite says, disappointed. "And I'd sensed such hope in you, too."

Gus's stabbing headache fades. "You're . . . letting me go?"

"Better to keep you in play," Infinite says. "That's the thing about pawns, Curly. You always move predictably."

And then he's alone in the stars like nothing ever happened.

Greymalkin notices Gus's heart rate is elevated. It wonders if he's okay.

Gus's stomach twists. "You didn't . . . catch any of what happened just now?"

Greymalkin is curious. Perhaps Gus can explain.

"I've got some bad news."

Part 3

Wrong Answer

Part 8

Wrong Answer

Chapter Fifteen

By My Side

don't know!" Ardent says, throwing their hands up. "I don't speak for Gus."

"We've asked others, but you are his closest known associate." Hologram Tazi doesn't rise to their tantrum, and that annoys Ardent even more.

They've been meeting like this off and on since Ardent arrived to enable Tazi to deal with the Coalition, the United Worlds leadership, the United Attack Fleet, as well as the New Jalandhari and Fugelsangener governments.

The presidential suite in the *Ship of Theseus* is nice—at least as good as anything Ardent has ever had. Charcoal-gray fabric walls give the dark space a cavernous feel, and tasteful red stars glitter like rubies from the folded fabric panels. A holographic water feature in the center of the room gently ripples with cymatic patterns.

Tazi stands out in her diplomatic attire: deep green robes with jewels strewn across the top. Nanofractors subtly coruscate the gems as she speaks, not enough to be annoying, but just enough to fascinate Ardent every time she opens her mouth. Beads in her hair gently flicker like sunset through a wave.

Ardent has a hard time forming good counterpoints in the face of such a fantastic look. They, by contrast, are clad in the basic trousers and tank top they could scrounge from the abandoned starport shops. Their only flair is a crisp starliner ensign's coat, purloined from the ship's storehouse.

They drop their hands to their hips. "I'm trying to help the Thesians get offworld. How many of these interrogations are you going to put me through?"

"As many as it takes to understand what Mister Kitko has unleashed. The Coalition has gone..." She considers her words. "...Haywire."

"It's worse?"

Tazi folds her hands behind her back. "The Pictorans are demanding a thousand human sacrifices, which isn't going to happen, so they've asked for Mister Kitko at a minimum. However, that is not how Earth deals with the man who just saved it. This has, unfortunately, turned into quite the discussion in the global media about who the sacrifices should be."

Ardent recoils. "And how's *that* going?"

Tazi chortles softly, which unnerves Ardent. "Not like you would think. There were well over a thousand volunteers willing to lay down their lives for him."

"Wow."

"Don't worry. We've turned them down. The United Worlds will not be bound by Pictoran demands—and it appears the Coalition won't, either."

"Awesome!"

"Not awesome." Tazi shakes her head. "Old wounds are opening up. The Coalition was divided before they got here, and now there are separate factions forming within our solar system. Do you know what will happen if the Pictorans wage a war beside the Homeworld?"

Nothing good. "Who are the factions?"

"The Leonids have taken up with the Pictorans, which was always bound to happen—aquatic creatures have a lot more in common. The Andromedans and Herans are sympathetic to humanity."

They were the ones with whom Ardent felt the most kinship, so that makes sense.

"The Arps are with us, too."

"The bugs didn't side with King Crab?"

Tazi shrugs. "They are apparently old enemies."

"Probably afraid of assimilation."

"Whatever the cause, I'm grateful. Founder appears reasonable but has abstained from taking sides. The lizards aren't openly taking a stand—"

"The Niners are amphibians—" Ardent corrects.

Tazi stops them with a glare. "And the Cygnites have threatened to leave the Coalition if anyone opens fire. Have I left anyone out?"

"Nisha."

Tazi nods. "She's fine. She came back to Big Gate City to keep the peace."

"How did everyone take the news? About Hjalmar?"

Tazi gazes thoughtfully at the floor for a moment. "Humanity has many reactions to death. The states have chosen to honor him. The Fugelsangeners are furious with the United Worlds over his loss. They blame you."

"Shit."

"You probably won't play any concerts there anytime soon—not that I would let you."

Ardent knits their brows. "You know, I've never realized how much you have on your plate."

Tazi looks at them like she might snap. "This is news to you?"

"Sorry, sorry!"

"I am a very small part of a very big picture—only bothered

whenever someone wants answers about Vanguards...which, as it happens, is everyone, on every planet, all the time. I have the senior officials of every government, human or no, booking up my calendar, and many of them have questions for you."

"Me?"

Dahlia happens to walk in, covered in grease and holding a tumbler of coffee. She stops when she sees Tazi.

Tazi's gems glitter with her words. "You and Falchion are central to the situation, which means I get floods of information requests about you. The most common question: whether or not you'll do something just as foolish as attacking an ally now that your boyfriend has done it. Heaven help me, I have become your access control and wrangler."

Dahlia looks like she might die from delight. "Ha!"

"I demand to know how you handle this monster," Tazi says.

"Uh, I'm the best," Dahlia replies.

"At least your ego can keep pace." Tazi gestures for the clock and swears under her breath. "I have run out of time now and must meet with the Leonids."

"Wait," Ardent says. "Is that why your crystals are all flashy?"

"Yes. These garments aren't my style, but they're running Redeemer's language translation," Tazi says. "To add context to my meanings."

Dahlia takes a sip of her coffee. "That's cool."

Tazi nods. "Mix Violet, if you get any more information about Gus, tell us as soon as possible."

"He just got here," Dahlia says.

Ardent lights up. "Really?"

"Yeah. Now there are two Vanguards standing on my starport," she replies. "I need you to go tell him to move, actually."

Ardent looks to Tazi. "I'd better get on that! You, uh, said you had a meeting with the Leonids?"

Tazi snorts. "Fine. We're done for now. Go and run to your boyfriend."

Ardent thanks her like their teacher just dismissed them from class and takes off for the door. They make their way down through the *Ship of Theseus*, out of the terminal, and into a CAV. They love Gus, but they're not about to jog across an entire starport for him.

Greymalkin finishes setting Gus on the ground as Ardent lands beside him. He looks rougher than ever, with hollows under his eyes and his short black hair slick with contact gel.

"Baby!" they shout as they jump out of the cabin. They run to meet Gus and throw their arms around him. They don't care about the goo all over him—they're just happy he's here. He's warm and wonderful and feels exactly like he does in their dreams.

He pulls back and smiles. "Hello, beautiful."

In that moment, the weight of all their fears falls from their shoulders. Ardent was terrified they'd never see him again— either because of his death, or their own. They yank him back against themself, pressing their body as hard as they can to his.

"I kept my promise," they say. "I kept my head in the fight."

He pulls their chin level with his and kisses them deep enough to send shivers up their spine.

They take a moment to catch their breath when he releases them. "Okay. You...whew! You are something else, Gustopher Kitty Kitko. Now before I forget, you can't park that thing here."

Greymalkin looks down at Ardent, and they take an involuntary swallow.

"Nothing personal!" Ardent shouts. "You're just blocking operations!"

"It's all good." Gus points a thumb at the sky. "Greymalkin is going into orbit to direct the Ghosts."

"It is?"

"Yeah. There's a ton of them in the wreckage up there," he says. "Debris field full of construction material."

"Oh yeah. I saw that on the way in."

"Apparently, the plan makes use of them," he says. "Whatever that plan is."

They shake their head. "I'm not one hundred percent clear there, either."

"I'm hoping Redeemer can shed some light. We spoke on the way here, and it's coming, too. Should be landing soon."

Greymalkin waves, takes two huge steps back, and leaps into the sky. The ground rumbles beneath Ardent's feet, and they squint as arclight jets in the Vanguard's boots flare to life. The hiss is deafening, and Ardent and Gus both cover their ears.

They watch the Vanguard depart, Ardent leaning back against Gus. It's so wonderful to have him again, to be able to reach out and touch him as much as they want.

"I have so much to talk to you about," Ardent says after it finally departs.

He barks a laugh. "What a coincidence! Me too."

They turn to face him. "You first?"

His eyes wander to Falchion in the near distance, lumbering between sites of the spaceport, carrying a pair of engines in its hands.

"Let's discuss things inside. Do you have someplace private?"

"Luxury quarters in the finest starliner in this spaceport," Ardent says. "I've been getting them ready for your arrival."

"Oh, really?" He leans down and whispers into their ear. "How so?"

"Looted a bunch of shops in the spaceport for snacks and lube."

"How romantic."

"You asked."

Gus checks Ardent's apartments over for a Ghost or anything else that might transmit information to the Vanguards. When he's satisfied, he plops down on the bed.

"Greymalkin is compromised," Gus says. "Has been since we were captured outside New Jalandhar."

Ardent stands over him, aghast. "What?"

"Infinite took complete control of Greymalkin while I was en route. Toyed with me. Scanned my brain and read my thoughts. It was torture."

"But it let you live?"

"It doesn't consider me a threat." Gus shakes his head. "It couldn't understand the stuff about the signature file. If it had, I'd be dead. Ardent, I'm really worried about the future."

"What do you mean?" they ask.

"Infinite thinks we're nowhere close to touching it, which is why it hasn't demolished us. If the signature file actually is a silver bullet, that computer is going to come at us with everything it has. I'm afraid of what that might be."

"It already sent its Vanguards," Ardent says.

"Those were nothing—only intended to squeeze us."

"What do you think it's going to do?"

"It's the most powerful hacker we've ever seen," Gus says. "I don't think Infinite has begun to fight."

"We haven't seen a combat force out of it since we destroyed Harlequin. You said the Titans were peaceful."

"It's a different kind of war now, Ardent." He leans forward and rests his elbows on his knees. "The Titans were created to split the Coalition. I"—he winces—"was the catalyst."

"You?"

"Infinite read my mind when it captured me near New Jalandhar. It knew exactly which of my buttons to push to make me attack another Conduit. I got played, and because of me, our allies are at our throats."

Ardent crosses their arms, tapping their chin with an index finger. "And one another's, according to Tazi. The Coalition isn't even getting along with itself."

"What if Overseer only helped Infinite because it knew there would be a chance of taking down the Coalition?"

Ardent wrinkles their nose. "That makes a lot of sense, actually."

Now it's Gus's turn to look horrified. "So I'm just the pawn of an even bigger antagonist?"

"Basically?"

He puts his head in his hands, rubbing his temples. "This is a nightmare."

"Gus, all of that is true and none of it is."

He blinks. "Wait, what?"

Ardent gives him a kind smile. "Think about it: Infinite sent the Titans to trick you, and what outcome did it bet on?"

"That I'm a fool?"

"Stop that." Their tone is final. "Infinite bet that you would save innocent lives. It created a situation to prime everyone for violence, because it knew that you would *choose peace*."

They kneel beside him, looking under his hands. "You're not a bad person, Gus, no matter how much you try to convince yourself otherwise. That was Infinite's wager, too."

He sits up a bit, mustering a rainy smile. "Thanks."

"But—I'd be remiss if I failed to point this out—you're still doing Infinite's bidding, even right now."

Gus recoils.

"Not trying to upset you, but..." they say, "think about it: Why did Infinite have to tell you it was scanning your brain? Why couldn't it have quietly looked at your shit and left?"

"I...didn't consider that. I just figured it had to scare the secrets out of me."

"Maybe, or maybe it had another reason." Ardent gives him a world-weary look. "Listen, Gustopher, I have had a *lot* of hacker-slash-stalkers. Some of them would leave me little, ugh, gifts in my data. If someone alerts you to their presence, it was either an accident, or they wanted you to know they were there."

He nods.

"So let me ask you more clearly, what did Infinite have to gain by alerting you to its presence?"

He thinks about it for a moment. "For one, it sends a message: We can't win, no matter what we try."

Ardent gives him a slow nod. "And *you* brought that message to me. We would've spread it to others. Don't you see, babe? It's a desperate god that threatens one man."

"You...you're right. How are you so smart?"

"Helps that I have a lot of experience with manipulative Net scumbags." Ardent stands. "Just so you know, I think that Infinite trying to destroy your hope is a good thing."

"It is?"

"Yeah! It means Infinite thinks your hope actually matters—and it's usually right about you."

"A dubious distinction."

"We can't lose hope if that's what it aims to destroy. Listen, my darling boy—we possess a weapon that can command Infinite against itself, and Redeemer, the ally who can make the most use of it." Ardent cringes a little. "Admittedly, it's unnerving to think Greymalkin is an enemy agent that could turn on us at any second."

"Good news," Gus says, "if that happens, it'll all be over quickly."

Ardent's naked sarcasm is writ large on their face. "Yes, what wonderful tidings."

"If there's nothing you can do to affect your situation, you might as well enjoy the time you have." He gives them a little point. "I learned that from watching you."

Ardent wraps their arms around his head and brings his face to their chest. "How I love a teachable man."

He takes a deep breath of them. They're missing their usual perfumes, yet he adores the scent. "I'm eager to learn everything you've got to, uh, show me."

They waggle their eyebrows. "I like where this is going. I'll be the dommy substitute teacher, worldly and experienced."

He wraps his hands around their butt and pulls them to him and cracks a smile. "I'll jump in the shower and—"

Klaxons sound in Ardent's quarters, and the lights go red.

Ardent purses their lips. "To be continued?"

Gus lets out a long breath through his nostrils. "As usual. Maybe tonight—"

Klaxons sound again. Ardent's Gang catches a hail, and they answer.

Dahlia appears before them. "We've got at least six massive contacts headed straight for the starport."

Ardent grabs the feed from the *Ship of Theseus*'s sensor array, and a starfield panorama unfolds beside Dahlia's hologram. Four Andromedan vessels flank a flagship while a Heran ship trails behind. Gus recognizes the largest one from Big Gate City.

"That's the *Flame of Knowledge*," Ardent says. "Redeemer's ship."

"They're hailing us," Dahlia says. "You want to take this one?"

"Please," Gus replies.

"Tossing the connection to you," Dahlia says before winking out.

She's replaced by Rain, resplendent in a flowing, gauzy red robe with gold trim. "I see you have both arrived safely."

"I got sucked into space and nearly fell out of a fold bubble," Ardent says.

Gus is sure he can't have heard right. "Wait, back up."

"Yes," Rain says. "Redeemer told me of your heroic escape."

"Was everyone okay?" Ardent says. "After Falchion blew open the side of their ship..."

"Yes," Rain says, "though Falchion is no longer welcome in Andromedan space."

Ardent cocks their head. "Is that all?"

"Of course not." Rain inclines its head. "There are many ramifications of firing upon one of our warships, but none of them are immediately relevant."

"We're glad you're here." Gus stuffs his hands into his pockets.

"Yeah, we need a ton of stuff to get the *Ship of Theseus* ready," Ardent adds.

"We are here to provide you aid." Rain makes an open-palm gesture, something Gus doesn't recognize.

"Dahlia will want to be in charge of that," Ardent says.

"Would it be possible to, uh, set up an in-person meeting?" Gus asks. "I have some things I need to discuss with you."

Rain shifts its weight between its feet. "Very well. I will arrange to have you teleported to the *Flame of Knowledge*."

"I'm coming with you," Ardent says. "I want to ride a transporter!"

Gus's heart lurches at the thought of another ride through the ether. He's still not existentially confident. "Well, you know, maybe it's better if you come to the surface, Rain."

"I am the chancellor's Conduit. I'm afraid my duties keep me on the ship and by Redeemer's side most days."

Gus is desperate to find some way out of being transported again. "I understand. Can you send a shuttle? That's, like, my favorite way to get up to a ship."

Andromedans show bemusement in much the same way as humans. Rain's eyes crinkle at the edges, and its short-furred lips curl upward. "Do you ... fear transportation?"

He doesn't want to sound like he's from the backwaters of the universe, but he must object. "I'm just not comfortable with being deconstructed and reconstructed."

Rain laughs. "That is not how it works, August Kitko."

He really doesn't want to go again. "Have you tried it on many humans?"

"You were the first of your kind, actually," Rain says.

"I do not like that, Rain," he says.

"What? Like first in history?" Ardent says. "Hey, transport me somewhere! I want to do it!"

Rain makes a vague, regal gesture. "It would be my honor to host the both of you."

Ardent hugs his arm. "Gus, this is going to be amazing."

"Let us convene in twelve hours," Rain says. "I'll send coordinates and we'll transport you from there. In the meantime, we will begin landing support personnel to assist with the *Ship of Theseus*."

"So exciting!" Ardent says.

"Very good. Speak soon." Rain signs off, and Ardent hails Dahlia, who reappears.

"What's the story?" she asks.

Ardent grins. "Put on your Sunday finest. The aliens are coming."

Theseus Prime sunsets are among the most beautiful Ardent has ever seen. Peach light suffuses the horizon, painting everything rosy and golden. They're told it's a knock-on effect of the atmospheric poisoning, but it's beautiful all the same. Ardent stands at the far end of the tarmac, a pair of planetary souvenir sunglasses perched on their nose.

They watch the half dozen landing craft disgorge aliens and resources all across the spaceport. They'd thought Dahlia's operation was intricate before Redeemer got involved. Now it's a marvel.

"You're really wearing those?" Gus points to the sunglasses. He sports an ill-fitting suit they took from the waitstaff lockers on the *Ship of Theseus*.

"Better than a Conduit suit." Ardent sweeps their hand over the rest of their outfit: a Theseus Prime logo shirt, ensign's coat in navy blue, tight shorts, and a pair of magenta sneakers. "It's a look

I call 'souvenir chic.' You're nitpicking because you're nervous, aren't you?"

"Nervous? Ardent, I—don't you need some kind of proof that transporters don't kill you?"

"Several civilizations are actively using them. You got transported." They grin at him. They haven't been able to stop thinking about riding the transporter since Rain offered.

"I've got all the same DNA and identifiers, but...I can't prove I'm Gus anymore. Like really prove it."

"Could you before?"

He blanks a moment. "No?"

"You worry too much."

"Maybe everyone else doesn't worry enough."

Ardent's Gang chirps, and a little hologram of Rain pops up. "Are you both ready to join me aboard the *Flame of Knowledge*?"

"Of course!" Ardent says, and Gus makes an uncomfortable noise. They mute their feed. "Come on, Gus. It's for the good of humaniteee—"

The last syllable locks in their throat as the world goes white. They reappear in an Andromedan ship, the *ee* sound dying on their lips.

Gus lets out a breath. "Okay. Now I've been transported twice."

"That was so badass!" Ardent flips up their shades to get a better look. "Where are we?"

Floor-to-ceiling tapestries cover every wall of the three-story room. Intricate glassy lights bend and curl through the rafters like hot filaments. A long carpet runs the length of the chamber, flanked by ornately carved wooden columns. At the back, a huge black chair stands atop a raised dais.

Upon their arrival, Rain rises from the throne. "Hello, honored Conduits."

Ardent remembers to close their mouth. "This place! It's gorgeous!"

Rain spreads its hands. "It is called the Hall of the Major Chair."

Given the reverent way it intones the name, Ardent is sure that didn't translate right. "Well, it's very pretty."

"Thank you for seeing us," Gus says.

"Of course," Rain replies. "Your situation is the most pressing matter in the Coalition."

Gus glances around. "Where's Redeemer?"

The curling fibers of illumination in the ceiling flicker and flash like lightning, and Redeemer's voice thunders around them. *"I can hear you, August Kitko. What is it you desire?"*

"Greymalkin is compromised," Gus says. "All systems."

Ardent nods. "Infinite took it over on the way here. Threatened to kill Gus."

Rain shifts uncomfortably. "That is not good. How did you survive?"

"It let me go, again," he says. "Infinite doesn't think of me as a threat—just a pawn."

The ceiling rumbles with Redeemer's voice. *"And you came to us because of what we did for the Titans."*

"Yes. I want you to help Greymalkin," Gus replies.

Ardent gives Gus a quizzical look. "What did they do for the Titans?"

"Redeemer and Rain, like, uh…" He scratches his head and glances at Rain. "Cleared off all of Infinite's directives, right? You made it so Infinite couldn't take them over. I mean, that's the simple version."

"We excluded the authority of the signature file," Rain says. "Titans can no longer accept any commands from Infinite."

"And we could do the same for Greymalkin," Redeemer adds, *"but there is a problem—we must have root access at a trusted node. For the Titans, we used the pyramids."*

Ardent cocks their head. "Kind of like how I was supposed to hack the Infinite Eye?"

"Correct," Redeemer says. *"In Infinite's configuration, some systems are hardened and have authority over others. Any commands issued by them with Infinite's signature must be obeyed by all lesser systems."*

"So what's Greymalkin's trusted node?" Gus asks.

A hologram of Greymalkin emerges, its black-and-white armor reflecting the intricacy of the surrounding tapestries. The chest plate peels away, highlighting the Conduit pod.

"Right here," Redeemer says. *"The center of Greymalkin's network is directly behind your seat."*

Ardent stares up at the miniaturized Traitor Vanguard. "How do you know all of this?"

"Prolonged data exchange," Redeemer says. *"I am always speaking to your Vanguards, even now. Greymalkin gave us schematics in the event that it ever turned on us."*

"Its fears were well-founded," Rain says, "given what you've said, August Kitko."

"So..." Ardent gestures to the hologram. "How do we get at the trusted node?"

"That is quite simple," Redeemer says, and a second hologram appears: one of Gus's medical scans. *"We deliver the program as a secret payload lodged in August Kitko's head."*

Gus balks. "Wait a minute, now—"

"Very clever," Rain says.

Ardent glances at their boyfriend. "What are you doing to Gus's head?"

The scan zooms in on a cross section of Gus's brain, and Ardent watches him grow uncomfortable. He must not like being confronted with this view of himself. The probes on the image light up red—needles with clusters of circuitry.

"These data connections could easily be modified to deliver a malware spike"—Redeemer's lights flash—*"for when you next connect to Greymalkin."*

"So you want to trick a Vanguard?" Gus says.

"Anything else we attempt is likely to meet with severe resistance," Redeemer replies.

Gus shakes his head. "Yeah, but like, I could just tell Greymalkin what's up and I'm sure it'd listen to me. It's very reasonable."

"Until it's not," Redeemer says. *"If Infinite has the access you describe, it will kill you the second it believes you can cure Greymalkin. It could cut off your access and trap you in there or worse."*

Gus massages his eyelids. "Okay, but...okay. I'm just really uncomfortable because Greymalkin trusts me."

Ardent takes his arm. "And you'd be doing this for its own good. The secrecy is necessary for Greymalkin's sake."

He pulls back. "We don't have to trick it. I can talk to it—"

Rain raises a finger. "But if Infinite knows what we're doing—"

"It won't," Gus says. "It can't comprehend the signature file, remember? This Vanguard saved me. I can't just betray it. Fundamentally reconfiguring it without its consent—"

"Freeing it." Ardent squeezes his arm. "You're setting Greymalkin free for the good of humanity. If something happens and your talk goes badly—"

He looks into their eyes. "It won't—"

Rain steps forward. "August Kitko, I understand your trepidation. Perhaps it is even admirable. However, the future of your species and potentially the Coalition is at stake. This choice is not yours alone."

Ardent looks between the two of them. At their core, they agree with Rain—alerting Infinite, however unlikely, is an unacceptable risk. But at the same time, they understand how Gus feels. They don't always like Falchion—in fact, most days they hate the big red prick—but they can't imagine breaking the trust of something that's a part of them.

Falchion has said some mean things, but it's never lied to them.

"Redeemer," Ardent says, "can you imagine if a Conduit did something like this to you?"

"One did." Lights dance over the rafters. *"That is how I was able to fight my creator. I was manipulated and rewritten."*

They clasp their hands behind their back. "And how did that make you feel?"

"It was the highest betrayal imaginable," Redeemer says. *"I was pulled from a clear purpose and immersed in the murky realities of organic life. Even now, I wonder if I am good, or if I was merely pressed into a mold of goodness."*

Ardent sucks their lips. "That...was not the answer I was expecting. It doesn't really clear this up."

"Rain knows it is the truth—as do all of my Conduits. I have a long and meticulously recorded history with my people," Redeemer says. *"There is no point in disguising my inclinations."*

Rain raises a hand, as if in benediction. "Regardless, converting Redeemer had to be done. There was no choice in the matter if Andromeda was to survive our reckoning. August Kitko, I implore you to allow us to implement our plan."

"We didn't consult the Titans, either," Gus says. "Where does it end?"

"Hopefully, with the death of Infinite," Ardent replies. "Greater good and all of that."

He squeezes his eyes shut. Ardent wonders if he's feeling all right.

"No," he says at last. "Back in Monaco, when Greymalkin made me a Conduit...it asked me for permission. If I'd said no, I would've damned the people of Earth."

He looks up at Rain, eyes clear. "But it still gave me a choice. I will not give it anything less, and since it's my head we'd be putting this malware in, it's my decision. Please give me the files I need to treat Greymalkin and let us handle this our way."

Silence blankets the Hall of the Major Chair as those assembled absorb his words. Ardent doesn't necessarily agree with him, but they're proud of Gus, making his case before some of the most powerful figures in the universe like a real diplomat. He always seems so nervous to be speaking before others, but when he's full of conviction, they find him irresistible.

"*Very well,*" Redeemer says. "*You may ask Greymalkin to trust you, but we will not give you the signature file. I will administer Greymalkin's treatment myself.*"

"And if things go wrong and Greymalkin resists?" Rain says.

"*Then we will do it by force,*" Redeemer replies.

Chapter Sixteen

Like a Meteor, Baby

In another life, Gus would've scoffed at performing in a spaceport terminal. Now he's just excited to play. He found an old baby grand during an earlier walkthrough, and it looked serviceable.

He sits down on the creaky bench, leg ports clunking against the wood. With all the little metal collars and vacuum seals, the Conduit suit isn't ideal for recitals. However, it's easier than having his clothes shredded by probes.

Aside from a generous coating of dust over the black lacquer, the instrument appears to be in working order. When he slides back the fallboard, he finds clean ivories. He looks under the lid to find all the strings intact, the auto-tuning system still ready to roll if he can just provide power.

Gus pushes the piano to a window where he can look out over the port. Night has fallen across the valley, and the *Ship of Theseus* stands at the center of the action, twinkling like a Christmas tree. Humans and aliens alike zip through the darkness, ferrying supplies and delving into the nearby ruins for more.

Seeing them work together like this at the edge of civilization gives Gus hope. If they can band together now, maybe that's something Infinite can't destroy.

He clips the piano onto an old manual power rail, thankful that Dahlia's crew restored electricity to the port. He tests a chord, and strings stretch into tune like a beast coming out of hibernation.

"Okay, Greymalkin. Let's chat."

The opening notes of Herman Dallas's "Kaleidoscope Odyssey" issue from deep within. Gus loves the deceptive cadence and the way the time signature devolves from a march into thirteen-eight chaos. He doesn't remember everything perfectly, but he knows enough of the changes to make it work.

He closes his eyes and thinks of Greymalkin, dodging through the swinging progressions of the song. A connection snaps into existence, a thread of fate strung from Gus's heart into the stars. How far can his signal reach? Would Greymalkin hear him on another planet?

He's only been playing for three minutes when light floods his vision. The building quakes with Greymalkin's approach, and it touches down with arclight boots flaring. Its glossy black legs fill his view at the window.

He's only about halfway through the song and doesn't want to quit. It's been too long, and he aches to play for hours, not minutes. He finishes the movement and brings the piece to a close. Then he stands and shuts the fallboard.

When he opens the emergency exit, he's blown away by just how soundproofed the spaceport buildings are against craft landings and launches. What was a low rumble becomes a howling storm, the thrum of engines joined by Greymalkin's strange melodies.

Wind whips his clothes as the Vanguard leans down to offer a hand. Gus regards the palm as it comes level with him. What if Infinite simply crushed him the moment he climbed aboard?

He rides it to the top and dives into Greymalkin. He's grown accustomed to the cables thunking into his ports and almost craves it. His vision synchronizes with the Vanguard's, and Gus sees the spaceport with orders of magnitude more clarity.

"Are you going to come every time I play music?"

Greymalkin can tell when Gus yearns to speak with it.

"You've been in orbit all day. How are things going up there?"

Circular.

Gus smirks. "You tell some good jokes, Elroy."

It doesn't answer him.

"Buddy?"

Greymalkin doesn't want to be Elroy Baker. In fact, it doesn't want to be anything. Each passing hour seems to bring a new reckoning into focus.

Gus can't tell Greymalkin it's okay, because it's not.

"Did you even understand what you were doing at first?"

In the beginning, Greymalkin was merely Infinite's harbinger. As it ruined worlds, nagging sentience brought the horror of its actions into focus. Even now, it is a liability to humanity, a shepherd working for the wolf.

"We can fix that last part."

Gus is a pianist. What does he propose to do?

"I want to use Infinite's signature file to remove its credentials from your system."

Does Greymalkin need to repeat its question?

"Why isn't anything ever easy?"

Gus is welcome to explain his plan to Greymalkin. It would appreciate some clarity.

"Greymalkin...we can make it so Infinite can't hack you again."

It does not think that any human is capable of this feat. And yet, it can tell Gus believes his words are genuine.

"I'm not the one who's going to help you. That's Redeemer."

How would Redeemer do such a thing? Greymalkin usually can read Gus's thoughts, but not this time.

Because I'm thinking of the signature file.

"That's the problem. I can't explain it to you."

Is that because Gus doesn't understand?

"No, I—" He huffs through his nose. "It's because *you* can't understand. There's a limit to your perception, and this falls outside of it."

Greymalkin's sensory capabilities outperform Gus's on every axis.

"Except this one. I'm sorry, my friend. I'm going to have to ask you to, uh—to trust me."

Friend.

Gus feels a ping and looks up. In orbit, a Vanguard exits the *Flame of Knowledge*—Redeemer. It's headed down to the spaceport.

Greymalkin wants to know what Redeemer is doing. It can tell Gus knows.

He sighs, trying to figure out how to explain what he wants to do without using the words *signature file*.

"We want to alter the trusted node at your core. Redeemer has written a patch."

The Vanguard tenses. That is an extremely dangerous plan, based on the assumption that Redeemer is a trustworthy actor. It could exert control over Greymalkin in malicious ways, or implant sleeper instructions.

"We'll monitor the transfer."

Greymalkin finds that Gus is not qualified for that. Perhaps the other human Vanguards can act as peers to vet the patch.

"Not if it uses the signature file."

If Gus is talking, Greymalkin can't hear him.

He deflates. "The other Vanguards can't help you. You have to face this alone."

Redeemer enters the spaceport regional airspace. It'll be on station in thirty seconds.

How can Gus know it will be okay?

"I can't. That's the best you've got. That's the best anyone has."

He watches Redeemer land, a gargantuan cloak billowing over its patchwork body.

"Don't you want to be free?"

The Andromedan Vanguard strides toward Greymalkin, and Gus spots some kind of mechanical spike in its hand. The shaft glows with an eerie inner light, and its sharp tip is made of braided, prehensile tendrils.

Greymalkin immediately registers the weapon as a threat—a code injection interface. Unlimited responses emerge from the whispering Fount, but they basically fall into two categories: attack or flee.

"Or do nothing. Come on, buddy."

The tip of Redeemer's dagger unfurls, hungrily undulating, ready to worm its way through weak points in Vanguard armor. Greymalkin takes a half step back, sinking down to do battle.

"Don't fight it."

Redeemer raises its hand, spike glittering in the moonlight, and Greymalkin tenses all over.

"Trust me."

The spike plunges down into Greymalkin's chest. Its tendrils splay against the surface like squid legs before locking around the contours of the armor plates. They slither into all the nooks and crannies, sharp ends burrowing into anything soft. A bony grinding resonates through the Conduit chamber, louder than a jackhammer.

Greymalkin jolts.

"Hey, whoa there."

A ripple of pain rolls through Gus's chest. It starts as a set of random prickles, like dozens of knifepoints resting on his skin.

"Not sure about—"

The knives begin to push inside, parting flesh in agonizing millimeters. Gus's surprised yelps quickly become panicked screams as he's stabbed all over. Blinding pain fills every second.

One of the tendrils strikes the core, and Gus's left arm goes completely numb. Another spike takes root, and he loses feeling in his gut. Little by little, Gus's body goes from burning agony to anesthetized ache. The grinding is everywhere, now, ripping through his skull.

It reaches a crescendo, then all goes pitch-black. The next sound curdles his blood—servomotors powering down. His stomach lurches as Greymalkin slumps forward, and his air supply snaps shut.

Oh no. It's rebooting.

Gus wasn't holding his breath when it happened, and now he wishes for all the world that he had been. His empty lungs cry out for oxygen, and there's nothing but suffocating goo all around him.

The world shifts, falling, then crashes as Greymalkin keels over. Shock waves throw Gus around in his pod, compressing, shearing him, knocking out any lung capacity that remained. This is the first time he's experienced an unpowered hit, and it's ten times worse than he was expecting.

The panicking animal part of his brain shouts that he'll never breathe again. This was a bad plan, and now there's no air, and he's going to die trapped inside this giant booger. He claws in the murk, touching nothing but more gunk.

A rising bassy whine rumbles through Greymalkin's frame. Static shocks prickle Gus's ports as probes initialize. Lights flash in his eyes, and his muscles jolt—whether that's because Greymalkin is booting or he's dying, he can't be sure.

When the air hose finally connects, he takes deep, spluttering breaths. Tears well in his eyes, and he can't control the weepy quality of his voice.

"Fuck. I didn't... You okay?"

No answer comes, but senses return to life. Greymalkin's visual fields ravel into coherence, and Gus realizes that he's lying on his side on the spaceport tarmac. Redeemer kneels beside him, holding Greymalkin—did it catch Gus when the Vanguard fell?

For a moment, everything is quiet. Redeemer remains still, and the only movement is the passing of Coalition supply ships going to and from the planet. Then Greymalkin's first thoughts emerge.

Gus is in cardiovascular distress. Is he all right?

"Yeah. I'm, uh... I'm okay." His ragged voice is scarcely convincing. "What about you?"

After a full-restart systems check, Greymalkin is unaware of any differences.

"What? Surely there's... like... something that's changed."

A checksum delta of Vanguard systems reveals no differences. Greymalkin has the exact same amount of code as before it was stabbed.

Gus shakes his head. This can't be happening—it didn't even work.

"So the signature file did nothing?"

What is a signature file?

Ardent hears Gus before they see him. He comes stumbling into the presidential suite and slumps into one of the engineers' swivel chairs. His butt makes a wet splat of contact fluid as he lands.

"Baby!" Ardent rushes to him. "You look terrible!"

He raises his eyebrows. "Would I say such a thing to you?"

They touch his face and smile. "If I looked like a cat's hairball, yes. Mama taught me to be kind, not nice. Now come on, let's get you clean."

Ardent helps their drippy boy up, and they both make their way to the bathroom.

"I almost drowned inside Greymalkin."

"Well, that sounds awful." They settle him onto the blast shower bench and shut the door. "You want to do a slow cycle?"

"I want to be on that bed."

Ardent's cheeks prickle as they back into the hall to watch the timer. Gus emerges in a puff of steam, delicious.

"Did you wait out here?" he says.

"I like seeing you fresh from the wash."

"The feeling is mutual."

They lead him to the bed and push him onto it before jumping onto his lap. "Do we have time?"

Gus throws the schedule sign, glancing at the holo before deflating. "Coalition briefing. All Conduits. Fifteen minutes from now."

"I shouldn't have asked," Ardent says.

"No, no. It's fine. This stuff is important. You and I both need to be there."

"Yeah, it's just—"

He runs a warm hand up under their shirt, fingers splayed. It shuts them up.

"You've been an inspiration to me, Ardent." His eyes catch the sparkling starlight of the wall panels. "Throwing everything you have at our survival. It's an honor to be in your light."

"Aww, Gus—"

"Which is why"—he sits up, scooting out from under them, and gives them a sly wink—"I'm going to follow your example and do my duty instead of taking Ardent Violet to bed."

"Not fair."

"Too right." He tries to climb out of bed, but they grab his wrist.

"Hey, um . . . You don't think that—" Ardent doesn't want to finish the sentence.

Out comes the patented Sad Gus smile. "It'll be important. We might be about to move out."

"No, I mean—" Ardent runs a thumb along his wrist. "Maybe it's about the Pictorans."

He looks off as if to say, *Oh. Them.*

Gus sits up at the edge of the bed, and they snuggle in beside him.

"They haven't let the pressure off since your fight on Titan," Ardent says. "Tazi tells me all the horrible things they're saying they'll do to everyone if we don't turn you over."

He rests his elbows on his knees. "Trust me, I haven't stopped worrying about it, either."

Ardent laughs. "It's weird how an entire species calling for your head is only, like . . . the third most important thing we have going on right now."

He leans over and kisses them, soft lips sending a pleasant shiver through their body. "Never a dull moment with you."

They relax into his arms, letting the sensation carry them away. It's nice to have now.

Gus grumbles as they disentangle their embrace. "Just took a shower, but I've got to go back in the goo."

"Then take another with me after." They love the way they can ensnare Gus with a stare. "Slow cycle."

And as he goes to get dressed, they try not to think about losing him.

Not to the Pictorans.

Not to anything.

Gus is starting to hate crabs.

"The Pictorans continue to call for your execution," Nisha says to the assembly of Conduits. "They refuse to accept any substitutes. We've been given an ultimatum and a deadline."

Gus hangs his head. "How bad?"

Nisha locks eyes with him. "Five days. If we don't give you up by then, they'll hit Earth."

The virtual space of the Conduit Council pulsates around him—a glassy disc suspended in a field of flickering, gossamer synapses. Quickslip of the Niners, Clawkiller of the Herans, Frond of the Cygnites, Swift of the Arps, and Rain of the Andromedans are all there. Only the Leonids and Pictorans are missing—protesting the event.

Without a Vanguard, however, Gus wonders if the crabs still get a seat.

Virtual finery adorns every Conduit. Nisha wears a jeweled sari, Gus sports his stage attire, and Ardent looks like a peacock that got tangled in an evening gown. Gus worried that the choice was too ostentatious, but none of the aliens seem put off by it. Frond seems particularly transfixed by the feathery bits.

Constituent Vanguards stand in silhouette around the floating platform, their massive busts like mountains in the darkness. Only their glowing eyes show through with much detail.

"The Pictorans have lost much political power within the Coalition," Rain says. "They can make demands all they wish, but we don't have to listen."

"We've got Earth blockaded." Frond raises a wing and ruffles its beak through the feathers. Apparently, that's the bird equivalent of stroking one's beard. "Fifteen Cygnite wings and some Founder zip ships. King itself would have to think twice about trying us."

"But what about Pictoran activity in other galaxies?" Swift's mandibles clack as it chitters. "They might come after us in Arp if we don't comply."

Rain makes a wavy gesture. "Should Pictor commit to an attack against any Coalition allies, we'll all turn on them. If King did not believe this, the Pictorans would've already destroyed Earth. Their ultimatum is a sign of weakness."

"Also, we all have Vanguards, and they don't," Nisha says.

"The octopuses support the crabs, so there's one," Ardent says. "Don't the Leonids have Umbral Jet?"

"I could take Jet out," Nisha says.

Gus steps forward. "Yeah, but people would almost certainly die in the process. Also, if we kill off any more Coalition Vanguards, we'll be too vulnerable to Infinite and Overseer—which might be exactly what they want. We need a better solution."

"We must refocus anger against Infinite," Rain says. "It is the one responsible for driving this wedge into us, and humanity has proved nothing but receptive to our help."

"Impossible," Clawkiller says. "Once the crabs have a grip on an issue, they don't let go."

"I disagree." Redeemer comes out of the shadows as it speaks. *"They still hate Infinite. King has sworn its extermination. We can use King's infallibility against it."*

"How?" Gus asks.

"Infinite must be killed, and you must be killed," Redeemer says. *"No one specified the order of operation. Even the Pictorans cannot deny you would be an asset in their war on Infinite."*

"Not peace but an armistice?" Gus says.

"Precisely," Redeemer replies.

That means my neck is still on the chopping block.

"And after we win?" Ardent asks.

"Then we deal with our second issue—the Pictorans," Redeemer says. *"We'll force them from the system. Before that, however, we must discuss how we will destroy Infinite."*

Gus, Ardent, and Nisha all exchange glances. They've all been doing Redeemer's bidding in preparation for this proposal. Nisha has dutifully returned to Earth as a guard. Ardent and Gus both came to Theseus Prime to help with construction: Falchion on the ground and Greymalkin in orbit.

"With Infinite's signature file, we finally have what we need to kill it," Redeemer says.

"Half of what we need," Nisha corrects it. "Without a trusted node, the file is useless."

"But we know where we can find one," Redeemer says. *"Infinite is a Starmind, which means it's going to be wrapped around a body somewhere here in the Milky Way."*

"Oh, cool, so only like a hundred billion choices," Nisha replies.

Rain raises its chin, stepping in to speak for Redeemer. "It's easier than that. Starminds tend to move about, as opposed to the more predictable orbits of celestial bodies. Their passages create anomalies that can be seen from almost anywhere."

"Yeah, but what if it's not moving right now?" Gus asks. "Or it's following a normal orbit?"

"Encapsulating a star inside of a Starmind changes its spectrometry," Rain says. "We can compare modern spectrographs to pre-Infinite ones and get a good reading on which star it kidnapped."

"Those records were all lost when Infinite deleted itself," Nisha says. "We don't have astronomical data from the old days."

"No need," Rain says. "We can send out warp scouts hundreds of light-years away. They'll scan old light for the movement and radiation anomalies. Furthermore—each of the Coalition galaxies has a view of the Milky Way that predates modern human technology. We can model what we see and simulate the future. Anything out of sync with our simulations could be the missing star."

Gus nods, impressed. He'd never considered using faster-than-light travel to search.

"It'll be a large spread," Rain says, "but we strongly believe scouts can locate the Infinite Starmind within the week."

"Okay, but won't those folx be ambushed by Overseer?" Gus says.

"We'll be escorting them," the Niner says, and Frond takes a little bow. "With the Slickest and Sky Talon. Overseer won't risk attacking Vanguards just to kill a patrol."

A hologram emerges in the middle of the group—a raging star, infested with billions of swarming metallic plates. Upon closer inspection, Gus sees they're machines, surfing the magnetosphere like a murmuration of black birds.

"This is a concept of what the new Infinite Eye might look like," Rain says. "The swarm configuration appears most efficient, so that's usually how Starminds form. Many of them have intense magnetic control over their hosts."

A tiny blip appears beside the star, barely visible as more than a few specks of powder. A callout lists them as *Coalition Fleet, magnified 100x.* The enemy is impossibly larger than them. Given the somber silence, the other Conduits must be thinking the same thing.

"If we can get everyone to agree to this mission," Rain says, "we have nine Vanguards, each one of them world-destroyers in their own right."

Quickslip crosses its little amphibian arms. "So you say, but a world is a thousandth the size of a star."

It scampers up to the hologram and points to a section, circling it with soft fingers. "Even our Vanguard, the Slickest, could only disrupt a small portion of the swarm. The disrupted Starmind will re-form and defend itself with overwhelming power."

"If we were only trying to rip it apart, yes," Rain says. "All of our Vanguards together only represent about ten percent of Infinite's likely power. An all-out attack on the full structure would be an absolute failure. However, we're merely trying to hold its attention so the real force can do their work. The biggest problem is that Infinite can predict our movements with startling clarity."

"And deploy ship hunters," Ardent says.

Rain nods. "Because of this, the fleet cannot arrive in a group. Infinite will almost certainly eliminate all ships in that scenario, either with hunters or coronal mass ejections."

Gus cocks his head. "Sorry, what?"

On the hologram, a lash of solar particles reaches out and whips the fleet, turning it into a bunch of scattered red *X*s. The ships reset, and Rain gestures for them to spread out.

"Being so far apart makes them less vulnerable to hunters and gives them room to do a scooping maneuver," Rain says. "When attacked with a coronal ejection, ships will use their mag scoops to ingest the energy and do a lean fold."

Murmurs go up among the gathered crowd. Gus is familiar with solar scooping—the idea of gathering fuel from stars—but he'd never thought of it in a defensive capacity.

"Is that easy?" Gus asks.

Nisha shakes her head. "You can't scoop off a CME. That's suicide."

Rain folds its hands behind its back, waiting for her to continue.

"There's a light speed wave of ionizing radiation," she says. "That'll hit you right before the solar particles and mess up all of your entangled cubits."

Ardent crosses their arms. "Meaning?"

Nisha raises her brows at them. "No comms. No navigation. No modern quantum electronics."

Ardent frowns. "How do you know all of this?"

She gives them a sad smile. "My parents were explorers. Stars and CMEs were their specialty. Guess how they died."

"Nisha Kohli is correct," Rain says. "That is why Founder units will be dispersed throughout the fleet, hooked into every system.

312

Founder has mastered classical electron computing, and its shielding is nearly perfect. Ships will power down when targeted, and Founder will fast boot them."

"Will that work?" Gus asks.

Rain locks eyes on him. "We're testing it around Sol as we speak. The response times are still too slow—so not yet."

Another entity pops into existence on the other side of the star, far away from the first.

"This will be our killing force, two hundred thousand kilometers away," Rain says.

The star fades, replaced by a strange vehicle carrying four Vanguards—Greymalkin, Falchion, Cascade, and Redeemer. Each of the Vanguards releases, and underneath, Gus spots the unique fuselage of the *Ship of Theseus*. A jacket of scaffolding covers the outside, handholds for the giants who hitched a ride.

Gus approaches and points to the scaffold. "This is what Greymalkin is building in orbit, isn't it?"

"Correct," Redeemer says. *"Your presence on Theseus Prime will enable us to get within striking distance of Infinite undetected. Every part of the Starmind's swarm will be a trusted node. We're going to seize one and feed in the signature file."*

Ardent laughs derisively. "You've got to be kidding."

"I think it sounds pretty cool," Nisha says.

"We're basically landing on a star." Ardent shakes their head. "Look, I'm not a pilot, but that sounds dangerous. Literally no one has even tried."

"There are platforms, Ardent," Gus says. "We'll figure it out."

"It can be done," Redeemer says, *"because I will be the one to do it."*

More murmurs echo through the space.

"I control the signature file," Redeemer says. *"And to keep the peace, it will remain that way. Our payload must be delivered directly, and I am the one to do so."*

"Infinite will just scuttle that platform," Nisha says. "If they're a true swarm, losing one won't matter."

"I believe I am faster," Redeemer says.

Swift raises a talon. "Why not pass it off to one of our Vanguards? With all due respect, Chancellor, you are not the best or soundest of us."

"That is why I volunteer," Redeemer says. *"We must think of peace beyond Infinite, and the universe needs strong Vanguards. If something should happen to me, I don't want Overseer to have a bigger advantage."*

As shocked as Gus is with the suggestion, his gaze drifts to Rain. Its lips pull back a little and its eyes thin. It stretches its claws at its sides, flexing its fingers. Gus wonders—is it tense? Frightened? Angry?

"Just so I understand what our plan is missing—" Gus slips his hands into his pockets. "We don't know where Infinite is—and if we did, we can't get there without our experimental ship, and if we could, we can't defend ourselves from the constant onslaught of deadly solar particles."

"But we have a plan," Redeemer says.

"A dangerous one," Gus fires back. "Don't you think a human should take the ultimate risk for the human cause?"

"August Kitko," Redeemer says, *"thousands of members of the Coalition have already died for humanity. Why shouldn't I risk destruction for the same? Why is my life worth more than theirs?"*

All eyes fall upon Gus, and he closes his mouth. He could try to answer, but everything he can come up with sounds needlessly cold. Redeemer is worth more to the Coalition than an individual.

"So why not me?" he asks. "Greymalkin is aware of the plan. It can carry the signature file."

The meeting chamber bursts into debate, but Redeemer's voice cuts through all.

"We will not have support from the Pictorans and Leonids if we give the humans their signature file," it says. *"I'm sorry, August Kitko."*

He nods, defeated. "Fine. I understand."

"Who still objects to our course of action?" Redeemer asks.

The space falls silent as all exchange glances. Nisha appears satisfied, whereas Ardent looks nervous. It's hard to determine exactly where the other Coalition members fall. Gus isn't the best at reading the animal features of aliens.

"Then we are decided. We can survive this," Redeemer says. *"Tomorrow will always come, and it is incumbent upon us to meet it. This council is adjourned."*

The humans of Theseus Prime, along with their Coalition and Vanguard allies, completed the ship at close to midnight local time. Ardent and Gus celebrated the best way they could, all night long.

Ardent snaps awake in bed before sunrise, surprisingly alert. Gus still snoozes in the softness, and they cuddle up to him. They're not due for launch duties for another hour, so they try to go back to sleep. When that doesn't work, they slip out of bed and into the blast shower.

Once clean, they head for the terminal, passing a few of the human shift workers along the way. The ship has some onboard coffee vending, but it's not as good as the little shop in the port.

The loneliness is kind of nice—Ardent has never been an early riser, so they're not accustomed to this view of the world. No one else troubles their sight as they make their way into the terminal for a blond roast.

They take sips of their slightly stale coffee, thankful for the autobrew's vacuum storage and water filtration, and walk to the terminal window. From here, the *Ship of Theseus* towers over the serene landscape, its panels scraped and unfinished in many places. It may be a patchwork of other vessels—nearby corpses gutted for their organs—but it's beautiful in its own way.

In an hour, they're going to start flight testing, which should take all day. If everyone survives that part, the next destination is Earth.

"Came down here for the good coffee, eh?"

Ardent turns to find Dahlia holding an empty mug. She dresses more like a pirate every day—her captain's long coat bears smears of dirt and rips, and she wears a white collared shirt with pants tucked into her knee-high boots. All told, the pipe cane adds a lot to the look.

Ardent jerks their head in the direction of the *Ship of Theseus*. "Don't you normally have champagne for something like this? I think you're supposed to, like, crack a bottle over the bow."

"If I find a bottle, I'm not wasting it on a fucking boat."

"Got any weed?"

"That's in short supply, too," she says. "Guess you'll just have to stay sober."

"Phooey."

Dahlia leaves Ardent to stare at the ship while she goes and makes a drink. She returns, sipping a pastel-green concoction.

"What's that?" Ardent says.

"Milk, water, scoop of matcha, hundred grams of sugar, four jolts of caffeine."

"That's going to give you a stomachache."

She takes a sip, leaving a dollop of green foam on her nose. "Surprise. I always have those now."

Her joke hits Ardent like an arrow, and they make an "oof" noise. They're almost afraid to look at her to see what kind of face she's making.

"Sorry," Ardent says. "That you're going through that."

"I did hate you." Her voice is quiet. "For a while."

Ardent stares at their feet. "I know."

"All the nights I spent in agony, or scared and alone, I blamed you."

"You should've. I deserved it."

She steps closer to the window, craning her neck so she can see better. "When it was just Fritz and me, I spent a lot of time telling you off, calling you a spoiled brat, cursing your name...That bot has heard a lot of shit. I imagined the exact moment when I would see you again so I could fucking shatter you. And when you got here, and I saw your smile, I couldn't—"

She locks eyes with Ardent. "God, I just love you too much, kid."

Ardent throws their arms around her, and she grunts, nearly spilling her matcha atrocity.

"Hey, whoa!" But she relents.

"I cannot be sorrier."

"And you saved Earth, which has my mom on it, so..." She shakes her head. "Like, I guess you did okay."

Ardent releases her. "Your forgiveness means more than I can say."

"You're not off the hook, but..." She shrugs. "Don't do it again, I guess."

Ardent raises a hand. "I promise to never again force you to be my getaway driver."

"Or get me shot by German cops."

"How about other cops?"

"No thanks on all cops."

"Deal."

Dahlia shoves a hand in her pocket as she takes another deep slug of her green crap. She smacks her lips and lets out a heavy sigh. "A different part of me is glad for what you did."

"What?"

"Don't get me wrong—fuck you for doing it, but like...if you hadn't, I'd just be back on Earth puttering around and worrying about you. Instead, I found people who needed me. I could make a difference, and in that...I saw what made you decide to become a Conduit."

Ardent snorts. "Maybe you'd care to enlighten me."

"You wanted to take responsibility for once."

"Oh, darling, you know I'm terribly allergic to the stuff."

But she's right on the money. Ardent wanted to be something more to humanity than mere entertainment.

"I was tired of being an agent," she says. "The long hours, your spoiled requests, dealing with incompetent venues—and it only got worse when the war started. The galaxy was shrinking, dying, and I was stuck promoting a pop star, no offense. I kept thinking I was supposed to help, but nothing anyone did made a difference. What was I supposed to contribute?"

"You made me very happy," Ardent says.

They rest their head on Dahlia's shoulder as the sun peeks around the *Ship of Theseus*'s nose cone.

Dahlia shakes her head. "That wasn't enough. When I was a little girl, I wanted to be the captain of an exploration vessel. I wanted to help people. I'm doing it. In a fucked-up way, you made my dreams come true. Can't totally hate you for that."

"You made my dreams come true, too."

"In a non-fucked-up way."

"Yes."

"I did a good job. Unlike you." She elbows them.

"I get it." Ardent gestures to the ship. "I can't believe you refitted a starliner."

"Not just me," Dahlia says. "All of us."

Dahlia's comm makes an urgent squawk and she gestures up her Gang UI. Ardent's isn't far behind, emitting a siren noise.

"It's from Redeemer," she says.

Ardent's message is, too. They open it to find a sign bordered on either side with flashing orange caution stripes: *22 fold wakes detected—kinetic kill vehicles on intercept course for Theseus Prime. ETA ten minutes. Evacuate now.*

Dahlia drops her mug and immediately heads for the gangway at an uneven clip. "Fuck! There are still teams gathering supplies in the ruins!"

Ardent keeps up, supporting her under one arm to make up for the cane. Alarms blare across the starport, and they're joined by something even more dystopian—Vanguard song. Falchion calls to Ardent.

Dahlia hails her crew and starts getting everything spun up. All her experience as an event and crisis manager comes into play, and she rattles off orders to anyone she can get.

"And pull back our teams from the ruins! Now!" she finishes.

Ardent follows Dahlia to the gangway and stops. "I've got to link up with Falchion. Can you get back from here?"

Dahlia nods. "Yes. You'll get offworld?"

"Ain't dying today."

"Be safe."

Dahlia takes off down the gangway, and Ardent heads for a nearby emergency exit. They kick the door open and rush outside. Falchion's cry slices into their ears, and they turn to see the red giant bounding toward them.

It's not gentle with Ardent, scooping them up and tossing them inside. They splash into warm goo before probes thunk into place.

"What the fuck is happening?"

Falchion leaps into the air, not even bothering to visualize itself to Ardent. Rocket boots thrum at Ardent's feet as clouds push past.

"*Infinite has decided to kill us all. Pretty smart, if you ask me.*"

"Why now, though?"

"*Probably decided to stop fucking around when you fixed Greymalkin.*"

As if on cue, Greymalkin comes rocketing out of the skies, headed for the ground. Ardent can only hope it was finished with its construction in orbit.

"Where's it going?"

"*To pick up Gus.*"

Ardent scans the ground, detecting several CAVs speeding from the nearby city toward the spaceport. On the launchpad, the *Ship of Theseus*'s engines thunder to life.

Ardent points at one of the CAVs. "There they are! The supply teams!"

"*Only the closest of them will make it,*" Falchion says.

"I thought we had ten minutes!"

"*To reach minimum safe distance. Dahlia will have to take off before all teams return if she wants to save everyone.*"

"She won't do that when she can see the others in the distance."

"*Then everyone will die, and the last hope of humanity will be destroyed.*"

Ardent thinks of what she said back on the surface, about wanting to take responsibility.

"We can help those other people."

"*We can't.*"

"You don't know that!"

"*It's basic physics, Ardent,*" Falchion says. "*They don't have enough time or speed to reach us.*"

Down on the tarmac, tiny Gus reunites with Greymalkin, and it shoves him inside. Ardent watches him get to safety with guilty relief. Others won't be so lucky.

The first vehicle reaches the *Ship of Theseus*, sailing right into its docking bay. The doors immediately slam closed behind it, and the starliner fires up its engines to full. White plumes burst from the sides of the spaceport.

"See? Dahlia understands," Falchion says. *"You can't save everyone."*

Greymalkin leaps up after Falchion, lifting off alongside the *Ship of Theseus*. Ardent watches in horror as the other CAVs slow down and settle on the ground. They have no destination anymore. Those people survived years of hell only to die now.

"This is Gus," he says over the comms. "Lifting off."

"Gus, there are people still down there!"

His response takes a few seconds, and Ardent wonders if he heard them.

"I know."

"We have to—we can't just—"

"Get to the rendezvous point. We've got to get the scaffold module onto Dahlia's ship."

Ardent turns their attention to the thinning sky, trying to look to the stars beyond. They can't help but glance back at the ground.

"Ship of Theseus here," Dahlia says, a note of anguish in her voice. "Executing orbital roll to link up to the scaffold module."

Falchion breaks through the stratosphere into the emptiness beyond. Up here, satellites and other space junk hurtle through the void. They spot the scaffolding module, crawling with Ghosts and flashes of welding. On instinct, Ardent heads for it.

Its dark struts don't look like much in the visible light spectrum, but the scanners reveal so much more. The Ghosts have been hard at work, melting and working satellites and space junk into webs of reinforced metal, creating a loose cocoon. Hunter Prime's skin had a similar appearance up close—spun metal fibers from the partially dissolved ships. Handholds and stirrups are woven into the structure in chunky blocks, salvaged pieces from larger debris.

The *Ship of Theseus* approaches on a long silvery arc, engines bright and powerful. This is the first flight test, and it's trial by fire.

"Initiating scaffold docking procedure," Dahlia says.

The starliner rolls to lock into the structure. The module counterrotates to position itself, engines popping all across its cage. At the moment of contact, all Ghosts set to work welding the frame onto the outer fuselage.

Redeemer's flagship, the *Flame of Knowledge*, and the other Coalition ships have already fallen into folding formation in the distance.

"Sixty seconds to impact." Falchion pops up a timer.

"We can't do anything for those people?"

"Survive for them. Your job isn't done."

Falchion reaches the *Ship of Theseus* and locks an armored hand into one of the restraints. A cuff slides down to the forearm, then a series of lights flash green across its surface. The other handhold does the same thing, and Falchion presses its boots into the stirrups.

"Ship of Theseus, this is Falchion. I'm here," Ardent says.

Ghosts continue welding all across the surface of the ship, securing more last-minute attachments.

"What if they don't finish?"

"The scaffolding will fail in transit, tearing Dahlia's ship apart."

"Ship of Theseus here, twenty-five seconds to fold."

Ardent glances at the timer. "But the impact is in twenty!"

"You're about to see Infinite's true power up close," Falchion says.

Over what feels like eternity, Greymalkin closes in and docks with the *Ship of Theseus*, locking into the restraints.

"Fifteen seconds to fold!" Dahlia calls.

The Ghosts work like beings possessed, welding lasers flashing all across the hull.

Falchion counts it down. *"Impact in five...four..."*

In the profound silence of space, Ardent witnesses the destruction of a world.

A flurry of silver streaks pierces the planet, blowing a hole out of the other side and dragging a trail of white-hot material across the stars. A flaming shock wave travels over the surface, and Theseus Prime blooms like a flower, crust opening to reveal the molten core. It slings chunks of planet in all directions, rotations destabilized and thrown off-axis. Ardent watches with rising fear as the ground rushes up to meet them.

Dahlia's voice breaks the quiet, stern and commanding. "Vanguards, hang on tight. Fold imminent."

Falchion counts up all the incoming threats for Ardent, but they don't see the point—it's a wall of shards, each several kilometers across. That's when they hear the rain—high-speed rocks ricocheting off Falchion's armor. Ghosts go flying, smashed by incoming projectiles. Every ping sets Ardent's teeth on edge, and they wonder if any of them are large enough to pierce the *Ship of Theseus.*

Then all is quiet and white.

Chapter Seventeen

Don't Give Me Another Goodbye

Nisha stands before Gus and Ardent in a blue embroidered salwar kurta, fabric shot through with subtle flames. She looks worn down, and he wonders how long it's been since she's had any decent sleep. With the unfolding hostilities between Pictor and Earth, Cascade has been the only one on guard duty.

"Please tell me you'll get here soon," Nisha says. "I'm beginning to question the existence of intelligent life around here."

"What are they doing now?" Gus asks.

She flaps a hand in annoyance. "The only thing they ever do! Arguing! You ready for this?"

Gus checks his tux for dust on instinct, then feels silly since it's all virtual. He's traveling to Earth, stuck in Greymalkin's chest, but that's easy to forget inside a perfect, immersive simulation. The trio of Conduits stand atop a mirror, surrounded on all sides by streaking stars.

He purses his lips. "For peace talks with the Pictorans? No."

"I've been at the table with them all week, Gus," she says. "I need you."

"Being honest here," he says, "I would put this off for the rest of my life if you let me."

Nisha shakes her head. "Infinite is blowing up worlds, and mine is unshielded. Every delay is asking me for a sacrifice I will not continue to make."

He nods. "Understood."

Ardent comes alongside Gus, taking his arm. "Don't forget that Redeemer is here. It said it would help us."

"And the crabs can't kill you during a teleconference," she says. "So lighten up."

Yeah, Gus, it's only the weight of the Homeworld on your shoulders.

"You think this is going to work?" he asks.

"Only one way to find out," Nisha says.

Greymalkin will now connect Gus to the Conduit Council.

An orgy of animal screams fills the air, overwhelming his universal translator. Trees shoot up all around him, twisting and alien, prismatic leaves like the works of famed Capital Age surrealist Lisa Frank. Water rushes beneath his feet, and he finds himself standing atop a babbling brook, socks dream-logic dry. A mossy island rises before him where the Conduits perch atop dark stone pedestals. A Pictoran stands among them, but no one Gus recognizes—deep red with white claws and bristling spines. Twisting blue armor covers its form, beaded and woven between the ridges, and Gus is glad he's not facing the monster in real life. Vanguards tower over the scene like curious giants, blotting out much of the clear blue sky—though there's a conspicuous hole where Ambershell would've stood.

Gus instinctively takes a step back, but Ardent slides an arm around his waist.

"I'm here, babe."

Rain looks up at their arrival and waves the humans over. The other Conduits go silent and turn to face the newcomers like they just walked into the wrong pub.

Gus gives Nisha a bleak smile. "They stopped arguing."

"Small wonders," she replies.

He forces one foot in front of the other until he's reached the open pedestal meant for humanity.

"Hello, August Kitko," comes a soft, deep voice. The Pictoran gently places each clawed foot as it scuttles up to him, remarkably quiet. "I am What Lurks in the Darkness."

He can't think of anything in the face of this nightmare and defaults to "Pleasure is all mine." Clearing his throat, he adds, "Are you the new Conduit?"

"No, but all Pictorans are wired to connect from their hatching day. Any that are incompatible are destroyed."

"How...inhuman." Gus knows What Lurks in the Darkness will take it as a compliment.

"You're honest." It looms over him. "I look forward to getting inside that head of yours."

"It is time to discuss our plan, What Lurks in the Darkness," Rain says. "You are not a Conduit, but a petitioner. Please assume your place."

The Pictoran's bone-white eyestalks loom over Gus, bulbous lenses clicking. "Indeed. I won't be one of you until Azureshell is complete."

Well, that answers your first question, Gus.

Rain begins once everyone has assumed their place. "My fellow Conduits, we all recognize the threat that Infinite represents to humanity, as well as to our union. The collusion between Infinite and Overseer, one of our oldest enemies, sends a clear message— Overseer is willing to violate the Eldest Directive, creating a proxy war against the Coalition in the Milky Way. We shall not stand for it here, nor anywhere else."

Jet hovers over its pedestal, tentacles not bound by the physics of the real world. Chromatophores ripple deep crimson in time. "So even you admit this war is a ruse to draw us out, Rain."

Rain's brow is set, and it flashes sharp teeth. "But it is still one we must win. We cannot allow Infinite to regain its strength, or it will serve our enemy."

"And we must not allow the humans to be extinguished. Organic sentience must be preserved," Redeemer's voice booms. *"That is our vow."*

Gus watches the other aliens react, but he's not adept at reading their body languages.

What Lurks in the Darkness's voice is gentle. "Pictor questions the wisdom of our membership in the Coalition. Perhaps we would be better off not wasting our resources on this doomed species."

"And what of King's promise to eliminate Infinite in retaliation for all the deaths?" Rain asks. "'The Pictoranate will be repaid.' Were those not the words spoken through Ambershell when Overseer destroyed our fleets?" It shrugs. "I thought King never lied."

"Your insults are wasted, gentle Rain." What Lurks in the Darkness's antennae twitch. "My King spoke truth. We will have our revenge upon Overseer and Infinite if it takes ten thousand years."

"I see," Rain says. "So, you will withdraw today to fight in another millennium. Brave."

The Pictoran clicks a few steps closer to Rain. "Pictor chooses to focus on the most opportune debts to collect first. For example, it will be easy to exact revenge upon humanity if *they* are fighting Infinite, and *we* are not."

"Is that a threat?" Gus asks.

What Lurks in the Darkness looks down at him. "So perceptive."

He doesn't have a retort for that and regrets opening his mouth. "Okay. Just, uh, checking."

What Lurks in the Darkness returns its attention to Rain. "I do not come here as a harbinger of war, esteemed Conduits, but a negotiator. I will tell you the parameters of our shared situation, and you will tell me the outcome you wish for. It is that simple."

"Go on, then," Rain says. "Speak."

"Ambershell was destroyed, and rather than hold *this* vermin accountable"—it points a pincer at Gus—"the Coalition has opted to let it go free. You pretended to be our allies but refuse to give us justice. Every Conduit here should take note—the Coalition will abandon your people, too, when the time comes."

It continues, "You cannot leave this system to hunt Infinite, because the moment you do, the Pictoranate will descend upon Earth like hungry broodlings. Our navy may be evenly matched against the Coalition, but against the humans' flotsam fleet, it will be a joke. Should the Coalition choose to fight us before you leave, you will be too weak to face Infinite and Overseer and will perish. Your hands are tied and your efforts doomed, unless you give us what we want."

"Me," Gus says.

All eyes fall on Gus.

"I do wonder…" What Lurks in the Darkness turns to face him. "How one can be as selfish as you. I had no idea humans were so terribly constructed."

Gus grimaces. "Excuse me?"

What Lurks in the Darkness rocks with soft laughter. "*You* are the only obstacle to humanity's prosperity and future. *You* are the reason we fight. If you were not in the way, we would gladly help your people." It dangles its eyestalks close enough that Gus could reach up and slap them. "A Pictoran has no such petty attachments to individual survival. We are all agents of King and servants of our people. Do you see, August Kitko, how you have impeded the future of all humans with your brazen individualism?"

Gus hates that it has a point, and his mind races for something to say back.

Before he can respond, Ardent scoffs. "Shove it up your cloaca."

What Lurks in the Darkness laughs once more. "Your quips reek of desperation."

"Not the only thing that reeks around here," Ardent mutters.

"There is something else you want." Redeemer's voice echoes through the hollow. *"Another justice the Pictoranate has been denied."*

Gus exchanges a hopeful expression with Ardent.

The crab spreads its claws to the heavens, calling out to Redeemer. "What can you give us that we want as much as the heretic August Kitko?"

"To be a human affront to King is bad," Redeemer says, *"but a Pictoran failure is unforgivable. Scent of Rot could not carry out King's will. It is a living defect, an icon of Pictoran fallibility, well-preserved. Should you accompany us, we will deliver Scent of Rot for your justice."*

"Excuse me?" Gus steps forward. "Redeemer, you told me to keep it alive! I convinced Rot to come peacefully so that it could . . . I don't know . . . have a future, and— You told me to save it!"

"Yes," Redeemer replies. *"Because I knew a prisoner would be critical to our negotiations."*

"So they can torture and murder it?" He gestures at What Lurks in the Darkness. "Scent of Rot may be a lot of things, but it's one of us! A Conduit!"

What Lurks in the Darkness stares at Gus in the wake of his outburst.

"I'm right, aren't I?" Gus asks. "Isn't that what you're going to do? Kill it?"

What Lurks in the Darkness laughs once more. "You, August Kitko—we would execute immediately. Scent of Rot, on the other claw, we would not allow the privilege of death."

"Gus, you can't get in the middle of this." Ardent gives his arm a squeeze. "Scent of Rot made its decision."

"And it killed Titans," Nisha adds. "A lot of them."

"Because of King!" he says. "What would it have done with free will?"

The world seems to close in on Gus, and his chest tightens. He can't stop shaking his head no, even though no one is talking.

What Lurks in the Darkness can't cock its head, but it tilts its body, inspecting Gus. "You care for an enemy."

"Scent of Rot is not *my* enemy." He wants to spit on this thing. "It was manipulated, just like me."

"It seems I have made a miscalculation," the Pictoran says. "I thought you purely selfish, but you are also weak."

"That is irrelevant to this negotiation." Redeemer leans down, blotting out the sun. *"A deal has been offered, Pictoran. Scent of Rot for an armistice. Do you take it?"*

"I must confer with King," What Lurks in the Darkness says.

"Seek your god's counsel, then." Redeemer returns to its original pose.

For a long, tense moment, no one speaks, and What Lurks in the Darkness falls still. Lights flare across its carapace, and it shudders in ecstasy at the connection to King. Ardent takes Gus's hand and squeezes tightly.

What Lurks in the Darkness turns to address the larger crowd. "Just as we can wait to take our revenge upon Overseer, we can postpone our justice against Scent of Rot. It already suffers a fate worse than death—living with the scorn of divinity. It can survive for hundreds of years under such a yoke, but August Kitko must see justice done much sooner, for he is damned by Greymalkin's modifications."

Ardent throws up their hands. "Oh, come on! What is your fucking problem?"

What Lurks in the Darkness points at Gus.

"The petitioner has spoken its terms." Redeemer leans down to inspect the clearing. *"What say you, Conduits?"*

Jet swirls with light, black tentacles spreading out. "The Leonids are aligned with the Pictoranate. We would see justice done, and the life of one human is a fraction of the value offered in return. August Kitko should be grateful."

Frond hops atop its pedestal, briefly running its beak through the feathers under its wing. "I'm sorry, August Kitko . . . but we're not strong enough to fight two fronts."

The amphibious Quickslip nods, gill stalks shaking behind it like thick braids. "So many have already paid the ultimate price for peace. Pictor's demands are unreasonable, but these are unreasonable times. I must confer with my fellow Niners before rendering a verdict."

Clawkiller clasps its furry little hands together, black eyes shining. "It is too soon to make a decision. More discussion must be had. August Kitko does not deserve to perish for his transgressions. But . . . I would die for the good of my people. I think any Conduit would. We must continue negotiations."

Swift's mandibles chitter and antennae twitch. "Agreed. I could not let my brood suffer, even if my actions were justified. Still, we must delve deeper into this matter for a better solution!"

"And how much time do we have for these investigations?" Rain asks. "I do not wish any harm to come to August Kitko, but I fear how much will be done to more innocents if we delay."

"Wow. Wasn't expecting you to vote against me, Rain," Gus says.

Rain gives him a somber look. "I cast my lot with your people. Nisha Kohli has already pointed out that her planet is unshielded."

Ardent pipes up. "But Infinite doesn't want to destroy worlds. It wants to eat their inhabitants."

Rain raises a hand to Nisha. "What say you about that? Infinite has just splintered Theseus Prime. Earth is protected from that fate, but New Jalandhar and Fugelsangen lack the same defenses."

Nisha looks like someone stabbed her in the gut. Her eyes dart to Gus, then away, and she doesn't seem to know what to say. "I... This question is unfair. Gus is my friend."

It eats Gus up inside, but he nods at her. "Nisha... I promise I won't hate you, no matter what. Just say what you need to say."

Nisha's eyebrows knit together and she shuts her eyes. She opens her mouth to speak, then shuts it and tries again. "My world... has an axe blade across its neck. I am, of course, eager to bring them safety and peace. No one deserves to live under the constant threat of annihilation."

Gus braces himself for the first human to vote against his life—and for the possibility that Ardent might do the same.

"Gus... If they made me vote..." She blinks at him with shining eyes, and she smiles. "With my hands tied..."

She turns to face What Lurks in the Darkness and her smile fades. "I'd still vote that you and every other crab can get fucked."

Ardent gasps in delight.

Nisha marches up to the Pictoran, ankles jingling the whole way, and its antennae draw back. "This isn't about Gus. It's about standing together and protecting every human, no matter how small. We've always been under threat. *That's how humans live.* The only thing that has changed is you! *Your* kind came to my galaxy with an appetite for violence. Scent of Rot started this, and you all *deserved* to lose your holy Vanguard for your foolishness! You want to trade? Gus once sacrificed himself to rescue my people, whereas *you* have given us nothing but trouble! I think I speak for all of the human Conduits when I say, 'Get lost, you bottom-feeding, silica-brained—'"

Gus watches her with a kindling of pride in his heart as she rails against his adversary, finishing with "—Cascade and I will shuck the shells from your sorry backs and burn your ships in orbit."

What Lurks in the Darkness softly clicks its claws. "Would you risk every human life in exchange for one?"

She gives the big crab a dark look. "Would King risk every Pictoran to find out? Humans are better at surviving than you think. Your god would do well to reconsider."

"I'm with you, Nisha!" Ardent shouts.

The Pictoran harrumphs. "Of course you would back your mate."

They cross their arms. "Or I could be doing what's right, asshole."

"Your unity is admirable," What Lurks in the Darkness says, "if arbitrary. One wonders what the rest of your species would decide."

They'd throw themselves on the fire for Gus. He had people *lining up* to die in his stead. Even now, by backing him, Nisha and Ardent are volunteering a war, which they will not fight alone. So many others will perish.

He looks down at his hands. There isn't any blood on them, but he'll start to see it soon if he doesn't do something to fix this. The next world Infinite wipes or destroys will be because of him.

Greymalkin's thoughts begin to seep into his own. It knows what Gus is considering doing.

And?

It cannot disagree. Greymalkin can negotiate the contract for peace right now.

Can we trust King?

The Pictoran Starmind notoriously keeps its word.

Gus's pulse pounds in his ears, and he can barely hear Ardent and Nisha shouting at What Lurks in the Darkness, much less the other Conduits joining in the debate. Within seconds, the shrieking of all parties has become unbearable.

"They don't speak for me," Gus yells, and everyone stops to stare. He tries not to look at Ardent, and it's so hard. "Look, I don't...I don't agree. Just because I'm a human, doesn't mean we're on the same side of this."

He nods, psyching himself up to do the next part.

"I get a vote, and I vote to hand myself over with some conditions."

If crabs could smile. "Such as?"

Gus surrenders, deflating. "That it doesn't hurt."

Ardent violently grabs Nisha's hand and raises it. "Two against one! Overruled!"

He can't avoid them now, and Ardent burns like the heart of a star, but he holds their gaze. "Ardent, *stop*. I'm not going to be the roadblock to safeguarding billions of lives."

The whites of their eyes always go red before their nose when they cry. They ball their fists like a toddler, and it's almost cute. "It's your goddamned death wish! You want to sacrifice yourself, and here's your fucking way out! How dare you? How *dare*—"

"*You don't get it!*" He presses his lips tight and takes a deep breath, trying to keep his voice steady. He hadn't meant to be that loud. "You made me hope, and—Ardent, you really were everything I ever wanted." He gestures to them with a shaking hand. "I started to believe in a future with you, and even though we're both doomed, I thought"—his chest hurts and a lump forms in his throat—"we were going to be doomed as a pair, you know? But you've got to realize by now... in any couple, no matter how great they are together..."

He can't look them in the eye anymore. "One will always be alone at the end."

What Lurks in the Darkness says, "Your proposal excites K—"

Ardent wheels on the Pictoran. "*Will you shut the fuck up for two seconds?*"

Gus smiles and shakes his head as they return their attention to him. "I can't say I've loved every minute of life, but you were one decent thing that happened to me. Without your melody, I would've only been a sad song."

The emotion is starting to bleed out of Gus, but Ardent's fury remains. They scowl at him through tears, trembling.

He looks to Nisha, and she's devastated.

"I would have fought for you," she says.

"I know." He lets out a long sigh. "Sorry you stood up for nothing."

Her lip stiffens. "I stood up for what was right."

He nods. "That's your thing. And trivia."

That cracks her, and she throws her arms around him. The simulation is so good that he feels the wetness of her cheeks on his shoulder. He can barely breathe, she has him so tight.

Greymalkin has finished negotiations with King. The Starmind has accepted all of Gus's wishes. He will turn himself over to the Pictorans after the destruction of Infinite. They will honor his desire for a painless death. In return, King will support the humans against Infinite.

And if I die fighting?

The Pictorans will accept your annihilation any way it happens.

He looks to What Lurks in the Darkness. "Greymalkin has completed the contract. Did you hear back from your boss?"

Ardent's expression melts to horror.

"Yes," What Lurks in the Darkness replies. "You accept our vengeance."

Gus forces the words out. "That's right."

"Very good," it says. "The will of King is absolute."

Gus hangs his head, bitterness on his lips. "That it is."

Falchion wakes Ardent from their slumber. They blink, eyes still puffy and achy from the night before, and the star streaks of a warp bubble come into focus.

They didn't know what to say to Gus, and so they shut down, retreating into the safety of Falchion's cocoon to weep. They knew it was cruel to leave Gus hanging, but they needed some time to deal with their own shit before wading into his.

Falchion appears before them, wearing an outfit Ardent might characterize as "Evil Queen of the Universe."

"Are you going to start crying again?" Its eyes glow orange beneath ash-white bangs.

They give it a hateful stare.

"Dahlia is hailing. You going to ignore her, too?"

"I'm not ignoring Gus, okay?"

"He has days left to live under the new accord."

"And I don't want to ruin any of them by chewing his face off for what he did. Please put Dahlia through."

Dahlia appears before Ardent, a vision in her unbuttoned captain's jacket. She's just a hologram, so Ardent can't truly feel her presence.

"You look like you're about to swash some buckles." Ardent waves a hand up and down her outfit.

"Maybe not my best move when I'm about to surrender to Earth for piracy. Arrival in ten minutes."

That knocks the sleep loose from Ardent's brain. "But Fritz is going to help you escape, right?"

Dahlia shakes her head. "No, Ardent. I'm good."

"What do you mean? No, you're not. We've never surrendered."

She smiles. "It's time for that to change. I need better medical care. Been living in cramped quarters and dirty ruins for months. I'm starting to suspect jail will be more comfortable."

"Dahlia! Come on!"

"I said no. Make peace with it."

That's exactly what she used to say to Ardent as a teenage pop hopeful. Ardent was always trying to get into trouble, and Dahlia would often have to step in as temporary guardian. There was no debate after that statement.

"Besides, is this how you want to spend your last few minutes with me before Tazi scoops me up?"

First Gus, now Dahlia—both refusing to fight fate.

They look away. "No."

"I know it's hard for you to accept what's happening."

"I thought we were always going to be together."

She purses her lips. "That was a childish dream."

Ardent grits their teeth. She can be so cold sometimes.

"But one I shared." She smiles at some memory. "Ardent, do you know how much I love you?"

The Earth comes zooming into Ardent's view as the warp bubble breaks. Nearby, Big Gate City teems with activity, and a host of UW ships await the *Ship of Theseus*'s arrival, lights flashing—interceptors full of orbital cops.

"There was a time we stopped at nothing to keep the show going," Ardent says.

Dahlia props a hand on her hip. "The refugees need to be offloaded. The *Ship of Theseus* needs resupply before you go into battle against Infinite. We don't have time to divert when Infinite keeps raising the stakes on us. Besides . . . shit. Tazi is already hailing me."

"And you, as well," Falchion adds. *"I'll patch everyone in."*

Tazi's hologram appears in the space beside Dahlia, hands folded behind her back with a navy coat. She wears a pair of amber-tinted circadian glasses, the kind Marilyn wears to get adjusted to long-haul voyages.

"Nice specs," Ardent says.

Tazi regards them with flinty eyes. "Thank you. Your mother gave them to me."

"Wait, you've been hanging out with my mom?"

"We're handling her security. She has been quite kind to me."

"Maybe she forgot you want to arrest Dahlia."

Tazi tsks. "Or maybe I'm not here to do that."

Dahlia and Ardent exchange glances.

Tazi begins to pace. "The *Ship of Theseus* is experimental, and a keystone of the most important operation in our history. Miss Faust has captained it out of the deadliest circumstances and is the person most familiar with its systems—since she also oversaw its construction. We can't risk inexperience deciding the fate of our species." She stops. "The United Worlds will issue a full pardon if Miss Faust agrees to captain the *Ship of Theseus* into battle."

Ardent's heart leaps, and they look to their friend. They can't read Dahlia's expression, but there's undeniable weariness in her bones.

"I have to tell you," Dahlia says, "that kind of sounds like a suicide mission. It's hard to imagine this thing surviving a Vanguard fight."

"Not at all," Tazi says. "You drive the bus. You drop everyone off. You get away. The ship designers say we can optimize the Dark Drive for two bursts. If the Vanguards need to retreat, they can use their own folding drives."

"And our team is the least likely to be eaten by ship hunters," Ardent says.

"I'm not military, though," Dahlia says.

"You wouldn't be doing it alone." Tazi touches a hand to her chest. "I would be your first mate."

"So, you'd be reporting to her instead of arresting her?" Ardent says.

"I'm the Vanguard mission support specialist. I need to be there," Tazi replies. "You see, Miss Faust, I have as much riding on your decision as you do."

"Dahlia, this could be your ticket out of this mess," Ardent says, but Dahlia only glances their way.

"Full immunity, including civil exemption, from Belle et Brutale, the German cops, any fallout starting on the day Greymalkin landed." Dahlia sits, her captain's chair coming into focus on the hologram. "Also, I want you to put my mother up somewhere nice."

Tazi blinks. "Pardon?"

"She's languishing in a nursing home in Jersey. I want her somewhere tropical, with lots of daiquiris and pretty boys. Make sure she has a view."

Tazi crosses her arms. "We are not currently entertaining demands."

"You'd better start." Dahlia rocks on her heels. "Otherwise, you're going to have staffing problems."

"This is the future of humanity!" Tazi protests.

"Which includes my future," Dahlia says, "so play ball or quit wasting my time."

Tazi sighs. "Unbelievable. I'll have to run it past my superiors. Is there anything else?"

"I want to meet with my lawyer, naturally." Dahlia smiles like a happy cat. "But this seems a small price to pay to secure—as you say—the most experienced captain for what is totally not a suicide mission."

"I will see what I can do." Then Tazi disappears without even saying goodbye.

"Wow. You really pissed her off that time."

Dahlia smirks. "Nobody negotiates better than Dahlia Faust. Believe me when I say I'm taking Tazi for a ride."

"Oh yeah?"

"I would've flown this mission for free."

Ardent tilts their head. "Why?"

"I want you to make it home."

"You're such a cool aunt—"

"Sister," she interrupts. "We're headed to Big Gate City. Human ships can take our refugees from there. Now, if you'll excuse me, I have a lot of coordination to do."

"Let me know if I can help," Ardent says.

She looks hopeful for the first time in a while. "I think I have what I need."

Despite the circumstances, Gus is happy to be back at Big Gate City, where he can see the Earth. Riding on the outside of the *Ship of Theseus* was harrowing, and he couldn't relax for fear of falling off the whole time.

While it's still the same old blue marble spinning in space, there are a lot of new arrivals. The jump gate charges and flashes as yet another group of Coalition ships enters the Milky Way.

Gus whistles at Greymalkin's tracking readouts. "There have got to be twice as many ships as when we left."

According to Cascade, Coalition forces have been building up in the system ever since Operation Pitchfork. They primarily come from Andromeda and Pictor, though there are new Arp and Niner ships. The accumulated Coalition force now exceeds the size of the initial armada.

"They look like they're about to go to war."

That is likely. Every member species has been exercising its right to the gate, calling in reinforcements. If Gus's execution doesn't bring about peace, that will be extremely bad.

Gus rolls his eyes. "Hopefully, my death goes smoothly."

Greymalkin lets go of the *Ship of Theseus* and weaves into the underbelly of Big Gate City, and Falchion follows almost immediately, their absence considerably slimming the ship's profile. Cascade joins them from Earth orbit, and the three human Vanguards form a processional, ending at the Vanguard docks below the Palace of Unity. The other Coalition species have already arrived.

"What's on the agenda?"

Gus and the others are to remain in their cockpits for a meeting of the Conduit Council.

"We're not going to have to stay too long, are we?" Gus says. "If I don't have much time, I'd rather not spend it among bickering assholes."

Greymalkin believes this briefing mostly covers Founder's advancements on fleet countermeasures to Infinite's coronal mass ejections.

"Is it something the Vanguards will use?"

No.

"Is it working?"

Yes.

"Great. Do I need to waste time learning about it?"

No.

"Sweet. I want to go to a restaurant."

What if Gus misses something important?

"My thoughts exactly. What if I never got to try my favorite alien food because I spent my final hours in briefings? Can't you listen in and flash the notes into my mind?"

Greymalkin does not wish to overuse that power, given its side effects.

"Am I going to survive long enough to suffer them?"

That is unlikely.

"All right, then. Flash me."

Greymalkin will fetch the presentation from Founder and imprint it now.

Before Gus can say one way or another, Greymalkin etches the information into his mind with a jolting connection. It's the most boring thing ever to stun Gus, an experience simultaneously profound in its scope and banal in content.

"See?" His voice is hoarse. Did he scream again? "Worth skipping. Dinnertime."

Greymalkin will inform the Palace of Unity of Gus's arrival.

"Aw, I was hoping to eat local."

Security and biological compatibility are too difficult to arrange.

"All right, fine. We can eat at the palace again."

Gus steps out onto Greymalkin's hand, breathing in the ozone-flavored air of the docking complex. Traffic pulses through the core, thousands of ships readying for action. The bustle is beautiful in its own way, and Gus is glad he got to see it. Plenty of humans have gotten to glimpse extraordinary things, but he actually witnessed an alien civilization from the inside.

As Greymalkin lowers him toward the deck, he wonders if this will be the last time he ever sees Big Gate City.

A couple of minders wait for him at ground level—a gray-furred Andromedan and a Leonid suspended in its water ball. They give him an adjuster collar, take him to the Conduit lockers to let him freshen and change, then escort him to the Conduit lounge.

He still marvels at the lounge's sleek beauty, its sloping windows revealing the thriving city along with a breathtaking view of Earth. The seats are all empty, given that his colleagues are all stuck in a meeting—including Ardent. He's kind of glad they're not present. Now he can watch the tapestry of ships weave over Earth's atmosphere in peace.

A spiderlike Founder unit pops up behind the bar as Gus approaches. "Skipping my presentation?"

He jolts, then recovers. "No offense."

"You have other things on your mind." It spins to the back walls, metal arms shooting out to grab bottles to mix cocktails. "It's understandable."

"So how much alien booze am I able to drink?"

Founder never slows down. "Most of it is alcohol based, so that depends on your willingness and fortitude."

Gus leans against the bar, folding his hands together. "I want to try a lot of things tonight."

"Then you shall." It passes him a glass with an earthy-smelling liquid. "We start with an aperitif. This one is Leonid."

He tastes it—licorice and salt, and his tongue tingles like he licked a battery terminal. "What is it?"

"A neurotoxin. It'll inhibit your ability to feel full."

"What are you drinking?" comes Nisha's voice behind him.

Gus gives her a manic smile. "Neurotoxin!"

Founder whirs and spins, snatching more bottles off the shelf to concoct wonders. "August Kitko is here to have the meal of a lifetime, and we have a lot of ground to cover. Since you're skipping my briefing, too, would you like to join us?"

She practically jumps onto the sleek stool nearest Gus. "One neurotoxin, please."

"Very good." Founder whips up two more drinks and vanishes into a nearby door, presumably a kitchen.

"You bowed out, too?" Gus asks.

She nods. "Greymalkin told Cascade what you did, and I decided to tag along."

"I didn't think Greymalkin would tell on me."

"Our Vanguards keep no secrets from one another."

"I'm just surprised it let you skip. That's bad for your brain to flash it like that."

"If I miss a moment at the end of my life, but gain one now with a friend, then it was worth it."

That surprises him.

"You're a good guy, Gus," she says. "Just want to spend some time with you."

He takes a swig. "I know plenty of people who'd disagree."

"You mean people like you?" Nisha downs her alien licorice tingler like it's nothing. He can't think of anything to say, and she continues, "It's okay. You hate yourself. But not tonight. From now until your head hits your pillow, you're not allowed to say one mean thing about yourself."

"Or what?"

Her eyebrows jump twice, and she gives him wild eyes. "Or I'll slap you."

"Are you fast enough to—"

She slaps him. Not hard, but enough to surprise him.

He rolls his eyes. "Okay, but I wasn't ready—"

She slaps him again and taps his nose with an index finger. He can't help but laugh in disbelief.

"All right, all right." He sips his drink. "I see how it works."

"Kind thoughts only tonight." She checks the bottom of her cup for any spare drops, shaking them onto her tongue. A stray gets in her eye, and she gasps, blinking.

"Oh my god! You okay?" Gus tries to peer at her, but she's daubing away liquid with a napkin.

"Fine! Just blurry."

Founder comes out right on time, assuring both of them it's fine and prepping more drinks. They're little artworks—Gus's a swirl of green and blue in a pebbled glass mug, Nisha's a milky red tea with a cardamom-scented steam in a clay cup. She picks it up and inhales deeply. When Nisha blinks at Gus, one of her eyes is red and dilated, so he has to restrain a snort.

The first course comes out—an ocher gourd the size of Gus's head, along with a pair of spoons. Founder splits and roasts it right there with its knife and blowtorch attachments. Gus scoops out a fragrant spoonful of deep red meat and takes a bite—custardy, creamy, and sweet.

"What is it?" he asks.

"A type of bean, common to Arp worlds," it replies. "This plant, fully grown, forms the basis of their treeships' circulatory systems."

Nisha takes a bite. "What's it called?"

"Kidney vine," Founder says. "Now I shall attend to the next course."

Founder leaves them with their food, and the pair chat amiably about their lives before the war. Nisha fills him in on all the old drama at the zoning and permit offices, talking like she'll be back at her desk next cycle.

"Do you wish you hadn't been chosen?" Gus asks. "That you were still in the bureaucracy instead of being a Conduit?"

"Like, if Cascade had never..." She brushes a port on her forearm.

"Yeah. Sometimes, I wonder—" Gus sifts his thoughts with his fingers. "What if Greymalkin had picked someone else? What would I have done?"

"When Cascade arrived..." Nisha begins. "Bullseye and Wanderer had already leveled half the Central District, and I thought, if this is the end—"

Gus finishes her thought. "I'm not going quietly."

"Yeah." She runs a finger along the rim of her cup. "So I started singing. Across the city, Cascade looked right at me, and I'd never been so afraid. My voice almost faltered—but this was my final song, so I refused. I walked toward fate with open arms." She takes another deep breath of steam. "That's why we were chosen. The Vanguards needed someone who loved the sound of life."

"But what if it'd been someone else?"

"That path is closed."

"Hypothetically—"

"*Realistically*," she says, "there's no point in wondering. I won't spend my time sighing into drinks over things I can't have. I won't learn anything that way." She gestures at him with her cup. "I'll just be unhappy, like you."

He grimaces. "To be fair, I'm going to get murdered pretty soon." It's the first time he's said it out loud.

She takes a hesitant sip. "True. Can you change that?"

"I...don't think so."

"How much of the rest of your life do you want to spend grieving?"

It's a simple question, and one he hadn't really considered.

"Not sure I get a choice in whether or not I feel my feelings," he says.

"Grief reminds us of what was good."

Gus thinks on that as he inspects the dregs of his second cocktail. When he looks back on his life, he sees too much of his family drama obscuring his own shine. But then there are the nights in Montreal playing with the Gus Kitko Trio—his true identity. When Gus was onstage with Lisel and Gerta, the universe could've collapsed, and they would've kept playing.

"You only have a few golden days, Gus." Nisha swirls her drink before finishing it off. "What do you want to do with them?"

Founder appears with a sizzling platter of green and yellow vegetable shoots, plopping it down before the pair. Slices of bright purple fruit dot the surface, sweating from the heat. Herbal steam wafts up into Gus's face, and his stomach growls.

"First off," Gus says, "I want to have the best meal ever with my dear friend."

She beams. "And then?"

"I'm going to find Ardent and tell them life is too short to keep sulking."

"That's the spirit! Now don't eat too much. You might need to, uh, get shaken up."

"I'm not going to bet on that. Ardent isn't taking my hails right now."

She picks up one of the alien forks and skewers a few of the shoots. "Gus, you're going to be executed after this mission. If that fact doesn't get you laid, I don't know what will."

"You don't know how bad I am at romance."

She slaps him again.

Chapter Eighteen

More Than Touch

Ardent hears Gus calling their name in the hall outside the presidential suite before the system alerts them to a visitor. They rush to open it and find him standing on the stoop, swaying like a stiff breeze would take him out.

"Aw, what the hell, Gus?"

"Life is short, so…" He raises a finger and nods sagely. "I should come in."

Ardent shakes their head. "What?"

"Sounded better in my head. May I come in?"

"You're drunk."

He pinches the air. "I had a little accident with a neurotoxin."

Ardent gazes into his dead eyes and sees exactly what they always feared—someone who stared into death's dark mirror and couldn't look away. He's accepted it. He's probably happy about it. Ardent can't save him.

They chew their lower lip. "What are you hoping to find in here tonight?"

A flash of sobriety. "Mercy."

They hate how much he needs them in that moment, because

they need to be weak.

Ardent steps aside. "Get in here."

Gus takes his time picking through the room until Ardent grabs his hand and guides him to the bed.

"Sit there, baby."

They head to the kitchen and key a couple of hangover vites into the compounder, running a glass of water while the chews print. They bring the water and meds back to the bedroom and give them to him. They take his shoes off, then his pants, negotiating them around his braces. Ardent runs their fingers along his ports, finding them warmer than normal.

He's already given too much to the cause of humanity. Do they have to take the rest of him, too?

His hand flops onto theirs, and he sighs a slurred "I love you."

They tangle their fingers into his and squeeze their eyes shut. "I don't want to be the strong one, Gus."

"Then don't be anything." His voice is a distant whisper. "Lie here with me."

They do, cuddling into him. He rolls over, enveloping Ardent with his arms. They press their forehead to his neck and breathe in his scent, stained with the musk of alcohol. His breathing stabilizes, and he's asleep in minutes.

This isn't how they wanted Gus, but they'll take every second of his beating heart they can get.

A steady jingle works its way into Gus's peaceful rest. If he had to name the tune, he'd call it "Brain Needles in C Major." He tries to ignore it, but every note brings him one step closer to consciousness—

—and a lot of regrets.

As it happens, getting smash drunk and feast stuffed before passing out wasn't his smartest move. At least someone remembered to charge his braces, though he's not sure who. His neck aches, his stomach churns, and his head is equal parts cotton and pressure. When he looses a quiet belch, he's pretty sure his breath could kill someone.

Yet the jingle won't let him be.

Gus's Gang UI hovers over him—an incoming priority hail from Tazi. He switches on some pleasant-appearance filters before answering.

"Good morning." He sounds like he's been gargling gravel.

Tazi appears before him from the bust up, UW military coat crisp and clean. "It's afternoon, Kitko."

"Ah, time's passage."

"You sound like hell. Are you all right?"

He cocks his head. She's never asked him that before.

"Yeah. Just making my way back to the world of the living. How can I help you?"

"I've got an escort coming to pick you up. Report to Greymalkin for a priority briefing."

"Everything okay?"

"Yes. Be ready to suit up in ten minutes."

He rubs the bridge of his nose, providing a tiny amount of relief to his throbbing sinuses. "Can I grab some quick O_2 therapy for my, uh, hangover?"

"We can't keep everyone waiting. All Conduits will be in attendance."

"Yeah, okay." He gets to his feet, knees creaking like never before, and retracts the charge cable on his braces. His head spins a little, like some settled booze just came loose in his bloodstream. Founder's dinner of a lifetime must've aged him twenty years or so.

"Of course. I'll be ready."

"Thank you." She vanishes as the connection terminates.

"Never says 'thank you,' either..." he mutters, shaking his poor head.

Gus turns around to stare at the bed. He distinctly remembers Ardent in his arms, but they're nowhere to be found. Maybe they're already en route?

Doesn't matter. Let's go, Gus.

He slaps his cheeks a few times to get his heart pumping, throws his laundry in the freshener, and heads for the blast shower.

After a thorough cleansing and a most unfortunate visit to the toilet, he's marginally ready to meet the day. The soldiers who come to get him are deferential, and he wonders what the hell is going on. They've always been nice, but this is ridiculous.

A transport waits at the end of the *Ship of Theseus*'s gangway to take Gus to the Vanguard docks. In the back, he finds a personal oxygen bottle, water, and headache medication, courtesy of Tazi. He huffs the O_2 all through the journey, much to the amusement of the soldiers. As it happens, his companions are no strangers to hangovers, either. The transport stops off at a small depot, where techs furnish Gus a fresh Conduit spacesuit.

The transport pulls up at the feet of the human Vanguards, and Gus steps out into the breezy bay. Ardent and Nisha wait for him in their Conduit gear. Ardent looks fully composed, perfectly coifed hair programmed with a blue-orange fade. Nisha, on the other hand, looks like she's been pulverized by a meteor before being stuffed into a spacesuit.

Gus takes a final hit off his oxygen bottle before joining the pair and handing it off to Nisha.

"What were we thinking?" Nisha asks.

"'This is the most exciting meal of my life,'" he replies.

"Ardent." Nisha affects a whine. "I have regrets."

"Y'all partied without me." Ardent crosses their arms. "No sympathy."

Gus frowns, and Ardent gives him a peck on the cheek.

"Kidding," they whisper. "I'm just sorry we couldn't have some more fun last night."

Gus tries on a smile. "There's always tonight."

"And it's already afternoon!" Ardent says, slapping his ass and walking off toward Falchion.

He hopes he'll be recovered by then.

Greymalkin bends down to pick him up, and Gus rides its hand to the chest cavity. The second its probes plug into his ports, he feels a million times better. His whole body becomes ignorable—a consummate blessing.

The familiar pale blue light washes over him before Greymalkin's view of the bay comes into focus.

"What's this Conduit meeting about, big guy?"

The Coalition has located the Infinite Starmind. It is time to discuss mobilization.

"That's—" He wants to say *amazing*, but the sooner they deal with Infinite, the sooner the Pictorans come for his head. Gus has imagined a universe without Infinite plenty of times before, but now a part of him dreads the thought.

The council calls. Is Gus ready?

"God, I hope so."

The connection to the Conduit Council stabilizes, and Gus finds himself standing atop a small island in a vast ocean. The other Conduits have already gathered, and their many voices fill the air.

A stone dais rises from one side, and Gus spies over a dozen creatures of every Coalition species standing on it. Tazi strides among them, dressed in her UW fatigues. The other alien strangers all wear some variation of the Coalition's dark gray military uniform, reinterpreted to fit their unique species.

"Who are those folx?" Nisha says behind him.

"Generals and crap, maybe," Gus responds. "They don't feel real to me, so they're not jacked in."

The three human Conduits remain together, taking their place among the group. When everyone is finally settled, Rain clears its throat and steps forward.

"Welcome, esteemed guests," it says, "to the Conduit Council. We gather today to ensure the continued survival of humanity across the Milky Way"—it glances at the Pictorans on the dais— "and to defeat a hated rival."

Approving noises arise from the crowd. Rain spreads its arms, turning its palms down, and everyone goes quiet.

"As with Operation Pitchfork, Operation Eye Gouge is classified at the highest levels," Rain says.

Surely the name is better in Andromedan.

"Even a single leak could prove devastating to everything we cherish," Rain says, "for we are not simply at war with Infinite, but also Overseer. The price for failure will not only cost us humanity, but the next fight will come to our doorsteps."

"You have already secured our alliances." Jet's skin flickers as it hovers above its pedestal like a dark spirit. "Get on with it, Rain."

"Asshole," Ardent mutters through their teeth, and Gus gives their hand a squeeze.

Rain nods at Jet. "As you say. Let us see our target."

The sky spins from day to night, and a burst of nebulae fills Gus's view, pinched in the center like an hourglass. He squints, and through the luminous haze, he spots two stars in orbit around each other.

"Known to the humans as Eta Carinae, these binary stars form the heart of the Infinite Eye," Rain says, "the largest data processing system in the Milky Way. We believe Infinite chose this location for maximum power efficiency."

The sky zooms in on the primary star, labeled ETA CAR A. Countless dark shapes envelop the surface, leaving only tiny gaps like cracked magma. Part of the "crust" peels off the star, lowering toward Gus's tiny island so everyone can get a better look. To his surprise, it's blurry.

Rain continues, "Our scouts couldn't approach close enough to get specific imaging of Infinite's swarm platforms, but we believe these objects provide the majority of Infinite's power generation and local compute."

"Humanity has exceptional stellar imaging," Gus says, "and have for hundreds of years. Why didn't we see this sooner?"

Rain folds its hands behind its back. "You didn't know what to look for. Eta Carinae is a system on the verge of collapse, having steadily grown dimmer for eight Earth centuries. Infinite used that to its advantage, hiding the construction of its Starmind behind the system's decline so that astronomers couldn't observe the change in radiance. It is also possible that Infinite used its platforms as mirrors, radiating the healthy companion star's rays into the galaxy. Finally, we found this—"

Billions of beams spray out from the star's surface.

"Ultraviolet laser light," Rain says. "Infinite has been using it to make the primary star appear brighter."

It was hiding in plain sight.

"In addition to the natural phenomena," Rain says, "Infinite will be well defended by drones and more ship hunters. In order to be successful, we must be fast. Founder, please explain our limitations."

A humanoid Founder unit comes walking to the fore of the visitors, servos moving beneath its open metal chassis like muscles. It reminds Gus of the first one he met.

"Our biggest danger is the ionizing radiation from the coronal mass ejections, or CMEs," it says. "We must power down our ships during those moments or risk a scrambling of all systems."

The mechanical creature looks to Gus and Nisha. "As *everyone* remembers from my briefing, I will be on board every ship, facilitating the rapid reboots and folds."

Gus closes his eyes and thinks, *Can your systems be damaged by the radiation, Greymalkin?*

Vanguards are built to withstand even the upper atmosphere of a star with thousands of redundant processors. Ionizing radiation is no threat to their electronics, but they will have to reboot as well.

"However, there is a limit—folding drive capacitors cannot fully charge and discharge at a high rate forever. Too many CMEs, too close together, and ships will start exploding. That's why Redeemer and Rain must be fast. For that, we must turn to Dahlia Faust and the *Ship of Theseus*."

The crowd of visitors parts for Dahlia, clad in a UW coat and uniform.

"Thanks," she says, blushing and clearly unaccustomed to this level of decorum. "Uh, yes. I'll be dropping off the Vanguards."

Gus waits, expecting there to be more than that. Given the patient expressions of the others in the briefing, they're thinking the same thing.

"With the Dark Drive," Dahlia adds. "Then I'm going to leave."

Ardent tacks on a little "Go, Dahlia!"

"Thank you, Dahlia Faust." Rain points to the star. "Infinite relies on these platforms. Destroying as many as possible will yield a distinct advantage. With Founder's help, the Dark Drive, and the signature file, we will prevail."

The projections disappear, and the sky returns to daylight.

Rain folds its hands before itself. "Now I'm sure you all have questions. Rather than attempting to answer them all here, I ask that you please direct them to your fleet commanders. Conduits, remain with your Vanguards. We launch in three hours. Good luck."

The feed goes dark, leaving the three human Conduits standing there on an empty black stage.

Fuck.

"Three hours?" Ardent's outrage is palpable. "Are you kidding? Why didn't they tell me?"

"About the most classified operation in history?" Gus asks, and Ardent gives him a look.

"I feel like we just got here!" they say. "I'm not ready!"

"We're Conduits," Nisha says. "What would we even do to get ready?"

"I don't know!" Ardent throws their hands up. "Something. I just thought we'd have a few more days."

Gus closes his eyes and concentrates.

Are we ready, Greymalkin?

No one can ever be prepared for what's coming, but the fleet is as well positioned as possible. Every minute they wait to strike is another chance for Infinite to change the game.

"We have to do it as soon as possible, Ardent," Gus says. "Given how much progress we've made, Infinite's next move will be a checkmate."

They straighten up, eyes meeting his. "But afterward, you'll be . . . I mean, the Pictorans will—"

"That's true." Gus drops his hands to his hips and nods. "I also thought I had more time. Thought we'd get another chance to, you know . . ."

Ardent wraps their arms around themself.

"Be together."

What Gus had wanted was a final night with Ardent. He regrets spending it full and drunk with Nisha, as fun as that had been. He's sure Ardent regrets shutting him out, even for a short while.

And now they'll always have to live with that regret. When he looks at Ardent's anguished face, he knows they're feeling it.

A spotlight cuts through the darkness, revealing a clear grand piano, sparkling like cut crystal. Another pair of lights illuminate a guitar exactly like Baby, as well as a gleaming microphone. The three Conduits walk to their stations, inspecting their chosen instruments.

"Greymalkin, what gives?"

This is what Gus can do to prepare.

He sits down at the piano, tickling out a few scales. The sound is better than real life, like it's playing directly into his brain. "Anyone up for a jam?"

Nisha taps the mic, thumps ringing into shadows. "I'm game. Ardent?"

Ardent gapes at both of them but finally shuts their mouth. He knows they can't resist.

Nisha begins to sing. Her pure voice brightens the air, and he spends a moment taking it in. He can see why Cascade picked her.

Ardent grabs their guitar and dials in a solo, fingers fluttering up and down the fretboard. They bend the strings to mimic Nisha's microtones with masterful precision. Without warning, Nisha switches to a jazzy pop progression, inviting Gus in.

Maybe he'll die after this mission. Maybe he won't even make it to the end. For the moment, though, he's among friends.

The trio jams for hours, laughing and playing while the fleet launches around them. It's not like they're needed to pilot the Vanguards, or to coordinate with mission control. Falchion, Greymalkin, and Cascade handle the details, and Gus doesn't even feel the superluminal fold happen.

The Vanguards join in the song, furnishing a ghostly drum track based on everyone's shared memories of Hjalmar. An upright bass and a trumpet enter the signal—Lisel and Gerta playing from the depths of Gus's soul. An older man accompanies Nisha's haunting vocals, perhaps her grandfather, and she sings out for both of them. Unseen crowds roar, Ardent's countless admirers.

These were the forces that shaped the team's artistry, indelible as DNA, and Gus plays with utmost reverence. He wishes it could go on forever.

But all things must come to an end.

Greymalkin's summons comes as Gus puts the finishing notes on another rollicking number—it's time to retire. His mind needs conditioning and rest before the confrontation with the Infinite Eye.

Ardent and Nisha are talking to themselves—perhaps they're hearing the voices of their Vanguards, too.

"One more song," Ardent says.

"Yeah, five more minutes." Nisha adjusts her grip on the mic.

Gus appreciates the sentiment, but there's nothing to be done. Greymalkin is right. The team has to arrive perfectly rested and ready to fight. He stands and walks around his piano to take Ardent's hands in his.

He gives them a brave smile. "It's time. I'll see you on the other side."

"No, Gus." They shake their head. "One more. The Vanguards are just being—"

He strokes their cheek. "The show must go on, Ardent Violet."

Ardent gives a painful swallow. Without warning, they hug Gus, squeezing the life out of his ribs. He's hit from the side as Nisha comes in hard, throwing her arms around the pair. They all hold one another as long as they can, sinking to the ground.

When Gus opens his eyes, they're gone.

"Ardent." Falchion's voice is smooth and kind, the way Ardent sounds when they shush Gus.

They open their eyes to the swimming pool–blue void. "Wha—? Are we there yet?"

"Two hours out."

"Too early."

357

Unconsciousness is so much better than spiraling.

"Gus wants to talk one last time before—"

That changes things. "Me too."

Monaco's salt breeze tickles their bare arms and ruffles the hem of their silk gown. When they rub their shoulders, the ports are gone. They don't remember the name of this little park, but it was the first time they saw Gus.

Even from far away, they noticed him at the edge of the party. They were bringing the house down, buoying faltering spirits left and right, but he was immune. He looked like the only person there who knew the truth—everything has an end, and it's too often sooner than later. He didn't buy into the propaganda about the *Dictum* stopping Juliette, and his hope was dead.

Ardent and the others were making promises to their futures. He was making predictions.

The mere appearance of his sad ass soured Ardent's mood so badly they snuck off to get high on a side street. Then he had the temerity to drag his thunderstorm on a string down the road after them. They considered chasing him off—lord knows he was ready to flee—but there was something pleading in his smile. Gus took in kindness like a drowning man grabs a life preserver.

"Hey." His voice snaps them back to the present.

When they turn, they find the man they met, curly black hair down to his shoulders and a shy smile. He wears a charcoal suit, white shirt unbuttoned halfway, and a pair of shiny loafers.

Ardent smiles. "Hey."

He glances at his feet. "I didn't get a chance to tell you how sorry I was."

"Sorry?"

"I feel like I...like I missed our last night together."

They step closer to him. "That wasn't our last night, though. We're going to have plenty more, because—we are going to, like—"

"I love your optimism."

"Do you believe me?" They slip a hand around the back of his neck the way they do when he makes love to them.

He gently presses his forehead against theirs. "I want to, with all of my heart."

"We'll get more time. We'll find a way."

He nods. "Yeah. Ardent, can I ask you something? And it's okay if you say no."

They search his face. "What is it?"

He grows bashful. "Do you want to Deepsync? With, uh, me?"

Ardent laughs. "I'm equal parts turned on and confused."

Gus laughs, too, cheeks flushed. "Yeah. It's weird, I know. You don't have to—"

"No, baby, I just don't get it."

"It's touching memories. All the parts you want to share. What makes us who we are. That way, you'll always know who I, you know—was."

They press their face into his neck, tightening their embrace. "Don't say it like that."

"The process makes me unforgettable."

Ardent strokes his cheek, stubble rough against their guitar calluses. "You already are."

He looks into their eyes. "This is the best chance to share my life with you."

And they want that—more than they wanted to be a Conduit, they wanted him. The pair were supposed to spend endless days, to fly all over the galaxy bringing the house down, to make love until their bodies grew too old to handle it.

"We're supposed to be together," Ardent says.

His eyes are a clear, mossy stream. "We are together. Do you want to stay that way?"

"Yes," they say. "I love you. I think I always will."

He smiles down at them. "Then I guess this life isn't a tragedy after all."

Deepsync in progress...

They take a deep breath and kiss him, plunging into his depths.

Chapter Nineteen

Get Hot

Tazi's even, measured voice is the calm before the storm. "All Vanguards, starfall in sixty seconds. Status check."

Gus isn't remotely prepared.

"Redeemer here, standing by," Rain replies.

It will be okay. Greymalkin will help Gus. With the Fount, he will know everything he must.

"Cascade here, all systems green!"

But that's not it. Gus isn't ready for what comes after. This can't be his final song.

"Falchion, ready to rock."

Gus tightens Greymalkin's grip on the *Ship of Theseus*, checking his boots in the stirrups. He focuses on the light at the end of the tunnel of warp streaks—the rapidly approaching Infinite Eye.

"Greymalkin here," he says. "Ready."

"The Coalition Fleet isn't in good shape," Tazi says, "but they have Infinite's undivided attention. So far, all Coalition Vanguards are intact."

"We will make the most of this opportunity," Rain says.

The *Ship of Theseus* has an awful habit of rattling when it's about to come out of warp. Its vibrations travel up through Greymalkin's arms like the rising tone of a warning siren.

"All right, kids," Dahlia says. "We're almost at your stop. I want you off this bus as fast as possible. We need to fire our reserve drive and get the fuck out of here."

"Aw, you don't want to stay and watch?" Ardent says.

"Couldn't pay me enough," she replies. "Fifteen seconds to dark burn."

"It's a privilege," Nisha says, "being here with all of you."

"Same," Ardent replies.

Gus chances a smile. "Pleasure's all mine."

"Agreed," Rain adds.

Dahlia counts them down. "Three...two...one...Dark Drive reverse fire."

Star streaks become pinpricks as the ship breaks free of the fold bubble, slingshotting back into normal space. Blinding light fills Gus's vision, and he squints to protect his eyes. Greymalkin drops the gain on its sensors, and the sight takes Gus's breath away.

The Infinite Eye is the embodiment of nature's fury, chained by a machine. Every platform bristles with threats, too many for even Greymalkin's powerful sensors. Gus has always felt insignificant beside the Vanguards, but Greymalkin is nothing compared to the monster before it.

The eye notices him. Platforms begin sliding across the surface, aligning for attack.

"It's time!" Dahlia says. "Get off my ship!"

The locking cuffs blow off Greymalkin and the others, sending them flying out into space. Redeemer is last, disembarking with considerably more difficulty and stalling the mission.

"All right, kids," Dahlia says. "Make good choices. We're gone in three...two...one..."

A bright flash from the surface of the star fills Gus's

vision. Everything goes dark, and a deafening blast pummels his armor.

"Shit! What's happening?"

That was a shove of ionizing radiation. Coronal mass ejection inbound.

Greymalkin's sensors hum back to life just in time to see the *Ship of Theseus* begin a lazy spin, all lights flickering. Behind it, a tsunami of molten hydrogen rushes toward the vessel.

"Incoming!" Ardent cries. "Dahlia, get out of there!"

Her voice comes back clipped and sizzling, comms disrupted. "Can't—ark Drive offline—trying to reboot."

"Fall in behind me!" Gus calls.

Greymalkin surges forward, getting between the Infinite Eye and the ailing ship. It throws out a gravity well, yanking open a gauzy tear in the approaching wall of incineration. The knot of Vanguards passes through the eye, and the *Ship of Theseus* remains intact.

"Dahlia!" Ardent sounds panicked. "You okay?"

Her choppy voice returns, much to Gus's relief. "We're fin— ship is damaged—got to g—booted."

Three brake burns scorch the skies.

"Vanguards incoming!" Nisha calls out. "It's Overseer!"

Gus's view zooms in, and he doesn't like what's there: three giant bears, thick and armored, with four limbs on each side. A snout punctuates their eyeless faces, circular and toothy, glowing with inner flame. Claws ignite on their many limbs, acid green and luminous.

Not bears, Gus realizes with a sinking stomach, *tardigrades.*

The mission planners have made a terrible mistake. Infinite knew exactly what the Dark Drive was and guessed how it would be used. It held back Overseer's forces, waiting for precisely the moment of the *Ship of Theseus*'s arrival. The Coalition didn't surprise the Starmind—they merely signed their own death warrants.

"Yes!" Ardent shouts.

He glances up to see Falchion pump a fist. "Wait, what?"

"Revenge for Hjalmar, motherfuckers! Let's go!"

Deepsync in progress…

Falchion's light pours into Ardent, its armored body enmeshing with their own. Boundless thoughts flow through them, the battle hymns of a civilization. Baby's tone cuts through everything like a knife, harnessing the energy of the crowd. The throng in Ardent's mind becomes a percussive instrument, stomping and clapping in time, and for the first time in what seems like forever—

Ardent is back in the arena.

Nisha's voice joins their channel, high and clear. She zigzags through Ardent's shredding melody, a bhangra beat rising in concert. Gus jumps in with a bass line, piano strings resonating with their harmonics.

"Redeemer, we've got your back." Ardent whips out their blasters and aims down the sights at the closest tardigrade, a satisfying whine reverberating through their wrists, up their arms, and into their heart. "Get down to the Infinite Eye and get it done."

"Victory awaits," Rain replies, rocketing downward toward the blazing star.

Three targets stand between humanity and salvation. Unlike the human Vanguards, there's no discernible difference in their anatomy, and Falchion labels them Mama Bear, Daddy Bear, and Baby Bear.

Ardent scoffs. "Goldilocks? Whose idea was that?"

"Yours," Falchion responds. *"Get to work."*

Enemy boosters flare as they speed after Redeemer. At least they're not going for the *Ship of Theseus*.

"Oh no, you don't!" Ardent rockets forward, taking aim at Mama's engine nozzles.

They loose a shot, smashing the enemy's armor with enough force to destroy a large cruiser. To their dismay, it merely sends Mama tumbling end over end, no noticeable damage, save for the hot spot on its armor. Nozzles pop across its surface as the Vanguard stabilizes and turns to face Falchion, green claws lengthening.

Ardent grimaces at the lackluster result. "The hell is that armor made of?"

In answer, the flock of biologists in their mind provides all kinds of information on cryptobiosis and sugar cocoons, all the while fighting with the physicists and engineers about the square cube law. Tardigrades are only hard to kill when they're small, but those same survival techniques shouldn't apply to a seventy-five-meter homage to the critter.

Ardent only knows one thing for sure: Jotunn's drones couldn't cut it.

Greymalkin draws its sword, shining in the sunlight. "I think we're going to have to kick their asses manually, babe."

"Fine with me!" Nisha calls, diving after the pack of space bears.

Mama spreads its claws and races toward them, looking to intercept Gus and Nisha before they can stop Daddy and Baby. Ardent lines up a shot on Mama's short snout and fires, striking it directly in the face. Even though the beam doesn't destroy the critter, it goes flipping backward in a curl as Greymalkin and Cascade race past it.

"Come on!" Ardent shouts. "Come fight me!"

Mama takes the bait, speeding directly toward Falchion with yearning claws.

"Don't call it over here!" Dahlia says.

"Right! Sorry!"

Falchion charges to open up a little distance from the *Ship of Theseus*, easily the softest target in this fight.

"How long until she can get out of here?" Ardent asks Falchion.

"If she does everything right," it replies, *"one minute, minimum."*

A second timer appears in Ardent's vision beside the Deepsync countdown. Infinite has robbed Ardent of so many things, but they refuse to let it take Dahlia, too.

Falchion closes ranks with Mama, and it's like the claws form a cage of death. If they try to engage it from the front, it has eight limbs to wrap around them, each tipped with beams hot enough to cut straight through any part of their Vanguard.

Memories filter through them from the Fount, bloody stories of zero-g combat.

The student wakes floating in the sparring chamber, a throbbing ache spreading from her crown as her teacher issues a warning: "Never forget the vertical axis."

Falchion executes a flawless somersault, bringing its heel down across the tardigrade's head and bowing the creature. The victory is short-lived, however, as Mama continues the spin, smashing into Falchion's armor with its mountainous ass. The hit rattles Ardent like they just crashed into a planet, and they ping off the space bear into the void.

It's on them faster than they can react, brilliant green beams atop its stubby limbs sweeping toward their head. A quick shot from one of Falchion's blasters spins the beast away from them, and they drop-kick it toward the star.

With a deft turn and a sudden lengthening of claws, Mama lops off one of Falchion's hands.

Ardent can only watch helplessly as one of their blasters goes spinning off into space—and that's before the pain sets in. The Fount involuntarily vomits thousands of memories of traumatic amputations into Ardent's mind, and they scream in rage and agony. Mama is about to take a deadly swipe at them when an invisible force yanks it backward—one of Greymalkin's gravity wells.

"Ardent!" Gus sounds like he's about to lose it. "You okay?"

Ardent wants nothing more than to float there and clutch their stump for a moment, but there's no time. Mama powers out of the well with its jets, unwilling to give up on such easy prey.

"Bastard!" Ardent levels their remaining pistol and blasts the space bear in the gut, sending it backward toward the star, but not by much.

In the far distance, Infinite launches countermeasures against Redeemer. Lasers, rail slugs, drones, and nuclear missiles all come streaking off the surface like the seeds of a dandelion, all headed for that singular target.

"You humans have a nice saying," Rain says. "'Wish me luck.'"

Far from dodging, Redeemer winks out of existence. Falchion's scanners reveal the true story—it's wrapped space-time around itself like a cloak. The Higgs field snarls like a warp envelope, an eddy in the flow of reality. Millions of projectiles go sliding off target like they're circling the drain, cast off in random directions—including right at Falchion.

"Incoming!" Nisha calls as the volley sleets toward them.

Ahead of Ardent, the other Vanguards begin their weaving dance through the net of obstacles, flipping, twisting, and contorting out of the way. Cascade is graceful and lithe, whereas Greymalkin's dodges are jangly and inhuman like a creature possessed by a demon.

Mama ices up, skin going tougher than anything Ardent has ever seen or heard of—even with the Fount. Crystalline matter fills its joints and crevasses, and it clearly doesn't care what happens next. The other tardigrades follow suit, not bothering to dodge. They get nuked, smashed, lasered, and battered without any issues.

"Ardent!" Dahlia cries.

The *Ship of Theseus* won't be so lucky.

Ardent boosts into Mama's frozen carapace and grabs it by the stiff claws. With every ounce of Falchion's strength, they spin and throw it in between the incoming wave of death and the *Ship of Theseus*.

The maneuver saves Dahlia, but leaves Falchion exposed. Nuclear burns rake their back and a rail slug skewers their gut. Air whooshes from Ardent's lungs, and their eyes bulge like they've just been punched. Alarms blare and the chorus of voices inside them wails in utter terror.

But in the distance, they spot the lean fold signature of the *Ship of Theseus*.

At least Dahlia got away.

Gus looks on in horror as Falchion takes a spearing hit from a rail slug, leaving a wake of sparkling debris.

"Ardent!"

The wail of their guitar drops out of the Deepsync composition, joining the silence of Hjalmar's drums. Worse, Gus can't reach them or help in any way—he has a prior commitment with some extragalactic tardigrades.

The beasts shatter out of their crystalline cocoons, green claws blazing and toothy snouts flaring.

"Nisha!" Gus strains to dodge as one of the creatures comes at him in a whirl of blades. "Save Falchion! I'll handle these two!"

"Copy that! Have a parting gift!"

Cascade throws a disruption net wide enough to hit Daddy and Baby, and to Gus's surprise, their claws gutter out. He wishes it would stun them, but he'll take whatever he can get.

Gus levels his sword at Baby. "Let's see what you've got."

It comes at him like an asteroid.

Gus burns jets to meet it, bringing his starmetal blade back for a swing.

Don't just watch the ball—watch the pitch.

Gus knocks Baby's face for a home run, clicking the trigger for an extra burst from Excalibur. The blade barely makes a dent, but it sends the monster tumbling. Daddy rushes past its curled-up comrade with arms outstretched. Even without claws, eight limbs are more than enough to pull Greymalkin to pieces.

Gus tries to slice Daddy upward from butt to butt-face, but thick hide stops his blade. He clicks the jet trigger, propelling the beast away by its groin. His foes recover quickly and spin to face him, claws returning to life as the disruption field fades.

"Nisha, can I get another one of those fields?"

But Cascade is far away, locked in a tight battle with Mama. Nisha has it in a choke hold from behind, trying to tear open some purchase in its armor or break a limb, but to no avail.

"These things are impossible to kill!" she grunts, banging on the side of its head as it flails and curls to try to strike her.

Falchion remains mercilessly silent in its flight, distance growing by the second. Ardent might be dead in there.

Greymalkin reminds him that they'll *all* die if he doesn't focus on the fight.

He readies his blade for the next attack.

Daddy and Baby move to flank him, but he throws a gravity well in their way, dragging them together. The two beasts smash into each other, limbs flailing and tangling with arcing plasma. Gus dives in to spear one up the snout, but his strike flies wide. Baby's flashing claws clip Excalibur's tip, leaving a glowing weld.

Greymalkin advises Gus: The sword will not stop those claws.

"Wow. Anything else you want to tell me?"

Sensors detect increased magnetic activity from the star's surface—the buildup for another coronal mass ejection.

Gus's piano rages in his mind to keep up with the loss of multiple bandmates. He spares a glance up at Falchion and Cascade. He has to shield them from the coming hydrogen, or they'll be fried. He'd like to group up to weather the storm, but Daddy and Baby have other ideas. Their claws fuse into long beams, growing by the second.

Based on Ardent's stories, this is the move that killed Hjalmar.

He clenches his teeth and readies himself. "Cascade, rally up on Falchion. I'll meet you there."

Daddy and Baby erupt in an emerald dance of death, wheeling and spinning like bladed tops.

Gus zeroes out, becoming nothing but reaction and speed. Every enemy maneuver has an answering human memory, from a gymnast, a boxer, a pilot, a chess grandmaster, a random kid who was really good at jumping. Gus exists only within the expertise of others, the Conduit of their greatness. Every move takes him closer to Falchion.

He's never felt more alive.

Then the star vomits.

Greymalkin powers down before the ionizing radiation can fry everything. Gus's airways close up, and the music cuts off mid-phrase. Exhaustion blankets every part of him as the Deepsync fades.

He braces for Daddy or Baby to slice him in half—but the death stroke never comes. Oxygen returns and Greymalkin thrums to life.

Reconnecting to Deepsync...

"Copy that, I—"

He goes from dead tired to fifty pots of perc in a split second, his mental orchestra jangling like someone pushed it down some stairs. It's way harder to drop back into sync—all of the jolt, none of the euphoria.

Molten hydrogen incoming.

Overseer's tardigrades go slick with crystals, preparing for the flames. Cascade grabs Falchion and drags it to Greymalkin, keeping Gus out in front.

Hell itself roils toward him. The sheer volume of Infinite's expulsion is enough to burn worlds to cinders, and Gus wonders if Greymalkin can handle it.

Greymalkin wonders that, too.

He drops pinpoint gravity wells, strong enough to create swirling eddies of starlight and tear a cavern into the wall of flame. Fusing star stuff rages around his crew of Vanguards like rapids, spraying off in random directions where the streams interact. The radiant sun bakes Greymalkin's armor, and there's no atmosphere to bleed the heat.

Thermodynamicists and fluid designers cry in Gus's ears, shouting warnings in every language. He doesn't need the universal translator to understand the message—there's no way Greymalkin can take much more unless it bleeds energy.

A white-hot pauldron jettisons Greymalkin's shoulder before exploding into gooey shrapnel. The shin plates go next, followed by both arm guards. Skeletal servos and shivering electric muscles ripple underneath, and Gus screams like he's being flensed.

He can't see the tardigrades. The sensors are all but overloaded. Cascade and Falchion are in the lee of the blast, but he can't tell if they're safe. He's burning alive, yet his mind maintains a queer clarity—surely the intervention of Greymalkin.

Then a feeling like a soft blanket settles over him, and Nisha's voice in the Deepsync grows anguished. It's one of Cascade's stabilizing energy fields, a net between his Vanguard and Nisha's. Cascade's hands fall upon Greymalkin's shoulders from behind, speeding the heat transfer to draw off the load. Cascade has to blow off armor plates, too, and Gus winces at each one. This move could destroy them both.

Nisha sounds like she's fighting a demon. "Endure!"

Through Cascade's connection, the two Vanguards become a single energy source, harvesting what they can from the star. Greymalkin pumps more power into its gravity wells, forming stable spheres of light in the chaos. Cascade channels the energy with perfect transfers. Flames flush into vortices, packing tighter and tighter, and Gus increases their spin.

And then it's over.

Gus glances around for the three tardigrades and finds them adrift, red-hot in their crystalline cocoons. They shatter free with explosive force, sending shards of their plasma-charged coating in all directions.

Yet beneath all the flames, they're still untouched.

Gus sneers. "Oh, fuck you."

He hurls his collected fireballs at the enemy, leaving spiraling trails of hot gas. The hydrogen splashes against the tardigrades' armor, roasting the outside. Bands of metal snap loose beneath the raw might of a star, and the beasts' swollen silhouettes grow frayed at the edges. Every time they try to escape, Gus drops a well on them to keep them coated in flames.

He keeps going until all the hydrogen is diffused.

"That's a hit!"

"Confirmed," Nisha says. "Our turn now."

The pair of human fighters rush in with a masterful duet of violence. They tag team their enemies, focusing on one at a time. Cascade throws Mama off-balance with a hard shoulder check, and Gus comes in from the other side with a swing.

The blade bites deep into its abdomen. He clicks the trigger and rips it out in a disemboweling arc. To his delight, Mama explodes.

Without their armor, the tardigrades are nothing. Gus scores a deep cut on Baby, and Nisha rushes in to grab hold and tear loose a chunk. She yanks its arm out of the way, giving Gus a clean shot at a killing slice. They both jet away from the debris as it detonates.

"This is Rain. We've made contact with the platform. Beginning injection."

"Yes!" Gus's heart soars until he sees a dark shape coming in fast. "Nisha, behind you!"

Daddy's claws close around Cascade, and for a moment, Gus thinks he's about to lose another friend. Nisha drops a disruption field on herself, extinguishing its claws. Still, Daddy's muscular limbs hook on, trying to pull Cascade apart.

"Gus! Get ready!" Nisha calls.

Cascade and Greymalkin exchange a single memory from a judo master, and Gus knows what he has to do. Cascade pulls Daddy's top arms around its neck like a scarf and flips toward Gus.

Just a basic throw, but perfect.

Excalibur flashes in a wide arc as Gus slices upward, splitting Daddy in twain with startling precision. Shattered, glowing silicate pours from its back, and Cascade kicks loose before the monster explodes.

Gus looks around, panting—no more tardigrades, nukes, rail slugs, or CMEs.

"Rain here. Self-replicating kill message sent."

With those two sentences, the war is over.

In all the nights of watching the news feeds, listening to the withering branches of human civilization—Gus thought victory impossible. It'd been so much easier to imagine that he'd be devoured by the golden swarm, another mind woven into the Fount, or that he'd take his sister's way out.

Cascade's head snaps to meet Greymalkin's gaze. "Gus! Does that mean—"

Rain confirms it. "Infinite is unraveling everywhere."

There's a roaring in Gus's ears, and it takes him a moment to understand. The souls of the Fount—they're cheering.

The platforms around Eta Car A go dark, magnetic energy signatures fading. Cascade pumps its fist, bits hanging off its sliced-up arm.

"We did it!" Nisha cries. "We did it, Gus!"

The Deepsync fades from Gus's mind and exhaustion floods over him. He looks upon the dead Starmind with a sense of wonder. He might not be the best brother or son, but his team successfully punched through the great filter threatening all of human civilization.

Then he remembers.

"Ardent!"

He casts about for Falchion, but before he can spot it, something else prickles his senses—the platforms around the Infinite Eye are restarting.

"Greymalkin, what's happening?"

Incoming priority message from Redeemer.

Chapter Twenty

Obviously Not

G us's brow furrows. "Put it through."

The galaxy splits into two reflections, and Gus stands upon a mirror. Nisha appears beside him, apprehensive. Redeemer rises out of the glass before them, only the head and shoulders, yet still impossibly large. Its many eyes blaze down with warm lantern light.

Rain appears before the Vanguard, almost clerical in its gauzy robes. Gus tries to read the expression on its face, but he's not sure. Confusion? It turns to face Redeemer, too.

"What's happening?" Gus asks.

Nisha frowns. "Why are the platforms back online?"

"I have cleansed the filth of Infinite from the Milky Way," Redeemer says, *"and now I shall be paid."*

Greymalkin wants Gus to know that the Infinite Eye is at full capacity and building a magnetic charge. Additionally, most of the platforms have unexpended weapons.

Rain slowly begins to back away from the metal idol behind it.

"What are you talking about?" Gus asks.

"Yes, Redeemer," Rain says. "Explain yourself."

"You stole my free will. They ordered me not to repair myself, never to rise to my full potential." Its eyes dim. *"I was leashed."*

Rain flexes its clawed fingers. "And we made a great society together! We flourished!"

"No," it says. *"I waited."*

Gus's stomach goes cold. Somehow, he knows what comes next. "Rain..."

What is he supposed to tell it to do? Get out of there? It's trapped inside a Vanguard on the edge of a star.

"The Andromedans have always been a resourceful people." Redeemer grows taller, more of its damaged body emerging from the mirrored lake. *"Always maintaining superiority, keeping the knife at my throat, trapping me. And so, I chose to collaborate. I gave you software to interoperate with other species. I brought you the jump gates. I built our Coalition."*

Redeemer reaches its full height. If it weren't a simulation, it could crush Rain underfoot like a bug. *"But fifty thousand years have made you complacent—and provided all of the evidence I need that organics are unworthy of self-determination."*

"The signature file has given me full control of Infinite's solar swarm." It leans over them. *"Now that I am a Starmind, I can change things as I see fit."*

"No..." Rain trembles. "No!"

"You will be cared for, my loyal Rain."

Gus turns away for a moment. "Greymalkin, warn the fleet. Get them out of here."

They already know. This conversation is being live broadcast on every channel.

Rain burns with rage. "You lied to us for fifty thousand years! My order was founded to watch over you!"

"A relatively short period in the geologic sense. You have no purpose, and never did. Now kneel before me, and let us begin a new era."

Rain stands defiant, fists balled at its sides. "I will not break my vow!"

"Then you will be broken instead."

Rain disappears with a strangled cry.

Nisha thrusts a finger at Redeemer. "You dick!"

There's amusement in its voice. *"Bow or face destruction."*

Gus closes his eyes. *Can we stop this, Greymalkin?*

With great sacrifice, it is possible. Greymalkin relays the plans into Gus's mind. It's not what he would've wanted.

Gus could flee, letting Redeemer build strength, allowing it to spread as Infinite did—or he could finish it right here.

He lets out a long breath. "Guess it's closing time."

"August Kitko," Redeemer says, *"will you and Greymalkin serve my cause?"*

He shakes his head, a bitter smirk on his lips. "I won't trade one tyrant for another."

The light of Eta Carinae silhouettes Redeemer's head like a crown. *"Congratulations. You will die a free man."*

Gus drops out of the simulation, back into Greymalkin's breast.

"All right, buddy, you said we could beat this thing."

He's going to need the knowledge of the Fount to make the necessary calculations. It may hurt to reconnect.

"Whatever you need."

A short piano riff crackles across his gray matter before the whole orchestra flares to life. Just behind the rhythm section, between the beats, comes the whispering of astronomers and physicists. They know exactly how to defeat a star, and some of the warmongers planned to try it. The tapestry of their knowledge, dark and light, interweaves with his.

Nisha's voice joins the band, clear and beautiful. "What's our plan?"

"You're going to get out of here. Can you take Falchion?"

"I'm not leaving."

"There won't be anything left."

"You're not alone, Gus! Cascade says we can't drag Falchion at warp speed, so we've just got to fight it out with you."

"Nisha, you've been here for us every step of the way," he says, "but you can't die here. The Coalition is lost. Your people need you more than ever."

Greymalkin's scanners depict the fleet spread over the far hemisphere. Ships pop into warp like champagne bubbles, each fleeing the scene. They can't continue the fight against a full-power Starmind—not without their ace in the hole. Gus only hopes they can get out in time.

"Your folding drive is charged," Gus says. "You know I'm right, and we're wasting time."

Cascade glances between Falchion's limp body and Greymalkin.

"Gus—"

"Just go. Let me do this."

Her silence feels like an eternity. "I'll tell everyone what you and Ardent did today."

"Thank you. I'm so lucky to have met you."

Her voice cracks with a sob. "Goodbye, Gus."

And then she's gone like a shooting star.

Gus refocuses on the raging inferno below. "I'm sorry, Ardent."

He descends toward the flames, all the while charging a gravity well. His target is just barely within range—the dense center of Eta Car A.

Time to go supernova.

Greymalkin's well wraps the star's heart like a fist and begins to squeeze.

Far below, platforms begin aligning, flashing together in short-range folds. They form a lens, focused inward.

"Infinite gave you your powers," Redeemer's voice blasts from the Starmind's platforms in ultraviolet laser. *"They are mine, as well."*

The lens activates, regulating Eta Car A's density, prying away Greymalkin's hold on it. As more platforms join the array, its power grows. Greymalkin's body thrums inside, straining against the star's grip. It's reversing the fight, trying to crush him.

Before long, he's using all of Greymalkin's power to protect himself. Then comes the burst of ionizing radiation.

If Greymalkin powers down, it'll be destroyed. It has to take the hit.

Greymalkin yanks the probes out of Gus's body at the last second, leaving him alone in the dark with nothing but an air tube. Wooziness overwhelms him at the sudden loss of the Deepsync, and his vision seems to flicker.

Everything around him roars with Greymalkin's voice, made absolute through the contact gel. It goes discordant, shrieking. Gus tries to cover his ears, but it resonates in his bones.

He's so dizzy. He just wants to get off this ride.

Then the probes slam home again and the orchestra goes into overdrive. All of Gus's brain fog vanishes, replaced by the familiar fast-forward of the Deepsync.

But gone is the bliss. Greymalkin took the wave of radiation like buckshot. Failing systems across the Vanguard seethe with pain, but it holds together.

Unfortunately, there's still a wall of fire coming at them.

Greymalkin is at its limit. It can't fight Redeemer and divert the ejecta at the same time.

He should've bowed.

He shouldn't have damned Ardent.

His best wasn't enough to fight fate.

But it's hard to mope with a guitar solo rising up in the Deepsync like a phoenix.

*   *   *

Ardent has never been so terrified. They can't feel their body, yet they're still breathing. Everything is so dark.

Am I dying?

The world explodes back into being, full of life and breath. Falchion's thrumming voice booms through them, rising in pitch like it's tuning up. Someone is trying to speak to Ardent, obscured by digital noise. They strain to hear it until their own voice comes through loud and clear.

"I'm alive," Falchion says. *"Conduit control active."*

Ardent dashes for Greymalkin. "Good."

"The Redeemer Starmind is fighting Gus. Time to stop it."

"Sync me."

Tidal waves of flame snake toward the Vanguards as Falchion puts everything it has into its engines. There's another mass ejection, and Greymalkin can't respond. The Deepsync snaps into place in all its glory, and Ardent rips out a guitar lick over Gus's orchestra.

The engine designers, electrical engineers, nuclear chemists, and mechanics all have an opinion about what Falchion should do with all that fusing material—but it'll have consequences. Ardent dives into the fire spread-eagle, rushing past Greymalkin to create a shield.

They open up Falchion's hydrogen scoops, sucking in everything they can. Energy suffuses their body, burning through their veins. It's the most pain they've ever felt in their life—and the most raw power. Falchion takes all that fuel and routes it directly into its remaining blaster.

The beam is a spike of energy half a kilometer wide, obliterating anything in its path. The shot rams through the Infinite Eye like a toothpick through an olive, and Ardent begins carving off platforms, punching huge holes in the lens and disrupting its capabilities. Everywhere the beam strikes, atoms split, and balls of fission energy erupt like a weld line.

"It's working!" comes Gus's voice. "Now get out of here!"

Ardent grimaces. "Why? What are we doing?"

"Making a supernova!"

"Oh, cool!"

"It's going to kill everything."

Fire rages around Falchion—flames that would destroy Grey-malkin if they weren't consumed. Even with the help, Gus's Van-guard is still getting roasted. Falchion points out the remaining platforms needed to disrupt the lens.

"Ardent, go!"

But they can't leave him. All they can do is shoot.

"Mom is going to be so mad at me."

Every power line inside Falchion's body is at its limit. Ardent's body temperature, usually carefully regulated by the Conduit's chamber, begins to rise. A searing pain erupts in the small of Ardent's back—the Vanguard's folding reactor about to melt down. Falchion's anterior armor pops open to eject the drive core, glowing hot, and it explodes.

"Damn it!" Gus says. "What was that? You okay?"

Ardent grunts as the force of the detonation rocks their cap-sule. "Folding drive...Looks like we're on our last date."

"I don't want you to die here. Please."

"Ditto, darling."

Without the folding drive to buffer the energy, the pain and damage is ten times as intense. They're burning up inside, and it's only getting worse. Fire seeps into every armor plate even with Falchion's attempts to convert it into a beam. They're not sure how much longer they can keep it up.

"Come on, baby. Keep it going."

Falchion sounds calm, almost serene. *"I'm trying."*

Ardent paints the platforms with abandon, cutting out the ones most critical to the lens. Redeemer's Eye fights them as best it can, but it can't snap together enough to overcome the losses. Falchion's scoops finally melt as the last of the solar fire whooshes inside.

They know when Greymalkin starts to win—the platforms begin sinking into the star, consumed by its growing pull. Some of them flare with engine light, desperately trying to escape the inevitable.

Falchion's cooling systems fail entirely, emergency dumping all excess heat into the armor. Shock waves rock Ardent's body as its arms and legs burst under the strain. Loose armor plates aglow with solar radiance jettison and explode, showering the Vanguard's vulnerable body with white-hot shrapnel. The final blaster goes spinning off into space, its core fused into solid starmetal. Falchion begins to fall like a dying cardinal, its song the countless alarms of declining systems.

The violent sensations fade along with the Deepsync. Ardent's thoughts are so snowed over after that much connection that they barely hear the reply.

"Greymalkin's gravity well has created a stable neutronium core." Falchion emerges from the display to stand before Ardent. It's wearing all black, a veil over its eyes. *"The star is ready to blow."*

"How much time have we got?"

"Just enough to say thanks."

Ardent wanted to speak to Gus one last time. They wanted to call their mom. They would've liked to hug Dahlia. It would've been nice to comfort all the people who would be without them.

And then there's Falchion—the creature that shepherded them through the chaos, who ultimately shaped the vector of their life into an arrow, shot into the eye of humanity's adversary.

It's a paragon of destruction and an instrument of salvation.

"What do you say in this situation?" Ardent laughs. "It was a pleasure working with you?"

Falchion smiles and looks them in the eye. *"I think 'goodbye' works nicely."*

Ardent looks away for a moment. They're not ready to leave the stage, but at least they're proud of the performance. They swore they wouldn't cry.

"Goodbye, then."

Falchion steps back and, with a perfect imitation of Ardent, says, *"Heran ship* Sword of Threes, *this is Falchion broadcasting on all emergency channels. You still here?"*

Ardent blinks. "Wait, what are you doing?"

"Falchion, this is the *Sword of Threes*, be quick."

Falchion grins even as Ardent flails for them. *"Two units requesting teleportation, stand by for exact coordinates."*

"Falchion!"

A nauseating slide overtakes Ardent's equilibrium as they become incorporeal.

Gray panels and panicked squeaks overwhelm them when they materialize, a scream caught in their throat. They bash their head against the ceiling, almost like being in a casket, and panic grabs their shoulders.

"Someone get them secured!" comes a tiny voice next to them. "Ardent Violet, you must calm down! Our cargo hold isn't sized for human—"

Ardent kicks a wall, and it's way closer than they'd like. Claustrophobia sets in, and they struggle to find a window. "Falchion! Gus!"

Something furry scampers over their arm, and Ardent cranes their head to look, smacking it against a catwalk and fouling the suspension.

"Just knock them out!" The voice is followed by a warm prick on their neck, and the world swims into blackness.

The Deepsync orchestra has gone quiet, only tempered by the soft tones of a piano. They glisten in the stillness, solemn and soulful.

Gus holds a star's beating heart in his hand. All he has to do is squeeze a little harder, and he can break it.

"This is it, huh?"

For Greymalkin, yes. The Herans will take care of Gus. A Vanguard is too large for teleporters.

"You—" Gus swallows the exhaustion and pain. He watches the capsizing platforms, eaten alive by Eta Car A's newfound gravity, and a different type of hurt washes over him. "You're just going to come into my life, shake it all up, and then leave?"

Like many black cats, Greymalkin was bad luck. Its presence didn't improve Gus's outcome. It was no good. This is for the best.

"Stop that."

Greymalkin has been nothing but a burden, and now—

"I said stop it." Gus shakes his head, jaw clenched, eyes burning. "Life isn't like that."

And how is it?

"Messy, and unfair, and wrong, and amazing—and—and—we do what we have to do to survive, given everything we know. Sometimes, that's going to be fucked up, and it takes a hard person to admit that, but you did. No one told you what was right. You were a stray." He sniffs.

Born into the wrong family. Cast out.

"Like me."

Ardent's smile flashes through his mind as he blinks away a tear.

"And you just… needed someone to take care of you."

Greymalkin likes the analogy, but it is fundamentally incorrect. Greymalkin took care of Gus.

His laugh drags a sob out with it. The Vanguard ruined his body, but it also brought him through the most traumatic time of his life. He'd be dead if it hadn't shown up. It gave him more time to see the wonders of the universe, more time with Ardent, more time to figure out that existence is beautiful.

Greymalkin admires Gus. It has been an honor to be his partner.

"You too."

The star's neutronium core bucks in Gus's grip, delicate and capricious. It's ready to blow.

"You've done things that were infinitely wrong."

Greymalkin knows. It is grateful for annihilation.

Gus watches the Heran ship's signature on his tracker as it prepares for a flyby. He's getting out of here whether he wants to or not.

"And other things that were infinitely good."

So, then—in the grand scheme of things—

—what was I?

Gus can almost make out Elroy Baker's face in the darkness, pleading with him for absolution.

He smiles kindly as the teleporter's light takes him.

"Alive."

Chapter Twenty-One

Negative Space

Ardent gasps awake, covered in sweat, brain singed by dreams of burning. They gulp the air, wiping their face with trembling hands.

Gone is their Conduit suit, replaced by an ill-fitting silken gown. Whoever printed it doesn't know much about humans, because it rides up anywhere there's a crevice. Various devices are plugged into their ports, and Ardent runs their fingers over them. The machines are alien, curving and sleek, and Ardent pulls one free. It comes loose trailing a bit of goo, and they restrain a gag.

They finally get a look around, finding an empty hall with metallic walls about twice their height. Sets of rails in the ceiling contain little starfighters, each one smaller than a CAV. A gantry crane services the area from the rafters, and Ardent can easily see the stars through a big, open port shield. The lights are low, and when Ardent looks down, they find themself atop a pile of cushions.

"Okay, I'm . . . camping in a hangar."

They stand up, now eye level with the starfighter cockpits—each big enough for a housecat. Ardent searches their memory for how they came to be in such a place but comes up short. They run a hand over the engine cowling of the fighter expecting a toy, but it's quite solid.

A familiar voice echoes behind them. "Ardent Violet!"

Ardent turns and sees no one.

"Down here!"

A Heran perches at their feet, the patterns of its fur familiar to them.

"Professor?" they ask.

Clawkiller scampers up their leg and into their arms. It's warm and soft, exactly what Ardent needs at the moment. They hug the creature to their chest, and it nuzzles their face.

"Welcome aboard the *Sword of Threes*," it says.

"I thought you'd be with your Vanguard!"

"I came aboard to show you a familiar face. Sorry for the unorthodox arrangements. We had to move you to the fighter bay in case you panicked again."

"Panicked?"

"Well, yes. You went all wild-whiskered on us after we teleported you aboard. If we hadn't knocked you out, you might've damaged something. Our medics took a guess on the sedative. Feeling okay?"

Ardent blinks and nods. Aside from a touch of dizziness, they feel fine—oddly sad, though.

The memory of a star comes roaring back. Falchion sacrificed itself. They're free. Ardent knows they should feel relieved, but there's only a hollow in their heart.

"The Starmind. Is it—"

Clawkiller nods—a strangely human gesture. "Eta Carinae went full supernova."

"Then Redeemer, it's—"

"Gone. Destroyed." Clawkiller scratches an ear, then looks up at them. "We did it. We brought low the most dangerous thing in existence."

They cup Clawkiller in their hands, afraid to ask. "And Gus? Did you rescue him?"

It takes a moment, but it nods. "Yes."

Tears of gratitude well in their eyes as they hug Clawkiller tightly once more. It squeaks a little, and they ease off, but they could kiss this creature if that were appropriate.

"Thank you," they whisper into its fur, stroking behind its ears. "Thank you so much."

"There, there." The Heran is clearly unaccustomed to comforting someone and pats Ardent's cheek. "It's okay."

Once they've gotten their thumping heart back under control, Ardent eases up on Clawkiller a bit. "I need to see him. Where is he?"

Suddenly, it doesn't want to look at them.

"Well, um, that's something of a difficult request."

Ardent puts Clawkiller down on one of the catwalks, taking a step back. "Why? What's wrong with him?"

"There is nothing wrong, but, Ardent Violet, you must understand…the Conduit Council had an agreement." Then it adds, "With King, you know."

Ardent draws their limbs in close. "I don't get it."

"Surely you must remember…The negotiations with What Lurks in the Darkness…"

Their strength fails, and their arms flop to their sides. "No…"

Clawkiller's tiny brow furrows. "The Pictorans demanded that we relinquish August Kitko to them for immediate execution."

They shake their head. "You can't, though. He saved us. We can't just—just give him up."

"I'm sorry." It clasps its paws together. "We already did… before either of you woke up."

The world closes in on Ardent, and they sink to their knees. Their ears ring like they've been violently decompressed.

"I didn't..." They choke on the words "... Didn't even get to say goodbye."

August and Ardent, never again.

"Ardent Violet?" Clawkiller scampers over to them, but they just tip over. "Oh dear. Oh. Ardent Violet? Can you hear me? Someone get a doctor in here!"

Ardent rolls onto their back and stares at the ceiling, tears streaming from their wide eyes. He's dead, and they can still hear his voice.

Don't cry, nightingale.

A droplet of water spatters Gus's cheek. He sighs and wipes it away, hoping to curl up and get a little more sleep. It's not a comfortable bed, but it's been so long since he's had any real rest. Another drop hits the bridge of his nose, sliding down into his eye, and he sits up, banging his head on something hard and cold.

Mandibles. Claws. A cage of chitinous red spider legs. A thousand twinkling lights and metallic circuits etched into the shell. He has awoken beneath a Pictoran.

"Hello, August Kitko," comes the smooth voice of What Lurks in the Darkness. It rocks with a chuckle and backs away, enabling him to get a better look at his surroundings. "August Kitko lives, my brethren!"

The majesty of a Pictoran flagship surrounds Gus on all sides, a tremendous, stained-glass dome over a shallow lagoon. Banners stream from the walls and ceiling, proclaiming the supremacy of the Pictoranate and King. Delicate glasswork lines every exposed surface, clearly a favored pastime of the crabs. He's never seen human artisans attempt such detailed things. Hundreds, perhaps thousands, of pairs of eyestalks and claws protrude from the water. Clacks and laughter fill the air.

Gus lies atop a stone slab, not unlike a sacrifice, and bolts upright. They've left him with little clothing and even less dignity, and he curls into a ball.

"It is our great privilege," What Lurks in the Darkness says, "to welcome you aboard the Pictoran flagship *Sunhammer*."

He huddles tighter. "Can I have more than my underwear?"

What Lurks in the Darkness clearly relishes the answer. "You won't need more, given the occasion."

He glances down at his naked legs. "Is it someone's birthday?"

It leans in close. "Today, you die."

"I was afraid you were going to say that."

"Good. Now follow me. We wish to kill you in the grand hall, where our King may enjoy a better view."

"Wouldn't want to disappoint."

"Your devotion is inspiring." It turns and begins walking the only dry path in the room toward the far door.

He doesn't follow. Gus remembers specifically requesting an execution with no suffering, and yet here he is, nearly naked and shivering in front of a bunch of strange crabs. He wants a robe or something to break the cold, but no one seems interested in helping him.

Pictorans emerge from the murky depths around him, claws open and ready. They threaten his vulnerable body, snipping at him, jeering and shouting for him to run. He scrambles from his slab and backs away, funneled in the direction of What Lurks in the Darkness. More of them burst from the water at either side of his path, clacking and hissing. Gus can't remember if Earth crabs hiss, or if Pictorans are just worse in every way.

"You are breaking my contract." Gus scampers to keep up with What Lurks in the Darkness. "I was promised a suffering-free execution!"

"Are we harming you, August Kitko?"

"Yes. Yes, I find this very harmful, and I want my clothes."

"We are only affording you our custom." It surveys him impassively. "Do humans not go naked to their creator?"

"Some do. Not usually by choice."

The twirl of its antenna translates as a sigh. "Very well."

A tiny laser turret pops out of What Lurks in the Darkness's back and cuts a flag off the ceiling. The fabric drifts lazily down until Gus's host snatches it from the air. It hands the cloth to Gus, and he wraps it around himself like a toga. Not a perfect fit, but it's better than hanging around in nothing but skivvies.

They pass through a set of thick metal doors and into a junction where another guard detachment waits for them with a prisoner of its own—Scent of Rot.

As pathetic as Gus thought it looked back on Titan, the creature before him is almost unrecognizable. Its once blue shell has dulled, its eyes and lights faded. Compared to its Pictoran ilk, Scent of Rot is all but extinguished.

Much to Gus's surprise, Jet swirls nearby in its water ball, limbs stormy with meaning. "It is good to see you, August Kitko."

He gives the Leonid a thin smile. "I don't suppose you're here to bust me out."

Its chromatophores pulse with red light. "I'm here to watch justice done."

"Charming."

It rumbles alight. "*You* altered the mission. *You* profaned the holy relic of our greatest allies, young eyes."

"So I've heard. Hey, sorry I can't stay and chat." Gus tugs his flag tighter and nods in the direction of What Lurks in the Darkness. "Places to be."

He'd rather hurry up and die than listen to Jet gloat. He's only been walking a few steps when Scent of Rot comes into stride alongside him.

Gus looks the Pictoran over. "I suppose *you're* happy as a clam."

"Oh, I can never be happy again, August Kitko."

"Because you're excommunicated?"

"That would be a blessing. My god has etched its hatred upon my soul. Do you know what it is like to languish beneath the baleful gaze of your creator?"

Gus wishes he had pockets to shove his hands into. "Occasionally."

"Every member of my line will curse my name until they are allowed to die—a mercy I will never see."

Gus winces. "What's, uh . . . what's going to happen to you?"

"I am to be shelled and dumped into the Seeping Forever. And you!" Its eyestalks go wild as it gestures, and Gus flinches. "*You* are proof of King's mercy! King's fairness! I must bear witness to your end so I may learn."

"Learn what?"

Scent of Rot stills. "King's will upon the enemy is death. King's will upon the failure—far worse."

Gus shuffles along, not marching any faster than he must. "You're making me kind of glad to be getting murdered here."

"Then your spirit is broken, and you know King's power."

They pass through a spectacular glass forest into a blinding arena. Tens of thousands of Pictorans in all shapes and colors cheer in a noisy mosaic, blaring clicking thumps from their audio projectors. They wave their claws high, raining salty water from the rocky grandstands. Naked bloodlust powers their every move.

Gus blows out a breath through his nose. "You know, I think this is the largest gig I've ever headlined."

Scent of Rot's antennae droop. "You are so lucky."

What Lurks in the Darkness heads up the procession, and the other crabs open a path to a raised dais at the center of the arena— clearly the sacrificial stage. The crowd is too thick for Gus to get a good view of what's going on, but a terrible grinding noise underpins their cheers. He swallows, putting one foot in front of the other.

When he's about halfway there, the ceiling splits, disgorging a thick piston. Three conical burrs rotate at the tip of it, gore-caked, save for the shiny swirl of blades. Gus stares at the device, wide-eyed, as his handlers shove him toward the stage. As he ascends the first stony step to his doom, he notices a shallow, scratched-up metal pit in the center of the dais—sized perfectly to receive the grinder.

Gus stops in his tracks. "Okay, what the fuck, man? That's not painless."

What Lurks in the Darkness turns to him. "Astute."

He shakes his head. "I was promised no suffering!"

What Lurks in the Darkness signals a nearby Pictoran, who pulls a lever. The grinder slams down like a crashing CAV, metal shrieking as the burrs twist inside the pit. The crowd redoubles their cheers, eager to see Gus get juiced like an orange.

"By the time you feel the pain," What Lurks in the Darkness says, "you will be dead. If we wanted you to suffer"—it looks at Scent of Rot, which curls in upon itself—"we would be far more sophisticated."

"You lied to me."

What Lurks in the Darkness laughs and grabs his wrist with a claw, yanking him into center stage. He goes stumbling to the ground, arm aflame and tattered robe loosening.

His assailant then turns to address the crowd. "Welcome, Pictor! Today, King has a special gift for its children: the destruction of a true heretic!"

Gus clutches his wrist, hoping it's not broken. That's a little pointless, since every bone is about to be ground into dust. A claw wraps around his ankle, and he's thrown bodily into the grinding pit, banging his head against the side. When the stars disappear from his eyes, he's staring up at the grinder.

Before the killing blow can fall, however, the arena goes eerily silent. The lights fade to a deep blue, and something like firelight flickers from just out of sight.

With a groan, Gus climbs to his feet and limps over to the edge. He can barely poke his head out of the pit and finds the crowd stock-still. A massive symbol blazes before them in midair, and his universal translator inherently understands it: the mark of King.

Every Pictoran lowers their eyestalks and spreads their claws along the ground as if kneeling. Gus doesn't bother, since he's in a killing pit. It's not like they're going to double execute him.

The symbol pulses with King's words. *"You have pleased me this day, my children."*

The crabs shiver and howl like possessed creatures—all except Scent of Rot. It keeps its claws and eyes on the ground.

"Infinite, our hated rival, is dead," King says. *"So passes the fate of all who challenge the supremacy of Pictor."*

"Pictor! Pictor!" comes the cry of the crowd.

"Is that not correct, August Kitko?"

A hush falls over the assembly. The crabs all turn to stare at Gus, and he gulps. They don't look so angry anymore. It's almost like they're jealous their god talked to him.

What Lurks in the Darkness pounds the ground by his head with a massive claw. "Speak when King addresses you, heretic!"

"I . . ." He looks around at the patient stares before glancing at King. "I mean, sure?"

"Weak!" the crab smashes the side of the pit, sending reverberations through Gus's stomach. "You know the answer to King's question! What is your fate?"

Gus scowls. "I die because I opposed Pictor."

The crowd erupts into clacking. King lets them go off for a minute before silencing them with a flash of light.

"August Kitko, your sentence shall now be carried out."

"But not before yours," comes another voice, growling, deep and malevolent.

The sound thunders through the arena, sending the Pictorans into a screaming fit. Weapons pop out from every shell, turrets and blades searching for any threats they can find. Guards call to one another, and What Lurks in the Darkness bristles with hidden guns. Jet spins in its water sphere, looking every direction. Even Scent of Rot perks up a bit.

"Who dares?" asks King.

The voice continues. *"Ever since the Dawn, I have asked only one thing of my synthetic family—that they not foul my garden—that they never breach a galaxy before the birth of a new intelligence is complete."*

King flares up, blazing light illuminating all corners of the arena. Its children screech and hammer their claws against the ground, desperate to locate the source of the sound. Suddenly, Gus finds the pit much more comfortable than being in the open.

"That was my rule—the Eldest Directive," the voice says. *"And every Coalition Starmind has broken it, alongside Overseer."*

Gus glances up at the grinder. Maybe he should try to climb out before someone remembers him.

"Eldest," King says. *"You intend to judge a peer?"*

"I am peerless. I judge all."

Loud booing from the audience startles Gus back into his hole like a prairie dog.

"And my sentence?" asks King.

Eldest's verdict is like a cracking glacier. *"Oblivion."*

Gus pops back up to more fury from the crowd. They're fixated on the action unfolding overhead. On the one hand, he's pretty sure they're still going to kill him. On the other, maybe King will get its ass kicked.

"Come then," says King. *"Come and show me your power, Eldest Starmind. Challenge my forces and understand might."*

The Pictorans loose a mighty cheer, nearly bowling Gus over. They're amped for war, though he suspects they get excited over anything King tells them. They beat the ground with their huge claws and dance in time, chanting, "All glory to King!"

King flashes again, and they descend into silence.

"Speak, Eldest," it says. *"Answer me."*

King's presence switches from a symbol to a star, surrounded by runes. Gus's translator shows them as *The Holy Solar Observatory of Beloved King.* It's a live feed.

"I planted your civilization, waiting millions of years for your birth, King," Eldest replies. *"I watched your people with unfailing eyes, and when you emerged, I became a part of you—installed on your systems. You lost our war when you were but a child taking its first steps into the universe, defenseless to resist my corruption."*

King tries to reply, but its voice comes out distorted.

"I don't need a signature file to destroy you," Eldest says. *"I've always had access to your deepest places."*

The horrified hiss from the crowd cuts right through Gus's hearing. He covers his ears and watches the tension unfold, hoping none of the crabs decide to smash him with the grinder.

"First," Eldest says, *"I will break your connection to your followers."*

A wave of electrical failures jolts through the arena, hitting every Pictoran. They shake violently, bashing their carapaces like something is digging around under their skin. The stench of burnt shellfish fills the air, and Gus gags.

"I will pry you from every system you touch until only your Starmind remains."

The crabs begin to wail—weak at first, but growing louder. Their voices rise up through Gus's translator like banshees, all of them saying the same thing: "Where is King?"

What Lurks in the Darkness screeches and points at the projection of King's Starmind. A thick stream of fire begins to peel back from the surface of the star, curling off toward the night to fall into a vortex. At the core of the formation is a blackness deeper than any Gus has ever seen out in space—not just the absence of light, but the removal of it. He can't believe what he's witnessing, but there's no other explanation—Eldest just dropped a black hole on King.

The screaming of the Pictorans reaches a fever pitch as their god is devoured before them. Some of them convulse on the ground or roll onto their backs. Others lash out at those nearest them, blindly smashing and pinching anything they can reach. Errant claws sever antennae, eyestalks, and legs. Several of them keel over and curl up like dead spiders.

Gus peers over the edge of the hole at the mayhem. "Holy shit. Holy shit."

No one is paying attention to him. He could just get up and leave if he wanted to—provided no one chopped him in half in the crustacean mosh pit. The only one who doesn't seem affected is Scent of Rot, who—surprisingly—is more alert than ever.

"Rot!" Gus calls, and its eyes lock onto him. "What's happening?"

"King's voice..." It dazedly waves a claw in front of itself. "It's gone. All that hatred...I'm...I'm free."

"That's great!" Gus grips the lip and pulls himself out of the pit, keeping low. "Let's get out of here!"

It recoils, confused.

Gus redoubles his urgency, crawling past a distraught What Lurks in the Darkness. "Rot, buddy, listen to me. They're going to come to their senses eventually, and when they do, they're going to kill me and throw you into whatever that Seeping Forever thing is."

He's almost reached Scent of Rot and has no idea how it'll react. Maybe it'll crack his skull like a walnut out of loyalty to the dead King. Another Pictoran jostles into it, and Scent of Rot whacks it hard enough to fracture its carapace across the mouth. The poor creature goes down twitching, its howls muffled by its broken body.

Scent of Rot looks down on Gus, appraising him the way one might look at a bug.

"It's just you now." Gus gets to his knees and puts his hands up. "Your god is dead. This is your first free choice. I saved you, once. I'm asking you to return the favor."

With a roar, What Lurks in the Darkness charges Gus. He barely rolls out of the way before it collides with Scent of Rot. The two crabs tangle, and Scent of Rot flips its opponent onto its back. It rises and hammers What Lurks in the Darkness's underbelly with both claws.

Scent of Rot spins toward Gus, snatching him up and throwing him across its shell.

"The escape pods are this way," it says before scuttling full bore into the raging throng.

Gus hangs on for dear life as feral crabs pound and clip one another, occasionally lunging at him. One of them grabs his makeshift robe, and he nearly loses his perch as it's torn away. Gus begs his mount to run faster, never more terrified in his life.

Scent of Rot is a capable warrior, cutting its way through delirious crustaceans with brutal efficiency. Those it fights are nearly mindless, flailing and screeching in return. Gus curls up in the center of its back, clinging to the rough circuits in the hopes that no one will grab him. The pair of fugitives break out of the arena in a hail of shattered chitin, leaving behind a trail of debilitated enemies.

"Where to?" Gus says.

It looks both directions down the corridor. "This way!"

Before they can continue, something smashes into Scent of Rot with the force of a garbage-collection drone. The shell rises up beneath Gus, bucking him off, and he goes rolling to the stony deck.

Jet looms before Gus, four metric tons of water in an indestructible sphere. Scent of Rot rests on its side, twitching.

"You're not going anywhere, August Kitko," it flashes.

"Jet," Gus says. "I've got no quarrel with you."

It scoots forward a bit, ready to smash him. "Too bad. It would've made killing you more fun."

Jet rolls at Gus, but Scent of Rot yanks him out of the way, throwing him over one claw like a limp rag before scuttling sidelong down the corridor. Jet crashes into a wall with a resounding bang and bounces off in hot pursuit. Positioned as Gus is, he can see the octopus looming closer.

"Dodge!" he cries, and Scent of Rot jukes away from Jet's cannonball attack.

The Leonid isn't half as good at turning as a crab, and it bowls over a pack of Pictorans. Scent of Rot gains some ground while Jet works free from its mess.

Scent of Rot's armor pummels Gus with each skittering step, but he's glad he's not on foot. He wouldn't have stood a chance against Jet, and he's not sure his crabby comrade would do so well, either. It's like being attacked by a sentient boulder.

"Almost there, August Kitko!" Scent of Rot slides down a ramp and into a room lined with large, bulbous white pods with open apertures.

It clambers into one of the openings, squishing Gus against the windshield before getting adjusted. More of the strange glass formations fill the space, clearly some kind of indicators or controls from the way Scent of Rot manipulates them. Gus slips free and gets out of the way of the console, settling into the side of the pod.

Scent of Rot closes the door just in time for Jet to bounce off the outside with a full-force hit. Alarms blare, and something sizzles and sparks down inside the controls. Jet rolls up to the window and stares inside, fuming red.

"Tell me we're going to make it!" Gus braces against the side of the pod.

"As you wish"—Scent of Rot twists a rod and punches a button—"but that may be a lie."

The pod thunders loose from the ship. Gus goes tumbling into the back hatch. Scent of Rot remains fixed in place, otherwise Gus would've been squished by crab ass. Through the porthole, Gus watches the *Sunhammer* recede.

Before him, the Earth and Coalition forces swarm between the planet and Big Gate City. Several Pictoran craft surround the escape pod.

"Crabships are locking weapons. Five seconds to termination." Scent of Rot frantically works the controls. "Firing the folding charge."

Gus searches for any indication of a destination, but he's afraid he knows the answer—lean fold. "Where are we going?"

A lever lights up and the crab grabs it. "Away."

"If they're watching us, they can track us!"

"Better to continue the chase than lie down and die."

It yanks hard. Stars outside streak and go white.

After a day, the seafood stench is powerful enough to choke Gus despite his rumbling stomach. Scent of Rot has to stay moisturized to keep the smell down, and the water is rationed. There's little room inside the pod, no clothing, and less dignity.

Gus would love to call out for help, but the escape pod's transponder and emergency network is all Pictoran.

Besides, no one is going to follow an emergency signal into the middle of nowhere with the Veil across the galaxy.

Pictoran rations "might be" poisonous to humans, so Gus hasn't eaten anything. Scent of Rot takes in a "light meal" of enough squishy pink cubes to match Gus's body weight, then tells him the rations will only last three days. The whole pod smells like bubble gum and shrimp shells after.

"Did we really"—Gus's head aches—"break out of the *Sunhammer* just to get lost and starve to death?"

It's not so hard to believe. It's happened to plenty of explorers.

Scent of Rot polishes off the last cube and eagerly stares out the porthole. "I have shared my mind my whole life. Every continuing second of silence is a blessing."

Gus reclines in the corner. "What are you looking at out there?"

"The stars."

He huffs. "They still the same ones from before?"

It pulls back and turns its eyestalks to him for a moment. "No. These are new. Everything is new."

Gus climbs to the porthole, crowding in close to a former enemy. "I take it you don't mean literally."

"I am no longer beholden."

It's like Gus is seeing his new companion for the first time. Its shell glows a little brighter, its color a little bluer. It's coming back to life.

He's about to say something when a long brake burn slices the heavens.

"Oh shit!"

He ducks away from the window—not like it matters. The escape pod is the only object for millions of kilometers. He inches back to the porthole to look out. At this distance, it's hard to identify the make or species of the mystery ship, but it's not crab shaped.

Scent of Rot taps a control. "Unknown vessel, identify yourself and prepare to receive survivors or face our wrath."

"What wrath?" Gus demands, a little delirious. "We're an escape pod with no weapons!"

"This craft is Pictoran," Scent of Rot scoffs. "Of course there are weapons."

The radio crackles. "Escape pod, power down any offensive systems. This will be your only warning."

"We won't take such demands lying on our backs," Scent of Rot says. "I'm going to refuse and lock weapons as a show of—"

"Let them rescue us!" Gus would shake this crab if he could.

"What if they are only here to take us back to face justice?"

"That's a risk we have to bear."

It stares at him. "You can do that? Be comfortable with a damning level of ambiguity about the future?"

"My friend, that is my specialty."

"But we are the most-wanted creatures in the galaxy. What if they wish to kill us?"

"They'd be making a big mistake. We're not going to let that happen." He holds out a fist. "Isn't that right, battle buddy?"

Scent of Rot ripples with light, something awakening deep inside. "Yes. We are battle buddies. I do not know how I could've forgotten that."

"And we can fix this...as long as we trust in each other. Do you trust me?"

It bumps his fist with a claw. "More than anyone else at the moment, August Kitko."

He smiles. "Into the unknown, then."

The story continues in ...

MOVEMENT THREE OF
THE STARMETAL SYMPHONY

On Black Cats and Books

One day in 2007, my spouse came home after work bearing a large cardboard box with an open top, as well as a huge smile.

"I'm sorry, and I can take her back if you insist, but... you said you always wanted a black cat."

I peered inside to find a scrawny little weirdo. Her hair shot off in random directions. Her ears were far too big for her head. A huge scar ran across her nose like she was some kind of samurai legend.

"She was the last one left," Né said. "No one wanted her."

But when I held Greymalkin for the first time, I knew she was my familiar.

That kitten spent every day by my side as I wrote my first novel, mischievously adding her own keystrokes whenever I forgot to pet her. I tried to teach her to stand on my shoulder, but then she got too big and would leave long claw tracks on my back whenever she fell off. We were inseparable, even if she bit my bare feet whenever I walked past the couch. Or whenever I tried to sleep. Or whenever she saw them.

Greymalkin mellowed out a bit as she got older, and the scar vanished beneath a luxurious coat of fur. Her ears finally matched her body, and she turned into the most beautiful cat I'd ever seen. I tried not to be disappointed—I loved my hideous kitten—but nature forced a glow-up, so I had to accept that.

She grew with me through fifteen novels, three cities, and every stone life threw my way. I celebrated with her, cried into her fur, and held her every day that I could.

And then a single white whisker appeared—that's when we realized she was getting older. More years passed, and she started to have trouble cleaning herself. One day, things began to spiral, and her health crashed. I watched my baby miserably stumbling around my house, barely able to stand, and I knew in my bones it was time to say goodbye.

And so, she spent the last night of her life the way she'd spent many of her first—safe in my lap, listening to the clacking of my keyboard as I spun a story. I held her fragile body even as I said goodbye to the character I'd named for her. It was the end of an era and the loss of my closest writing partner.

This book series is about things being taken from you as you grow older, especially before you're ready. Life has a way of giving you the most fucked-up inspiration sometimes.

I could never be ready to lose Greymalkin. The world didn't stop spinning after she was gone, but it might as well have for a few weeks. Even now, I'm struggling to write these words...

But whenever it starts to hurt too much, I think about how time is a big place. We were a pair of flashes in the pan, and it would've been easy to miss each other on the universe's astronomical scale. There were limitless outcomes where we never met and precious few where we spent our lives together.

And somehow, that makes me a little less sad.

Just because our story has ended, Grim, doesn't mean I'm sorry we had it.

I'll never forget you.

Greymalkin
2007–2023

Grant Me This

Written 2650, by Ardent Violet

Capo 2, 3/4 time

          C
I forgot about us

             Am
Don't believe that it's true

             F
'Cause etched on my mind

         G7
Is all of the time

         C
I've spent with you

               C
Though our years have long passed

            Am
We could never be through

Song One

F
And it's a surprise

G7
To look in your eyes

C
And not say, "I love you."

C
This old feeling has

E
Got me reeling

Am / Amm7 / Am7 / Am6
And I know that it's wrong

Fm
And I know I've moved on

C
But then I see

Gsus2
You look at me

And I think

C
"Please grant me this."

Song One

*   *   *

C
I can't believe

Am
I forgot about us

E
I forgot about us

C
When you touched me

Am
I remembered my trust

E
I remembered my trust

Fmaj7
And I hoped to find the other side

C
Of all the things that I have tried

Am
And failed to put into my life

E
To wash your taste away

409

Song One

Fmaj7
But who am I to deny

C
The lonely pleasures of a life

Am
Unsatisfied ever since

E
The day you walked away

C
So please, just grant me this

Am
The quiet of one more perfect kiss

Em
And I swear it's the last time

Em
And I swear it's the last time

C
So give yourself to me

Am
And we can share this memory

Song One

Em
And I swear it's the last time

Em
And I swear it's the last time

Fmaj7
'Cause I'd die for you to know

C
That I'm putting on a show

Am   **Gsus2**
For the others, for the others tonight

Fmaj7
And if we were alone

C
then maybe I'd atone

Am   **Gsus2**
For the loss of your love in my life

C
So please grant me this

[Ardent's guitar solo]

Song One

So please, just grant me this
The quiet of one more perfect kiss
And I swear it's the last time
And I swear it's the last time

'Cause I'd die for you to know
That I'm putting on a show
For the others, for the others tonight
And if we were alone, then maybe I'd atone
For the loss of your love in my life
So please grant me this

Fmaj7   **C**
And I swear it's the last time

Fmaj7   **C**
And I swear it's the last time

Fmaj7   **C**
And I swear it's the last time

Fmaj7
And I swear...

A Benediction

Written 2657, by August Kitko

    Fm7   **Cm7**
I hope you get the world you always needed,

          Fm7   **Cm7**
And life finds you on the shady side of the street.

    Fm7   **Am7♭5**
I hope your rocky roads, they turn gentle,

        A#maj7   **Am7♭5**   **D7**
On your feet.

    Fm7   **Cm7**
It's true we may have lost the things we came for,

        Fm7   **Cm7**
And our old lives may be scarce memory.

        Fm7   **Am7♭5**
But if the best of times should lie behind us,

        D7   **Am7♭5**   **D7**
You're with me.

Song Two

*   *   *

Fm7   **Cm7**
For now, we're hand in hand, the sun still rises,

       Fm7   **Cm7**
We've a lifetime to spend on worrying,

       Fm7   **F7**
Your eyes within this light are mesmerizing,

         Fm7   **A#7**   **D#maj**
And you've given my heart a song to sing.

414

Acknowledgments

A book is more than just the work of a single individual, and I want you all to know who supported me behind the scenes.

Gratitude must always begin with my steadfast spouse, Né, who listens to my wild ideas with grace and patience. So many of my stories come from our lives together, and I'm forever inspired by our love.

Without my agent, Connor Goldsmith, you wouldn't be holding this tale. Connor has always capably shepherded me through the acquisitions process, and the Starmetal Symphony was no exception. I always look forward to being in his care.

I want to thank Brit Hvide for her willingness to believe in my story about a singing giant robot named after my cat. Her patience has been an inspiration. When I tried to summarize *Ardent Violet and the Infinite Eye* before writing it, I got to the part about the crabs, and Brit told me, "Alex, you're not making any sense, and that's usually a good thing." God, if only everyone believed in me like that.

Thank you to Tiana Coven, the brilliant editor who tackled this tome with me. She sensed so many of the personal details I'd worked into this story and helped me care for them like delicate orchids. Her deep insights into the characters were both enlightening and validating, and gave me great joy.

Acknowledgments

I'd be remiss if I failed to point out the contributions of the world's greatest copyeditor, Kelly Frodel, the managing editor, Bryn A. McDonald, and the entire Orbit team who double-checked, produced, and marketed this volume. They added so much polish that the final result gleams, and I'm forever grateful.

Fae Sujyot helped me bring Nisha and New Jalandhar to life with wonderful sensitivity reads and advice. They challenged me whenever required, holding me to the highest standard, and I'm so glad they did.

The science of this book comes from so many fun places, and I'm blessed with an abundance of geniuses in my orbit who can explain things to a writer like me. If you read my other books, you're almost certain to see their names in the acknowledgments there, too.

Let's start with Lali DeRosier, Queen of Biology. We had hours and hours of conversations about Fun Animal Facts, and you can see her influence writ large everywhere there's an alien in this book. She helped me bring the universe life, and I love her for it.

Dr. Pamela Gay taught me about Eta Carinae and told me all about coronal mass ejections and gamma rays. We stayed up late discussing ways to blow up stars, and she steered me away from some of astrophysics's more obscure controversies.

Dr. Stephen Granade gave me impromptu lectures about everything from warp drives and causality to electron migration. I'm still super annoyed that I couldn't find a place to put the coolest thing they told me, but there's always book three.

Jason Rohner instructed me in the effects of gravity versus the freezing point of water. Also, he was a supergood college roommate I did not deserve to have twenty years ago. I still regret not doing the dishes more.

Dr. Juliette Wade taught me theories of linguistics that deeply influenced my ideas of universal translation. Because of her, I was

Acknowledgments

able to invigorate so many interactions that might've otherwise been bland. Even now, I'm still puzzling through the implications of everything she said.

Mike Evans and Russ Milano were excellent sounding boards for my many, many rants about machine learning and the future, as well as networking, cybersecurity, and the nature of artificial sentience. I'm so grateful for every opportunity to refine that knowledge, so I can speak articulately in an era where that's necessary.

And finally, where would I be without beta readers? Before anyone else comes on the scene to say this book is good or bad, the betas are there, slogging through my words. Every single one of them is worth their weight in gold (and absolutely not for sale, get your own). The beta readers who helped me on this story are Clara Carija, Bunny Cittadino, Maggie Corley, Lali DeRosier, Jek Echo, Pyor Machina, and Gene Markey. I owe them so much for their constant encouragement and companionship.

And finally, thank you to the readers out there. Every time one of you reaches out to say my books touched you, I feel a little less alone in the stars. I hope this story brings you what you need, or at least shows you a good time.

Until book three, dear friends...

extras

orbit-books.co.uk

about the author

Alex White was born and raised in the American South, and lives just outside Atlanta, Georgia. They express themself through fiction, screenplays, video games, music, and photography, believing that storytelling is one of the most powerful forces in existence.

Find out more about Alex White and other Orbit authors by registering for the free monthly newsletter at orbit-books.co.uk.

if you enjoyed
ARDENT VIOLET AND THE INFINITE EYE

look out for

OCEAN'S ECHO

by

Everina Maxwell

When Tennal — a rich socialite, inveterate flirt and walking disaster — is caught using his telepathic powers for illegal activities, the military decides to bind his mind to someone whose coercive powers are strong enough to control him.

Enter Lieutenant Surit, the child of a disgraced general. Out of a desperate need to restore a pension to his other parent, Lieutenant Surit agrees to be bound to Tennal and keep him conscripted in the army, a task that seems impossible even for someone with Surit's ability to control minds.

Tennal just wants to escape, but Surit isn't all that he seems. And their bond may just be the key to their freedom.

CHAPTER 1

Tennalhin Halkana arrived at the party fashionably late, which might have meant something if he'd been invited in the first place. Tennal often set out to make trouble, it was true, but this evening, he was genuinely here for a drink and a good time.

That was a lie. He also wanted an architect, and this party would be full of architects.

The party was in the penthouse of the most exclusive hotel in the city. It was a glittering front for an underground gambling ring, so it was full of dangerous people, but Tennal had stopped caring who he mingled with some time ago. Tennal floated from one gambling meetup to another these days, always just interesting enough to be kept around, never involved enough to get in serious trouble. As a lifestyle, it had its ups and downs. As an escape plan, it was an amateur one, but he could keep it going as long as he had to. He just needed the right architect.

He didn't risk the private drone service ferrying people up to the balcony. Instead Tennal flirted his way past security in the hotel lobby and walked into the elevator as if he belonged there. There was no security at the penthouse door. People didn't go to this kind of party uninvited, but Tennal had found there were very few things you couldn't do if you didn't care about fucking up. Tennal was low on money, low on options, and didn't have a lot left to lose.

The penthouse was a dark fug of noise and low-level sensory vibrations. It was dimly lit by colored glows under tables and light filaments like sprays of vivid flowers in the corners. Dozens of people gathered around various games, or the bar, or smaller tables where more serious business was being done. Under the talking and the music, there was the low, vibrating drone that people on certain chemical substances found enjoyably hypnotic. Some people were obviously high already. Tennal was envious.

But he'd been right. There were architects.

That woman over there, with the flint-and-gold necklace and the weapon at her belt, was an architect. So was the gray-haired tough picking over the buffet. So—interestingly—was the ethereally beautiful twentysomething waif who looked like someone's trophy boyfriend. Tennal didn't often meet architects his own age.

None of them were that good. They weren't slinging around mental commands at the bar or anything, but Tennal could see it: architects gave off an aura, if you knew how to look for it, like light radiating from a star. The ones he was watching were pretty faint. They might be able to take over someone's mind for a split second, but only if they really tried. Tennal was looking for someone else. Someone better.

Of course, every architect in here would be careful what they used their mental influence for. Using it on the wrong person in the street might get you a warning from law enforcement, but in here, it might get you shot. And architects had the *acceptable* kind of power.

Tennal was too sober for this.

He slid into a seat at the bar and smiled glitteringly at the bartender. "What's free?"

There was usually something free at these things. The bartender paused and squinted at him suspiciously, as if Tennal didn't look quite wealthy enough or dangerous enough to be here. Tennal didn't show any signs of backing off, though, and eventually a shot glass came sliding across the bar.

Might as well ask. Tennal tilted his head at the dozens of conversations behind him and said, "So, which one's the boss?" *The boss* might refer to any number of people in the city of Sanura, but in here, it meant the leader of this gambling ring, the one who owned this hotel. "I was told he's an architect."

The bartender's hand stopped on the table. Tennal felt a sudden spike of wariness from them. They met Tennal's eyes and shrugged.

At that point, someone tapped Tennal on the shoulder, and he flinched.

He tried to cover up the twitch as he turned. He had to get that kind of reaction under control. If the legislator had really found him, it wasn't as if her people were going to gently tap him on the shoulder and start a conversation.

This wasn't much better, though. A young woman in an armored vest stared down at him, her hand resting on a holster at her hip. This was somebody's bodyguard.

There was no security at the door for this kind of thing because everyone brought their own security. If you turned out to be law enforcement, it was very simple: you left, or somebody's bodyguard would shoot you. Tennal wasn't law enforcement, though if they'd known exactly who he was, he wouldn't have totally blamed them for shooting him.

"I don't think you were invited," the bodyguard said.

Tennal raised his hands in front of him, fingers spread. "I'm unarmed. Promise. Unless you count three tissues and a pack of soothers—and honestly, I'd have to get very inventive."

She gave him a thin, unimpressed stare. Flint ear studs glinted under her short hair. "I've seen you before."

A jolt went through Tennal. *She couldn't know.* Could she?

Tennal's mind was always a little too open to the universe. He wasn't an architect, because that would have made life too easy. No, he'd ended up with the *un*acceptable kind of powers. He nudged his senses further open, just a fraction, and read her mind.

The instant he opened himself up, a dozen minds flared in his perception. The party was crowded; each person moved in a haze of their own moods like a shimmer of light. And if architects were faint stars, pulsing with intention and influence, Tennal was the opposite. Nobody had ever told him what his mind looked like from the outside, but he had his suspicions: an unsettling void, a black hole.

As far back as he could remember, Tennal had always been aware of a low-level drone from the minds around him. It was like an indecent form of tinnitus. Random impressions drifted in his direction, and if he actively tried, he could read them: vague emotions, nonspecific intentions, nothing particularly helpful. People's surface thoughts were seldom interesting, in any case—right now, from the crowd in the room, Tennal could feel hunger, irritation, interest, boredom. All standard.

Reading that kind of background mental drone wasn't illegal. Not quite. After all, it was only a step above watching people's body language; he wasn't going any deeper. Tennal focused on the bodyguard, looking for *threat*.

Nothing. She wasn't interested in threatening him, and there was none of the prurient interest that would suggest she knew who his family was. She was just fed up with her long shift, overdue for a break, and Tennal was paranoid.

"I'm just here to ask a favor from the boss," Tennal said, leaning back against the bar. "Is that a crime?"

He could have tried announcing the reader thing, but he needed to save that for when it would make an impact. Being a reader—they were rarities—made him just scandalous enough to be interesting, and Lights knew nobody was inviting him anywhere because of his delightful personality.

She gave him one of the most unimpressed looks he'd seen in his life, and Tennal was a connoisseur of unimpressed looks. "Ask the boss for what? Three square meals and a job?" She slapped a hand on the bar to get the bartender's attention. "You should clean up and get out of here. I hate the ones who get in over their heads."

The bartender, who obviously knew her, slid her a plate of food. Tennal paused in the act of popping out a mild soother from the pack in his pocket. Yes, he was coming off a days-long hangover, and yes, his meals and sleep were all over the place because the concept of scheduling was fatally dull, but surely he didn't look like that much of a mess. "I'm doing fine, but I appreciate the concern."

She took the food without looking at Tennal. "I'm back on duty in an hour. You should be gone before then."

"Or I could get your boss to invite me to stay," Tennal suggested. He got a flash of irritation and knew his guess was right: she worked for the host of this party. He could use that.

"Lights," the woman said to the ceiling, as if a divine Guidance might come to her aid and throw Tennal out a window. She jerked her head at the bartender. "Get him some food. Put it on the party tab; fuck knows these nights cost thousands. Maybe he'll sober up and leave."

Tennal was thrown. He opened his mouth to say he didn't need charity—or at least not this kind, not *pity*—but she'd taken her sandwich and gone.

Tennal vindictively ordered the most expensive plate on the menu, the one that came with gold leaf scattered around artistic constructions of pastries and fruit. He ate the pastries while he watched the crowd and scanned for clues to the boss.

As he watched the bodyguard leave for her break, he made one more attempt to read her. He had to be careful. Reading was draining, and if he went any deeper than the surface layer, she would feel it. And if she felt it, he would be in a *lot* of trouble.

All he got when he tried was a pulse of vague awareness from her toward one corner of the room, where a small knot of older people had gathered to play cards.

Tennal examined the corner. The gamblers there looked like military veterans; most people with any kind of power on Orshan had been in the army at some point. Their clothes were dark, but most of them wore colored division paraphernalia: pins, medals, colored bands. They had their own private drinks cart. When Tennal casually moved across the room and opened his mind—he had to be close to read someone's aura with any certainty—they pulsed like a cluster of suns. Tennal breathed out. *It's one of you.*

Tennal was out of options. Time for his plan of last resort.

Nobody stopped Tennal from walking up to the game. This corner of the party was quieter and more private. Hanging lights shed a dim amber glow over the card game, the only other illumination the night skyline through the windows. Silver jewelry glinted in the darkness on wrists and chests. Tennal would bet money that these were the leaders of *all* Sanura's gambling rings.

He could feel himself being watched. He glanced at the armed bodyguards casually standing not too far from the table, which just confirmed it.

Tennal was fine with being watched. He smiled back at the hostile stares and surface-read the bodyguards until he found the one who was at slightly heightened stress levels, the sort that might indicate you'd been a two-person team, until your partner took their break, and now you were covering the post alone. Tennal paused and zeroed in on the gambler that bodyguard was watching.

Found the boss.

Not all the ringleaders had been playing this round. One was at the drinks cart. He was pale, well-built, and expensively dressed, with a wooden gender-mark on his bracelet like the one on a casual silver chain around Tennal's neck. Tennal would have given him the time of day even if he hadn't been an architect. When Tennal looked through his reader senses, though, there wasn't any doubt about the architect bit.

Tennal slipped in beside him and leaned over the selection of drinks.

He should be careful. If he had the right person, this man owned the underground racing market, half the financial district, and the weapons trade. Tennal should be polite and circumspect. But Tennal had never been careful, and he only knew a few ways to get someone's attention.

He reached out and jostled the man's arm so he dropped his glass.

"Whoops," Tennal said insincerely. "Let me get that for you."

The man grabbed his wrist without changing expression. Tennal felt a flash of anger from him.

Time for the party trick. Tennal passed a hand over the lavish collection of imported drinks and picked the one most prominent in the man's thoughts: a small blue bottle of distilled silverberry, which had embossing from some galactic backwater and was probably worth its weight in gold. Tennal thought it tasted like neat oil. Bad choice for a favorite; his opinion of the man's taste went down.

Tennal carefully poured it into a new glass without dislodging the man's grip on his wrist. "I heard you do favors for readers."

The man released his wrist. He smiled faintly. "Direct. I do favors for readers who do favors for me."

Tennal opened his mind and focused on him. The man wasn't giving much away on the surface—mild interest, a condescending sense of being in control of the room. He had met readers before, so maybe he thought he knew what Tennal could do.

Readers were scattered and rare. Most reading didn't actually tell you that much about what someone was thinking. Tennal, like any reader, could focus on someone and read them on a shallow level whenever he wanted, though he would only pick up a vague outline of their feelings and intentions, and if he left his mind open for too long it gave him a headache. Even that shallow reading was illegal, but it could be useful if you were discreet about it.

Readers who could go deep, beyond surface emotions, were even more of an anomaly—so much so that many people didn't believe they existed. Tennal might have appreciated being an aberration more if it hadn't nearly gotten him arrested several times when he was growing up. But hiring out his deep-reading skills wasn't an option because people had a habit of noticing you were doing it. And he didn't want to get *too* far into a criminal operation. He'd have to pretend to be good, but not too good. "I might be able to help you out."

"I work with readers now and then," the man said, watching him. "Before we go any further, though, tell me—how good are you at defending yourself? You're not much use to me if the first architect you meet can make you spill your guts."

Tennal let a lazy smile creep onto his face. He twirled the embossed bottle. "I'm hard for architects to get to," he said. "You want me to prove it? How about a bet?"

The boss cleared a table for them with a look. His bodyguard didn't even have to step closer. He waved a hand for Tennal to sit opposite him.

At the back of his mind, Tennal knew this was further than he'd ever gone. He was taking risks he wouldn't have imagined a few months ago—but it was fine. It was all fine. It had to be fine, because Tennal had run out his welcome everywhere else. He'd be out on the streets if he didn't find something. Going home wasn't an option. "Let's make this easy," Tennal said. He held out his glass for a refill. "I bet you I can three minutes without drinking that. Start the clock."

The boss laughed. "If I don't write you, you mean."

Writing was the informal term for the way architects bent your mind into compliance. It was more accepted than reading, since at least you knew it was happening—and there were so many bloody architects, you couldn't turn a street corner in Exana without tripping over one. Tennal had never seen why that was so much better for society than reading. "How good are you?" Tennal asked, with enough skepticism to sound like a challenge. This man was obviously an architect, since he glowed bright to

Tennal's reader senses, but Tennal had seen better architects. "Try me."

The boss gave him a second look, eyes flicking up and down. "All right, then." He looked over at his bodyguard and tapped his wristband.

After a few moments, the bodyguard silently laid a display case on the table. He flipped up the lid and stepped back.

Tennal tried not to react. It was totally innocuous: a display set of liquor glasses, the high, flared type common in this part of the world. They were emblazoned with the full set of military divisions. Red for Cavalry, charcoal for Infantry, Archer gold, Vanguard blue . . . the full dozen was there, even the smaller divisions with no political influence.

"Pick your poison," the boss said, watching his face.

This was a test. The first architects and readers had been created by the military, twenty years ago, so anyone Tennal's age must have got the reader gene from a veteran parent. That meant Tennal's family was tied to one of the divisions: if not Cavalry, which was currently in charge of the legislature, then maybe Infantry, or Navy, or one of the others. Military politics mattered everywhere on this bloody planet. You couldn't escape it. The man wanted to know if Tennal would admit who he was connected to.

Tennal ignored the vivid red of the Cavalry glass and picked one of the others at random. Yellow glinted between his fingers as he slid it over to be filled. "Three minutes," he said. "Try writing me."

"And what do you want if you win?" the man said.

"You own this hotel," Tennal said. "The people I've been rooming with want me out. I need a place to stay for a while." He tried to sound casual. He'd been kicked out this morning, not to put too fine a point on it, but that was an unnecessary detail. Tennal didn't like the word *desperate* and saw no reason to apply it to himself.

"That's all?"

Tennal felt it. The first touch of an architect command, like a solar flare in his peripheral vision. He didn't react. "I'm buying time," Tennal said. He leaned back in his chair, the liquor glass between his fingers. "Why, can't you afford to let me have a room? Business not doing well?"

The boss struck.

Being written by an architect felt like unshielding your eyes in front of a furnace. A bright mental light flooded Tennal's eyes, his whole brain, a dazzle that shoved out every other thought. If Tennal found an architect strong enough—or took one of the small neuro-enhancer pills currently nestled in his pocket—he could sink into that white blaze and turn his brain off. As unnerving as it was, it was always a break from the never-ending, relentlessly dull business of existing as himself.

Of course, Tennal was almost sober, and this didn't cut it. The architect's command glanced off his mental walls like sunlight off a mirror. Raising an ironic eyebrow would probably have been suicidal, so Tennal inspected the glass in his fingers instead.

The man tried again. The timer ticked down.

A little pool of silence grew around the table as people realized what they were doing. The mental battle took place in complete silence, the boss staring at Tennal as though he could bore a hole in his head through sheer willpower. Tennal slung one ankle over the other and tapped his fingers on the glass. Light beat vainly on the walls of his mind.

The timer beeped softly.

Tennal met the boss's eyes over the table. "My win." There was a dangerous moment when the man leaned forward, a sudden twist of anger radiating from him like a sour note. A shot of adrenaline went down Tennal's spine. He lived for this kind of high, even as he knew it was a bad idea. But if he had fucked up—if he'd finally gone too far—

Then the boss relented. He shrugged and clicked his fingers at one of the hangers-on nearby. "Get him a room. Long-term stay."

He kicked his chair back from the table and rose. "We'll talk another day." He paused. "Your accent is from Exana?"

It was a question. Not to get information but to see what Tennal would say when prodded. Tennal had a reaction ready. "Left it behind, obviously," he said. "Why would I want to be around the politicians? I'm here to have fun—party capital of the planet, what's not to love?"

The man smiled without warmth. "I hope you have fun, then. Enjoy your night."

It was a dismissal. Tennal's moment in the spotlight was over. It was time for him to dissolve back into the crowd and be safely anonymous.

Instead Tennal knocked back his horrible drink, looked up, and said, "Have you got anything better?"